EIGER: WALL OF DEATH

OVERLEAF: *The Eiger (showing the North Wall in shadow) and the Mönch*
RUBI PHOTO

ROLLING PLAINS CAMPUS - LIBRARY
SWEETWATER, TEXAS 79556

EIGER: WALL OF DEATH

Arthur Roth

W · W · NORTON & COMPANY · NEW YORK · LONDON

FRONTISPIECE: *Robert Seiler (foreground) and Marcel Hamel on the Second Icefield of the Eiger North Wall. The hotel and railroad station at Kleine Scheidegg are visible in the valley.* JEAN FUCHS PHOTO

PHOTO CREDIT: The photograph of the Eiger North Wall on pages 32, 34, 86, 250, and 294 is by Ernst Schudel.

The text of *Eiger: Wall of Death* is composed in photocomposition Baskerville. Display type is Typositor Windsor. Manufacturing is by the Maple-Vail Book Manufacturing Group.

BOOK DESIGN BY MARJORIE J. FLOCK

FIRST EDITION

Library of Congress Cataloging in Publication Data
Roth, Arthur J., 1925–
  Eiger, wall of death.
  Includes index.
  1. Mountaineering—Switzerland—Eiger—History.
2. Eiger (Switzerland)—Description. I. Title.
GV199.44.S92E357 1982   914.94'7   81-9658 AACR2

ISBN 0-393-01496-7

W. W. Norton & Company, Inc. 500 Fifth Avenue, New York, N.Y. 10110
W. W. Norton & Company Ltd. 37 Great Russell Street, London WC1B 3NU

1 2 3 4 5 6 7 8 9 0

For my twelve-year-old son, Mark,
who is already beginning to lead me on climbs:
"Wait for me.   Pull!   Pull!"

Contents

Acknowledgments

The author wishes to acknowledge that he borrowed freely from the following books that deal mainly with the Eiger: *Eigerwand* and *North Face in Winter* by Toni Hiebeler, *The White Spider* by Heinrich Harrer, *Der Eiger* by Rudolf Rubi, *The Eiger* by Dougal Haston, *The Climb Up To Hell* by Jack Olsen, *Straight Up* by James Ramsey Ullman, *Direttissima* by Peter Gillman and Dougal Haston, *Um Die Eigernordwand* by Harrer and Heckmair, and *Eiger: Kampf um die Direttissima* by Jörg Lehne and Peter Haag. In addition he used material from chapters about the Eiger that appeared in published accounts of such climbers as Chris Bonington, Mick Burke, Don Whillans, Ian Clough, Dougal Haston, Brian Nally, Leo Dickinson, Terry King, Gaston Rébuffat, Lionel Terray, Ludwig Vörg, Kurt Diemberger, Hermann Buhl, Reinhold Messner, Walter Bonatti, Riccardo Cassin, Peter Habeler, and others. He read extensively and used material from the Alpine journals of half a dozen nations, climbing magazines such as *Mountain, Summit, Climbing,* and *Der Bergsteiger,* as well as scores of English, French, Swiss, Italian, and American newspaper and newsmagazine accounts of various climbs, for all of which he is indeed grateful.

He wishes to acknowledge the help rendered him by such mountaineers as Layton Kor, Anderl Heckmair, Heinrich Sedlmayer, Michel Darbellay, Joe Tasker, Ludwig Gramminger, Martin Epp, Paul Nigg, Eric Jones, Alex MacIntyre, and all the others who filled out an extensive questionnaire on their Eiger climbs. Thanks is also due to Mrs. Marilyn Harlin for photos and information about John Harlin's climbs; to Nicholas Kagan and Ian Wade of Great Britain and to Larry Bruce and Steve Shea of Boulder, Colorado, for their interviews following their successful Eiger climbs in 1979; and to Tom Frost, John Harlin III, Hugo Hartenstein, Jocelyn Del Monte, David Brashears, Roger Briggs, Miriam Fryggens, and Joe Threadgill for their help in various matters.

Thanks are hereby tendered to Pat Fletcher and Franc de la Vega of the American Alpine Club Library in New York for their research help and their patient operation of an often balky copying machine; to Maja Grau of the Grindelwald *Echo* for clippings from that newspaper; and to the librarians of a dozen libraries; in particular the New York Public Library, the Boulder Public Library, the University of Colorado Library, the Denver Public Library, the public libraries in Berne and Interlaken in Switzerland; and the author's hometown library in East Hampton, New York, where many books and other publications were obtained on interlibrary loan through the good offices of Beth Gray.

Thanks are also due to the following: the officers and pilots of the Schweizerische Rettungsflugwacht (Swiss Air Rescue Service) for their photos and information on the many Eigernordwand rescues in which that organization was involved.

The Bayerisches Rotes Kreutz, Munich, for information and addresses.

Sybil Costello for a transcript of a TV show that involved the Eiger.

Gary and the staff at Neptune Mountaineering in Boulder, Colorado.

Helmut Klee and Walter Bruderer of the Swiss Tourist Office, New York, and the Swiss tourist offices in Geneva, Berne, and Grindelwald for their help with photos and innumerable details of research concerning the Eiger.

The Swiss Federal Railways for a three-week first-class ticket that made possible the author's many back-and-forth journeys to various sites in Switzerland.

To Grindelwald guide Edi Bohren for photos and information on Eiger helicopter rescues.

To Rudolf Rubi, of Grindelwald, author of *Der Eiger,* for photos and information on Eiger history.

To Peter Boardman, director of the International School of Mountaineering in Leysin, Switzerland, who made his extensive Alpine library freely available.

To the International School of Mountaineering guide Gordon Smith (who climbed the Eiger's north face at age eighteen) for taking the author up on his first modest Alpine climbs in Leysin and Chamonix.

To Gus Morin for his unflappable calm while leading the author up some fearsome 5.7 climbs in Boulder and El Dorado canyons in Colorado.

To Jeff Long, who read the manuscript for errors and who pointed out several glaring mistakes in mountaineering technique and terminology, and who also led the author on climbs in Colorado and Yosemite.

To Adams Carter for reading the manuscript and making many invaluable corrections and suggestions.

To climber Harris Tallan, who introduced the author and his son, Mark, to the climbing world of the "Gunks".

To Helga Meyer and Henrika Hadjipopov for their help in translating material from German language books and publications, and to Vania Murpurgo for help in translating from the Italian.

To Mr. and Mrs. Häsler-Eggler, Hotel Sans Souci, Grindelwald, for their hospitality and their help in setting up interviews with local guides and other authorities on the Eiger.

A heartfelt thanks to all those "adrenaline junkies" in the Shawangunks of New York, in Boulder and El Dorado canyons, Colorado, and in Yosemite, California, who patiently answered a thousand and one questions about equipment and techniques, and who put up with the author's all too often ham-handed and lead-footed climbing style while he was being coaxed (and sometimes dragged) up various cliff faces.

And, finally, the author acknowledges responsibility for any mistakes that may have crept or blundered into the text (one climber's name is spelled differently in three separate accounts of his climb) and apologizes for omitting, in the interest of brevity, the names of many climbers who did that awesome north wall of the Eiger.

OVERLEAF: PHOTO BY CHRIS BONINGTON

In this short span
between my fingertips and the smooth edge
and these tense feet cramped to a crystal ledge,
I hold the life of a man.

— GEOFFREY WINTHROP YOUNG

From death in valleys, deliver me O Lord!

— A MOUNTAINEER'S PRAYER

That mist is a mountain—and that mountain must be conquered.

— VLADIMIR NABOKOV

And it shall! It shall!

— PETE POMEROY

1

Too Difficult! Too Dangerous!

On June 3, 1950, the French mountain climber Maurice Herzog and his climbing companion, Louis Lachenal, became the first men to stand on the summit of Mount Annapurna in the Himalayas. It was then the highest point on earth, in fact the first mountain over 8,000 meters (26,247 feet), ever to have been climbed.

The descent, however, turned out to be appallingly dangerous, marked by crevasse breakthroughs and avalanches. Herzog and Lachenal, both crippled as a result of previous falls, their hands and feet badly frostbitten, were finally half carried, half led to safety by fellow climbers Lionel Terray and Gaston Rébuffat, who themselves were sightless from snow glare. It was literally a case of the blind leading the halt and the maimed.

Herzog's feet were so badly frostbitten that all his toes had to be amputated. When told by Lionel Terray that he would never climb again, Herzog, who had just mastered the highest mountain ever ascended by man, burst into tears and said, "I'll never do the Eiger now, Lionel, and I wanted to so much."

The Eiger North Wall dwarfing the hotel and railroad station at Kleine Scheidegg below.

RUBI PHOTO

Four years later Tenzing Norkay, coconqueror, along with Edmund Hillary, of Mount Everest, got partway up the feared Nordwand of the Eiger with a young American climber before the two turned back. This famed Sherpa guide, whose courage was and is unquestioned, said of the Eiger's north face, "Too difficult! Too dangerous!"

The Eiger is a mountain in the Bernese Oberland of the Swiss Alps. The name means "ogre" in German and goes back at least to 1252, when a Latin document was drawn up describing the borders of a piece of land as running to the foot of the "Egere" (Eiger).

The mountain was well named. So far over forty of the finest mountaineers have been killed on its north face alone. That number may seem trifling when compared to the fifty to seventy-five that are killed annually on Mont Blanc, but those killed on the Alps' highest peak include hikers, skiers, Sunday strollers, and climbers of every degree of competence or ineptitude. The Eiger is another Alp entirely. You just don't start up its north face until you've earned your credentials as a mountaineer. Almost without exception, those killed on the Eigernordwand (Eiger North Wall) were climbers of above-average skill. They had to be; there are no easy routes on the Eiger's north face. The Eigernordwand drew the best climbers, and often the best perished on it. They have fallen off it and been swept off by snowslides. Their brains have been dashed out by plummeting rocks. They have been frozen to the mountain's walls in slabs of ice. They have been caught on ledges, unable to move up or down, doomed to die of cold and hunger. They have been trapped in their gear, their bodies hanging in space for as long as three years. They have been strangled to death when their ropes fouled around their necks. They have been a couple of feet from the summit when a cornice broke off, hurling their bodies 5,000 feet to the base of the wall.

Imagine a mountain that looks like a scoop of ice cream with a pointed summit. Now imagine that you pick up a spoon and with the tip slice downwards straight through the peak, cutting away at least one-third of the ice cream. The face that is left is like the north wall of the Eiger—concave, scooped out, somewhat hollow. One climber compared it to a scallop shell standing on edge. Like a triangle, the Nordwand, to give it the local name, narrows from a broad base one mile wide to a pointed tip one mile high. And it is this difficult and dangerous north face that draws mountain climbers to the Eiger like—well, like tourists to the pretty Swiss village of Grindelwald that crouches at the mountain's foot.

By world standards the Eiger is not high. At 13,026 feet it has less than half the altitude of Mount Everest (29,028 feet). It is not even the highest of the quintet of peaks for which it forms the centerpiece, the

Wetterhorn (12,143 feet) and the Schreckhorn (13,380 feet) lying to the east and the Mönch (13,449 feet) and the Jungfrau (13,642 feet) to the west.

Climbing mountains, especially the Swiss Alps, as a sport is an idea only a little over 150 years old, although hardy Swiss guides were leading tourists on mountain hikes long before then, or guiding travelers through Alpine passes—for a fee, of course. Official certification of Swiss guides goes back in Berne to 1856, when a set of regulations was drawn up governing the rights and duties of guides vis-à-vis patrons. In Chamonix, the great mountain-climbing center of France, the local company of guides was founded in 1821.

Actually, up to the early 1800s, Swiss peasants believed that all kinds of eigers, or ogres, inhabited the peaks of the Alps, much as certain people today believe that the Abominable Snowman galumphs around in the Himalayas and that Bigfoot romps in the Pacific Northwest, strewing their Patagonian pugmarks all over the landscape.

Early exploratory rambles through the Alps were not always viewed in the same spirit in which they were undertaken, as witness this letter, written by the inveterate Alpine traveler and scientist Horace Bénédict de Saussure of Geneva, in 1778, to his wife: "In this valley I have made observations of the greatest importance, surpassing my highest hopes, but this is not what you care about. You would sooner, God forgive me, see me growing fat as a friar, snoring every day in the chimney corner after a big dinner, than I should achieve immortal fame by the most sublime discoveries at the cost of reducing my weight by a few ounces and spending a few weeks away from you." It brings to mind another sorely tried wife who railed at her husband, "There you go again, you old daredevil! You don't care about home. What will happen to me and the children?" Old daredevil, Tenzing Norkay was off on his seventh, and finally successful, attempt on Mount Everest.

De Saussure, incidentally, made four separate attempts to be the first to climb Mont Blanc and was beaten back each time. To combat snow blindness, he carried a parasol and swathed his head in a veil. Other climbers prudently brought along bottles of smelling salts to revive them after the expected ecstasies or terrors of *la haute montagne*. De Saussure made it to the top of Mont Blanc in 1787 and was so delighted with his achievement that he stayed on the summit for three and a half hours,

---

OVERLEAF: *The Eiger, showing the scooped-out nature of the north face, on the left. On the right the West Flank, and in the lower left-hand corner the buildings of Kleine Scheidegg.*

SWISSAIR PHOTO

making scientific measurements and observations. The peak had first been climbed the year before by Jacques Balmat and Michel Paccard, both of nearby Chamonix and both in their twenties.

In 1838 one Mme d'Angeville, jealous of the Baroness Dudevant (George Sand), who was then visiting Chamonix and scandalizing local society by parading around in men's trousers, proceeded to climb Mont Blanc and, in the words of Claire Engel, a noted historian of Alpine mountaineering, "simultaneously displayed a virile courage, hysterical tendencies and a climbing costume of checkered material complete with wide trousers, long coat, feathered beret and a long black boa." When Mme d'Angeville subsequently claimed to be the first woman to climb the Alps' highest mountain, it was brought to her attention that Mont Blanc had previously been climbed by a hardy and venturesome eighteen-year-old Chamonix maidservant, Marie Paradis, who very sensibly used her accomplishment to advertise a tearoom that she started right after her exploit. Mme d'Angeville immediately responded by saying she was still the first *lady* to have climbed Mont Blanc, thus bringing the class element into mountaineering—alas, not for the last time.

Many of the early explorer-travelers faced considerable difficulties in their perambulations through the Alps. One story is told of an unlucky wanderer who barely escaped with his life from an avalanche at the foot of the Eiger. His compulsive note taking and sketching led to his subsequent arrest at the Swiss-Austrian frontier as a spy. He managed to talk himself out of that charge only to be rearrested a few days later as a Pan-Slavist agitator. When that matter was cleared up, he returned to his beloved mountains—one presumes with a sigh of relief—only to be nearly burned alive when the mountain hut in which he took refuge one night was struck by lightning.

These exploring forays were next taken up by foreigners and became a favorite pursuit of certain nineteenth-century English gentlemen who came to Switzerland every summer to take the temperature of glaciers, to measure their thickness and rate of flow, and to explore ice caves, seracs, crevasses, and other high Alpine phenomena.

One A. D. Inglis, an English naturalist, wrote in 1833 of a possible attempt to climb the Grossglockner: "It is a positive act of egregious folly, for one not moved by scientific motives, to endure the pain and dangers of an ascent greatly above the line of perpetual congelation."

Mountain climbing was thus seen as an adjunct of scientific endeavor, but this state of affairs did not last very long. Assaults on the Alps soon became a favorite sport among young English gentlemen. Of thirty-nine major Alpine peaks climbed between 1854 and 1884, British climbers and their local guides accounted for thirty-one. For some reason many of these young bloods were clergymen who took to bagging peaks just for the heaven of it. It was an age of muscular Christianity; more than one-quarter of those applying to join the British Alpine Club when it was founded in 1856 were clergymen. "Nearer, My God, to Thee" seems to have been taken rather literally.

There's no doubt that natives in search of chamois, or of rock crystal, climbed many of the lower Alps as a matter of course, or because they were in the way of getting from here to there. Mountain climbing for utilitarian purposes goes back to man's earliest beginnings. One band of Neanderthal men, for example, buried the skulls of six bears in a stone box placed in a cave halfway up a cliff, at 8,000 feet elevation, near Drachenburg in east Switzerland.

The first historical record of climbing a mountain simply "because it's there," to give George Leigh Mallory's famous and perhaps tongue-in-cheek reason for climbing Mount Everest, was in 1492 when King Charles VII of France ordered his court chamberlain, the lord of Domp-julian and Beaupré, one Antoine de Ville, to have the 6,900-foot Mount Aiguille, outside Grenoble, climbed just to see what the top of that soaring, prow-shaped, flat-topped mountain was like. The ascent of a large company of climbers, using ropes and ladders and various "subtile means and engines" was duly made. No monsters were discovered inhabiting the meadow on top, simply a small herd of chamois. Three crosses were erected, a mass said, and a report of the climb made to King Charles. The use of ladders and "subtile means and engines" gives de Ville a good claim to being the father of direct-aid (artificial) climbing. Undoubtedly his engineers adapted military methods of scaling fortress walls to help solve the problem. The climb of Mount Aiguille, previously known as Mount Inaccessible, is still considered a difficult one, though guide ropes have now been fixed along the more dangerous parts of the climb. Some 342 years were to pass before the climb was repeated, this time by a local peasant.

Whatever about the Lord of Dompjulian and Beaupré, to the English must go the credit for having invented the *sport* of Alpine climbing. They paid a price too. The beautiful graveyard in Grindelwald contains memorials to half a dozen English climbers who lost their lives on nearby peaks, as witness this marker: "In memory of Robert Burton Fearon, M.A. Oxon, age 30, and Henry Charles Digby Fearon, H.B.M. Inspector of Factories, age 29, who with their guides were killed by lightning on the summit of the Wetterhorn, 20 Aug. 1902. 'They were lovely and pleasant in their lives and in their death they were not divided.' " The two guides were Samuel Brawand and Fritz Bohrens of Grindelwald. One brother's body was found, with that of a guide, near the peak, while the other brother and guide were discovered some 2,000 feet lower down. All of their bodies showed lightning burns.

The Grindelwald cemetery contains, too, an appreciable number of graves of native guides that show a broken ice axe or a frayed-edge coil of rope looped over a knob on a monument carved from limestone, indicating that the guide lost his life in a mountaineering accident. The broken ice axe or the frayed rope, to symbolize a life cut short, is similar to the broken ship's mast in seaport cemeteries in America that symbolizes a life lost at sea. These guide gravestones invariably contain one brief, brutal line: "Fallen from the Jungfrau" or "*Verunglückt am Grünhorn.*" A twenty-three-year-old Austrian climber's gravestone gives a single chilling word to explain his death, "Eigernordwand." Another Grindelwald bergsteiger's (mountain climber) gravestone is actually a carved miniature replica of the Eiger.

The Golden Age of Mountaineering is generally considered to have started in 1856 with the publication of Alfred Wills's book *Wanderings Among the High Alps,* a work that details a number of his climbs, including the ascent of the Wetterhorn in 1854. Then too, it was in 1856 that the British Alpine Club was founded; the British *Alpine Journal,* the world's first periodical devoted to mountain climbing, started publication in 1863. And in 1865 that most idealized, most romantic of all Alpine peaks—the Matterhorn—was climbed by Whymper.

The prototype of the hearty Victorian climber, the twenty-five-year-old Edward Whymper, along with three guides and three other Englishmen, including the eighteen-year-old Lord Francis Douglas, led the first successful ascent of the Matterhorn, barely beating an Italian team to the summit on July 14, 1865. The Italians were only 600 feet or so from the summit when the English party topped out. To let their rivals know that the mountain had been mastered, and probably to taunt them, Whymper and his party playfully rolled stones down on them from the summit. Whymper wrote, "We drove our sticks in and prized away the crags and soon a torrent of stones poured down the cliffs." The Italians turned tail—small wonder!

Tragedy stalked Whymper that day. While the party was climbing down, a rope broke, precipitating Lord Douglas, the Reverend Charles Hudson, the nineteen-year-old Douglas Hadow, and the veteran guide Michel Croz off a precipice and into a fall of thousands of feet, their bodies bouncing off rocks and ice crags until they were shredded. As a result of these deaths, Whymper and the two surviving guides were embroiled in controversy for the rest of their lives.

Not everyone hailed these muscular Christians. John Murray's *Handbook for Travelers in Switzerland,* published in 1854, warned against such follies as mountain climbing, charging that those who had already climbed Mont Blanc "were of diseased mind."

Charles Dickens poured scorn on what he called the "Society for the scaling of such heights as the Schreckhorn, Eiger and Matterhorn" and claimed they "contributed about as much to the advancement of science as would a club of young gentlemen who should undertake to bestride all the weathercocks of all the cathedral spires of the United Kingdom."

John Ruskin, an essayist whose style was much admired, severely admonished climbers in his book *Sesame and Lilies,* published in 1865, with these words: "The Alps themselves, which your own poets used to love so reverently, you look upon as soaped poles in a bear garden, which you set yourselves to climb, and slide down again, with shrieks of delight. When you are past shrieking, having no human articulate voice to say you are glad with, you fill the quietude of the valleys with gunpowder blasts, and rush home, red with cutaneous eruption of conceit, and voluble with convulsive hiccough of self-satisfaction."

Among Ruskin's "your own poets" was presumably Lord Alfred Tennyson, who, on first catching sight of the Grindelwald glacier that lies near the foot of the Eiger, is said to have remarked, "That is a filthy thing!"

Notwithstanding criticism and an occasional tragedy, mountain climbing was considered a lark in those days. It was not uncommon for a pair of English climbers to be escorted, not only by three or four guides, but by a score of porters who, like Sherpas a century later, would haul all sorts of accoutrements up to the mountain peaks, on which picnic hampers would be unloaded, tableclothes spread, and magnums of champagne broken out while the climbers enjoyed their lordly view. All of which led one English alpinist to write, "It's not advisable to drink too much strong liquors while climbing in the Alps. If, however, you are going to fall over a cliff, it's advisable to be thoroughly intoxicated when you do so."

Which brings us, in a very roundabout way, to someone else who wanted to climb the Matterhorn. In 1858 an Irish sportsman, Charles Barrington, was on holiday in Grindelwald looking around for an Alp to climb. He did a few easy local peaks but wanted something memorable to finish off his vacation. He first thought of the so-far unclimbed Matterhorn, but his funds were running low, his time was running out, and anyway here was this mountain named the Ogre right in his hotel's backyard. The locals assured him that the Eiger, "that monster in the act of bounding from the earth," as another English writer was to describe the peak, was still unclimbed.

Charles Barrington promptly set out to correct that state of affairs.

2

Up Here I Am Master!

Charles Barrington approached veteran guides Christian Almer and Peter Bohren, who had accompanied him on some of his earlier hikes. Had the Eiger ever been climbed, he asked them. No, it hadn't. Would they consider trying it with him? They would.

A story is told about the time Christian Almer and another local guide decided to climb the Wetterhorn just outside Grindelwald. They carried a young chopped-down fir tree to stick in the summit snow as proof of their success. As they neared the peak they were astonished to run across three strangers, Englishman Alfred Wills and his two favorite Chamonix guides. The French guides talked of giving the Grindelwald men a few *"coups de poing"* to dissuade them from attempting the summit, while in turn "the Grindelwald guides were indignant at this invasion of their backyard," as Wills later wrote of the incident. "My guides at first talked of giving them (the strangers) blows but eventually they gave them instead a cake of chocolate and declared that they really were good fellows after all. Thus the pipe of peace was smoked and tranquillity reigned between the rival groups."

The five men reached the summit and there planted the fir tree and a flag. Astronomers in Berne later spotted the flag in their telescopes, as well as the fir tree, which they took to be an optical illusion of some kind, because the summit of the Wetterhorn was well known to be far above the line where any plants grew.

To celebrate his golden wedding anniversary, Almer reclimbed the Wetterhorn in his seventieth year, accompanied by his seventy-two-year-old wife, who had never before climbed any of the local peaks. Along with the pair of celebrants were their two sons, their eldest daughter, two porters, a photographer, and, presumably to be on the safe side, a doctor. Almer died two years later, after having pioneered scores of first routes and ascents in the Alps of both Switzerland and France.

Peter Bohren, Barrington's other guide, was also to become a legend for his mountain-climbing prowess. Because of his swift, effortless pace, he was called *Der Gletscherwolf* (The Glacier Wolf) by his fellow guides. It was Bohren who first enunciated what was to become a guiding principle of Swiss bergführers (mountain guides) when he told a recalcitrant patron one day, *"Herr, Sie sind Meister im Tal, hier oben bin ich es."* ("Sir, you are master down in the valley. Up here I am master.") Bohren died in his sixtieth year of an embolism suffered while on a climb of the Wetterhorn.

Early in the morning of August 11, 1858, Barrington, Almer, and Bohren started up the west flank of the Eiger. But let Barrington, whose writing style was lively and down-to-earth ("Spent the night in a small hut occupied by a goatkeeper. I was eaten up with fleas."), tell of the ascent in his own words, taken from a letter he sent to the British *Alpine Journal* in May, 1877.

"In the evening of the next day, the 10th, I made a bargain with the same guides for the Eiger, and walked up to the hotel on the Wengern Alp, stopping to play cards for an hour on the way, and found it quite full at 12 o'clock at night. Threw myself on a sofa and started at 3:30 A.M. on August 11 for the Eiger. We took a flag from the hotel. When we came to the point where one descends into a small hollow, I looked well with my glass over the face of the Eiger next to us, and made up my mind to try the rocks in front instead of going up the other side, which had been tried twice before unsuccessfully. Almer and Bohren said it was no use and declined to come the way I wished. 'All right,' I said. 'You may stay. I will try.' So off I went for about 300 or 400 yards over some smooth rocks to the part which was almost perpendicular. I then shouted and waved the flag for them to come on, and after five minutes they followed and came up to me. They said it was impossible. I said, 'I will try.' So, with the rope coiled over my shoulders, I scrambled up, sticking like a cat to the rock, which cut my fingers, and, at last got up to say fifty to sixty feet. I then lowered the rope and the guides followed with its assistance. We then had to mark our way with chalk and small bits of stone, fearing we might not be able to find it on our return. We went up very close to the edge, looking down on Grindelwald, sometimes throwing over large stones to hear them crash down beneath the clouds. We got to the top, the two guides kindly gave me the place of first man up—at 12 o'clock, stayed about ten minutes, fearing the weather, and came down in four hours, avoiding the very steep place as, looking down from above, we found out a couloir, down which we came, and just saved ourselves by a few seconds from an avalanche.

"I was met at the bottom by about thirty visitors, and we went up to the hotel. They doubted if we had been on the top until the telescope disclosed the flag there. The hotel proprietor had a large gun fired off, and I seemed for the evening to be a 'lion.'

"Thus ended my first and only visit to Switzerland. Not having money enough to try the Matterhorn, I went home. Nothing could exceed the kindness of Almer and Bohren. Both were splendid mountaineers, and had I not been as fit as my old horse, 'Sir Robert Peel,' when I won the Irish Grand National with him, I would not have seen half the course. I may add that when leaving Grindelwald for the Eiger I was surprised to see the families of the guides in a state of distraction at their departure for the ascent, and two elderly ladies came out and abused me for taking them to risk their lives."

Because of the traditional rivalry between Celt and Saxon, one suspects that Barrington, a noted horseman who sometimes raced his mounts in England, derived an extra dollop of satisfaction from his Eiger triumph. Switzerland was full of Englishmen dashing around snatching off one unclimbed peak after another. The Eiger, however, was one Alp an Irishman had beaten them to.

In 1864 a Miss Lucy Walker of a wealthy Liverpool family well known for its interest in Alpine mountaineering made, along with local guides, the fourth ascent of the Eiger and the first by a woman. A formidable figure, Lucy ate nothing but spongecake and drank nothing but champagne when engaged in climbing. She later became the first woman to climb the Matterhorn.

In 1865, seven years after the original Eiger climb, Christian Almer was asked by Whymper to join him in a Matterhorn attempt. Almer declined. Whymper instead turned to Michel Croz who, as we've seen, lost his life on the descent. Whymper was to climb often with Almer and once said of him, "There isn't a truer heart or surer foot in the Alps." On one occasion Whymper and Almer went to Chamonix to try a first ascent of the Aiguille Verte. They took a local porter with them to help set up a tent at a place called the Couvercle. They left the porter to look after the tent and the food while they went ahead to climb the summit. They duly arrived at the peak, congratulated each other on another first, then started down again. "Snow began to fall heavily before we were off the summit rocks, our track was obscured and frequently lost, and everything became so sloppy and slippery that the descent took as long as the ascent," Whymper wrote. "The schrund was recrossed at 3:15 P.M. and then we raced down to the Couvercle, intending to have a carouse there; but as we rounded our rock a howl broke simultaneously from us for the porter had taken down the tent and was in the process of moving off with it. 'Stop there! What are you doing?' He observed that he had thought we were killed, or at least lost, and was going to Chamonix to communicate his ideas to the *guide chef*. 'Unfasten the tent and get out the food.' Instead of doing so, the porter fumbled in his pockets. 'Get out the food!' we roared, losing all patience. 'Here it is,' said our worthy friend, producing a dirty piece of bread about as big as a halfpenny roll. We looked solemnly at the fluff covered morsel. It was past a joke—he had devoured everything; mutton, loaves, cheese, wine, eggs, sausage, all was gone—past recovery. It was idle to grumble, and useless to wait. We were light and could move quickly—the porter was laden inside and out. We went our hardest. He had to shuffle and trot. He streamed with perspiration; the mutton and cheese oozed out in big drops; he larded the glacier. We had our revenge and dried our clothes at the same time and when we arrived at the Montenvers the porter was as wet as we had been upon our arrival at the Couvercle. We halted at the inn to get a little food, and at a quarter past eight re-entered Chamonix, amidst firing of cannon and other demonstrations of satisfaction on the part of the hotel-keepers."

In 1867 Englishman John Tyndall and two guides repeated the climb of the Eiger's west flank. He commented, "A wilder precipice is hardly to be seen than this wall (north face) of the Eiger, viewed from the cornice at the top. It seems to drop sheer for 8,000 feet down to Grindelwald." (It is actually 9,800 feet from the tip of the Eiger down to the village.) Tyndall, one of those Englishmen of scientific bent who were so prevalent in those days, actually took blocks of glacier ice back to London, where he conducted scores of experiments trying to determine why ice sometimes melted from the inside out. He had noticed blocks of ice with bubbles of water trapped in their interiors.

In 1876 Richard Barrington, a brother of Charles, and a more experienced climber, repeated the west-flank ascent. During the 1880s an English aristocrat, Sir Peter Campbell, who had been blind since boyhood, also climbed the west flank of the Eiger, as well as Mont Blanc and the Matterhorn.

The Eiger had been mastered. What next? One of the constants of mountain climbing is that as soon as one challenge is met, a new one takes its place. True the Eiger had been climbed, but on its easiest, west flank. How about the other approaches? One by one they fell.

In 1876 the south ridge was climbed by Englishman G. E. Foster and his Grindelwald guide, Hans Baumann. Eight years later the Eiger was climbed from the southwest ridge via the saddle connecting it with the Mönch by guides Ulrich Almer and Aloys Pollinger, and English mountaineers Anderson and Baker. In 1885 local guides roped down the Mittellegi Ridge after ascending by the normal west-flank route.

In 1921 a young Japanese climber, Yuko Maki, arrived in Grindelwald and hired guides Fritz Amatter, Fritz Steuri, and Samuel Brawand for an ascent of the Eiger using the Mittellegi Ridge that rises just above the village. The four men, making one overnight bivouac, reached the summit the next day. Thirty-five years later Yuko Maki was to lead a successful Japanese assault on 26,760-foot Manaslu in the Himalayas, one of the world's ten highest mountains. The Japanese were back again in 1927 when S. Matsukata and S. Uramatsu, teaming up with guides Emil Steuri and Samuel Brawand, climbed the Hörnli Ridge of the Eiger's southeast face to the summit.

One more of the routes considered possible remained, and that fell when two Swiss climbers, Dr. Hans Lauper and Alfred Zürcher, with

their guides Josef Knubel and Alexander Graven, climbed the northeast ridge to the peak in 1932. That line was immediately dubbed the Lauper Route in honor of the great Swiss alpinist and mountaineer. Actually Lauper was considered to have solved the Nordwand of the Eiger, and he wrote in 1932, "it is a source of gratification to us that the north face of the Eiger, the last important problem of the Bernese Oberland, should have been solved by this unsurpassed all-Swiss party." Presumably he considered the true north face, between the Lauper Route and the west flank, unclimbable, and he indeed referred to it as that frightful abyss.

Two years later the first winter traverse of the peak was made by the Grindelwald guides Fritz Amatter and Fritz Kaufmann Almer, who ascended via the Mittellegi Ridge and came down the west flank. What magnificent men that generation of Grindelwald guides must have been! Amatter was sixty-eight when he accomplished the winter traverse.

In Grindelwald the local guides rested on their laurels as far as the Eiger was concerned. They had been involved in almost every successful ascent and attempt on the peak. The mountain had no challenges left— all possible routes had been mastered.

Except, of course, that the stark north face was still unclimbed, but then that route was clearly impossible. Only a madman would attempt its series of sheer rock walls linked to each other, like slanting step risers, by long steep icefields.

The Eigernordwand—clearly impossible, and yet men dream and invent new challenges. As far back as 1882 Johann Grill, a German mountaineer who made many winter climbs in the Tyrol, speculated on the possibility of doing the Eiger's north face. Then in 1931 the north face of the Matterhorn, another big north wall, was climbed by the Schmid brothers of Munich, who bicycled one hundred miles to Zermatt, started off up the north wall of the Matterhorn, bivouacked once on the face, climbed to the peak in a raging snowstorm, and then down climbed the Hörnli Ridge, a route with which they were unfamiliar. They reached the Hörnli hut, slept eighteen hours, descended to Zermatt, mounted their bicycles, and rode the hundred miles back to Mun-

---

THE NORTH WALL OF THE EIGER

1. Bivouac Cave	*5. Death Bivouac*	*9. Lauper Route*
2. Stollenloch (Gallery Window)	*6. Traverse of the Gods Bivouac*	*10. Mittellegi Ridge*
3. Swallow's Nest	*7. Longhi Ledge*	*11. Summit*
4. Eigerwand Station windows	*8. Corti Bivouac*	*12. West Flank*

ich. Four years later a second "impossible" north wall fell to German climbers Peters and Maier—the north face of the Grandes Jorasses in the Mont Blanc massif. Now, of all the great faces in the Alps, only the Eigernordwand remained.

Conservative climbers pronounced it unscalable. It was too steep, too high, too demanding. It was a mile-high haul straight up over rock, snow, and ice—a climb that would test to the breaking point, and even beyond, the skill and courage of the best mountaineers. In addition to big-wall experience, what qualities did you need for the Eiger? One climber said that it called for the strength of a gorilla, the agility of a cat, the nerves of a high-wire walker, and the endurance of a marathon runner. You had to be constantly alert and cheerful. Men hanging over a mile of yawning space couldn't indulge in temper tantrums or a moment of carelessness. One's first mistake on the Eiger was usually the last.

The best climbers knew how to handle rock and ice. The real difficulty of the Eigernordwand climb came from the "objective" dangers it posed, those perils that no amount of equipment or skill can guard against. The giant north face, largest in the Alps, is composed of black limestone that is crumbly and cracked by eons of freeze and thaw. The lower third of the face has been scoured smooth by falling rock and grinding ice. Every little bump and projection has been filed down so that it is cliff after cliff of smooth polished rock with, if one is lucky, a crack here and there to hold a piton. The upper third of the face is covered with a skin of rotten, crumbly limestone that is constantly flaking off, or being shivered off, by frost and sun. The sun does not rest long on the north faces of mountains in the northern hemisphere. But when the rays of the westering sun finally touch the upper reaches of the Eiger's north wall, ice lets go its grip on stone, and a rock barrage begins. Climbers face sudden rockfall on almost every section of the climb. Icicles from the higher snowfields whistle down like gleaming

---

WHERE THEY DIED

1. Sedlmayer and Mehringer (Death Bivouac)	10. Nothdurft and Mayer	19. Travellini
2. Angerer, Rainer, and Hinterstoisser	11. Adolf Mayr	20. Eske, Kalkbrenner, Richter, and Warmuth
3. Kurz	12. Brewster	21. Herzel and Reichardt
4. Sandri and Menti	13. Derungs	22. Weiss
5. Gollackner	14. Marchart	23. Ursella
6. Körber and Vass	15. Carruthers and Moderegger	24. Masahiro and Miyagawa
7. Gonda and Wyss	16. Rabada and Navarro	25. Knowles
8. Moosmüller and Söhnel	17. Watabe	26. Stör
9. Longhi	18. Harlin	27. Pechous and Siegl

spears, while melting snow turns cracks and chimneys into waterfalls. The water in turn makes footing slippery and loosens even more stones. Each rock begins to hum a deadly song as it falls, from a thin, high, eerie whistle to the clattering shatter sound of collision with the great rock face. Whole sheets of ice, like huge panes of opaque glass, come slicing down through space.

A noted English mountaineer succinctly described the north face of the Eiger in these terms: "rotten limestone hung with snow and icefields, hidden in mist and clouds, wracked by furious storms, frequently swept by avalanches of snow and rotten rock." A French climber took one look at the rocks that came whistling and bounding down that fearful precipice and complained, *"Pas une ascension cela, c'est la guerre"* ("That's not climbing, that's warfare").

And then there's the weather. Because of the north wall's scooped-out shape, and its position in the Alps, storms brew up on the face in a matter of minutes. It is the first great thrusting bulwark in the Alps to catch a storm coming in over the plains of France, westward from the Atlantic and southward from the Baltic. Climbers soaked from a struggle up rocks streaming with snowmelt may suddenly find themselves in a howling blizzard, their clothes stiffening into garments of ice. Holds and ledges fill with powder snow, rocks are glazed with ice, ropes become as stiff as broom handles, and avalanches hiss down with suffocating force. Lightning frequently plays over the scene, sometimes striking the metal pitons that hold climber's ropes to the wall. Fierce winds are common on the Eiger. Gusts of over a hundred miles an hour have been recorded on its flanks. In fact, hailstorms and snowstorms frequently rage on the Eiger's north face while Grindelwald, at the mountain's foot, is bathed in sunshine. Tourists sunning themselves on terrace deck chairs can look up at a white shrouded Eigernordwand and be unaware that a ferocious thunderstorm is raging behind those curtains of cloud.

There is one more interesting fact to note about the Eiger. In 1912 the Jungfrau railroad drove a tunnel across the heart of the Eiger's north face on its switchback journey to the Jungfraujoch, the saddle between the Mönch and the Jungfrau, where Europe's highest railroad station is to be found. From this tunnel five huge windowed openings of the intermediate Eigerwand Station pierce through the north wall itself. These openings were used to dump waste down the mountain when the cog railway was being built. Lower down and to the west of the Eiger-

Stollenloch (*Gallery Window*).

wand Station, there is another breakthrough hole in the face that is cus-
tomarily kept closed with a pair of stout wooden doors. The Eigerwand
Station and the Gallery Window (*Stollenloch*) were to play dramatic roles
in many of the attempts on the Eigernordwand—did in fact play such a
role in the first recorded attempt on the north face when, in the summer
of 1934, three German climbers, K. and G. Lowinger and W. Beck, got
2,000 feet up the wall before they came to grief. They hung in their
ropes several hours before local guides crawled out the Eigerwand Station windows and managed, at no small risk to themselves, to rescue the
marooned men.

Finally there is the open-air theatricality attached to any Eiger climb.
The north face is visible from almost any part of the village of Grindelwald, as well as from the hotels at Kleine Scheidegg, low down on the
Eiger's western flank. In clear weather, climbers on the face can be followed with field glass and telescope from scores of hotel balconies.

A journalist once described the Eiger as the White Cobra. It was a
particularly apt coinage, because it graphically conveys the concave
nature of the face and the darkly menacing aspect of the broad, flared
shoulders that rise hoodlike to a small, poised malevolent head.

The locale is set, the scenery described. Center stage the White
Cobra waits.

Enter Sedlmayer and Mehringer.

3

Death Bivouac

In 1935 Max Sedlmayer, twenty-four, and Karl Mehringer, twenty-
six, two German climbers from Munich, arrived at the foot of the Eiger
and made their headquarters in a small mountain hut. For a week the
two men studied the bleak soaring face through their binoculars, trying
to find a good line up those sheer cliffs and icefields. One day Mehringer
climbed the "easy" west-flank route in order to deposit a precautionary
cache of food on the summit, in the event that he and Sedlmayer
reached the peak in a half-starved condition, their food supplies already
consumed. He also thought it prudent to learn the west-flank route in
case of a forced descent at night, or in a snowstorm.

---

*Max Sedlmayer and Karl Mehringer chopping wood in Grindelwald the day
before they started their climb.*

SEDLMAYER PHOTO

The two men now waited for a good-weather forecast, four or five clear days in a row, if possible. At the end of each day's climb they planned to camp up on the mountain face, attaching themselves to the wall with pitons, if necessary. They hoped to make the summit in three days but, as a precaution, would take enough food to last twice as long.

Sedlmayer and Mehringer belonged to a new breed of mountain climbers—the extremists, so called because they used extreme or artificial methods in their attempts to conquer mountain faces. For the most part these climbers, scornfully called rockscramblers or *Kletterfritzen* by the purists, were German, Austrian, and Italian. They had invented and adapted new tools and methods to attack supposedly unclimbable cliffs.

The purist or Victorian mountaineers used only a rope and an ice axe to help them reach the summit. The rope was used mainly as protection against a fall. One was tied to a guide, or another climber, with anywhere up to a hundred feet of rope between both parties. If one fell, the other man on the rope would theoretically brake the fall and hold his rope mate. The rope had been used in this fashion by peasants for hundreds of years in the mountains, usually when crossing glaciers, as a safeguard against plunging into an unseen crevasse. The ice axe, with a pointed metal tip at one end and a chopping blade at the other, was a combination of two earlier tools— the *Alpenstock,* a stout walking stick with a pointed metal ferrule for jabbing into ice or snow, and the ordinary chopping axe that was often taken along to chop footholds in steep ice slopes. The earliest climbers, before 1840, say, also used light wooden ladders and grappling hooks, but these were gradually discarded as being too cumbersome or too dangerous.

The extremists used such items as pitons, spikes of various sizes that could be driven into narrow cracks in the rock walls. These spikes had an eye or a ring at one end through which a snap link, called a carabiner, could be attached. A rope, tied around the climber's body at the waist, was then snapped into a carabiner via its spring-loaded gate. In this way a climber was held safe on a wall while he decided what his next move was. If a climber slipped and fell while climbing beyond a piton through which his climbing rope ran, the spike would hold him because his weight would be counterbalanced by the weight of the climber, or climbers, on the lower end of the rope. Extremists climbed on 100- to 450-foot-long combined "ropes" of two, three, four, or more climbers. Sometimes pitons, also called pegs, pins, and spikes, were used as steps or handholds, but generally they served as anchor points to hold climbers safe in their progress up a wall. Sometimes instead of, or in addition to, using a piton, a lead climber, finding a good "stance" or safe place on which to plant himself, looped the climbing rope around a rock knob and then around his waist so that he was braced to hold a possible fall by his partner. This was called a belay. The next climber then moved up with the rope to join his companion, safe in the knowledge that the belay anchor and his partner would hold him if he fell. As the second climber moved up, the lead climber took in the slack so that the climbing rope was always taut and ready to instantly hold the following climber should he come off. Similarly the second man on the rope was always ready to hold the first climber should the former fall while leading the way up a rope length, or "pitch." As the lead climber got higher and higher, the rope length increased, and therefore so did the distance he could fall. However, the dangers of such a fall were lessened by the climber's periodically banging in pitons, into the eye of which carabiners were clipped, and the climbing rope was threaded through each carabiner in turn. If the climber fell, he would now be brought up short at the nearest piton, instead of falling all the way to his climbing partner's stance.

Pitons were a natural development of the practice of some early climbers of taking along a pocketful of tenpenny or twelvepenny spikes.

Some climbing gear: Clockwise from extreme left, waist harness, Figure-8 descender (used for rappels), various ice and rock hammers, pair of crampons, various ice axes, carabiners, slings, étriers. In center, helmet, rope, and boots. Not shown, rock and ice pitons. A. ROTH PHOTO

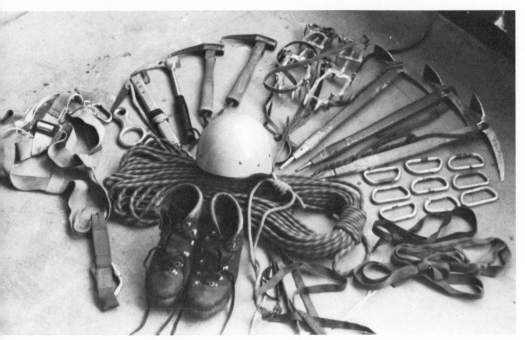

One of these large nails was driven into a suitable crack, the rope looped over the spike, and the end of the nail hammered upwards to form an angle that would contain the rope. In the early days of such use, climbers simply picked up a suitable stone and used it to pound in the nail, but gradually hammers became a standard part of a climber's equipment. Some climbers took to using eye bolts, with the eye opened just enough to take the rope, but in time special long, shafted iron pegs, with a ring at one end, were made and the piton was born. However, the piton had one big drawback. To get the climbing rope through the eye or ring in the end of the piton, it was necessary for the mountaineer to untie the rope from his waist, thread the end through the piton's eye, then retie himself into the end of the rope. It was an awkward, time-consuming, and dangerous procedure. A shortcut was soon found, a separate five-foot length of rope, called a sling, that was tied through the piton's eye and then around the climbing rope in a loop that permitted the climbing rope to feed on through, yet would hold the climber to the piton in the event of a fall. The last man on the climbing rope would untie and collect the slings as he reached each one. Even this proved too time consuming, and the carabiner, an oval-shaped snap link that could be easily opened and closed, soon became a standard part of a climber's equipment. The carabiner was, in effect, a short, rigid metal snap hook that held climbing rope and piton together, but one that could be quickly engaged and disengaged. Carabiners are thought to have been first adapted for mountain climbing in the early 1900s by a German climber Otto Herzog, who noticed them being used by Bavarian firemen in their various rescue maneuvers. As a piece of fire-fighting equipment, they go back to the 1850s. A further development came with the locking-gate carabiner, which when its swinging portion was locked shut via a threaded thumb nut, could not be accidentally forced open again by a buckling rope or by pressure from a spike of rock.

Extremists were also called Grade-VI climbers, in reference to a rating scale that was drawn up in the 1920s by Willo Welzenbach, a superb German climber who lost his life on Nanga Parbat in 1934. Climbs were classified according to length, degree of difficulty, physical agility required to make the hardest moves, degree of "objective" dangers, and so on. Grade VI came to denote artificial or direct-aid climbing of the highest standard, calling for the free use of pitons, bolts, *étriers* (three- and four-step rope ladders), pulleys, and other mechanical aids to hoist one upward. The last three grades were further subdivided into plus and minus, thereby giving a greater degree of discrimination. Thus a route might be graded VI−, VI, or VI+. Last year the UIAA, an umbrella group of Alpine associations, sanctioned the use of Grade VII, in effect adding another three levels of difficulty.

Sedlmayer and Mehringer, both Grade-VI climbers, loaded their backpacks in the small hours of the morning of August 21, a Wednesday, checked each other's ropes and hardware, and started to hike up the mountain meadows that led to the foot of the Eiger.

Meanwhile word had spread through the valley that two German climbers were already working their way up the lower reaches of the Nordwand. There was no lack of discussion among the local guides about the attempt, and, in general, the German climbers were dismissed as madmen. The Swiss guides were highly professional, philosophically opposed to the ideals and methods of the extremists. Safety was their paramount consideration, and there was nothing safe about the Eigernordwand. Still, there had to be some envy on the part of the Grindelwald guides. Back in the good old days *"der Lords und Ladies, der Grafen und Herzoge, mit Gefolge und Säcken voll Geld"* ("of the lords and ladies, of the counts and dukes, with their attendants and bags full of money"), as a current history of Grindelwald mountaineering puts it, the local guides were involved in all attempts on new routes on the Eiger and other local peaks. But in 1935 the Great Depression had gripped Europe, and the extremists were generally working-class youths (often unemployed) who couldn't afford the local hotels, let alone the services of guides. They often slept in tents or in cow huts in the mountain pastures, and for transportation generally relied on their thumbs or bicycles. The luckier ones had eccentric motorbikes that often tried to do in their owners before the mountains had a chance at killing them. And although there may have been little sympathy for the German pair on the part of the local guides, there had to be a certain amount of admiration for their audacity in tackling the Eigernordwand. In 1924, and again in 1932, local guides had tried the Nordwand, but without the newer techniques and equipment of direct-aid climbing, they had been unable to get any higher than the windows of the Eigerwand Station, a not inconsiderable achievement under the circumstances.

When daylight came, Eiger watchers crowded around the telescopes on the terraces of the hotels in Grindelwald and at Kleine Scheidegg. They soon spotted the pair of German climbers. Sedlmayer and Mehringer were climbing into unknown territory. However, they had studied the face for days and knew they had at least four towering bands of cliffs to master. In between these cliff bands, where the mountain face was not straight up and down, there were icefields. These were frozen ice and snow shields that clung to the side of the mountain. In addition to the rock bands and icefields, there were the usual "overhangs," "traverses," and "chimneys" to be negotiated on the cliff faces themselves.

In spite of the difficulties, the two men steadily nailed their way up the wall. All day the telescope watchers marveled at their skill. This was

high-wire climbing, moving constantly on that thin edge where climbing often shaded into acrobatics. The pair mastered the first steep band of cliffs, climbed above the five windows of the Eigerwand Station, and, when dark came, were 2,500 feet above the base of the wall. With their axes they hacked snow and ice away from a shelf of rock, sat down, and prepared a hot drink and some food. In high spirits they decided to leave a memento of their passing and, on a scrap of paper, penciled in a few brief words. Folding their message, they placed it inside a tobacco tin that they thrust into a crevice in the rock face. There, they left proof that they had gone higher on the face than anyone else. Then, pulling their sleeping sacks up to their shoulders, they prepared to wait out their first night. They must have felt pleased with their progress. With 2,500 feet of the wall below them, they had only 3,500 feet left, and still had two full days on their three-day schedule.

The next morning dawned cloudless. The forecast was holding up. The first watchers to man the telescopes spotted the two climbers already hard at work. Even through a scope the men looked like tiny flies against the immensity of the rock face. As the day progressed, the climbers cut their way up the First Icefield. It took them hours. To make matters worse, they constantly had to dodge falling rocks, previously loosened by the sun's warmth. There were no safety helmets then, so whenever the climbers heard or spotted rocks on the way down, they placed their rucksacks on their heads for protection against the projectiles whizzing by them.

To climb the First Icefield, Sedlmayer and Mehringer had to hack a staircase of steps out of the granular ice. It was slow, laborious, and physically as well as emotionally exhausting work. The icefield had a fifty-five-degree slope, and it was like climbing the steep roof of a house, where one slip could prove fatal. However, they reached the upper rim of the icefield and here found a sheltered spot to bivouac. Using pitons, they roped themselves to the wall for safety, fixed food (bread, pork sausage), and a hot drink (tea), and tried to catch some sleep in their bivouac sacks. They were sitting up—there wasn't enough room to stretch out full length.

The next day, Friday, watchers down in the valley noted that the climbers had slowed considerably. Were they weakened from their exhausting efforts of the previous two days? It now looked as if it would take them at least four days, perhaps even five, to reach the peak. The pair still had several cliff bands and at least three more icefields to mas-

Max Sedlmayer.
SEDLMAYER PHOTO

ter. And one of the little surprises the Eiger had in store for climbers is the fact that, generally speaking, its icefields are arranged in ascending order of difficulty. The Second Icefield is steeper than the First, the Third steeper than the Second, while the Fourth, the Spider, serves as an avalanche chute for the whole upper quarter of the face.

As the day wore on, Sedlmayer and Mehringer seemed to be moving slower and slower. Often they were motionless for as long as fifteen to twenty minutes at a time. The Second Icefield proved to be twice as hard as the First. Not only was it nearly twice as high, it was also appreciably steeper; to make matters worse, the men were exposed to rockfall every step of the way. Again and again they were seen to halt, burrow their bodies into the ice, and dodge the rocks that came bounding and whirring and chittering down the mountain face. They were still climbing when clouds drifted across the Eiger and hid them from view.

That night a storm blew up, bringing high winds, thunder, and lightning. Rain down in the valley was often snow up on the Eiger. It could not have been easy for the climbers, as the storm sent down avalanches of loose snow and unpredictable volleys of falling rock. The Grindelwald guides were now discussing the climbers' chances of ever getting down off the wall alive. Morning came, but the storm still raged. All day Saturday the elements were in a fury, and all day clouds piled up against the Eiger wall. Night fell, and people could only guess at the torments of the two men on the Eigernordwand.

On Sunday morning the weather showed some signs of abatement, though there were still occasional showers and plenty of clouds blanketing the face. At midday the veil of clouds parted briefly, and one of the telescope monitors spotted two tiny figures climbing across a snowfield. The Munich men were approaching the Flatiron, a prow-shaped ridge, thrusting out from the face, that resembled a front-on view of an old-fashioned flatiron for pressing clothes. The lead climber, presumed to be Sedlmayer, seemed to be still strong, but his rope mate, it was noticed, often slumped in his ropes from exhaustion.

Experienced Swiss guides now feared the worst. They knew it would be suicide to try and climb down. One problem in climbing sheer cliffs was getting back down again. It was often easier and less dangerous to climb up than to climb down. But an old method of getting down cliffs was adapted to mountain-climbing purposes, the abseil (German) or rappel (French) descent. The climber looped the midpoint of his rope around a tree or rock knob, so that both ends hung down the cliff face at an equal length. He now straddled the rope, his face to the cliff. He brought the doubled rope up into his crotch, then up behind his back to his right shoulder, thence down over the shoulder and across his chest to his left side. His right hand held the rope out in front of him; his left

hand held the doubled rope at his left hip. By leaning backwards at an
angle of forty-five degrees, he let his body weight pay out the rope, his
right hand guiding the amount of payout and his left hand acting as a
brake. The climber now walked himself down the cliff face, his feet
braced against the rock wall to lower himself in a series of smoothly
controlled moves. By taking an extra loop of rope around his right
thigh, he could even rest on the rope, both hands free to check a previous piton placement, or to sort through his gear. When he reached a
safe stance, he could retrieve the rope by pulling on either of the two
strands, the rest of the rope running up and around the rappel knob at
the head of the cliff. The abseil method had been used for centuries by
mountain woodcutters. A fifteenth-century illustration shows a wood-
cutter, his rope looped around a sawed-off stump of a tree, going down
a cliff in a classic abseil. Before that, in the Middle Ages, jugglers and
acrobats putting on a show in the town square, had sometimes climbed
to the top of a church steeple and rappelled back down, to the delighted
astonishment of the onlookers. It helped to draw a crowd for the subsequent pitch—to pun on a mountaineering term.

The important thing about the rappel was to make sure you had a
ledge to stand on when you came to the end of the rope—or the second
fastest way down a cliff, as rappelling has been called, could quickly
become the fastest way.

Unfortunately for Sedlmayer and Mehringer, falling rubble, snow
avalanches, and ice-glazed rock made a descent to the lower reaches of
the wall extremely difficult. It would take as long to get down as to go
up, and the climbing would be just as perilous, if not more so. They
probably felt that their only hope was to get as high as possible, then
somehow to find a traverse line across to the Lauper Route on the northeast flank. From there they could probably manage a safe retreat to
Grindelwald.

Clouds closed in again and another storm-wracked day and another
long, cold night passed. It was Tuesday before the weather finally
cleared. Sedlmayer and Mehringer had now been on the wall six days
and five nights. Their food was all used up. And without food their
strength and endurance had to be running out.

Watchers eagerly manned the telescopes. But no matter how metic-
ulously they searched, they could find no trace of the Munich climbers.
In the days that followed, small planes passed and repassed the north
face of the Eiger, looking for signs of the climbers. Nothing was spotted.
Hometown friends of the two men, including Sedlmayer's brother Heinrich, who had cut short a climbing trip in the Dolomites when he heard
that Max was in trouble on the Eiger, arrived at the scene, but rescue
attempts were hopeless. The recent storm and its snow burden had left

the north wall impossible to climb. And there was no way of lowering rescuers from the peak, even if men climbed up there via the west flank. Heinrich Sedlmayer and his friends actually did climb the west flank, but could see no trace of the missing pair of mountaineers. Nobody knew where the climbers were, and no one except Sedlmayer and Mehringer knew what to expect up there. Among the guides the consensus was that rescue attempts would only result in more deaths. "The two adventurers had just scrambled from piton to piton. . . . it was impossible to send out a guides rescue party," the British *Alpine Journal* reported. Sedlmayer and Mehringer were given up for dead.

A month passed. In mid-September a German pilot, Ernst Udet, flew a small plane back and forth across the Nordwand, trying to locate the bodies of the missing climbers. With him was Fritz Steuri, a local guide with an encyclopedic knowledge of the Eiger. The plane flew within a hundred feet of the wall. Finally, higher than they had expected, they spotted a body. The man was standing up in a crouch, facing the wall, half-buried in snow. He looked as though he were engaged in some grotesque congress with the face. The men in the plane couldn't see the climber's features, which were hidden under the hood of a storm jacket—couldn't tell whether it was Mehringer or Sedlmayer. Nor did they spot the body of the second climber. The place on the Eiger where that frozen body was noticed, the overnight camp above the Flatiron, was ever after known as Death Bivouac.

A year later Heinrich Sedlmayer and some friends arrived in Grindelwald to look for the bodies of the missing climbers. They climbed up the lower reaches of the wall and spotted four fingers sticking up out of a patch of snow a short distance below the Eigerwand Station. They dug out the corpse, which proved to be that of Max Sedlmayer. His waist carabiner was still in place, as was part of his climbing rope, evidence that he had been climbing when an avalanche had swept him away. The body was in the direct fall line of the position, much higher up, where the pilot Udet had, the previous September, reported spotting a climber facing the wall. Sedlmayer's body had to be dismembered of both arms and legs before it would fit in the body bag brought along by the retrievers, who themselves were climbing to the very limit of their capabilities. However, they managed to effect a retreat from the wall with their grisly burden and eventually brought the body back to Munich for a proper burial.

Heinrich Sedlmayer speculates that Mehringer probably died of exposure and exhaustion at Death Bivouac sometime Monday night, and that his brother buried his rope mate's body in snow, then continued climbing in the morning. This would explain why only one body was spotted by the pilot in his reconnaissance flights back and forth across the face several weeks later. Max Sedlmayer must have known that his position was hopeless. He still had over 2,000 feet of rock face and ice-fields to get up, yet something compelled him to continue climbing until his heart and body gave out and he died in his final footsteps, now married to the wall forever.

Mehringer wasn't found until 1962, when his dessicated corpse was discovered on the Second Icefield by a pair of Swiss climbers, Claude Asper and Bernard Voltolini. That was twenty-seven years after the initial attempt. Undoubtedly his body had been carried down to the Second Icefield from Death Bivouac by an avalanche sometime in the intervening years.

In the spring of 1976 Karel Prochazka, one of a four-man rope of Czech mountaineers climbing the rock face above the Eigerwand Station, found a small rusted tobacco tin. Inside there was a laconic note from forty-one years before, a brief yet somehow poignantly gallant message that marked the first bivouac place in that 1935 Eigernordwand attempt by two young men from Munich. The note read, "Biwakplatz am 21.8.35. Max Sedlmajr, Karl Mehringer, München."

4

The Wall Is Ours

The deaths of Sedlmayer and Mehringer ignited a controversy. One commentator wrote, "Even had the two Munich scramblers succeeded in their attempt, it would still have been a mockery of classic alpine climbing," and went on to call it "an evil demonstration on Swiss peaks. They knew full well that the severity of the face required continuous mechanical aid, hammers and nails, methods happily not recognized in Switzerland as yet. Let us hope these acrobats will find no imitators in Switzerland." He charged that Sedlmayer and Mehringer "would have inflicted a degradation on a great Alpine peak; mountaineering perverted into monkey tricks (*Affenlarve*)."

This remarkably harsh judgment on the two dead climbers was reprinted in the British *Alpine Journal* with the following editorial comment: "with which sentiments, while expressing sympathy for the relatives of the young climbers, every British mountaineer will concur." Another writer called the attempt "a flagrant example of the neglect of every sane principle of mountaineering in an attempt to gain cheap notoriety by accomplishing mechanized variants to former routes."

One now suspects that part of the outrage sprang from the fact that

Sedlmayer and Mehringer were working men. Some are called to the foot of the mountain, some to the peak.

Although the cantonal authorities in Berne actually issued a ban on climbing the Eigernordwand (rescinded a year later), the controversy eventually subsided, and the climbing world went back to its quotidian pursuits. Perhaps the extremists would now accept defeat and demonstrate their *Affenlarve* on other peaks, in other countries. The Eigernordwand was unclimbable, in fact suicidal; surely that was evident by now.

The professional corps of guides in the nearby towns of Grindelwald and Wengen certainly hoped that no more attempts on the north wall would be mounted. For the most part the professional mountain guides thought that the daring new climbers were more than a little touched. It's easy to see why. The local bergführers, who were hired by clients to conduct them on climbs in nearby mountains, generally sought the safest way up a slope. The extremists, on the other hand, wanted to test themselves and their new methods and equipment on the sheerest cliffs and the most dangerous icefields. A problem that bothered the guides, therefore, was the near impossibility of rescuing anyone in trouble. Mountain rescues had always been part of their tradition. Yet there were times when the weather and the conditions on the face made it impossible to climb. Though brave men, the Swiss guides had little experience with the iron hardware and new techniques used by the extremists; that was not their way of climbing. How, then, could they rescue an extremist? It was like rescuing a steeplejack. Only another steeplejack would try. And if foolhardy climbers like Sedlmayer and Mehringer died on the face, their bodies frozen to the rock, or perhaps hanging in their ropes, what effect would that have on tourists? Might not visitors, seeing those corpses turning in their ropes, decide that mountain climbing, even with professional guides, was much too dangerous a pastime for people who simply wanted healthy exercise and perhaps a small triumph? It was no wonder the local guides looked on the young Grade-VI climbers—those hotheads and Eiger "crazies," those amateurs—as a threat to their livelihood, if not to their very lives.

After the deaths of Sedlmayer and Mehringer no more attempts were made on the Eiger that summer. The tourists in the hotels of Grindelwald and Kleine Scheidegg, the two stations at opposite ends of the valley railway over which the Eiger reared its menacing height, no longer gathered around the telescopes.

In May of the following year, another pair of Munich climbers, Hans Teufel and Albert Herbst, appeared at Kleine Scheidegg. Some said they were friends of Sedlmayer and Mehringer, come to look for their as yet undiscovered bodies. Others said they were there to reconnoiter the Nordwand for a later attempt. Teufel is reported to have boasted,

"You Swiss are worthless. We will accomplish the deed." Whatever the truth, the two climbers left the Eiger in late June, probably because the mountain wore too heavy a snow burden from the previous winter. The pair decided to try some other peaks and perhaps return later in the summer when conditions for an Eiger attempt might prove more favorable. They never did come back. On climbing down from a first ascent of the north face of the Schneehorn, Teufel slipped on an ice bulge and was swept 600 feet down a snowfield, dragging his partner after him. Teufel was killed outright while Herbst was badly injured and had to be rescued by Swiss guides.

The summer of 1936 also saw the arrival of a formidable Swiss lady, one Loulou Boulaz, with her guide, Raymond Lambert. The pair had solid credentials. The previous summer they had followed two Italian climbers up the north face of the Grandes Jorasses in the Mont Blanc region, a climb nearly as difficult as the Eiger. The Italian climbers ungallantly reported that, had it not been for their help, the Swiss pair following them would never have made it to the summit. Boulaz was the first woman, and she and Lambert the third rope, to do the north face of the Grandes Jorasses. Some time later Boulaz was also to become the first woman to do the Walker Spur on the Grandes Jorasses, and, in a climbing career that spanned decades, she was the first woman and sometimes the first climber up scores of different Alpine routes.

But here she was in Grindelwald, purportedly ready to tackle the Eigernordwand. She and her partner evidently made a reconnaissance climb of the lower cliffs, getting as high as 2,000 feet before they retreated, to fade from the scene, if not from Eiger history, where Loulou Boulaz surely deserves her place. She was the first woman to try climbing the Eigernordwand. And she would be back! As for Raymond Lambert, he went on to a brilliant climbing career, capped when he and Tenzing Norkay, part of the 1952 Swiss expedition to Everest, reached 28,215 feet before bitter cold and jet-stream winds forced the pair to turn back, a heartbreaking 800 feet from the summit. It was the highest point man had ever climbed until then.

Early in July two experienced Austrian bergsteigers from Innsbruck, Edi Rainer and Willy Angerer, arrived and camped at the base of the north wall. They made several scouting climbs to test various routes. Knowing that Sedlmayer and Mehringer had found the going very tough on the sheer rock bands below the First Icefield, Rainer and Angerer looked for an easier line and opened up a new route to the west of the First Pillar, which they climbed past, and on up to the Shattered Pillar above it, another familiar landmark on the face. They continued climbing up the Difficult Crack, an eighty-foot pitch, to the foot of the *Rote Fluh* (Red Crag), a sheer rock cliff rising about a thousand feet, a smaller wall within the north face itself. Here they were stymied. The Rote Fluh seemed unclimbable. But how, then, were they to get to the First Icefield? The way to the left was barred by eighty-degree slabs of rock. The way up was barred. Yet somehow a line had to be forced. They bivouacked where they were that night and came down again the next morning. They were soaked and tired, but determined to try again as soon as the weather improved. While waiting, they met two German soldiers from Bad Reichenhall, Anderl Hinterstoisser and Toni Kurz, both twenty-three and on leave from their mountain regiment. They too wanted to try the Eiger. Both were experienced climbers who had pioneered many new Grade-VI routes in the Berchtesgaden Alps and had done such big walls as the north face of the Grosse Zinne. Their experience with multiday mixed rock and snow climbs, however, was somewhat limited.

By now the whole valley was humming with rumors of another north face attempt. At least four extremists were eyeing the Eigernordwand. Newspaper editors, remembering the deaths of the year before, sent reporters to the scene. Reporters sent back stories, some of them actually true, and it wasn't long before most of Europe knew that another Eigernordwand attempt was being mounted. Tourists and reporters were ready with their field glasses, their cameras, and their telescopes. Would the climb be a repeat of the year before, or would the Eigernordwand finally meet its match? Were the Germans and the Austrians in a race against each other, or would they climb together?

Of the four, Toni Kurz was the youngest. He had also been a professional guide in the mountains of his native Bavaria before entering the Army, and still had his guide's certificate. Thus he could sympathize with the Swiss guides and their feelings about the extremists. But Toni was young and had a devil-may-care attitude and a quick laugh, and he loved the spice and danger of the new style of climbing. Of the four men, he was probably the most popular among the Swiss guides and tourists who met him that summer. His laugh was always ringing out, he seemed absolutely fearless, and with his black curly hair and blue eyes, he had the stunning good looks of a movie star. His boast, *"Die Wand ist unser—oder wir bleiben in ihr"* ("The wall is ours, or we die on it"), could be dismissed as a bit of youthful braggadocio. Despite Kurz's popularity, it was generally felt that Hinterstoisser was the better climber of the two.

The German pair also made exploratory climbs, on one of which Hinterstoisser fell when a piton tore loose. He plummeted over a hundred feet but fortunately landed on a snow ledge with nothing worse to show for his fall than a sprained knee. On August 17 the weather cleared, and a favorable forecast of three or four days of good weather decided the climbers, who started packing their gear. Reporters were present, and Kurz told a long comic story of Hinterstoisser's fall several days before. Hinterstoisser, packing things not needed on the climb in a duffel bag he was leaving behind, shoved some photographs of himself and Kurz away in the sack and jokingly told the journalists that if anything happened to them, they knew where to find photographs for their stories.

Finally, at 2 A.M. on August 18, the four men shook hands all around, then headed up the meadows for the face of the mountain. With them they had sixty of the old-fashioned ring pitons, twenty of which were the foot-long pegs used on the snow fields. They had a dozen or so carabiners, hammers, ice axes, a spirit cooker, 240 feet of extra rope and a four-day supply of food, including two pounds of bacon, half a dozen loaves of black bread (you could drive pitons with them after twenty-four hours), cans of sardines, tea, and sugar. They roped up in two pairs, Hinterstoisser and Kurz on one, and the Austrian pair on the other. They climbed swiftly and surely and by 9 A.M. had reached the place where Rainer and Angerer had bivouacked on their earlier scouting foray. Here the climbers clipped in together on one rope of four. Though it would slow them down a bit, it would provide greater safety. If one fell off, there were three others to hold him.

Now they faced their toughest test so far, the overhanging bulge of the Rote Fluh, a face so smooth that it was doubtful whether even pitons could be used on it. There seemed to be no way up at that point; so Hinterstoisser decided to "traverse" across the middle of the broken cliff band to his left until he found an easier upward line.

A traverse is a sideways, horizontal move. Belayed by your companion, you edge over as far as you can, hammer in a piton, attach a snap link, thread your rope through the metal loop, then edge over some more. With the other end of the rope held firmly by your companion, the piton will bear your weight in case you fall. You go as far across as you can, hammer in another piton, clip in your rope again, then repeat the process until you find a couloir or a chimney or an icefield, some natural line that lets you start climbing upward once more. Here you stop and belay your companion while he repeats your traverse and joins up with you. There are various techniques that can be used on a traverse, including a tension traverse and a pendulum. The latter occurs when the next horizontal hold is too far away to reach. You climb up as high as you can, hammer in a piton, drop down again until you have ten or fifteen feet of rope between you and the piton, then start running back and forth across the cliff face, swinging like a clock pendulum on your rope until you've managed to reach the desired hold or step at the extreme end of one of your swings. You then find a stance, drive in a piton, and belay your partner. "Belay," incidentally, was originally a nautical term meaning to take a few turns around a pin or cleat with the end of a rope in order to hold something secure.

It was this traverse that opened the way for future climbers to make it to the First Icefield. Led by Hinterstoisser, the other three balanced their way safely across the 130 feet of rock face until the First Icefield was reached. And it was here that an error of judgment was made that later proved to have dire consequences. Instead of leaving the rope fixed through the pitons the full length of the traverse as a running belay, in case they had to retreat that way, the climbers pulled the rope in after them. They probably felt that it was too early in the climb to be leaving ropes behind. They would need them all to reach the top, or possibly for a long rappel on a retreat. In truth, retreat was probably far from their minds. They had every intention of reaching the summit, then walking down the easy route on the west flank. In any case, having opened the traverse, it may have seemed that they could retrace their steps if they had to, even without a fixed rope. But the Eiger never stays the same; nothing can be taken for granted on its north face. The dry walls over which one has picked one's way on boot toe and fingertips may be glazed several hours later with ungrippable ice.

The four climbers strapped spiked, metal crampons to the soles of their boots to give them a good grip on the icefield. For increased speed they split once again into two ropes. The icefield slopes were less steep than the rock faces, and with the aid of an ice axe, one could sometimes kick one's way upward without actually cutting out steps. However, the icefields posed another danger—falling rock. Rocks coming down cliff faces tend to bounce off a knob or bulge and go sailing harmlessly out into space. Climbers can hug the cliff face during these barrages and be relatively safe. But rocks on snowfields or icefields follow the downward slope or line of the field, gathering speed as they go, the larger ones coming down in great bounding hops that, at point of contact, can wipe the climber completely off the mountain. Sometimes such falling boulders hit a projecting rib or knob of rock with such shattering force that the boulder literally explodes like an artillery shell, and with the same potentially lethal result. It required constant attention to dodge this mountain cannonade and was not unsimilar to crawling up a bowling-alley lane, never knowing when an invisible bowler would let go with a strike.

All four made it up the First Icefield to the cliff face that was like a giant step between the First and Second icefields. And here the telescope watchers sensed the first hint of trouble. The Austrian climbers on the second rope were following much too slowly. Then it was noticed that Rainer was supporting Angerer, who seemed to be holding his head as he climbed. He must have been hit by falling rock while coming up the

First Icefield. The climbers took off their crampons and once again linked into a single rope for the difficult climb up the hundred-foot step, called the Ice Hose because it was frequently frozen with meltwater from the Second Icefield. But now their climbing was much slower. Finally, on the lower left-hand edge of the Second Icefield, they found a good bivouac cave for the night, safe from falling stones. Down in the valley everyone assumed that Kurz and Hinterstoisser were giving the Austrian climbers time to recover. Perhaps it was a slight concussion and by morning Angerer would be feeling fit again.

Most of the Eiger watchers felt that the four men might well be satisfied with their progress. They were well up on the face, higher than Sedlmayer and Mehringer had climbed on their first day. With any luck they would be at Death Bivouac, or perhaps even higher, at the end of their second day. And so the Eiger spectators went to their tables in the hotel dining rooms, looking forward to hot meals followed by cigars and brandy, then to warm feather beds to sleep in that night.

And high on the north face, the four climbers prepared food and hot drinks, before squirming into bivouac sacks for the night. The weather was still favorable, their spirits high, their chances excellent.

5

I'm Finished!

The next day, a Sunday, drew bigger crowds than usual to the hotel telescopes. The question on everybody's mind was whether Angerer would be fit enough to continue climbing. The answer was not long in coming. At 7 A.M. the black patch on the Second Icefield broke apart to become four black moving dots. Two of the dots, Hinterstoisser and Kurz, started off, making a colon against the snow. Double space down a second *Doppelpunkt* appeared. Angerer must have recovered. Soon the four men were crawling up and traversing left across the long slope of the Second Icefield, the largest one on the face. Clouds intermittently obscured the wall, but watchers noted that progress seemed very slow. Hinterstoisser and Kurz were presumed to be alternating the lead, laboriously hacking out foothold steps with the ice axe, an exhausting, time-consuming job that would soon take its toll. The four men had about reached the head of the Second Icefield when massed banks of clouds curtained off the view. The climbers were now faced with some tricky rockwork in order to bridge up and across to the top of the Flatiron, that bulging arête guarding the entrance to the Third Icefield. All afternoon they attacked the rock pitches on the Flatiron, working higher and higher. Finally they made it to the crest and did a short traverse to the left and across to the start of the Third Icefield. Here they found an indented ledge that offered protection from falling rock. They settled down to their second night on the mountain. They were now only a few hundred feet below Death Bivouac, where Sedlmayer and Mehringer had perished the year before.

At seven on Monday morning the climbers were seen to leave their bivouac stance. Again Kurz and Hinterstoisser took the lead. But the second rope of Rainer and Angerer was clearly in trouble. The Austrians were hanging back, making little or no progress. After a while the climbers on the lead rope stopped. For half an hour the two ropes appeared motionless. Obviously the climbers were debating whether to go on or turn back. Finally Hinterstoisser and Kurz turned around and began to descend. It must have been a bitter blow for the German climbers. They were almost two-thirds of the way up the face, and with a bit of luck they might have topped out on the peak that day. In any event they surely would have reached the summit by the following day, making it a four-day ascent. But Angerer must have been too sick to continue. And Rainer by himself would have found it very difficult to get his companion back down the face. It could be done, but it could be done much more safely with all four working together. At least the weather had stayed fair. They weren't like the climbers of the year before, condemned either to climb up and out or to die. So Hinterstoisser and Kurz made the tough decision to give up their attempt on the Eigernordwand in order to nurse their wounded comrade back to safety. Had the German pair gone on, it was more than likely that they would have gained the summit before the really bad weather set in. Hinterstoisser and Kurz were probably sick at heart. Despite all their hard work they could not even say they had gone higher on the face than anyone else. That honor still belonged to Sedlmayer and Mehringer. Hinterstoisser especially must have felt the disappointment. It was his brilliant lead on the traverse that proved to be the key to solving one of the major problems of the climb—a route to the First Icefield. Kurz was another matter. Everyone agreed that he probably laughed away his disappointment with a cheerful or ribald word to the others. They were young, and the mountain would not go away and hide. There would be other chances, other days, a return engagement with the north wall. The important thing now was to get Angerer down to the valley and his injury treated.

The men dropped down to their bivouac site, where they rested for an hour or so while they brewed up a hot drink and ate some food. Then they started the descent, and at first all went well. They got down the steep and dangerous Second Icefield fairly quickly, but it took all after-

noon and lots of hard work to get down the rock band and Ice Hose
separating the Second and First icefields. But now the weather broke; it
began to rain, mist covered the face, and the climbers were soaked
through. Also, to the watchers down in the valley, it appeared that
Angerer was getting weaker and weaker.

Dark was coming on, and the four men decided to quit for the day.
They prepared a bivouac at the top left-hand edge of the Rote Fluh and
settled down to their third night on the mountain. Surely the following
day would see them down off the Nordwand. The worst part left would
be the return of that traverse. Once across that, and down the Difficult
Crack, they would practically be home free.

All that night a freezing rain fell. The next morning the climbers left
their cold and wet bivouac, drenched to the skin, their strength sapped.
Nevertheless they made it back down the First Icefield without mishap,
but they were then halted by the 130-foot traverse. Meanwhile the wind
rose and rocks whistled down the face. They were in great danger. Both
the First Icefield and the traverse were natural paths followed by avalanches, water, and rock coming down from above. The conditions for
getting back across the traverse were also much worse since the rain and
cold weather had combined to form a thin glaze of ice on the rock face.
Hinterstoisser, in opening the traverse on the way up, had been able to
make good use of his boots and fingertips on every slight knob and cleft
on the dry rock. But ice had now rounded off those knobs, filled in those
clefts, and he was faced with rock nearly impossible to get a grip on. All
those slight irregularities, those rogosites, that a good climber makes use
of, all were now hidden beneath the ice. Hinterstoisser must have bitterly regretted not having left a fixed rope on the traverse. With such a
rope, pinned here and there with pegs, they would have had a handrail
to hang from, their feet braced against the face while they made a return
across the smooth slabs to the bottom of the Rote Fluh.

Nevertheless Hinterstoisser attacked the traverse while the other
three waited. Down in the valley the Eiger watchers caught occasional
glimpses of the drama through their telescopes. Below the icefield there
was a band of broken cliffs that dropped some 600 feet. The climbers
might rappel down but would they find ledges or safe stances at the end
of each rope length? One or more of them might be left hanging in
space, unable to move up or down, or even move into the rock face itself.
No, they had to retrace the traverse, if they possibly could. To make
matters worse, the weather became even colder, the wind rising and
blowing snowdrift into the climbers' faces. The watchers now lost track
of the four men, but they noticed one thing. One climber was inactive,
taking no part in the attempts on the traverse. That surely had to be
Angerer. And the climber who again and again balanced his way out

delicately on the rock, reaching for a hold, rejecting it, reaching for another—that surely had to be Hinterstoisser. But the face gave him no footholds or handholds. His boots scrabbled off the ice; his nearly frozen fingers kept slipping helplessly. Even crampons were of no use, because the ice was too thin for the points to stick. Again and again he attacked the glazed wall with his hammer, trying to clear ice away from possible handholds and footholds. It was incredibly exhausting and dangerous work, and a couple of times he must have fallen, to be saved from disaster by the belay stances of Kurz and Rainer. Undoubtedly in order to rest Hinterstoisser, Kurz tried to lead the traverse, and just as surely failed. Finally, after hours of numbing effort, after exploring every possible way of making the return, they had to admit defeat. The traverse simply could not be forced. They would have to abseil down the cliff band, fixing pitons and retrieving their ropes as they descended. They could only hope that the ropes would be long enough, that falling rocks or sheets of ice wouldn't sweep them off the wall, that an overhanging bulge wouldn't jut out so far as to stop them from getting close enough to the rock face to hammer in anchor pitons, that their frozen fingers wouldn't betray them at a crucial moment. But they had no alternative, and so they prepared their ropes and gear for the long climb down.

Albert von Allmen was a sector guard on the Jungfrau railway. His job was to patrol the tunnel that ran inside the north face of the Eiger, to watch for rock that might have fallen from the tunnel roof down on to the tracks, to check the score of details that sector guards were responsible for. He reached the Gallery Window at a spot called kilometer 3.8 on the cog railway. Here there was a storage room, where he put on a kettle to make himself a cup of tea. Across the way there were two great wooden doors that led out to the north face. Allmen knew that four young men were somewhere on the heights above him, trying to make their way down. Perhaps he would open the doors and look out. He had heard of the difficulties facing the German and Austrian daredevils. He had heard all the arguments about the crazies who thought the north wall was climbable. Still, he had to admire their courage, even their skill. Perhaps he would catch a glimpse of them somewhere on the rock.

He managed to get the pair of doors swung open. Then he stepped outside on the rock sill for a moment and looked up at the black overhanging face, here and there annealed with thin plaques of ice. Mist and blowing spindrift cut visibility to the point where he could barely see ten feet in front of him. Every once in a while a rock would come humming down through space. He would hate to stay where he was for five minutes, let alone try and climb down that wall. He was about to go in again when it occurred to him to shout. Perhaps one of the climbers would hear him. It couldn't hurt for them to hear a welcoming word, to be reminded that the Gallery Window could be used to get in off the wall. Cupping his hands around his mouth, Allmen leaned his head back and let out a traditional Swiss yodel. He was amazed when overlapping voices immediately answered, cries that rang down from the heights above and to the left of him. At first he had trouble making out the words, but then, quite distinctly, he heard someone shout, cheerfully it seemed to him, "We're on the way down. All's well!"

Allmen went back inside to put more water in the kettle. He was sure the young climbers could use a cup of hot tea. From the sound of their voices, he guessed they were only a couple of hundred feet above the gallery window. And give them credit, they seemed to know what they were doing. At least there wasn't any hint of panic in their voices.

Half an hour passed, and Allmen grew anxious. What was keeping them? Surely they should have reached the gallery window by now? On the other hand, it had to be very difficult climbing, especially since dark was coming on. Finally the guard opened the doors, stepped out on the rock sill, and shouted up the face. This time only one voice called down from the heights above. "Help!" Toni Kurz cried weakly. "The others are all dead. I'm the only one alive. Please help me!"

"I'll be right back," Allmen shouted; then he raced inside to the tunnel, found a phone, and called the Eigergletscher railway station at the bottom of the Eiger's west flank. He knew there were three guides there, working on a film for a movie company.

Despite the ban on climbing the north wall, the Swiss guides, Hans Schlunegger and the brothers Christian and Adolf Rubi, responded. They could not stand by and watch a fellow guide freeze to death on the face. A special train soon brought them up to kilometer 3.8. The trio went out the Gallery Window and into the teeth of fierce winds and blowing sleet. They made a chancy zigzagging climb up to the left and reached a spot a couple of hundred feet directly beneath where Kurz was hanging in his climbing rope. Their way upward was now blocked by a cliff face too steep to climb. They could not see the young Bavarian, though they could hear his voice and he could hear them. Shattered with horror, Kurz shouted down that Hinterstoisser had fallen off a hold, all the way down the cliff face. He had been leading the way down and had just untied from the climbing rope when he lost his footing and fell. The suddenly loosening rope had somehow pulled the weakened Angerer off his stance, and he strangled in a coil of rope as he fell. Angerer's body was hanging some fifteen feet below Kurz on the end of the same rope. Above Kurz on the rope, Rainer had been jerked tight against a piton by the weight of Kurz and Angerer below him. Unable to move, he had swiftly frozen to death.

The guides asked whether Kurz could lower a rope to them. Then he could haul up some food and whatever else was needed. Kurz shouted back that he had no rope. He had also lost his hammer, and he had no pitons or snaplinks, for Hinterstoisser had been carrying them. The guides were stymied. It was almost dark, and even now it was dubious whether they could make it back to the railroad window. There was absolutely nothing they could do for Kurz at the moment. He would have to stick it out where he was until first light in the morning. They shouted up to him, telling him to tough it out until daybreak.

"No! No!" Kurz screamed. "I'll freeze to death here. Don't leave me!" The unfortunate climber had lost one mitten, and his left hand was useless, a dead lump. In fact his whole left arm was as hard as a frozen log.

But the guides could do nothing. In the dark, and without special equipment, there was simply no way they could reach the stranded climber. They tried to tune out the cries of the youth as they made their dangerous way back and down to the Gallery Window. The three men's hearts must have been wrung with pity. Each one of them had, at one time or another, gone through his own moment of hell on a mountain, and each knew what it meant to have a friend nearby—knew, too, what it meant to be abandoned. They must have had grave doubts as to whether the young German could last through the night. Still, the guides discussed various means of rescue, readied their plans and equipment for the morning, then caught a few hours of sleep that must have been shot through with nightmares of what Kurz was going through on the face.

When daylight came, the rescuers had Arnold Glatthard, dean of the local guides, along with them. Once again they made the dangerous climb up from the Gallery Window. Stones and snowslides descended ceaselessly all around them, and Glatthard narrowly escaped death when a large boulder shattered to bits on a stance he had just vacated. Now aided by better light, the guides were able to get a bit higher on the wall and wound up beneath a bulging overhang, about a hundred feet below the young Bavarian. They shouted up, half expecting no reply. But incredibly enough Kurz was still alive and conscious. The guides now told him that, because of the overhang, there was just no way they could get a rope up to him. Kurz obviously had no spare rope to lower down to his rescuers, or he would have used it to climb down. It was a stalemate, and, to make matters worse, the weather was even colder than it had been the day before, with wind-driven snow cutting visibility to practically nothing. Kurz asked the guides to climb up the way his party had originally come. He and his rope mates had left a few pitons fixed in the rock behind them. The guides could take advantage of those pitons and then rappel down the cliff face to him. It was only three rope lengths.

Then, with the extra rope the guides would bring, they could all abseil down to the Gallery Window level.

The guides looked at each other. Kurz didn't know what he was asking. They weren't extremists who knew the techniques and ironware of sheer-wall, direct-aid climbing. How would they get across that traverse? Anyway, the rock had been dry when the four young climbers had gone up. Now it was clad with ice. To repeat the climb would only be to repeat the loss of life, of that the guides were convinced.

But the rescuers now came up with an alternate plan. Could Kurz let himself down the rope to Angerer, cut his body loose, climb back up to Rainer, and, anchoring himself to the piton already fixed there, cut the climbing rope? By unraveling the strands of the forty-foot length of rope thus salvaged and by tying one strand to another, perhaps he could make a long enough rope to reach his would be rescuers? Then the guides could tie on fresh climbing ropes and a hammer and pitons for Kurz to haul back up again.

With one good hand, using his ice axe and his teeth, in an incredible display of tenacity, Kurz managed to do everything the guides asked, and do it all in the cutting edge of a bone-chilling wind and endless spindrift avalanches. When he cut Angerer's body loose, it stayed where it was, frozen to the wall. Somehow Kurz made it back up to Rainer's body. It was brutally difficult work, with his practically useless left arm. Then he had to unravel the rope, with near frozen fingers, and tie the strands together, knowing that if a knot worked loose it was the end for him. And do all this hanging in his sling, shakily attached to the rock face by one piton. It took him six hours, but finally a thin rope, its end weighted with a stone to prevent its blowing straight out from the face, began to dance and jerk into view below the overhang. One of the guides reached out with an ice axe and pulled the stone into the men on the ledge. Swiftly the guides tied in a hundred-foot climbing rope, a hammer, pitons, and carabiners. They shouted, then watched as Kurz started to haul up his fresh supplies. Now it was discovered that the climbing rope wasn't quite long enough to reach all the way. The first rope was lowered again some twenty feet and a second rope knotted to its end, and Kurz was instructed to resume hauling. A few feet further on and the upward progress of the rope ceased. Above them the men could still see the knot joining the two rope lengths, turning slowly in the air, just below the top of the bulging overhang.

Kurz now had to drive a piton into a crack to anchor his new rope. Somehow, with his useless left hand he managed to hold the piton steady and at the same time drive it in with his other hand. Below him the guides could hear the hammer thuds, the blows painfully slow and uncertain, the clear ringing sound when he struck the head of the piton, the mashing flat sound when he missed and struck the rock. The guides had a frightful, nightmarish moment when a body, its limbs splayed out, came sailing down past the overhang and disappeared below them. Had Kurz fallen off? They shouted up, expecting silence. But Kurz answered. It had been Angerer's body, breaking loose from its icy bond to the rock. Having finally fixed the spike, Kurz tied his new rope through the eye, then transferred his sling snap link from the old piton to the new rope. Cautiously he began to rappel his way downward, his right hand paying out rope as he went. Feet against the wall for balance, he steadily lowered himself, braking his fall by jamming the rope between his frozen left arm and his side.

The guides called encouragingly to the exhausted youth as he came slowly down in a series of bouncing jerks. Dimly, through the swirling snow, they saw a pair of boots scrape over the lip of the bulge. Kurz was only fifteen feet above them now, his legs plainly visible. Then all downward motion stopped.

"What's wrong?" a guide shouted.

"The knot!" Kurz cried. "It's jammed in the link."

The knot tying the two climbing ropes together had jammed in the carabiner that was attached to Kurz's waist. It would not go through and start paying out the second length of rope. Kurz hung there, unable to move up or down.

"Force it through!" a guide yelled. "Come on, man, you can do it!"

"It will go!" another guide called.

Kurz tried with his good hand, fumbling with the knot. But even his right hand was now half-frozen. His face, blue with the cold, bent to the carabiner, and the cold metal of the link chattered against his teeth as he tried to chew the knot into a suppleness that would allow it to feed through. Then an awful tiredness stole over his body. They were asking too much. He had solved all the problems. It wasn't fair to make a new one now, not when he was so close to being rescued, not after all he had been through. There was a limit. Still, he made one last desperate effort to worry the knot through with his teeth.

Below him, the guides feverishly thought up alternatives. After all, Kurz still had plenty of rope. It was just a temporary jam. Could he haul up the end of the second rope, tie it in above him, then somehow cut through the knot and come down the other half of the loop? Or could one of them climb up the rope and help Kurz push the knot through?

At considerable risk Arnold Glatthard climbed up on the back and then on the shoulders of a guide who was hugging the wall. Facing out-

Toni Kurz hanging from his rope.

ward Glatthard reached with his ice axe and was just able to touch the points of the young Bavarian's crampons. But that still did no good. Glatthard climbed down again.

A weak cry floated down from the exhausted and desperate climber. "What?" a guide shouted back.

"Ich kann nicht mehr," the youth said clearly. It was all over, he was finished, he could do no more. It was important that they understood. Then he slumped foward in his sling, head falling, all four limbs hanging downwards. Toni Kurz was dead.

The Eigernordwand had claimed its sixth victim. But never did it have a gamer opponent. Toni Kurz fought the wall to the very last flicker of life in his body.

6
Hanging an Eye in on the North Face

The deaths of the four young men rekindled the controversy over climbing the Eigernordwand. Could anything have better demonstrated that the extremists were suicidal risk takers? A Swiss correspondent to the British *Alpine Journal* wrote that a successful forcing of the Eigerwand, because of the objective dangers, was 90 percent a matter of luck. "Extreme forms of technical development, a fanatical disregard of death, staying power and bodily toughness, are of mere secondary importance. The incalculable elements of fate, chance, etc. are so overwhelmingly important that this face climb belongs far more to a degenerate form of the Children's Crusade of the Middle Ages."

Colonel Strutt, president of the British Alpine club, who called the attempt an insane deed, later wrote, "The Eigerwand continues to be an obsession for the mentally deranged of almost every nation. He who first succeeds may rest assured that he has accomplished the most imbecile variant since mountaineering began." (A "variant" is a route different from the one usually taken.) One irreverent mountaineer of England, parodying a remark of Oscar Wilde's about fox hunting, called those attempting to climb the Eigernordwand "the unbalanced in full pursuit of the insane."

Innovation in sport is often met with resistance. The Grade-VI climbers had developed equipment and techniques that enabled them to climb faces previously thought to be unscalable. Their answer to why? was the standard answer of all innovators: because it hasn't been done.

The battlelines became clear: the older generation versus the younger; the "gentlemen" Alpinists of the British and Swiss mountaineering establishments along with the professional guides whose livelihoods often depended on those gentlemen against the working-class German and Austrian (and, to a lesser extent, Italian) extremists. As Colonel Strutt put it, "The British and Swiss mountaineers are fulfilling the best traditions of their craft." Those who climbed free, without such direct aids as pitons and carabiners and stirrups, considered themselves purists. The extremists defiled the mountain with all their ironmongery; they were engineers, not artists. It was a split, artist versus engineer, that has endured to the present day.

This lineup, the English and Swiss democracies against the then fascist states of Germany, Austria, and Italy, naturally brought politics into the controversy, and it was soon being charged that the extremists were climbing to enhance the black swastika of the fatherland—"*Deutschland über Alles*," it was charged, had taken on a literal as well as a symbolic meaning for the German, and many of the Austrian, climbers who were out to prove some sort of racial superiority. Elements of the fascist press poured fuel on the fire. "Another climber has fallen. Let a hundred others spring forward for the morning!" brayed a party-line correspondent. It was reported that Hitler had offered a special medal, an Olympic Gold Medal for Alpine Valor, to those German climbers who first conquered the Eigernordwand. There were even rumors that Hinterstoisser and Kurz, soldiers on leave from their regiment, had been *ordered* to climb the face by someone very high up in the German government.

In his excellent book *The White Spider*, Heinrich Harrer, whom we shall meet again later, states that far from being ordered to climb the Eigernordwand, Kurz and Hinterstoisser were ordered *not* to climb it. Harrer writes that when the commanding officer of their Mountain Ranger (*Jäger*) Regiment, a Colonel Konrad, who had himself often climbed in the Bernese Oberland, learned that the two young soldiers were going to attempt the Eigernordwand, he telephoned Grindelwald and forbade the climb. The order was relayed to the climbers' tents at Kleine Scheidegg on a Friday evening, but it was too late. Kurz and Hinterstoisser had already left for the face. That this story is no postwar whitewashing afterthought is confirmed by a report in the British *Alpine Journal* of 1936 in which it is stated that Kurz and Hinterstoisser had been ordered by their commanding officer not to attempt the climb. But the pair went ahead, "in the teeth of every conceivable warning by local guides and experts," as one commentator put it.

As recently as 1950 a British writer said of the German climbers that "they were urged on by patriotic zeal inflamed by the fiery oratory of

Adolf Hitler in his efforts to arouse the Germanic people from the despondence of defeat . . . of World War I."

It is widely believed in Grindelwald to this day that the German climbers, and perhaps the Austrians, too, were subsidized by the German government. It probably is true that some of the German attempts were partially or fully sponsored. It probably is also true that the climbers, nearly all of whom were impecunious young men, would cheerfully have accepted the sponsorship of Mars or Saturn, or even the Universal Church of Flat Earth Believers, simply to get their hands on new ropes and hardware.

Whatever their reasons for climbing, the six young men who perished on the Eigernordwand in 1935 and 1936 were certainly not wanting in bravery, tenacity, and gallantry. Perhaps Harrer's comment on those attempts is as good a last word as any: "Let's grant courage and the love of pure adventure their own justification."

At about this time the German press, in a grim pun, began to call the Eiger north face the *Mordwand* (murder wall) instead of *Nordwand* (north wall). Perhaps no Alpine peak has earned so many names. Heinrich Harrer, in his book *The White Spider,* did much to popularize that name for the Eiger North Wall. The Spider is a snowfield about three-quarters of the way up from the base. Snow-filled cracks and couloirs seem to reach upward and dangle downward from the four corners of a squarish snowfield in such a way as to suggest the stringy legs and squat menacing body of a spider.

The Eigernordwand has been called the Final Exam by some climbers who claim that until you've traversed its walls and climbed its half-dozen shooting-gallery icefields; until you've spent a night bivouacked on a ledge a few inches wide, standing through the darkness, roped to the wall with pitons; until you've experienced the dizzying exposures of the Hinterstoisser Traverse, the Ramp, the Traverse of the Gods—until then you haven't really earned the ultimate credential as a big-wall climber.

The White Spider or the White Cobra, the Nordwand or Mordwand, the Final Exam or the Imbecile Variant, whatever it was called, the Eiger north face continued to attract climbers.

In the fall of 1936 the cantonal authorities in Berne revoked their ban on climbing the Eiger. The ban had been no hindrance to Angerer or Rainer, to Hinterstoisser or Kurz. As a ban it was about as effective as a ban on committing suicide. Having revoked the ban, however, Berne now tried to placate the mountaineering establishment by issuing a regulation specifying that parties attempting the Eigernordwand were to be warned that "in the event of an accident, no rescue operations were to be set in motion." This regulation made about as much sense as the previous ban on climbing the Nordwand. If men were in trouble on the face, there was simply no question that the local Swiss guides would do what they could to help. They might charge a huge fee for their services afterward, but some of them, at least, would respond.

Samuel Brawand, that grand old man of Grindelwald guides, stated, "It would be ridiculous to threaten not to go to the rescue of those in trouble on the face. If people call for help, then our guides will naturally respond and do what they can to bring that help, unless of course it is obvious that a rescue attempt has no hope of success."

This was the same Samuel Brawand who, along with Fritz Steuri and Fritz Amatter, guided the Japanese climber Yuko Maki on the first ascent of the Eiger's Mittellegi Ridge in 1921. However, Brawand went on to warn that there "were more important tasks in the world than climbing the Eigernordwand." One suspects that a successful ascent of the north face would have somewhat eclipsed his own achievement in reaching the Eiger's summit via the Mittellegi Ridge. Brawand later went on to become a member of the Swiss Parliament. He was a good example of the natural progression that often comes with age—young tiger to old pussycat in thirty years. Or, as it is often said of race drivers, deep-sea divers, and other followers of hazardous hobbies, there are old practitioners and bold practitioners, but no old, bold ones.

The summer of 1937 saw half a dozen teams camping out in the meadows of Alpiglen, one of which was composed of the veteran guide Anderl Heckmair and Theo Lösch, two Munich climbers who were studying the Nordwand carefully. There were also the usual number of charlatans who claimed to be either in training for a climb or about to start one. Heckmair later wrote that these Alpine crooks, as he called them, "were drawn to the Eiger as a moth to light and, with their posturing, succeeded in infuriating both the genuine climbers and the Grindelwald guides."

Having learned of the ban on climbing the Nordwand, Heckmair and Lösch rented a cabin in Interlaken and cycled every day to Grindelwald, where they found a well-hidden camping spot in the pastures of Alpiglen. They erected their tent and, when the weather was bad, as it often was that summer, retreated to Interlaken. Each time they returned to Grindelwald, they brought more equipment. They even enlisted the local alpenhorn player to warn them of anyone approaching their hideout. They laid plans to start up the wall early one morning but overslept, which turned out to be fortunate because at midday a bad storm blew up. That was it for Heckmair and Lösch. They had been hanging around for six weeks and were now broke. They packed up their gear, mounted their bicycles, and started on the long ride home to Munich. Heckmair, though, would return.

The summer of '37 was not a very good one; in fact it was wretched. As one climber put it, "When it wasn't raining, it was snowing and vice versa." In the meantime the climbers, in the manner of youth everywhere, cheerfully denigrated each other's climbing abilities, courage, and even manhood. An element of national rivalry was involved—down in the *Kuhalpen,* the cow pastures. But those who went up on the face, even on minor practice climbs, seemed to find and exercise a higher loyalty than patriotism—a loyalty to those who dared the big wall with them, whatever their nationality or the language they spoke. This transcendence of cultural and language barriers turned out to be one of the constants of Eigernordwand climbing, an attitude that was to lead to some unusual teams' roping up together on north-face climbs.

The first serious trouble of 1937 came when an experienced Italian rope, a pair of crack guides from the Dolomites, Giuseppe Piravano and Bruno Detassis, decided to climb the Lauper Route for a reconnaissance of the north wall. From the higher reaches of the Lauper Route they could, to quote one of the local guides, "hang an eye in on the north face." Piravano and Detassis climbed without incident and bivouacked at the end of their first day's efforts.

On the morning of the second day it began to snow. The new snow made the going treacherous, and although Piravano was a superb ice climber, a snowslide swept him away while he was leading a pitch. Fortunately his partner, with the aid of a solid ice piton, was able to check the fall, but Piravano suffered a bad leg injury that left him practically unable to climb. He could not traverse sideways, or climb down, but had to be constantly held, and hauled, by a taut rope from above. Somehow Detassis got his companion up to the top of the Lauper Ridge and then across a spur to the Mittellegi Ridge, where a mountain hut offered refuge and a chance to dry out. It was early evening when they reached the hut, and shortly afterward two Grindelwald guides, Peter Kaufmann and Peter Inäbnit, arrived. The next morning they brought Piravano down to safety. It was a close call, and there were some in the valley who feared that both climbers had already lost their lives in the snowstorm. Indeed one correspondent had already reported the Italian climbers to his paper as "probably fallen."

The next incident occurred when two young Austrian climbers from Salzburg, Franz Primas and the nineteen-year-old Bertl Gollackner, ignoring the difficulties experienced by the Italian team, decided that they, too, wanted to look in on the north face from the Lauper Route. They intended to climb up the east flank as high as they could and return before sunset—at least high enough to give them a good look at the upper reaches of the Nordwand. How did one proceed above the Third Icefield? Was that long, angled cleft called the Ramp negotiable all the way? Did one have to climb the length of the higher snowfield, better known as the Spider? If so, how did one get over to the Spider from the snowfield at the head of the Ramp? Perhaps a reconnaissance climb would answer some of those questions.

Primas and Gollackner started off with only enough food for that day's lunch, the standard fare then of penurious young climbers—*Brot und Wurst*—a chunk of bread, a hunk of sausage. They had no sooner started up the Lauper Route than the weather turned foul again. It had been a frustrating summer in that respect. If they had to wait for perfectly good weather, they would never get anything done. They pushed on. The weather worsened, and the pair was in constant danger from avalanches. By afternoon it was obvious, given the weather conditions, that retreat down the snow-plastered slabs would be more dangerous than going up and over to the Mittellegi Ridge and following that route back down to the valley. They climbed until the light ran out, then bivouacked for the night, a cold overnight stop without sleeping sacks or much more to eat than the few crusts of bread remaining from their lunch.

The next day the weather deteriorated to blizzard conditions, but Primas led pitch after pitch, and they climbed on, though Gollackner's strength was fast running out. By evening they had dug out a bivouac snow cave just under the top of the Mettellegi Ridge. The next day they hoped to reach the ridge and, like the Italian pair before then, take refuge in the hut. They topped out on the ridge the next afternoon. And now they made a fateful and rather strange decision. Instead of heading for the hut on the Mittellegi Ridge below them, they continued up the snowfield toward the summit. Perhaps Gollackner, in the manner of many a teenager testing his manhood, was unwilling to tell his older companion just how weak he really felt. Perhaps Primas thought it easier to reach the summit and go down the west flank, rather than downclimb to the Mittellgi hut. Their progress was pitifully slow, and once again they were forced to bivouac for the night in a cave dug out of a snowfield. The following morning, their fourth day on the mountain, Gollackner's resources ran out, and he died of exposure. Primas remained with his dead companion in the snow cave, shouting into the wind every few minutes in the hope that would-be rescuers would hear his cries.

And rescue efforts were indeed under way. Local guides, climbing on a nearby glacier, had noted that the pair of Austrian climbers were in trouble and set off up the Mittellegi Ridge. From another direction two Austrian climbers, Matthias Rebitsch and Ludwig Vörg, had also started up the east flank of the Eiger the day before, looking for their overdue compatriots. After a perilous, exposed bivouac on a cliff face, they made it to the Mittellegi hut the next day. They had no sooner gotten their clothes dried out than local guides reached the hut, leading an exhausted Primas, whose feet were badly frostbitten. He had been found passed out on the dead body of his comrade. He told them that Gollackner at one point, just before he died, had gone berserk and tried to hurl him off the mountain.

Vörg and Rebitsch, when told that Gollackner's body was still up on the ridge, volunteered to retrieve the corpse. They climbed up and hacked the frozen body free of the ice, then brought it down to the hut with them. Bertl Gollackner was the Eiger's seventh fatality in three years.

The teenager's death brought on a renewal of demands that all climbing activity on the Eigernordwand cease at once. The mountain, it was claimed, was becoming like one of those Japanese volcanoes that young people climbed in order to commit suicide by hurling themselves down into the fiery interior. There was complaining among the local guides as well. Twice already the rescue section had been called out to go to the aid of young extremists who had seemingly pushed beyond the limits of their skills and endurance. If such foolhardy attempts did not stop, it was only a matter of time before the law of averages caught up with the guides, who were now taking risks beyond the normal in their rescue forays.

All this talk didn't bother Rebitsch and Vörg. They coolly laid plans for their own attempt on the north face. Late in July, helped by another pair of climbers, they set about establishing a camp up on the face. They had hardly gotten started when one of the climbers spotted a body lying at the foot of a cliff. It had to be either Hinterstoisser or Mehringer, the only two still not accounted for after the tragic events of the preceding two years. Kurz had been cut down by guides who had climbed to the bottom of the overhang and, using a knife attached to a long pole, had sawed through the rope holding his body. Rebitsch and Vörg turned back and with the help of their friends, brought the corpse down to Alpiglen. It was the body of Hinterstoisser.

Nothing daunted by having had to retrieve two bodies from the Eiger's flanks in as many weeks, Rebitsch and Vörg renewed their assault on the Nordwand. On August 11 they climbed up past the First Pillar, past the Shattered Pillar, then up the Difficult Crack to the start of the Hinterstoisser Traverse. Here they fixed a pair of ropes in order to safeguard their return passage. At the end of the traverse they climbed up a couloir for some sixty feet and found a jewel of a bivouac spot, which they immediately named *Das Schwalbennest* (The Swallow's Nest). This was a ledge with a projecting roof that kept them safe from snowfall and rockfall. There was even room enough for two to sleep side by side, an unheard-of luxury on the Eiger. A tent sack, stretched from the edge of the roof to the ground, kept off the rain. They even built a low stone wall to enclose the front edge of their eyrie. Here they could rest in comfort, sitting down, safe from the elements and with a splendid eagle's eye view of the whole valley far below them, from Kleine Scheidegg on their left to Grindelwald on their right. Still farther away, Interlaken and Thun were visible. Up the flanks of the mountain there drifted the cries of cliff swallows, the hoarse croaks of ravens, the clang of cowbells, the piercing whistles of rock marmots, and the deep melodic lowing of alpenhorns.

The following day dawned fair, and they were at work before the sun had yet cleared the horizon. They put away the First and Second icefields, surmounted the tricky rock pitches to the Flatiron, and reached Death Bivouac by late afternoon. Here they half expected to find Mehringer's body, which still hadn't been found. But the only trace of the Munich climber of 1935 was a pair of pitons hammered into the wall. There was now a slight descent to the top of the Third Icefield and a traverse to the left in order to reach the Ramp, a long, forty-five-degree angled cleft running right to left across and up the face. A vicious rainstorm caught them at the foot of the Ramp, and it wasn't long before waterfalls were plashing down the rocks. The pair abandoned their attempt to climb the Ramp and retreated to the protection of a ledge near Sedlmayer and Mehringer's Death Bivouac. Perhaps the weather would clear in the morning and they could continue the ascent. On their insecure stance they waited out the long night, unable to see very much, but hearing plainly the terrifying rumble of unseen rocks thudding down the face.

In the morning the weather was so bad that continuing the climb was out of the question. But they knew their way back, ropes had been fixed on the Hinterstoisser, and the way down from there had been negotiated by both climbers half a dozen times before. As a consolation they could say they had been higher on the face than anyone else, had passed Death Bivouac, and had traversed the Third Icefield to the bottom of the Ramp. At the very least they brought back the information that the line was feasible up as far as the head of the Ramp.

Rebitsch and Vörg spent the rest of the day rappelling down the cliff bands and climbing down the icefields, now dangerously mushy from the two days of heavy rain. Time and again they had difficulty in finding ice solid enough to hold an ice piton for a belay stance. Nevertheless, by late afternoon they had put both icefields behind them and were once again comfortably lodged at the Swallow's Nest. Here they changed their wet underclothes and dried their outer garments as best they could. Compared to their last bivouac, the Swallow's Nest was a first-class hotel.

During the fitful spells of clear weather, when the Eiger curtains had briefly parted to allow glimpses of the face, watchers in the valley had been able to track the climbers. At no time did it seem that the pair was in trouble. The two men climbed deliberately, methodically, and their retreat showed that same quality of craft and competence. It was obvious that rescue attempts were not needed, though one never knew, of course, when rockfall or an avalanche would dramatically change the picture.

Since the weather was still bad the next morning, Rebitsch and Vörg decided to continue their retreat. Anyway, they were almost out of food. They roped down the couloir to the left-hand edge of the Hinterstoisser, successfuly negotiated the traverse despite the drenching water that poured down the rocks, and made it down to their tents in the Alpiglen meadows before dark. They had spent over a hundred consecutive hours on the wall and come back without a scratch.

Rebitsch and Vörg did much to still the criticism of Eigernordwand climbing, and, for the first time, people began to accept the idea that the north face might eventually be scaled. Had Rebitsch and Vörg been granted one more decent day after their highest bivouac, they most likely would have reached the Spider and from there climbed out the next day no matter what the weather. Despite apparent failure the summer had been well spent, particularly for Vörg. The knowledge he had gained would be put to good use the following summer, for Vörg would be back in 1938. In the December 1937 issue of Munich's *Der Bergsteiger,* he wrote of his and Rebitsch's attempts: "I do not underestimate the extraordinary objective dangers of the face and admit that we had luck. We young climbers can only contribute . . . by solving so-called last problems. If we have the luck to conquer the last and greatest face of the Alps, I will describe it as an inheritance from our Alpine Fathers." There were those who detected a hint of boasting in this, though it seems, on the face of it, a simple enough statement.

One other notable climb in the summer of 1937 helped to dispel the notion that the young Eiger climbers were all suicidal misfits—wall nailers and steeple jacks, as they had been called in the British *Alpine Journal.* After scrambling around on the lower reaches of the north wall earlier in the summer, two German bergsteigers from Munich, Otto Eidenschink and Ernst Möller, made a two-day first ascent of the south face of the Eiger. It wasn't quite the Nordwand, but the Eiger tigers were closing in.

7

The Traverse of the Gods

The climbing season of 1938 began when two experienced Italian climbers, Bartolo Sandri and Mario Menti, both twenty-three years old and members of the Italian Alpine Club, arrived in Grindelwald in mid-June and headed for the meadows of Alpiglen. After studying different lines up the face, and doing a reconnaissance climb of the lower bands, they started up the wall early in the morning of June 21. Though both climbers were highly experienced on rock and had done many Grade-VI ascents in their native Dolomites, they weren't all that familiar with the snow and ice conditions of the western Alps. Late June, even with good weather, was still too early to climb the Eiger. For one thing, not all of the winter snow burden had yet melted or sloughed off, which meant a higher than usual risk from avalanches pluming down the face. Then too, the previous season's snow, through the process of continuous melt and freeze, had still not melded sufficiently to the underlying coat of old ice and snow in those sloping icefields that retained this névé cover all year round. The unstable snow mantle meant that it was highly likely that slabs of new ice and snow would come off the underlying floor, especially when shear pressure was applied.

The Italian pair made another mistake. Probably because there were as yet few, if any, German and Austrian climbers in the valley to advise them, they decided to go up the Sedlmayer-Mehringer route in preference to the one pioneered by Kurz and Hinterstoisser. Perhaps they were wary of the Hinterstoisser Traverse because of its associations, or perhaps they preferred the older route because it meant less travel over icefields. They were more at home on rock.

Whatever their reasons, they started up the Sedlmayer-Mehringer line and actually climbed higher up on the face than the German pair had managed to reach on their first day. But that evening the Eiger was racked by one of its usual summer thunderstorms, by avalanching snow and rockfall. The next morning there was no activity evident on the face, or any sign of a bivouac spot. The telescope watchers searched the ledges, cracks, and gullies of the wall's lower reaches without sighting the Italian climbers.

Once again the Grindelwald guides sent out a search-and-rescue team. Fritz Steuri and his son Hermann searched the bergschrund at the foot of the wall, crisscrossed the avalanche snow fans and terminal screes that dressed the bottom of the Nordwand. Finally a dark smudge was spotted at the foot of a cliff. It was the broken body of Bartolo Sandri. Several days later Mario Menti's body was hauled up out of a 150-foot-deep crevasse at the foot of the mountain. Obviously both men had plunged to their deaths, though it was never determined whether they had fallen while climbing or been knocked off their holds by rockfall or snowslide. Sandri and Menti were the eighth and ninth Eiger fatalities, and the first Italians to perish on the Nordwand. Later a brass plaque was set into a rock at the base of the mountain to commemorate the two climbers.

In early July, Heinrich Harrer, a student just finished with his finals
at the University of Graz in southern Austria, arrived in Grindelwald
astride the usual mount favored by the chronically penniless climbers of
that era. He parked his motorbike and met a Viennese friend, Fritz Kasparek, who was waiting for him. They, too, had ideas of doing the Eigernordwand. The pair spent a week camped in the pastures, looking over
the face. They did an exploratory climb on the eastern flank of the
Nordwand, went up the Mittellegi Ridge, traversed the summit, and
came back down the west flank. Then, for good measure, they scaled the
Eiger's neighbor, the Mönch.

One afternoon they climbed to the bivouac cave above the Shattered
Pillar, where they left a rucksack of extra provisions and equipment,
clearly marked with their names, before down climbing to their tent at
the Eiger's base. This "cache" climb to the Bivouac Cave was becoming
a ritual of north-wall attempts. They waited several more days, until they
were satisfied with the conditions on the face and the prospects of good
weather. Finally, at 2 A.M. on July 21, they started up the wall, climbing
the lower slopes in the predawn darkness. Now and again they heard
other voices below them on the rock. The following rope, a pair of experienced Austrian climbers, Rudi Fraissl and Leo Brankowsky, caught up
with Harrer and Kasparek. For now, the four men decided to climb
together, but still moving as two separate ropes. They pushed on, and a
surprise awaited Harrer and Kasparek at their bivouac cache above the
Shattered Pillar. Here they found two climbers who had spent the night
on the face, just getting out of their tent sacks. The men were thirty-two-
year-old Anderl Heckmair and Ludwig Vörg, the latter back for another
crack at the Eigernordwand. Heckmair, a superb all-around ice and rock
climber, had wide experience in both the eastern and western Alps and
was well known for his climbing exploits. As early as 1931 he had
attempted the north face of the Grandes Jorasses outside Chamonix.
During the 1937 climbing season he had spent six weeks in the meadows
of Alpiglen, just studying the Eiger's north face. Heckmair belonged to
that school of Munich climbers who won most of their experience in the
Bavarian Alps and in the high peaks of the Austrian Tyrol. In his autobiography, *My Life As a Mountaineer,* he gives a gripping picture of what
his days were like as a climber in the 1930s. For a while he worked as a
gardener for the city of Munich. On Sundays he would do a Grade-VI
climb and then often help to bring down the victim of a climbing accident. On Monday and Tuesday he couldn't work very hard, because he
was still recuperating from weekend climbing exertions that all too often
involved a long bicycle journey. On Wednesday he would get the day off
to go to the funeral of the previous Sunday's fatality. On Thursday and
Friday he tried to conserve his strength for the climb on the following

weekend. It's little wonder that the municipal fathers in Munich decided to lay him off. Then it was "beg, borrow, and steal" his way through the Alps of half a dozen nations, once even ranging as far as Morocco in search of new peaks and pitches. The result of all this climbing was that he ranked as one of the top climbers in the 1930s, on a level with Willo Welzenbach or Riccardo Cassin.

His partner Ludwig Vörg was equally strong. He had been higher on the wall than anyone else and was one of only two men ever to have come back alive from above the Second Icefield. The other, Rebitsch, was off that year to Nanga Parbat in the Himalayas. Vörg, too, had wide Alpine experience and had also taken part in two expeditions to the Caucasus, where in 1934 he had been part of the team to make the first north-south traverse of Mount Ushba. Two years later Vörg did the first ascent of the gigantic west flank of Ushba.

Heckmair and Vörg, having found the cached rucksack with a note identifying it as the property of Harrer and Kasparek, had drawn the natural conclusion that the Austrian pair would be making a summit attempt the next day. Meanwhile Harrer was just a little bit in awe of the much older and more experienced Heckmair, who, among other eccentricities, was rumored to be actually staying in a hotel in Grindelwald. Among the impoverished climbers of the 1930s, an hotel was an unheard-of luxury. The rumor wasn't true. The Munich climbers were camped in their tent in the hidden location used by Heckmair the preceding year. It was noticed, too, that Heckmair and Vörg had all-new equipment, including the modern twelve-point crampons that enabled one to "front point" up ninety-degree ice walls. In order to save weight, Harrer had not brought any crampons—a mistake, as he later admitted—but he and Kasparek, who did have crampons, had agreed that the latter would lead all the ice pitches, and Harrer the rock pitches. It was up to Kasparek to cut steps on the icefields large enough to fit his partner's nail-studded climbing boots. As the men talked, daylight began to flood the face. Heckmair, studying his altimeter, concluded that the barometer was falling, a judgment reinforced by fish-shaped clouds low on the horizon, often a sign of bad weather. He quoted a country proverb to the others, "Fish clouds in the sky, brings rain by and by." He was sure that the weather was breaking and said that he and Vörg were going back down. Heckmair also felt that six men on the face at the same time, on three ropes, was at least two climbers too many. The north face rained enough rocks down around climbers, without climbers' themselves adding to the falling debris with their scrabbling boots.

So Heckmair and Vörg retreated while the other four continued with their climb. Harrer and Kasparek, each carrying a fifty-five-pound rucksack, had mastered the Difficult Crack (Grade V), and were coming up to the bottom of the Rote Fluh when they heard a cry below them. Rudi Fraissl had been hit on the head by a falling rock and, though seemingly not hurt too badly, was feeling too dizzy to continue the ascent. A quick conference between Fraissl and Brankowsky led to the decision to retreat. They didn't want to repeat the mistakes of the Kurz party when Angerer, hurt early in the climb, nevertheless continued in the illusory hope that his condition would improve.

Four out of six had turned back, but Harrer and Kasparek climbed on, as the sun was now breaking well free of the horizon. At the Hinterstoisser they found Vörg's rope of the preceding year still firmly attached to the wall, and they made grateful use of it to help them across the traverse. The rock face of the Hinterstoisser was glazed with ice, and without a fixed rope it would probably not have been negotiable that day. Even with the fixed rope, they occasionally had to resort to their hammers to hack ice away from the rock to give their boots purchase. On the traverse, Kasparek, who was leading, was able to leave his rucksack with Harrer, who clipped it into the fixed rope on a snap link and slid it along ahead of him.

The climbers must have felt a gratifying sense of relief when they put the Hinterstoisser behind them. In short order they were up the sixty-foot couloir and at the Swallow's Nest, enjoying breakfast. Then, no doubt recalling that it was exactly two years to the day since Hinterstoisser had tried, hour after numbing hour, to return on the traverse he had opened up, they left 300 feet of rope, and extra slings, pitons, and carabiners at the Swallow's Nest. They meant to assure their retreat directly down the cliff face if they were forced to turn back and if the rock of the Hinterstoisser proved impassable on their return. The ice on the traverse rock face was bad enough, but at least they had clear weather. Trying to reverse the Hinterstoisser in a snowstorm, say, on ice-glazed rock, would be a nightmare.

Their packs now considerably lightened, Kasparek and Harrer started out, Kasparek leading. Wearing crampons, he cut steps in the ice, and Harrer followed in his nail-studded boots. At the end of every rope length, Kasparek would bang in a long ice piton for a belay, hack out a platform, and lean back against the ice while he brought Harrer up to his stance, either looping the gained rope at his feet in loose coils or letting it trail down the icefield while his partner climbed to join him. With Harrer at the stance, Kasparek would set off again, protected by his partner anchored to the ice piton. When the rope ran out its full length, Kasparek would bang in a new ice piton while below him Harrer would pull out the low piton and again climb to his partner's position.

They reached the hundred-foot cliff band that separated the First and Second icefields. Here the natural line up this rock step was through a couloir known as the Ice Hose because it was inevitably iced-up with snowmelt that dribbled and dripped down the rock from the Second Icefield to freeze every night into the cleft and form a frozen waterfall. A difficult pitch, the Ice Hose can still be climbed in its entirety by good ice men, but it is often rendered even more difficult by water pouring down underneath the outer sheath of ice. A passage might have been forced up the cliff itself, had the rocks been dry, but they wore a thick skin of ice.

On this day the climbers' clothing and gear were completely sodden after they had successfully worked their way up to the bottom of the Second Icefield. The Ice Hose had given them a thorough drenching. By now it was afternoon, and the warming rays of the westering sun, touching the upper third of the wall, had melted the thin ice bonds that held loose rock to the face. The bowling alleys were open, and a steady procession of rocks, snow avalanches, and ice chunks came bounding down to be caught, though rarely held, in the huge, wide apron of the Second Icefield.

The two men wisely decided that the falling debris on the icefield was too dense to risk. Discretion called for tackling the Second Icefield in the morning, while rocks and ice were still anchored in place by the night's freeze. Then too, while climbing an icefield one's eyes are constantly searching for a spot to kick in crampons or drive in an ice axe. To have to do this while at the same time looking far ahead to the top of the field, trying to spot descending rocks so as to gauge their speed and direction, requires an exhausting degree of concentration. Kasparek and Harrer therefore decided to call it a day. They traversed to the right, off the icefield, and onto a rock bulge, where they hammered in a pair of anchor pitons and spent considerable time hacking a small platform out of the ice and rock. Using their coils of rope as cushions, they sat down and cooked supper. Then they settled back, prepared to wait until morning. It was their first bivouac on the face.

It must have been an uncomfortable night. Their clothes were soaking wet from having come up the Ice Hose. Although they had dry underclothes in their rucksacks, the confined space they were in and the way they were roped to the wall, made it more trouble than it was worth to try to change clothes. In any case, their outer clothes were so wet that the fresh underclothes would soon become as wet as the discarded ones. And so they wore the long night down. The next morning, half-frozen as they must have been, in their wet clothes, they set out on the Second Icefield. Again Kasparek led, hacking out step after step in the fifty-five-degree ice slope. Harrer followed, placing his foot in the niches already fashioned by Kasparek. It was physically exhausting work for Kasparek, who had to chop steps for more than twenty rope lengths, belaying his partner up each pitch. It took the pair five hours to go up and across the icefield, and it was here, while taking a rest, that they looked back down their trail of steps to see two men coming so swiftly up the long slope that they appeared to be running. Even though the newcomers were taking advantage of the steps already cut by Kasparek, their speed was phenomenal.

The climbers turned out to be their old acquaintances Heckmair and Vörg, who had started up the face early that morning. Of their previous day's descent, Heckmair later wrote, "As we descended the weather got finer and finer and our faces grew longer and longer." Then they had watched Fraissl and Brankowsky turn back. Overnight the weather had held reasonably fair; so the Munich men decided to renew their assault on the face and, if possible, catch up with Kasparek and Harrer.

Their speed up the icefield was also due to the new twelve-point crampons they wore. Crampons, a sort of metal overshoe, normally had ten sharp spike points that stuck straight down from the sole, a design that was invented in 1908. Metal crampons of one kind or another, sometimes known as ice walkers, had been used for a long time before being adapted by mountain climbers in the early 1900s. There is an Italian account of a battle with Swiss troops in 1478 in which it is recorded that the Swiss were victorious because they used metal spike attachments to their boots, enabling them to outflank the Italians on a glacier. In 1931 an Italian climber, Laurent Grivel, came up with the ingenious idea of adding two horizontal spikes to the metal lattice work of the crampon. This pair of front spikes stuck straight out and slightly downward from the toe of the crampon. They were called front points, and with such crampons it was now possible to climb vertical ice walls. Even overhangs could be negotiated with front points. The new design led to a way of climbing with a pair of ice axes that made it unnecessary to cut footholds or handholds going up steep icefields. One started out by firmly kicking the ice with one foot, then the other. Leaning slightly back and dropping the ankles ensured that the front points on the crampons would press upward and lock firmly into the ice. With the toes of both boots anchored firmly, one now swung the right arm and sank the pick end of a short ice axe into the frozen surface of the wall at shoulder height. Another swing with the left arm, and the sharp point of an ice hammer was similarly embedded. At this point one was attached to the ice wall at four places—two footholds and two handholds. To move up, one drew back and disengaged the right crampon, bent the knee, and with a firm kick sank the front points eight or ten inches higher on the wall. This procedure was repeated with the left foot. Next one withdrew the head of the right ice axe, then sank the point into the ice again eight or ten inches higher up. The left ice hammer was withdrawn, and it, too, was embedded higher on the wall. Pulling alternately on the ice axe and hammer handles, one hauled one's body up and found new purchase with the front points.

The trick of front pointing on vertical ice walls is to make sure that one always has contact with the wall at three points—either two footholds and a handhold, while one is loosening and getting a new bite with an ice axe, or two handholds and a foothold, while sinking in a new bite with the front points. Technically it's possible to stay on the ice wall with only one hold—that is, hanging by one hand from the handle of an ice axe or ice hammer with both feet free of the ice and the other hand clear of the wall. Naturally, such one-hold positions are chancy and rarely used. The front-point method of ice climbing, while roped to a partner on a good belay stance, gives a maximum degree of safety. Front pointing, too, is a lot faster than hacking out steps, and modern climbers can traverse the Second Icefield in little over an hour as compared to the five or six hours it took the older climbers to cut steps all the way across the traverse, which means four hours less exposure to rockfall.

After the four men met and exchanged greetings, Heckmair advised Kasparek and Harrer to retreat because, in his opinion, they weren't properly equipped for a long ice climb. Harrer had no crampons, and neither he nor Kasparek had an ice axe, the steps having been cut by Kasparek with an ice hammer, a much more difficult tool to use in step cutting. Kasparek replied that he and Harrer were going on, despite their inadequate gear. It would just take them a little longer, he said. It was Vörg who found the way out of a possible dispute when he suggested that both teams climb together. At first Heckmair was none too pleased with the suggestion, but he changed his mind as the ascent continued. The four men now in agreement, Heckmair and Vörg took over the lead, and Kasparek and Harrer followed on a separate rope. They all moved up the flanks of the Flatiron without incident and reached Death Bivouac, where they took a long and welcome break.

From Death Bivouac there was a slight downward pitch to the Third Icefield, with its sixty-five-degree slope, then a traverse left to the start of the Ramp, a long upward-sloping cleft that led to still another, smaller icefield. They could have taken to the cliff face directly above Death Bivouac, and there is some evidence that this was the route Sedlmayer and Mehringer tried to open. But patches of mist obscured the view upward, and they were fairly sure, from Vörg's climb of the year before, that the Ramp was negotiable all the way to its head. So the four men moved across the precipitous Third Icefield and reached the start of the Ramp.

Meanwhile, down in the valley, hundreds of watchers were following the progress of the climb. The quartet was now higher on the face than anyone had ever been before. Fieldglasses were trained on the four black dots moving slowly up the Ramp, and queues formed behind the half-dozen pay telescopes at Kleine Scheidegg.

And now the weather seemed to be breaking. After a clear, cloudless morning, scarves and veils of fog began to wreathe in and out across the face, filling the rocky cleft of the Ramp and often obscuring the climbers from view.

The four men were moving slowly into virgin territory. Although the line had long ago been picked out down in the meadows—up the Ramp, traverse somehow across to the Spider Snowfield, then up the Spider to the Exit Cracks and find the right couloir leading to the Summit Snowfield. But a line that looked good in the meadows was often another line entirely up on the face. The Ramp, for example, looked like a nice deep bench, but in reality the rock forming the floor of the cleft sloped outward and downward, and it wasn't long until one of the men took a fall. Kasparek came off while leading Harrer and dropped sixty feet, but the latter was able to brake and to hold the rope at the belay piton until his partner climbed back up and continued leading the pitch. Had Harrer not held at his belay, Kasparek would have fallen over 3,000 feet to the base of the mountain.

The two ropes, with Heckmair and Vörg still in the lead, reached the head of the 600-foot-long Ramp, where further progress was barred by a waterfall. The head of the Ramp funnels into a chimney that leads upward into a wide rocky bay overlaid with ice—in effect another icefield. Like the Ice Hose between the First and Second icefields, the chimney at the head of the Ramp is a natural bottleneck that funnels melt water down into the Ramp. At this point the four men decided to look for a bivouac spot for the night. They had no desire to get drenched to the skin going up through the waterfall and then to spend the night in wet clothes. Kasparek and Harrer had already done that the preceding night. The lower temperatures of the night hours should freeze the melting water into solid ice by early morning.

A bivouac spot was thus found and prepared. Heckmair and Vörg picked out a small platform and made themselves comfortable. A few feet below them, Kasparek and Harrer managed to clear ice from a narrow rock lip which afforded standing room. They drove in a single piton and rope anchored themselves to the wall. There wasn't enough room to sit down properly, but the use of slings and rope supports enabled them to make themselves halfway comfortable in a crouched, hunkered-down position. Next to them, jutting from the wall, there was a tiny flat boss of rock about the size of a saucer, on which they rested their cooker. Soon hot drinks were being brewed and consumed. None of the men were hungry, a not uncommon reaction after a strenuous day of climbing, but Heckmair opened a can of sardines and finished them off. The four men, in separate lodgments, chatted back and forth as the light gradually drained from the sky. Dehydrated after their exertions, they drank endless cups of tea. Between wisps of fog, they were able to spot the twinkling lights of Grindelwald, some 7,000 feet straight down.

Meanwhile, in the valley, speculation was rife that the climbers were in trouble and would have to retreat in the morning. Look how long it had taken them to climb that easy handful of pitches on the Ramp. Something seemed to happen to climbers once they got beyond Death Bivouac. Their strenth seemed to fail in the higher altitudes and their progress to slow. Moreover, the weather was turning bad; fog and mist almost totally obscured the way ahead. Chances were fifty-fifty that the climbers were in trouble and would have to rope down when daylight came.

And indeed in the middle of the night, Heckmair came down with a bad case of gastroenteritis when those sardines evidently began some sort of mass migratory movement. But after half a dozen cups of tea brewed by Harrer, and a breakfast of hot porridge and coffee, the stomachache subsided and Heckmair pronounced himself fit once more to continue leading the climb.

The men put on their crampons, stowed their rucksacks, and checked their gear. As they had hoped, the waterfall had frozen solid during the night, although the previous afternoon's snowmelt had left all the nearby rocks glazed with ice. Still, Heckmair, with a superb demonstration of ice climbing in his new twelve-point crampons, got through the Waterfall Crack and now found himself facing what appeared to be an insuperable obstacle, the thirty-foot-high overhanging Ice Bulge. He banged in a solid ice piton for protection and had almost reached the top of the bulge when he pulled something loose and peeled off. Fortunately the piton held, and, taking a deep breath, he tackled the ice cliff again, front pointing his way up. Once more he reached the overhang and once more came off. On his third attempt he had almost reached the top and was groping around for a handhold when he felt himself starting to slide again.

Many years later Heckmair was to tell the Italian climber Reinhold Messner what happened at that point. He suddenly lost his temper with himself and the Ice Bulge and, filled with a cold, loathing rage, somehow briefly held the slide, reversed course, humped his body upwards, found a hold, and one-armed himself to the top and wriggled over. Then he drove in a pair of secure pitons and belayed the others up to his stance. Last to arrive was Harrer, festooned with ironmongery, all the pitons, ice screws, and snap links that he had cleaned out on his way up to join his three companions.

The men now roped together for the ascent of the Ramp Icefield. Keeping well to the right, out of the direct line of falling rocks, they moved up and onto a brittle ledge, from which they hoped to traverse across to the Spider. Their progress was enlivened by an awful roar that seemed to presage an enormous rockfall. But it turned out to be an airplane that flew by so close that the climbers could see the passengers' faces. But now the way forward was blocked when the Brittle Ledge petered out and they had to climb a crack straight up a hundred-foot cliff to reach another ledge, where they hoped to find a continuation of the line to the Spider. Once again Heckmair, climbing superbly, led the vertical pitch and then safeguarded the others up to his stance.

It was now early afternoon, and snow avalanches and rockfall had started their daily game. Fortunately, the men were somewhat protected by overhangs on their traverse across to the Spider, a slightly upward-sloping climb that was technically easy (Grade IV) and gave such magnificent views of the valley below that it soon acquired the name *Götter-quergang* (Traverse of the Gods). Again Heckmair and Vörg led the climb, negotiated the last difficult step down from the traverse on to the Spider, then swiftly raced up the Fifth Icefield on their front points. Unfortunately, the weather had worsened. The Eiger Reception Committee now put on one of its *son et lumière* spectacles for the four climbers. Lightning slammed the rock ribs and cliffs around them, thunder rolled across the face, and sleety snow began to cut visibility down to an arm's length. Kasparek and Harrer, on a separate rope, now discovered that the Spider was, in effect, an avalanche trap. The dozen cracks leading upward from it channeled all the loose snow and rockfall coming down from the top one thousand feet of the face. These cascades of snow funneled into the head of the Spider to roar down the full length of its steep face and then plunge free another thousand feet to the Flatiron and Second Icefield. For a moment Kasparek looked at the snowfield. Heckmair and Vörg were already halfway up. They had the new front-point crampons, however, and Kasparek didn't. Also he would have to cut steps for Harrer, who had no crampons at all.

He stepped out and began hacking at the ice.

8

The Last Great Alpine Problem

Harrer, last on the rope, emerged on the Spider and hurriedly banged in an ice piton to safeguard Kasparek, who was already thirty

Anderl Heckmair, leader of the first successful climb in 1938.

feet ahead of him, cutting steps. Minutes later Harrer heard a fierce whistling sound and saw rocks and ice fragments, followed by a white cloud, come bounding down the icefield, heading straight toward him. He barely had time to jam the rucksack over his head for protection when the full force of the avalanche struck. For a full minute he kept expecting to be torn loose and wondered whether Kasparek, by now fifty feet above him, would be able to hold. Then he wondered whether he would be able to hold Kasparek, should his companion be swept from his stance. He would not have any warning of such an eventuality. He couldn't see Kasparek through the swirling snow, but kept expecting to spot a body go tumbling past in the masses of falling debris.

Harrer had barely recovered from the avalanche and was clipping a sling from his waist into the gate of the piton's carabiner as an added anchor when a second avalanche, even more furious than the first, came raging down. He was sure that the end had come, that he and the others would be swept to their deaths. The snow built up between his body and the ice slope, forcing him backward until he felt that he could hold on no longer and had to be torn from his position. But somehow he sur- vived even this second avalanche, and when its last rearguard ice fragments went whistling past, he shouted up the slope to his unseen comrades. Incredibly, their cries came floating back down to him. All were safe, though Kasparek had had the skin torn off the back of one hand by a falling rock.

Heckmair, on the upper rim of the Spider, was up to his waist in avalanche snow. He had somehow managed to sink the point of his axe into the ice when the first snowslide struck, and was holding onto it with one hand. With his other hand he gripped the collar of Vörg's coat, who was standing a step or two below him, with nothing to hold onto.

Heckmair, too, was incredulous that they had all survived and was later to write that an indescribable joy swept over him when he realized that his companions had come through this double assault without having been swept from their holds. The men now wasted no time in moving swiftly up to the head of the icefield and into one of the Exit Cracks that led upward to the summit. Here Kasparek's hand was bandaged, and they clipped once again into a rope of four, with Heckmair leading as he had all day.

To the watchers down in the valley, the suspense was unbearable. The climbers were briefly glimpsed on the Traverse of the Gods, then fog obscured the view. A drenching rainfall turned the lower half of the face into a vast lace curtain of plunging waterfalls while above, on the upper reaches of the face, it snowed. A Swiss correspondent wrote, "Conditions were dreadful and snowfall continuous. Ceaseless avalanches poured down the precipitous ice gully in which the party was embarked. One man in the party studied the face above so as to call out warning of slides to his companions." At 7 P.M. the clouds parted long enough for watchers to pick up the four men. To the amazement of everyone, they were already above the Spider and still climbing. It continued to rain or snow on and off for the rest of the evening, and, as dark was falling, around 9 P.M., the telescope watchers caught a final glimpse of the climbers preparing to bivouac.

Once again the four were separated—Heckmair and Vörg on one narrow ledge, Kasparek and Harrer on another close by. Once again there wasn't enough room even to sit down, and the men had to rope themselves to the rock. They nailed pitons to the wall to serve as hooks from which to hang their rucksacks and climbing gear. Their ledges were about a dozen feet apart, and they strung a rope between the two stances and brewed coffee for hours, sending the pot sliding back and forth to each other on a snap link hooked over the connecting rope. The men ate no solid food, the heavy adrenaline charges washing through their bodies for the past several hours having acted as an appetite suppressant. "We had Ovomaltine, dextrose, roasted pork, sausage, bread, sardines in oil, but we hardly ever touched it. In this respect we were very inexperienced," Heckmair later wrote to a friend.

Tent sacks pulled over their bodies, the men tried to sleep on their feet, leaning out from the wall, secured to pitons. The weather stayed unsettled, and snow avalanches hissed down all around them. But their bivouac ledges were under an overhang and thus somewhat protected. In the morning it was snowing once again, and they debated their situation. Should they stay where they were and wait out the weather, or should they push on, despite the bad climbing conditions? The problem with staying put was that there was no knowing how long the bad weather might last, or how long it would take after it stopped for the face to be clear of loose snow and once more fit for climbing. It could be days, and they couldn't afford to wait that long.

At all events they unanimously agreed to push on and try to make the summit that day. Although they didn't know what rock architecture they were climbing into, they were now less than 800 feet from the top, and everyone still felt fairly strong. Even Kasparek's lacerated hand was not paining him as much as it had on the preceding evening.

In an account of the climb in his book *The White Spider,* Harrer relates that he was quietly confident that they would reach the summit, so confident that, to lighten their load for the final test ahead, he emptied the rucksacks of all food, including a full loaf of bread, and threw it down the face. Throwing the bread away bothered him, he confessed, not because they might need it for sustenance, but because they were destroying food. These were still, very much, men of the depression thirties. Yet the act had its own value. If any further commitment to success was needed, throwing away their food was surely the final gesture. It could still prove to be an expensive gesture, however.

Once the decision to push ahead was made, they clipped into a rope of four, with Heckmair in the lead, followed by Vörg and by Harrer. Kasparek was placed last so that he would have the least amount of rope hauling to do with his injured hand.

Heckmair started up a steep and difficult chimney crack that was deep enough to be safe from snow slides. However, to add to the difficulty of the climbing, it was now snowing quite heavily, large wet flakes that coated all the rock faces with an extremely slippery and mushy cover, a sort of lubricating gel. Despite Heckmair's efforts, he couldn't continue the chimney line and was forced to retreat. This time he tried another line, an unprotected gully down which streamed incessant small snow avalanches. He ran out the length of the rope, then found footholds and a stance, whence he belayed Vörg up to his position. The other two followed in their turn. Next began a tricky series of pitches. The gully steepened, and the ice thinned out to the point where pitons wouldn't hold in the thin ice covering the rock. To add to the difficulties,

small avalanches were constantly coming down the couloir, drenching the men with wet snow. Now and again a heavier snow slide would slam into them like a load of wet cement. The men would hug the rock, hang onto their climbing ropes, and tough it out. Heckmair tried to time his moves so that he climbed only between avalanches, but the trains of snow were not always strictly on schedule, and the men were often swamped and buffeted about on their ropes as they moved from stance to stance.

And then, as the visibility was down to almost nothing, while he was trying to surmount a difficult overhang, Heckmair came off. Trying to straddle a crack, he had driven an ice piton in as far as the depth of ice would permit, about half an inch. He then swung his ice axe, and half an inch of the point bit in. He began his move. He had just crossed one leg past the other and was reaching for a higher hold when, for just a moment, his full weight rested on the ice piton. The shallowly placed piton pulled out, the ice holding the point of his ice axe popped free of the rock, and Heckmair started to fall down the gully. Quickly he twisted his body so that he was falling outward, preferring to see the terrain he was falling into, rather than to fall blind. When one falls facing the rock, it is all too easy to catch one's feet on a crack or a projecting flake of rock and suddenly be flipped backwards, head over heels, so that one is helplessly falling head first.

Although Heckmair was not falling through space, but rather down a steep gully, he still found it impossible to arrest his plunge. He now saw that he was going to hit Vörg and probably knock him from his stance. If that happened, the combined weight of Heckmair and Vörg would fall on Harrer, next on the rope and a hundred feet below. In the likely event that Harrer couldn't hold the two climbers, all four would be swept to their deaths, because there was little chance that Kasparek, with his injured hand, would be able to hold the weight of three plummeting bodies. Knowing all this, Heckmair let out a shout, and Vörg looked up through the swirling snow to see a body hurtling down on

---

———————— 1938 ROUTE

— — — — — — — VARIATIONS

1. First Pillar	*8. Second Icefield*	*15. Traverse of the Gods*
2. Shattered Pillar	*9. Flatiron*	*16. Spider*
3. Difficult Crack	*10. Death Bivouac*	*17. Exit Cracks*
4. Hinterstoisser Traverse	*11. Third Icefield*	*18. Exit Snowfield*
5. Swallow's Nest	*12. Ramp*	*19. Summit Snowfield*
6. First Icefield	*13. Waterfall Crack*	*20. Summit*
7. Ice Hose	*14. Ice Bulge*	

him. Reacting instinctively, he yanked in as much of the slack rope between him and Heckmair as he could, thereby shortening the length of fall. Then he braced himself for the impact. Heckmair slammed into his partner and both men went flying into the air in a windmilling explosion of arms and legs. Heckmair turned a complete cartwheel, then felt his crampons slamming into a slab of ice. They held, and for just a moment he was standing upright, but that moment was all he needed to grab the climbing rope below Vörg and hang on for dear life.

Although Vörg had been knocked loose from his stance, he had fallen only a few feet before the belay piton braked, then held his rope. Both men climbed shakily back to Vörg's stance. It was now discovered that Vörg was hurt. When Heckmair's body, sliding feet first, had slammed into him, one of the spikes of Heckmair's crampons had gone through Vörg's mitten and through the ball of his thumb, blood pouring from both entry and exit holes. Vörg got the glove off. The spike wound was bleeding profusely, and Vörg's complexion had turned green with a combination of shock, pain, and fright. Heckmair got his first-aid kit out of his rucksack and bandaged his partner's hand. Rummaging through the kit, he found a vial of drops that were meant to stimulate the heart in cases of exhaustion. He made Vörg drink half the vial. Heckmair took the tiny bottle back from his partner and looked at it for a moment. Though seemingly none the worse himself as a result of the ordeal, he was thirsty; so he knocked off the rest of the medicine and flipped the tiny bottle down the face. For good measure he followed the heart stimulant with a couple of tablets of glucose. "Ready?" he asked Vörg. The gully and its overhang were waiting, and the sooner they were up it, the better. If they rested too long, they might lose momentum or even nerve. Meanwhile another avalanche roared down with such force that it slammed Heckmair into the rock face, raising a lump on his forehead.

Meanwhile, below the pair of climbers and out of sight and hearing, Harrer and Kasparek had been waiting at a stance for word to start climbing. The wait seemed to last forever. Then an avalanche came down and Harrer was astonished to see the snow streaked with blood. What had happened? He shook the loose snow from his body and shouted up the gully. Silence. Something had obviously gone wrong. Then the paper cover of a bandage came floating down, followed by a tiny medicine bottle. Again Harrer shouted. Again silence.

Above, Heckmair decided to forswear the use of ice pitons on the overhang. Sometimes protection caused one to take chances that were better not attempted. Climbing cautiously, he finally surmounted the overhang and found a place that would take a solid belay rock piton. By now Vörg had brought Harrer up to his stance, and the latter learned the reason for the long delay. Vörg moved ahead, freely assisted by Heckmair, who was pulling on the rope to ease the strain on his partner's punctured hand. Then Harrer and Kasparek were brought to the stance and learned how close they had all come to peeling off the wall to their deaths.

A short time later the men heard voices shouting to them, although the clouds and snow made it impossible for them to see anyone. Nor could they tell whether the shouts were coming from the summit, from the west flank, or even from the Mittellegi Ridge. However, they agreed not to shout back, in case the cries were taken for distress calls that might set a rescue operation in motion. Because of the bad weather, they knew their progress had not been followed by anyone in the valley since yesterday evening, and with the snowstorm all that day, people were undoubtedly considering rescue attempts. But they were not in serious trouble; nor were they in need of rescue. They were tired, and Vörg and Kasparek were hurt, but the four-man rope was moving slowly and surely, pitch by pitch, foot by dogged foot, up the Exit Cracks to the Exit Snowfield, the sixth, and last one before the Summit Snowfield itself.

The Eigernordwand does not come easily. One of its challenges is that the climbing progresses from hard to severe to extraordinary. The icefields get steeper, the rock face sheerer, the rock itself more rotten, protection less easy to find, and the exertion required greater as the effect of the altitude and previous struggles deplete the climber's resources.

The men were moving much more slowly now, as cold and fatigue stole over them and a general debilitation set in. Still, they were making progress, and so far their worst fear had not been realized—that of coming to a great overhang that would bar all upward movement and force them to go back down, perhaps all the way to the Spider, to seek a new line.

Now once again they were startled to hear shouts, seemingly much closer this time. Once again they agreed not to answer lest their calls be misinterpreted as cries for help. So they remained silent. Later they learned that the first shouts had come from their friends Fraissl and Brankowsky, who, worried for their safety, had climbed to the summit prepared to let down ropes and do whatever they could to help the four men on the face.

The second series of shouts had come from Hans Schlunegger, a local guide, who had also climbed up the west flank to lend aid if needed. When both parties, traveling separately, returned to the base of the mountain and reported that they had heard no response to their cries, the report was taken in contrary ways. The optimists assumed that the four climbers had found a sheltered bivouac and had wisely decided to wait until the weather cleared before resuming their ascent. The pessimists were convinced that the four had either fallen off or died of exposure, their bodies still roped to the wall above some ledge or deep in a couloir.

But the four men were still climbing, Heckmair, as always, in the lead. Because of the poor visibility, he was unable to see where the summit was, but he knew that the Exit Cracks would take him up and into the Exit Snowfield, which in turn would lead them on to the Summit Snowfield. It was then but a few rope lengths to the top.

Heckmair found the slope of the gully easing off somewhat and the avalanches fewer and less fierce. He climbed the remaining few feet of rock and out onto an icefield. It was noon. An hour later all four men were moving up the Summit Icefield. It was climbing that required the utmost caution and careful placement of ice pitons and crampons. The new snow sheared off the underlying névé with treacherous unpredictability. For Harrer especially, who had no crampons, the climb was a nightmare. The winds up near the summit were fierce, and the men were bent double in order to retain their balance. Heckmair was so blinded by wind and snow that he almost blundered right over the lip of the summit cornice. Vörg, second on the rope, saw black shapes in the snow in front of them that he took to be rocks. He shouted to warn Heckmair. They were rocks, all right—rock ramparts thousands of feet below them on the south face of the mountain. Vörg was looking down through holes in the top edge of the cornice curl, and he and Heckmair had almost gone completely over the cornice and fallen on the other side of the mountain. They turned right, away from the cornice, and followed the line up the last few spiky feet of the summit ridge.

Soon the other two came up, and at 4 P.M. all four stood on the peak. The Eigernordwand had been climbed. Numbly they shook hands, congratulated each other and, for a few moments, engaged in the curious ritual of picking icicles and ice balls out of their eyebrows, nostrils, and mouths. Then, eager to get back to civilization before darkness fell, they started down the "easy" west flank.

The west flank, protected from the wind, was thick in new snow, three-feet deep in places, and the men plunged and slipped and slithered and fell and did a lot of swearing. Heckmair, now relieved of leading, seemed to go into shock with physical and mental exhaustion. He had been under greater strain than all the others on the ascent, constantly aware that the lives of three other men hung on his every move. Now that the summit was won, he discovered that he was weary right through to the marrow of his bones. His legs hurt all over. He had sprained both ankles with the slamming arrest of his fall in the Exit Cracks. His head hurt; his hands and arms were numb. Now last on the rope, he sat down at one point, glissading down a snow slope on the seat of his pants, to go shooting past the others, trusting they would hold him. It was a dangerous procedure, but half an hour later he was at it again, only this time he tore the suspenders off his trousers. And because high heroic moments are rarely without those mocking deflative touches that fate likes to slip in to remind great men that they're only human after all, Heckmair was now bedeviled by broken suspenders that kept dropping his trousers down around his knees. This daringly agile mountain goat of a climber was reduced to a Chaplinesque figure as he shuffled along trying to hold up his pants. Again and again he had to grab tiredly at his trousers to keep them in place. Harrer, who was in the lead because he supposedly knew the route, having come down the west flank in his earlier traverse of the peak, kept losing his way, for which he was roundly castigated by the others. On top of everything else, he was still without crampons and, of necessity, kept slipping and sliding all over the place. Their descent was becoming a farce, but who cared about that? Plaudits are earned for ascents, not descents.

As they reached lower altitudes, the cloud cover thinned out and the snow changed to rain. Soon the men were nearing the great glacier that leads to the saddle between the Mönch and the Eiger. Below the glacier they could see a mass of dots moving up the slopes. At first they wondered what was going on. Then a young boy, all out of breath and stammering with excitement, raced up to them and asked where they were from. Had they really come down off the face?

The four weary men looked at the excited lad and no doubt saw themselves but a handful of years before. Harrer smiled. Yes, they had all come down off the face. Suddenly the tired climbers were surrounded by friends and journalists and well-wishers who escorted them in a triumphal procession back to the hotel of Fritz von Almen at Kleine Scheidegg. Here they learned that a rescue party had been on the verge of setting out that afternoon when the four climbers had been spotted coming down the west flank.

The weary men were feasted and feted for the rest of the day, the first men ever to have climbed the dreaded Eigernordwand. A week later the four were hailed as heroes in Germany, where they took part in a triumphal parade at which they met and were individually congratulated by Adolf Hitler, who presented each of them with a framed picture of himself inscribed, "With Best Wishes, Adolf Hitler, 22/24 July, 1938."

The German climbers, the extremists, had proved their superiority by vanquishing the last-three great unclimbed Alpine north faces. First the Schmid brothers, Toni and Franz, of Munich, had done the north face of the Matterhorn in 1931. Then another pair of German climbers,

Peters and Maier, had mastered the north face of the Grandes Jorasses in 1935, and now, the last and most fearsome face of all, the Eigernordwand, had fallen to a combined German and Austrian team—or perhaps an all-German team because, since the Anschluss, Austria and Germany were federated in the Greater German Reich.

In a book written by Harrer and Heckmair, *Um die Eigernordwand,* published in 1938 in Munich, both writers wrote fulsomely of their reception in Germany after the climb. Interestingly enough, Harrer credits Heckmair with being the inspiration for the climb, with being at his best when the going was at its worst. There's little doubt that Heckmair led superbly throughout, and his determined persistence and brilliant route finding no doubt contributed most to the victory. For his part, Heckmair credits Harrer for much of the success of the climb and, praising his strength and durability, notes that Harrer consistently carried the heaviest loads. Indeed Harrer, without crampons, was laboring under a great handicap the whole route. Once across the Hinterstoisser, the others wore crampons all the way until the climb was finished. Also, coming last of the four, Harrer had to clean the route of rock and ice pitons, which added considerably to the normal weight of his rucksack and his climbing hardware.

In a recent letter about the climb, Heckmair said that the Ice Bulge at the head of the Ramp was the most difficult pitch, with several pitches in the Exit Cracks following hard on its heels. He called it the hardest of the Alpine faces, requiring not only climbing skill but also an instinct for route finding and a tenacity in the face of suddenly changing weather conditions. By comparison, the Walker Pillar on the Grandes Jorasses was "a real treat of a tour," Heckmair said.

In reply to the charge often made that the climbers had been subsidized by the German government, Heckmair says that Vörg, through connections in the Reich Ministry of Education and Sport, was able to get most of their climbing equipment free. Heckmair states that money was also offered several times, but that he refused it because he was afraid that it would hamper his freedom to make independent decisions regarding his climbs.

Harrer and Kasparek received no support of any kind. Harrer asserts unequivocally, in his account of the climb in *The White Spider,* that no one ordered them to make the climb, and that they got no medals whatever for their achievement. This doesn't quite jibe with Heckmair's account of the climb in his autobiography, *My Life As a Mountaineer,* in which he talks of "our reception and decoration by Hitler" and mentions that, just like anyone else, they (the climbers) "felt honored at being picked out of our obscure existence and presented to the most powerful man in Germany and being decorated by him." Perhaps Heckmair considered that signed photograph a decoration, perhaps the climbers later received a certificate of some kind that escaped Harrer's memory, or perhaps only the German pair was decorated. Whatever their attitudes at the time, decoration or no decoration, they climbed, according to Harrer, because of the challenge, the adventure, and they won out because they were an ideally balanced team. They richly deserved their victory; there can be little argument about that.

All of them paid for their adventure, though fortunately none was hurt seriously. Both of Heckmair's ankles were badly sprained from his fall in the Exit Cracks. Vörg had a deep puncture wound, and Kasparek a skinned hand.

Heinrich Harrer later went on to lead a full, rich, adventurous life. The following year, 1939, he was in India on a German expedition to climb Nanga Parbat when World War II broke out. The British promptly interned him, but he escaped from the camp and, still attracted to the mountains, made his way to Tibet, where he spent the next seven years in Lhasa as a confidant of the Dalai Lama. After the war he wrote a book about his experiences, entitled *Seven Years in Tibet*; he followed that with his popular history of the Eiger, *The White Spider*. He lives today in Kitzbühel, Austria, where he devotes much of his time to writing and lecturing.

Heckmair, who grew up in an orphanage, is also still alive, resides in Munich, and, at seventy-four, remains active in the mountains. In 1978 both Heckmair and Harrer attended a fortieth-anniversary celebration of the climb in Grindelwald, where they were guests at a banquet in their honor. Later they hiked together to the foot of the Eiger north wall. What were their thoughts on looking up again at that awesome face? Heckmair, too, wrote about his climbing experiences in several books. One originally appeared in German in 1938, under the title *Die drei letzten Probleme der Alpen* (*The Last Three Alpine Problems*). Another, his autobiography, he entitled, with disarming modesty, *My Life As a Mountaineer*.

The other two climbers were not so fortunate. Vörg was killed in action on the first day of the German invasion of Russia in June, 1941, while Fritz Kasparek fell to his death in Peru in 1954 when a summit cornice on Salcantay Peak gave way. Also killed during World War II was Rudi Fraissl. While serving in the German Army, he died in an attack on a Russian position.

Not everyone was happy that the climb had been achieved. On the same day that the four-man team came down from the summit, Italy's greatest climber, Riccardo Cassin, with two comrades, Ugo Tizzoni and Gino Esposito, arrived in Grindelwald to climb the Eigernordwand. Hearing that the wall had finally been vanquished, they turned away in disappointment, went to Chamonix, and there did the first ascent of what was now considered the newest last great Alpine problem, the Walker Spur on the Grandes Jorasses. But for a minor passport delay, they would have arrived in Grindelwald three days earlier and started up the face on the same day that Heckmair and his companions had, an interesting "what if?" possibility indeed. Cassin, however, would be back at the Eiger, nineteen years later, to take part in one of the mountain's great epics, the Longhi-Corti disaster.

It might be thought that the successful solving of the last great problem of the Alps would be hailed by everyone. And by and large the feat was acclaimed in most mountaineering circles. But there were exceptions: the British *Alpine Journal* noted the achievement and paid tribute to the "skill, endurance and modesty of the climbers," but in a sour comment it went on to state that the route climbed had "little or no mountaineering value. The true route up the Eiger's north face was discovered in 1932." (The Lauper Route)

Even the *American Alpine Journal* weighed in with a piece of advice. "Perhaps now that it has been demonstrated that this face can be climbed without the climbers meeting an untimely end, we shall have an end to attempts and accidents on the face." From this one might deduce that climbers should attempt only unclimbed faces.

9

I Would Not Repeat It

Now that it had been shown that the Eigernordwand could be climbed, one might have expected a flood of applicants determined to become the second team to master the Alps' most difficult great wall. But lunacy on a much vaster scale was stalking Europe. Because of World War II no further attempts were made on the Eiger's north face until 1946, when two Swiss guides, Hans Schlunegger and Edwin Krähenbühl, started up the wall on August 16. Schlunegger had been involved in the attempt to rescue Kurz and had, in 1938, climbed to the summit via the west flank in an attempt to find out what was happening to the Heckmair party. Hans Schlunegger and his brother Karl probably knew the Eigernordwand better than any other guides in the Bernese Oberland. They were from the nearby village of Wengen, about as far to the west of the Eiger as Grindelwald lay to the east.

Schlunegger and Krähenbühl started out magnificently, fixing ropes on the Hinterstoisser and front pointing up the First and Second icefields, negotiating the Flatiron and the subsequent traverse of the Third Icefield, going up the Ramp to the Waterfall Crack, surmounting that and the Ice Bulge at its head. They climbed the brittle band that led to the Traverse of the Gods and there found a good bivouac stance, a nice ledge that was later to be used by many other parties on the wall. The pair of local guides settled down to a reasonably comfortable night.

The next morning they did something that only local guides would have done. Instead of following the Traverse of the Gods to the Spider and then up the Exit Cracks to the summit, they decided to explore the possibility of reaching the northeast face, the Lauper Route, by finding a crack or gully leading up from the head of the Ramp Snowfield. If they could find such an early exit, it would considerably lessen the dangers of subsequent climbs. Should climbers find themselves in trouble, with someone hurt for example, a safety route out via the head of the Ramp might make all the difference between life and death. The knowledge of such an escape route would also be invaluable to local guides called on to rescue someone. Ropes or cables dropped from the Lauper Ridge to the gullies at the head of the Ramp Snowfield would greatly facilitate rescue attempts. And for climbers themselves, an escape up to the east ridge would eliminate climbing the last and hardest and highest one-third of the face.

The two guides spent most of the day following one crack after another up to the northeast ridge, only to be stymied time and again by beetling overhangs that barred any exit off the north face. Finally, in late afternoon, as the weather was turning bad, they admitted defeat and headed back down, effecting a safe retreat. There was no easy way off the face via a continuation of the Ramp line, despite the inviting cracks and gullies that seemed to offer every prospect of success. Schlunegger and Krähenbühl established that once climbers were committed to the face, it was either climb up and out, or climb down and off.

Hans Schlunegger and his brother Karl were to return to the north face the following year for another attempt. Edwin Krähenbühl never got back to the Eigernordwand and was subsequently killed when a ledge on the Engelhörner gave way, carrying him to his death.

Next year the French arrived in Grindelwald. So far there had been no serious French attempts on the Eigernordwand. But in the summer of 1947, Louis Lachenal and Lionel Terray, two veteran guides from that cradle of French mountaineering, *L'Ecole de Haute Montagne* in Chamonix, came to Alpiglen and readied their equipment. Both had won their *étriers* in the French Alps, particularly in the Mont Blanc area, with its Chamonix Aiguilles and its hundreds of splendid climbs, ranging from easy hikes to the Walker Spur of the Grandes Jorasses. Good Frenchmen, Terry and Lachenal started up the wall on the afternoon of their country's national holiday, July 14, Bastille Day. Weather conditions were excellent, and the Hinterstoisser, though streaming with water, was free of ice. Climbing swiftly, they reached the Swallow's Nest by 6 P.M. Here they found relics of the first successful climb in a pile of old pitons, shredded rope, rotting garments, and cans of sausage and sardines, part of the cache put there by Harrer and Kasparek in 1938 to safeguard their retreat in case of trouble. They also found a small metal tin containing messages, written in German, to which they added their own names and addresses and a few ribald comments for any French climbers who might come after them. The night was clear, and they could see the hotels and houses of Grindelwald. Ocassionally there drifted up to them the disembodied bark of a dog, a car horn, or a herdsman's cry.

At four the next morning they prepared breakfast and with first light launched themselves once again at the face. They scrambled up the First and Second icefields, front pointing all the way, belaying every rope length with an ice piton. Despite their fast start the pair ran into problems at the Flatiron, where constant rockfall and snow avalanches made the going hazardous. Their pace slowed as they carefully eased their way down to the Third Icefield and, though peppered with small stones up to the size of tennis balls, made it across to the relative safety of the Ramp.

The Waterfall Crack at the head of the Ramp was in full spate and Terray, who disliked intensely the idea of getting soaked, turned the crack on the right, making a small, high ledge with a final leap upwards from minuscule holds on the rock face. Had his leaping hand not managed to grab the ledge, he would have fallen thirty feet, but luck was with him, or so it seemed. But when he got up and looked around, the vertical rock was bare of holds, offering no cracks to take even an ace of spades (a short, thin piton shaped like the spade on a playing card). There was no way up. He was forced to rappel back down, but in doing so he found another line on the rock. He followed it and soon came out at the head of the Waterfall Crack. The ice in the Ice Bulge above was soft and porous, and Terray was able to knock handholds and footholds in it with his ice hammer. It now began to hail, but the men made it up the Ramp Snowfield and the subsequent Brittle Crack. By now it was 6 P.M., and the Eiger was in full bombardment with its usual afternoon rock salvos. Not only that, but the two climbers disagreed about the route. From the evidence in Terray's written account of the climb, he and Lachenal never climbed better than when they were arguing violently with one another. To end the argument, they decided to bivouac and tackle the Traverse of the Gods in the morning, when there would be far less danger of being clobbered by falling rock. It took them several hours to find a suitable ledge, and it was nearly midnight before they had finished changing clothes, making a meal, and arranging themselves for the night.

The next morning, with chancy-looking weather, they started climbing again at five, making their way over the traverse to emerge on the Spider. Because the ice was relatively soft, with here and there a rib of stone sticking through the surface, they made swift progress and were soon up into the Exit Cracks. But then an Eiger thunderstorm struck the face. The climbing at this point must have been tension ridden in the extreme, and it is to the credit of the two men that they didn't lose their poise but went on climbing. The rocks around them hummed with electrical charges; blue sparks crackled on the tips of their ice axes, crampons, pitons, and carabiners. Every bit of hardware on them invited a lightning strike. Yet there was nothing they could do except continue to climb. They were fully exposed on vertical rock above the Spider Icefield. Lightning savaged the nearby crags with earsplitting cracks of thunder and left a distinctively sulfurous smell in the air. They climbed to the continuous brattle of thunder and rattle of rockfall, wondering whether the next strike would be their last, thinking no doubt that at least they wouldn't hear the bolt, or even know what hit them. Below, waiting to receive their bodies, should they peel off, there was a yawning abyss of space, some 4,000 feet deep. To make matters worse, the previous night's hail and rain had frozen overnight, leaving the rock with a half-inch cladding of verglas.

It now began to snow large, wet flakes, which meant that Terray, who was leading, had to brush loose snow off the ice and break the ice away from the rock where he thought there might be a crack that would take a piton. Often there was none, and he would have to repeat the process in another likely spot. Whether prompted by the storm or simply eager to get the climb over with, the pair made it quickly up through the worst of the overhangs to a very wide sloping gully filled with rubble. Terray, still leading, was well up in the gully when he began to wonder why it took so long to run out the rope length. Turning around suddenly, he discovered the reason. Lachenal was not really belaying him, but was climbing when Terray was climbing, then freezing into position, pretending to be "on belay" when Terray looked back. Terray wasn't happy with the lack of protection, and another argument started. Thus jawing at each other, yet still climbing, they suddenly found themselves on the Exit Snowfield. An hour later, at 3 P.M., they were on the summit, the second team to have climbed the Eigernordwand. It might be thought all would have been elation at this point—but no. "I felt no violent emotion, neither pride nor joy. I was just a tired and hungry animal. Lachenal was obsessed with getting back to the valley to reassure his wife. . . . [he] ran in front of me, cursing his head off. Still roped together I had no choice but to follow. In the depths of my heart I began to hate him for being a hectoring tyrant," Terray wrote in his account of the climb.

Arguing their way down the west flank, the pair got lost in the poor visibility and treacherous four-inch mantle of new snow. For a while it looked as though they would be faced with a third bivouac, but then they broke out onto a long sloping snowfield that led down into the lights and life and *tout confort* of Kleine Scheidegg.

Terray was to make several interesting comments about the ascent. "It's the greatest climb in the Alps, you commit everything to it," he said. Then he added a remark that many a climber after him was to echo fervently, that one ascent of the Eigernordwand was enough: "I would not repeat it."

Actually Terray was to return to the Eiger several years later, amid rather dramatic circumstances. He made one other revealing remark about the climb, in reference to his feelings the night of their first bivouac at the Swallow's Nest. "Suddenly I was oppressed by our utter loneliness. The hostility of our surroundings and the insanity of our actions seemed horrifyingly plain." This deep depression was felt by almost everyone who climbed the wall. It was as though the men knew they were trapped within the face's concave sides and would never get out alive.

On their return to Chamonix the climbers found a congratulatory telegram from Anderl Heckmair waiting for them. They responded by inviting him to Chamonix as their guest. Heckmair wrote back saying that the immediate postwar conditions in Germany prevented him from accepting their invitation, but that some day he would be happy to go. A correspondence was initiated, and in response to a question as to how he was getting along, Heckmair wrote that as far as food was concerned, nobody was bursting out of his clothes. For a long time afterwards, Terray and Lachenal regularly sent food parcels to Heckmair. It was 1951 before Heckmair finally got to meet the two French climbers in Chamonix, where he arrived to climb the Walker Spur on the Grandes Jorasses.

The Terray-Lachenal triumph signaled the arrival of the French into the top ranks of Alpine climbing. Before the war the German, Austrian, and Italian climbers had been preeminent, so far as extreme technical climbing was concerned, but as a result of their nations' defeat in World War II, and the long period of time it took to get their war-ravaged economies back on a normal footing, the French jumped to the fore with climbers like Terray, Lachenal, Rébuffat, Desmaison, Franco, Ichac, Frendo, Herzog, Martinetti, and a dozen others. Suddenly the French were putting up new routes all over the Alps, as well as in the Himalayas, where their ascent of Annapurna announced the start of the end for the last virgin peaks on earth. Annapurna was climbed in 1950, the first of the world's fourteen 8,000-meter (26,247-foot) peaks to be mastered. In 1953 the British climbed Everest, and a year later K-2, the world's second-highest mountain, fell to an Italian team. Kanchenjunga, the third highest, was climbed by the British in 1955. Makalu, the fifth highest, was also climbed in 1955, by the French. By 1960, after the ascent of Dhaulagiri by an Italian team, the ten highest mountains in the world had been climbed.

Close on the heels of the French were the Swiss climbers who had scorned the extremist methods before the war. But the Swiss economy had come through the conflict relatively unscathed, and there were many young adventurous Swiss with plenty of spare time and a sufficiency of money to take up mountain climbing as a sport rather than a profession. Not only that, a lot of Swiss were beginning to ask what was wrong with their climbers that they had not yet demonstrated their dominance of the Eigernordwand. An answer wasn't long in coming. Several weeks after the French success, a trio of Swiss climbers, Hans and Karl Schlunegger and the gifted amateur climber Gottfried Jermann, started up the face at two in the morning of August 4, 1947. Hans Schlunegger had been as high as the start of the Traverse of the Gods the preceding summer, and his knowledge of the route no doubt helped the three climbers. Nonetheless, they were almost wiped off the face by a rock avalanche that narrowly missed them on the Second Icefield. Despite this, they swiftly disposed of the lower part of the face and, climbing with great speed and assurance, reached the bivouac site at the start of the Traverse of the Gods by 3 P.M. Knowing they would soon be exposed to the heavy afternoon rockfall and snowfall on the Spider, they decided to stop where they were, as Hans had done the preceding year at the same place. Their bivouac was well protected against anything that came down from above. Like Lachenal and Terray before them, they were now treated to one of the Eiger's afternoon thunderstorms. Drenched from their climb up through the Ramp's Waterfall Crack, they faced a wet, cold night as the temperature dropped sharply. Altogether they spent fourteen hours at the bivouac. To add to their discomfort, it snowed heavily during the night. At 5 A.M., wet and shivering, they resumed climbing and reached the Spider, where they had to battle their way upward through the usual snow slides coming down from the Exit Cracks. The cracks themselves were filled with ice and incessant snow plumes, up which the three men had to slowly force passage. The storm grew even worse, and their wet clothes froze into nearly rigid suits of armor. They climbed the Exit Snowfield in the teeth of gale-force winds and near-zero visibility due to the horizontal snow. They reached the summit in the late afternoon, however, and were back down at Kleine Scheidegg several hours later. They were the first Swiss team to climb the Eiger's north face.

The men were hailed in the Swiss press as heroes, by some of the same commentators who had earlier excoriated the adventurers and desperadoes attempting the Eigernordwand in the late 1930s. But these climbers, of course, were Swiss. And they had done the north face with only one bivouac night in the open, as opposed to two nights for the French team and three for the German-Austrian team of the first ascent. The Swiss had also made, according to some, a unique accomplishment, the first guided climb of the Eigernordwand—because the Schluneggers had supposedly been hired by Jermann to take him up. The truth is that Jermann, though an amateur, was an experienced climber, or he would never have been taken in the first place.

The Schluneggers did not, by a long shot, underrate the difficulties of the climb. Hans said he considered the route too dangerous for it to ever become a regular climb even for the best mountaineers. If the weather was cold, the rock face was enameled with ice too thin to take a piton, or even a crampon point, yet thick and slick enough to offer no adhesion to boots or fingertips. If the weather was warm, it meant constant rockfall on the face and the necessity of climbing through drenching showers of rain and snowmelt. Climbers were forever between a rock and a hard place on the Eiger.

The White Cobra had been defanged, and the spectators down in the valley were now talking about a new north-face challenge, the first climb without a bivouac stop. Mountain climbers in France, Germany, Austria, and Italy were also beginning to discuss new challenges: the first winter climb and the first "direct." However, these achievements were not to come for another few years at least.

For a while a lull seemed to settle on the Eigernordwand scene. There were several attempts by Swiss and German climbers in 1948 and 1949, but none were successful. Then, in 1950, a pair of twenty-one-year-old Swiss climbers, Marcel Hamel and Robert Seiler, made two attempts on the face, only to be driven back by severe weather conditions. On the second occasion they reached the rock band between the First and Second icefields when a blizzard forced a bivouac. The next morning they had to rope down, practically repeating Kurz's doomed descent, as far as the Gallery Window, which they used to get in off the Nordwand. They left most of their gear, including 300 feet of rope, on the face and were indeed lucky to get away with their lives (see the frontispiece photograph).

Another pair of young climbers from Austria, Karl Reiss and Karl Blach, next took up the challenge. They were on the Difficult Crack,

Blach leading the pitch, when a block came loose and broke his arm. Reiss splinted his companion's limb and helped him down to the Gallery Window, whence they made good their escape. Despite Blach's broken arm, both climbers walked down the railway tunnel to the Eigergletscher Station, to the consternation of the railway authorities, who didn't like the idea of people wandering around in their railway tunnels.

A second pair of Austrians started up the wall two days later. The twenty-two-year-old medical student Erich Waschak was a good friend and occasional climbing companion of Fritz Kasparek. Actually Kasparek had lent Waschak the same ice axe he had used on the first successful ascent of the face twelve years before. Waschak's partner was Leo Forstenlechner, a forestry worker and another excellent climber who had cut his climbing teeth on the cliff faces of the Gesäuse in Styria in his native Austria. Waschak and Forstenlechner had intended to do a "cache" climb to the bivouac site at the top of the Shattered Pillar, come down, grab a few hours sleep, then start up again around midnight with the rest of their equipment. Rockfall, however, forced them to stash their gear lower down. They retreated and, at the base of the mountain, watched four young Swiss climbers, Jean Fuchs, Raymond Monney, Marcel Hamel, and Robert Seiler, prepare themselves for a Nordwand climb. The Swiss quartet had already been up on the face and had strung ropes across the Hinterstoisser. For Seiler and Hamel it was to be their third try that year.

It looked as though a race between the Swiss and Austrians was in the offing. The Swiss team set off, but Waschak and Forstenlechner stuck to their original plan of not starting up the face until midnight. That afternoon, telescope watchers at Kleine Scheidegg announced that the Swiss rope had already reached the start of the Second Icefield. The Austrian pair guessed that the Swiss would spend that night at a sheltered overhang rather than chance the afternoon artillery barrage on the Second Icefield. They themselves went back to their tent, slept through the afternoon and into evening, then got up at midnight. At 2 A.M. they started their climb. At the equipment cache they redistributed their loads, roped up, and moved on. By early morning, when the alarm clocks in the valley were clanging everyone awake, the climbers had traversed the Hinterstoisser, finding it free of ice, and had mastered the First Icefield and the cliff up the Second Icefield. They were halfway up the Second Icefield when they heard voices above them and saw the four Swiss climbers on the other side of the Flatiron, embarking on the Third Icefield. The Austrian climbers were surprised. They had expected their competitors to be at the head of the Ramp by now, or even on the Traverse of the Gods. But it was evident that the Swiss climbers had slept late that morning. Confident now of their ability to catch up, the Austrians moved swiftly up the Icefield and onto the Flatiron, where Waschak was hit on the arm by a falling stone. Fortunately the blow was not disabling, and the pair scampered off the Flatiron and traversed the Third Icefield as swiftly as they could, in order to get out of the direct line of falling rock that now, at noon, was already starting to trickle down from the Spider and the rotten walls above it.

At the head of the Ramp, Waschak and Forstenlechner overtook the Swiss climbers. Here a delicate bit of climbing etiquette came into play. Would the Swiss let them go ahead? Or would they insist on their right to stay in the lead? As it turned out, one of the Swiss party, Jean Fuchs, had been hit on the head by a rock, and though his wound was not considered very serious, it meant a change in climbing order on the rope and a temporary slowdown of the whole party. At all events the Swiss waved the Austrian pair on through. Waschak and Forstenlechner went ahead, forced the Waterfall Crack, and hacked their way up the frozen Ice Bulge to the Ramp Icefield.

The Brittle Crack and the Traverse of the Gods tested their mettle to the limit. By now, in late afternoon, the rotten rock was loose and crumbly, and where there was ice, it was too thin to take an ice piton. They were forced to bunch and stack their pitons and to fix traversing ropes as they went. To make matters worse, the afternoon Eiger thunderstorm came through right on schedule. It was as though any human trespassing on the Traverse of the Gods called forth a retaliatory thunderstorm from the deities for whom the traverse was named. This storm was accompanied by snow and lower temperatures that soon began to stiffen their clothes, already soaked from their forcing of the Waterfall Crack. By the time the Austrian pair reached the end of the traverse they were out of pitons, which the second climber had not retrieved, because he wanted to safeguard the route for the Swiss coming after them. So Waschak and Forstenlechner were forced to wait at the doorstep of the Spider. It seemed to take hours, but finally the Swiss party showed up and handed over a sling full of pitons. Reassured that the Swiss party was in good shape, Waschak and Forstenlechner went out onto the Spider, which was, for a change, relatively free of snow avalanching and rockfall. The lower temperatures had frozen things into place. The pair made it quickly up into the Exit Cracks, where the rocks were now covered with a coat of ice. An occasional snowslide cascaded down, forcing them to grab hold and hang on. They alternated the lead and climbed steadily. Halfway up the Exit Cracks they briefly debated whether to bivouac for the night or to push on. The weather seemed so cold, and their wet clothes so uncomfortable, that they decided to try and make the summit before night fell.

They were in a race with the approaching dark—a race they barely won when they forced the Summit Snowfield and finally stood on the peak. It was almost nine o'clock. It was now too dark to go down the west flank, a route they had never been on before. So they found a sheltered spot just below the summit; there they hacked out a snow cave, got into their tent sacks, and brewed up some coffee. They were the fourth team to do the Eigernordwand and the first to make the climb without a bivouac stop, taking eighteen hours all told, a record for speed that was to stand for the next fifteen years. It was an interesting progression. The first team had bivouacked three times, the French twice, the Schluneggers once, and now the Austrian team, the fourth ascent, had done it nonstop.

That same night the Swiss party, necessarily traveling at a slower rate because they were a four-man rope, bivouacked on a ledge just above the Spider. The next morning they started up the Exit Cracks, assuming that they were within a couple of hours of the summit. But the weather turned vicious. It began to snow, and the wind rose to gale velocities. Raymond Monney, the oldest, led each pitch, and he had to battle ice, snow, and near-zero visibility for every foot won. Much of the time he couldn't even see the other climbers until they joined him on a stance. Despite the appalling conditions, the rope continued upward, admittedly at a very slow place. Meanwhile Waschak and Forstenlechner got down off the summit before the weather broke. Because of the blizzard, there was talk at Kleine Scheidegg of sending a rescue team up to the summit—if not that same day, then the following morning. But the Swiss climbers struggled upward and, thanks to Monney's skillful leading, finally reached the summit at 8 P.M. Like the Austrian pair before them, the Swiss were forced to bivouac for the night. They were down at Kleine Scheidegg by nine the next morning, just in time to stop a rescue team.

It was the fifth ascent overall and the second Swiss success on the Eigernordwand. Starting with the members of the first ascent, fifteen climbers in a row had now made it up the Eigernordwand without a fatality.

10
Tied Like Goats to a Stake

Despite several attempts by German, Austrian, and Swiss climbers in the summer of 1951, there were no successful ascents of the Nordwand. Nor, fortunately, were there any accidents on the face serious enough to require rescue efforts on the part of the local guides. But in

1952 the floodgates parted, and it seemed as though every Alpine Otto, Kurt, and Gaston was doing his stuff on the Eigernordwand. First came a pair of young French climbers, Maurice Coutin and Pierre Julien, who climbed the face on July 22 and 23, with only one bivouac stop at the head of the Ramp. Several days later, on July 26, a pair of Austrian climbers, Sepp Larch and Karl Winter, went up the face, bivouacked once, and topped out on the summit the following day. They achieved the sixth and seventh ascents of the face.

By now the meadows of Alpiglen were swarming with climbers from Germany, Austria, Italy, France, and Switzerland—the five major Alpine nations. Among those climbers were two who were reputed to be the best in Europe—Hermann Buhl of Austria and Gaston Rébuffat of France. Presumably both had been attracted to Grindelwald by the Eigernordwand's growing reputation as a very difficult, exciting, and testing climb, the Final Exam as it were.

Hermann Buhl was widely considered to be the finest of the German-speaking climbers and a man who loved to climb alone. Born of poverty-stricken parents in Innsbruck, he began to climb while still a boy. Too poor to afford the conventional climbing shoe of that period, rope-soled espadrilles, he climbed in stocking feet or barefoot. He did practically all of his apprentice climbing alone and developed a passion for soloing. He was soon doing winter solos of such difficult routes as the south face of the Marmolada in the Dolomites. He soloed the north face of the Piz Badile in four and a half hours! This was a route first done by Riccardo Cassin and four others in 1937. The five climbers had bivouacked twice on the wall before they had won the peak. On the descent, in the teeth of a blizzard, Molteni and Valsecchi had died of exposure.

Buhl also did a solo of the Salzburg Route on the Watzmann, a 6,000-foot precipice—in winter—at night! He was the Nietzschean superman of mountaineering, a strange, driven, enigmatic figure who made his own rules, went his own way, and was revered (if not exactly loved) by climbers everywhere for his phenomenal skill and courage.

With Buhl was Sepp Jöchler, another strong Austrian climber. They had hardly left Kleine Scheidegg when they were accosted by a woman who begged them not to climb that day—she had premonitions. In order to get away from her, Buhl said they were only going to the Eiger glacier. They started up the Nordwand in the late afternoon of July 25, and, at the bottom of the First Pillar, Buhl startled a hare, which bounded away. He was surprised to find an animal that high up and suggested to Jöchler that the hare was intending to climb the wall, too, and had been waiting for his partner. Joking, the pair climbed on, intending to cache equipment in the bivouac cave at the head of the Shattered Pillar, then come down again and start the climb proper with the rest of their gear on the following day. On the way they met two brothers from the Allgäu, Otto and Sepp Maag, who were coming down after having left some equipment at the Bivouac Cave. When Buhl and Jöchler reached the Bivouac Cave, the rockfall was intense and small boulders were shattering to bits in explosive puffs of dust on the ledges all around them. To climb down was to risk being knocked from the wall. To stay where they were was equally dangerous; they therefore moved up a hundred feet or so to a ledge under the overhanging Rote Fluh. Here they sat and listened to a cannonade of rockfall coming down the almost thousand-foot height of the Red Crag. The stones went sailing harmlessly past, well clear of their position. They waited for the rock barrage to lessen, so that they could descend for the remainder of their gear. But the mountain was in a particularly brittle condition that day, and the rockfall kept up until darkness fell; the men knew they would have to stay where they were for the rest of the night. Faintly, from the black void below them, calls came from Buhl's wife, Eugenie, and from Sepp's brother Hans, who were both worried when the men didn't come back down again as planned. Explanations were shouted down, and the pair below duly satisfied as to the climber's safety.

In the morning the two men were faced with a decision. Should they go down, sort out their remaining equipment and start up again the following day? Or did they have enough gear with them to continue the climb? Buhl even thought it possible, given the speed of the two previous ascents, to reach the peak that day. The decision was made to go ahead, and at the Difficult Crack the pair met the Maag brothers on their way up. Perhaps because of the inexperience of the two youths (Otto was only eighteen, Sepp twenty-three), Buhl and Jöchler did not rope up with them but climbed ahead on their own. They moved across the Hinterstoisser, Buhl leading and fixing a rope for his partner. They were followed by the Maags, who, perhaps thinking that Buhl and Jöchler needed the rope, retrieved the fixed rail that Buhl had installed to safeguard their retreat. Fortunately, the rock face of the Hinterstoisser was dry, though one never knew when a storm could change all that.

After some difficulty on the band that separated the First and Second icefields, Buhl and Jöchler moved up and took a quick rest. Below them they could see the Maag brothers, and below the Maags they spotted a string of five more climbers moving up—making a total of nine men on the face. Buhl and Jöchler couldn't have been too happy with that fact.

The new party of five was a French rope, led by Gaston Rébuffat and Guido Magnone, along with the veteran climbers Jean Bruneau, Paul Habran, and Pierre Leroux. Rébuffat was considered by many to be the best of the French mountaineers. He had already twice done the Walker Spur of the Grandes Jorasses and, should he climb the Eiger, would become the first to do the three great Alpine walls—the Eiger, the Grandes Jorasses, and the Matterhorn. Guido Magnone was considered to be barely a step behind Rébuffat. He had recently done a first ascent of the west face of the Dru. When the French came closer, Buhl recognized among the climbers some old acquaintances from Chamonix and shouted greetings down to them, congratulating Magnone on his spectacular performance on the Dru. The greetings were returned. Buhl and Rébuffat were, of course, aware of each other's reputations, and although neither would admit to competition, each man undoubtedly reassured himself that he would be first to the summit of the Eiger that day. That often difficult and solitary man Buhl was later to write, perhaps tongue in cheek, "I felt very small and unqualified in this company of international stars." It was unlikely that Rébuffat, a prima donna among climbers, shared his feelings.

Despite constant rockfall the Second Icefield was duly disposed of. Jöchler was later to say that he kept hearing cries of alarm as one or another of the seven climbers below him on the icefield was hit, or narrowly missed, by falling rock. Buhl and Jöchler climbed up and across the Flatiron and dropped down to the Third Icefield. Here they found a welcome surprise, a chain of footholds, large "buckets" hacked out by Larch and Winter the preceding day. It was still no easy climb though, as a thousand feet above them the Spider, catching rocks from the summit walls, dumped them straight down onto the Third Icefield. Jöchler was more than impressed, depressed even, and was to write that the insignificance of a single man on that awful face was like a nightmare. "One felt lost and lonely. There was not an inch of dead ground on the whole face, nothing but stones whizzing down from overhead." After having twice been nearly swept from their holds by falling rock, the climbers finally made it to the shelter of the Ramp and started up that ice-filled gully. Behind them the Maag brothers were advancing, and behind the Maags the five French climbers, on two separate ropes, were bringing up the rear.

Any idea Buhl and Jöchler had of stealing a march on the others was soon undone by the Waterfall Crack at the head of the Ramp, here frozen into solid ice. The pair tried to turn the Waterfall Crack by doing the Terray Variant on the outward sloping rocks to the right of the crack. They spent several hours on the variant and, even with the acrobatic ability of Buhl, who stood on Jöchler's head at one point, they were unable to reach the stance at the head of the crack, though they came within six feet of the position. After three hours they finally admitted defeat and abseiled down to find that the end of the rope hung far out

over the void. Jöchler mentally prepared himself to start swinging in and
out on the rope, in order to reach the walls of the Ramp, when the
French party arrived and took in the situation. Not wanting to appear to
be pressing the others, the French had taken a long, leisurely lunch at
Death Bivouac. One of the Frenchmen now reached out and with his ice
axe hooked the rope into the security of the Ramp. Buhl and Jöchler
came down safely, but it was now the turn of the Maags to spring into
the lead, and they straightaway went up through the Waterfall Crack,
more climbable now because the late afternoon sun had melted much of
the ice. The French rope followed, getting drenched as it forced its way
up the cataract. The Waterfall Crack is over a hundred feet long, and
the climbers had to force themselves up through the water, literally in
danger of drowning, because every time they opened their mouths to
draw a breath, they inhaled a mouthful of water and sometimes even
sand and pebbles. Finally all were through the crack and up safely over
the Ice Bulge that bars the way to the Ramp Snowfield. Everyone was
drenched to the skin—"hanging shakily from their pitons like drowned
rats," as Jöchler was later to put it. At this point Buhl and Jöchler swept
into the lead, never to relinquish it until the climb was over. Buhl may
have been smarting that he and Jöchler had failed on the Waterfall
Crack variant pioneered by the Frenchmen Terray and Lachenal.

Everyone now decided to bivouac for the night. It was 5 P.M., and as
rock was still coming down the face, the Traverse of the Gods would be
too hazardous. Anyway, the Frenchmen wanted to change into dry
clothing. The three parties settled down into separate bivouacs—the five
Frenchmen on one platform, fifty to sixty feet above them the Austrian
pair of Buhl and Jöchler on a narrow ledge, and the Maag brothers on
a separate but nearby stance. During the preparation of his bivouac site,
Jöchler was hit on the head by a falling stone, the third rock to hit his
head that day. Temporarily lightheaded from the blow, he didn't realize
how badly he had been hurt until he noticed blood dripping down onto
his trousers. Fortunately the bleeding soon stopped. It proved to be a
cold and uncomfortable bivouac for Buhl and Jöchler. They were soaking wet and could not even get their tiny cooker going, because their
matches were sodden. Buhl wrote that he hurled their pulpy matches
into the darkness below them with "an appropriate quotation from the
classics." He added, "We were racked by thirst and food stuck in our
mouths; even chocolate tasted like sawdust." One wonders, of course,
why he didn't simply borrow matches from one of the French party.
True the French were sixty feet below, but matches could have been
passed up in a sack on a lowered rope. One suspects that Buhl was too
proud to ask. Meanwhile the French, true to national traditions, were
assuring themselves of a good meal. The cooker was lit, Leroux pre-

pared hot drinks and a supper of sausage, bacon, and cakes, and all dined with Gallic gratification on this new kind of haute cuisine.

The Maag brothers were faring no better than Buhl and Jöchler, and they too passed the night without any food or hot drinks. Not only that, but the brothers from the Allgäu had no sleeping sacks. They were so poorly equipped that Rébuffat had earlier insisted on giving Sepp Maag a dry pullover to wear, because the German youth was clad only in a light shirt and ski anorak that had gotten soaked through on the Waterfall Crack.

With the first light of dawn the four leading men were climbing again, in a combined German-Austrian rope. The morning brought bad weather—another snowstorm with gusting winds and poor visibility. Meanwhile Rébuffat, leading the French team, ran into trouble climbing up the Brittle Band. He had a forefinger hold through a piton when one of the Maag brothers, a hundred feet above him, knocked loose a rock the size of a suitcase. The slab shattered on a bulge a few feet above Rébuffat's stance, exploding like a fragmentation bomb and peppering his head and shoulders with slivers and pieces. The shock knocked him out for several seconds. Fortunately his forefinger grip through the eye of the piton held the full weight of his body because he had now been knocked completely from his holds. The Maag brothers, realizing what had happened, quickly lowered a rope to Rébuffat, who thankfully grabbed hold and tied on. The rope of four was now a rope of nine—a European rope of German, Austrian, and French climbers. However, the conditions on the Traverse of the Gods were now fearful, every handhold and foothold had to be brushed clear of snow in order to make sure that the underlying rock was firmly attached to the wall. The men, though all tied in together, worked in almost total isolation, unable to see each other in the driving snow, seeing only a few feet of rope leading away from their waists on each side. Small snowslides came endlessly pouring down over their heads from the slopes above, filling their mouths and eyes with spindrift snow.

There was hardly one climber in the nine who hadn't a wound or a bruise somewhere on his body from having been hit by falling stones. Yet somehow they made it across the traverse, the 4,000-foot void below them hidden in the thick rolling clouds. Led by Buhl, the rope of nine emerged on the Spider and started up that icefield, hugging the right-hand side to avoid the central chute that snow and rock took in coming down the slope. Had one been able to see the line of climbers, it must surely have made a remarkable sight—a chain of nine flies in the Spider's web, a long rope with nine human knots tied into it, making its slow way up through the white maw of the Spider. Now and again a shout would come from Buhl in the lead, to be relayed by others lower down, a warning cry that another avalanche was sweeping down from the Exit Cracks. Nine dark figures would furiously drive axe points into the ice wall, kick in their crampons, press their bodies flat against the slope, and will every muscle to hold to the limit of endurance while the first shock wave of compressed air buffeted them on their ropes, followed by a wall of loose, suffocating snow particles. This happened time and again, for the avalanches came down roughly in five-minute intervals. Though the Spider is less than a thousand feet in length, it took all of six hours to get the nine climbers to the upper rim. A rope of nine made for a safer climb in one sense—any one climber coming off his holds would have eight others to brake his fall, any two swept away would still have seven anchors, and so forth. However, each man on the rope slowed the overall progress of the others, exposing them to the avalanche conditions on the Spider that much longer. It was probably for that reason, the pressing need for speed, that the rope of nine split into two ropes once again, a German-Austrian rope of four and a French rope of five.

Buhl, who had cut hundreds of footholds for himself and the others on the scoured, polished ice of the Spider, climbed on in the lead, one rope length, then two, and was working on the third pitch above the Spider when another and larger avalanche came sweeping down from the Summit Snowfield. It knocked Jöchler and Sepp Maag from their holds, but fortunately their pitons held. Rébuffat, too, was in trouble and was forced to shout for help. " *'Ermann Buhl . . . corde!'* " ("Hermann Buhl . . . rope!"), Buhl records having heard him cry. A rope was lowered to Rébuffat, and he clambered up to join Jöchler and Sepp Maag.

At this point the Maag brothers and Rébuffat decided to bivouac for the night, on two tiny ledges, barely a foot wide. The conditions were too appalling for them to continue climbing. Jöchler agreed, but he wanted to be with his partner Buhl; so he started up to where Buhl was, a hundred feet above. There the two men banged in anchoring pitons and pulled their sleeping sacks up around their bodies. They had nothing to eat and nothing to drink, except the snow that they scooped off the rock and melted in their mouths. It was their third night on the mountain, their second without hot food or liquids.

At the lower bivouac the French managed to get a portable stove going and to melt snow for a drink of lukewarm water. They shared the last of their food with the Maag brothers and made themselves as comfortable as they could. Five men sat on one narrow downsloping ledge, their feet dangling, while below them two more sat on an even narrower ledge. Rébuffat was to write, "We were all tied to pitons like goats to a stake, in case one of us slipped or went to sleep." A small tarp was stretched over everyone's head in a futile effort to keep off snow slides.

They were wet to the skin, their hands and feet half-frozen. Buhl and Jöchler in particular spent a very long night, their soaked condition preventing them from sleeping. According to Buhl the night seemed endless. Once he asked Jochler for the time. "Eleven o'clock," Jöchler responded. Hours later Buhl asked again. "Eleven-thirty," Jöchler said. "Night came and stayed a week or two," as a poet once wrote.

Sometime during the night the storm ceased, and, as often happens when the weather clears, the temperature dropped swiftly. Buhl guessed that it was ten below zero in the morning. Ropes were rigid to the touch, the hardware covered with a fur of white rime, clothing stiff, fingers and toes without feeling, and the climbers exhausted from their long bivouac night and the strenuous efforts of the preceding two days. Buhl reported that the hood of his parka was so frozen that he couldn't push it back and that his trouser legs were as stiff as rainpipes and bumped against his legs like tin. His gloves were frozen rigid, and he had to beat them against the rock before he put them on. The rock itself on the Exit Cracks was in nearly impossible condition, a thin skin of ice glazing every surface. On top of this ice sheath there were several inches of loose, unstable new snow.

Buhl led off, and once again all nine men tied into a single rope. The first pitch, a band later to be known as the Quartz Crack, was exceedingly difficult, even for a man of Buhl's dexterity and toughness. Again and again his feet skated off the surface of the rock, and again and again his hands slipped from holds. He fell off three times, held each time by protection pitons. But each fall jolted his whole body, shook him as a rat is shaken by a terrier, and each time he had to quickly get back on stance and then force himself to repeat the maneuver that had peeled him off on the rock just seconds before. Though technically not the most difficult pitch on the face, because of the condition of the rock and the exhaustion of the men, it was probably the hardest pitch the climbers had yet faced.

Jöchler watched Buhl come off yet another time, then hang in his rope from the waist harness, his arms and legs dangling, like a sheep being hoisted in a belly sling. He heard Buhl cry, "I'm finished!" and it shocked him, a chilling reminder of Kurz's last words, and the famous photo of Kurz's dead body dangling at the end of a rope, arms and legs and head hanging down. Yet somehow Buhl got back to the rock face and hoisted himself up to a decent belay stance. It had taken him four hours to climb the sixty-foot pitch. Because of Buhl's complete exhaustion, Jöchler now passed his companion and took over the lead. The French rope, meanwhile, was having its problems. One climber lost a crampon, while another was hit in the face by a rock. But after a few more pitches Jöchler brought Buhl, the Maags, and Rébuffat up to the Exit Snowfield. Here Rébuffat unroped and suggested that the Germans and Austrians go ahead to the summit. He would belay his four French companions up to his stance. So the great European rope of nine became two ropes once again.

The Germans and Austrians reached the summit, where worried friends were waiting for them. The peak was now bathed in sunshine. Buhl reported that he felt none of the joyous feelings that one might expect from such a triumph. "We were . . . incapable of grasping that the fight was over. We had only too recently fought our way back to life."

They were soon down at Kleine Scheidegg, where Buhl's wife, Eugenie, and Jöchler's brother Hans greeted them. After the usual press conference, they tumbled into a Jeep trailer and made their beds on a pile of ropes and rucksacks. They were asleep in minutes, and when they woke up it was past midnight and they were home in Innsbruck.

When the French climbers arrived at the summit, the peak was deserted, and Rébuffat thought it strange that Buhl and Jöchler had not waited for the rest of the team to come up. The French shared their last few fragments of food and were back down again at Kleine Scheidegg by evening. The eighth ascent of the Eigernordwand was something special. Buhl, the greatest of the German-speaking climbers, and Rébuffat, the greatest of the French-speaking climbers, met each other on the greatest face in the Alps. It was a showdown worthy of a high-noon movie, but something happens to national rivalries when climbers get up on the Nordwand. Instead of a confrontation between Gauls and Teutons, the climb became a cooperative effort, a daring adventure of nine men against a mountain and against their fears, their weaknesses, their vanities. And nine climbers emerged victorious from the ordeal. It was, in many ways, the greatest climb yet on the Nordwand. It was certainly the Eiger's busiest day. Never before had nine men made it to the peak within hours of each other.

The following year Buhl went on to his greatest triumph, the first ascent of Nanga Parbat in the Himalayas, a peak that had already claimed over thirty lives. He did the finish of the climb in a forty-hour solo epic that included a stand-up all-night bivouac at over 26,000 feet, without tent sack or sleeping bag. It was surely one of the greatest mountaineering feats ever performed. Before the final push he left his climbing partner Otto Kempter at the last campsite, as Buhl got up at 1 A.M. instead of the agreed-upon 3 A.M. Otto followed, several hours later, but never caught up with Buhl, who later in the afternoon spotted Otto on the Silver Saddle below him. Buhl wrote, "I saw him stop and then sink down. Otto had given up. This, in itself, was more or less immaterial to me, but with my throat parched and my stomach rumbling I could not but think of the bacon in Otto's rucksack, now lost to me." It was a chilling comment on the singlemindedness of Buhl's drive.

On June 26, 1957, this great mountaineer lost his life in an accident on Chogolisa in the Himalayas. He was with Kurt Diemberger on a retreat from the peak when a cornice lip suddenly broke off under him. The climbers were not roped together at the time. Diemberger, in the lead, saved himself by an instinctive leap to his right when he felt a movement in the snow under his feet. When he looked back to check on his partner, Buhl had disappeared, his steps leading right into the cornice break. He fell thousands of feet to his death.

On the Eiger, 1952 was not yet over. A week later three Austrian climbers, all in their twenties, Hans Ratay, Erich Vanis, and Karl Lugmayer, started up the face. Ratay and Lugmayer had already done the Lauper Route as a reconnaissance. The three climbers bivouacked on the Ramp. During the night it snowed, and just to prove that no Nordwand climb is ever predictable, the three almost got wiped off the face by an avalanche coming down the snowfield above the Ramp, an area generally free of such slides. They got into further trouble heading for the Traverse of the Gods when they missed the Brittle Band and started off too high. After following false leads, and ledges that petered out, they were forced to retreat, and by the time they found the right entry into the traverse, it was late afternoon and time to bivouac again. The next day Lugmayer got cracked on top of the head by a rock the size of a grapefruit while he was on the Spider. The day before Vanis had been hit by a rock on one of the lower snowfields. The concussion was temporary, a typical Eiger "headache," though for a good ten minutes Lugmayer was seemingly out on his feet, though still held to his stance. His worried partners were about to rope down to him when he came to and resumed climbing.

It was evening when they reached the summit, and rather than chance a descent of the west flank in the darkness, the trio dug out a snow cave for their third bivouac on the mountain. By midmorning of the following day they were down at Kleine Scheidegg.

A few days later a young Viennese chemist, Karl Blach, was back for another try at the Eiger. Two summers before he had broken an arm on the face when he and Karl Reiss had had to retreat. But now he was teamed up with Jürgen Wellenkamp, a Bavarian, whose partner, Bernd Huber, had come down sick and was unable to climb.

The pair made good progress and bivouacked their first night on the Ramp. The next morning they unsuccessfully tried to turn the Waterfall Crack via the Terray Variant. Despite several attempts they, like Buhl and Jöchler before them, were unable to force passage and finally had to half swim, half crawl up through the Waterfall Crack. They mastered the Ice Bulge above it, traversed across to the Spider, and bivouacked that night in the Exit Cracks. They were on the summit by noon of the following day.

Unknown to Blach, his old climbing partner Karl Reiss, who had nursed him down to the Gallery Window and safety two summers before when he had broken his arm, was also on the face, camped at Death Bivouac. Reiss had arrived at Alpiglen the day after Blach had started his climb. With Reiss was another young climber, Siegfried Jungmeier. The pair made a normal climb to Death Bivouac, then tried to climb directly up the Central Pillar to the Spider. They actually got to within 500 feet of the bottom edge of the snowfield, at which point they ran short of pitons. Rather than risk being caught without protection, they retreated back to Death Bivouac. On their variant, Reiss found a couple of old pitons on the route, evidence that Sedlmayer and Mehringer had gotten much higher than anyone suspected. No one else had tried to go straight up from Death Bivouac. Reiss's attempt was important for another reason; it added fuel to the idea of doing an Eiger "direct."

Reiss and Jungmeier returned to the regular route and, unlike Blach and Wellenkamp, were able to climb the rock-wall variant around the Waterfall Crack. There was another bivouac at the start of the Traverse of the Gods, and the Spider greeted them with its usual deposit of rolling eggs. Still, they made it up the Exit Cracks and on to the summit, to complete the eleventh climb of the Eigernordwand.

The summer of 1952 had been the most successful season yet on the Eiger's north face. It looked as though climbers were coming close to reducing the Nordwand to the status of an ordinary ascent. The year saw six successful climbs that put twenty men all told on the peak. No one had lost his life. In fact no one had been seriously injured; nor had the local guides been called out to go to the rescue of anyone. Counting the ascents of 1950, 1947, and 1938, a total of thirty-three climbers had now made it up the Eiger's north face without a fatality.

The Eigernordwand had finally been tamed by the men of the east, by the German and Austrian *Kletterfritzen*. Some commentators claimed that the next development would be guided tours, following fixed ropes all the way.

But 1953 was to tell a very different tale.

11
Falling! Hold Me!

On July 26, 1953, two German climbers, Paul Körber and Roland Vass, climbed the screes at the foot of the Eiger and embarked on the stepping-stone ledges of the face. They made their first bivouac on the prow of the Flatiron. That night it snowed and turned bitter cold.

The next day visibility was poor, and telescope watchers caught only brief glimpses of the German pair. They seemed to be moving towards Death Bivouac, but very slowly. Were they in trouble? It was impossible to tell. Clouds closed in again, and there was another overnight stay on the face, perhaps at Death Bivouac or even on the Ramp, though no one knew exactly where.

The next day, the twenty-eighth, the men were spotted descending the Second Icefield, obviously retreating after a change in plans. Was either of them hurt? Again it was impossible to tell. But the watchers kept following the progress of the two climbers as they traversed down and to their right across the Second Icefield, that ever dangerous chute for rockfall. Then the upper of the two climbers lost his holds, or was swept from them by falling rock. The body went sliding down the ice-field, gathering momentum as it fell. Would his partner's belay hold him? To shorten the possible length of fall, the lower climber furiously gathered in rope as his partner went sliding past. The line snapped taut as the falling body was brought up short by the runout of the rope. For just a moment it seemed that the belay would hold, then the second body was yanked upward out of its stance and bounced and jerked down the ice ramp. The dark knot uncoiled as it fell, hands and feet desperately flailing at the ice, trying to grab something, until in a great slow curve the rope seemed to loft the second climber off the icefield. A pair of bodies sailed, for a long, agonizing moment, down through the air to strike a ledge and bound upward and out into space again, one body now arresting the other, now jerking it free from a ledge.

Körber and Vass were the tenth and eleventh Eigernordwand deaths.

A month later thirty-year-old Uli Wyss and his younger climbing partner, Karl Gonda, started up the face on August 20. Wyss was a well-known Swiss climber from Zurich. Gonda, twenty-three, now resident in Switzerland, was originally from Dresden, in East Germany, where he learned to climb on the Elbsandstein range of hills that run all the way into Czechoslovakia. The Elbe's sandstone rock climbers were known for several peculiar practices, such as climbing in the soles of their bare feet, with the ankle and rest of the foot protected by a cut-off boot top. The climbers, by and large, scorned the use of pitons or artificial chockstones for protection, preferring instead rope slings the knots of which they would slot into cracks and tiny weathered-out holds on the cliff face. The Dresden climbers were considered by many to be the best pure-rock climbers in Europe, though their experience on snow and ice was limited.

Conditions for the climb were as normal as they ever get on the Eigernordwand. The usual misty rain hampered visibility, and the men could be spotted only during short breaks in the weather. They evidently bivouacked the first night on the Flatiron or the Ramp, and the second night somewhere on the Traverse of the Gods. On the third morning, when the clouds parted briefly, the pair could be seen making steady progress up the Exit Cracks. They seemed to be in fine shape and moving well, despite two cold and wet bivouac nights.

Toward noon the two figures were picked up by Hugo Wyss, Uli's brother, who was manning a telescope down in the valley. The climbers were on the last snowfield, 150 feet from the summit, and the watchers assumed that the worst was over, that they would soon be standing on the peak, congratulating each other. Clouds obscured the face for a moment or two, and when the view was clear again, the men's tracks were picked up. They led straight into a fan-shaped snowslide. Around this time a railway-sector guard at the Eigerwand Station, inside the mountain itself, happened to be looking out the huge windows that pierce the face. He saw an avalanche go by, masses of snow hurtling past, and in that snow he recognized the blurred dark outlines of two tumbling bodies.

It should have been the twelfth ascent. What went wrong? An avalanche breaking away at that height has had little time to gather force and should not have been strong enough to sweep the climbers away. Were they, with the peak now within a rope length or so, climbing unprotected, not having placed any ice pitons on the last easy stretch? Others had done the same. Or had the pitons been hurriedly and carelessly placed, the men now confident of making the summit? Or were they simply out of ice pitons? Whatever the cause, two lives were lost. Parts of bodies belonging to the two men were later recovered at the base of the mountain, in the fall line under the Eigerwand Station windows. Instead of making the twelfth ascent, Gonda and Wyss became the Eiger's twelfth and thirteenth fatalities.

The twelfth ascent went instead to a pair of Bavarian climbers, Eberhard Riedl and Albert Hirschbichler, who came from Bad Reichenhall and Berchtesgaden respectively. Eiger historians remembered another Bavarian team from those two towns, Hinterstoisser and Kurz, but this time the mountain gods were kindly disposed, and the pair of climbers made a more or less routine ascent of the Nordwand, with two bivouac stops.

Those who pictured streams of tourists wending their way in files up an Eigernordwand festooned with fixed ropes (like the Hörnli Ridge on the Matterhorn) must have been confounded by the climbing seasons of 1954 and 1955, during which no ascents were made, nor any serious attempts mounted on the face. Perhaps the four fatalities in 1953 had tempered the enthusiasm of those climbers who might have had ideas of making their first Eigernordwand ascent.

The summer of 1956 saw the arrival of two Munich climbers, Franz Moosmüller and Manfred Söhnel. The pair camped in the meadows of Alpiglen and started up the face on August 3. They reached the beginning of the Hinterstoisser Traverse, where they intended to string a fixed rope. However, they were met by a heavy storm that drenched them to the pelt and left the rock face above the traverse streaming with waterfalls. The better part was called for, and they discreetly withdrew to their tents down in the meadows.

Two days later the weather improved, and they started up again to prepare the Hinterstoisser. But once again the weather broke and forced them back down. On the eighth they started for the third time and were at the bottom of the Difficult Crack when they met two other climbers, Klaus Buschmann and Lothar Brandler from Saxony. Buschmann and Brandler had already bivouacked the previous night at the cave above the Shattered Pillar. Brandler was only nineteen, and Buschmann but a few years older, and neither was very experienced on great-wall climbing, particularly a route involving vast snowfields and icefields like those on the Eiger. For that reason they must have been delighted to meet experienced mountaineers like Söhnel and Moosmüller.

When the four came together at the foot of the Difficult Crack, they exchanged greetings and sought the usual information about each other—previous climbs, friends in common, conditions on the face, and so on. There was no talk of clipping into a single rope; there would be time enough for that later when they reached the icefields. For now the two teams would climb on separate ropes.

Söhnel and Moosmüller led the way up the Difficult Crack. Below them Brandler and Buschmann started up on their rope. Then something happened. Suddenly Moosmüller cried out a warning and fell from his stance. Dragging Söhnel with him, he struck Brandler on the way down. Fortunately Brandler had just clipped himself into a solid piton, and the peg held. But below him Moosmüller and Söhnel disappeared from sight as their bodies bounced off ledges and struck rock faces with the accompanying clattering clink of ice hammers and strings of pitons, interspersed with soft dull thuds that told of life being inexorably beaten out of two human beings.

Harrowed with fear and shock, Brandler and Buschmann stayed rooted to their stances for many minutes, trying to comprehend what had just occurred. Then they pulled themselves together, roped down, and eventually found the broken bodies of Söhnel and Moosmüller at the foot of the wall. They could hardly believe that two men with whom they had been joking only minutes before now lay dead at their feet. It was a brutal introduction to the Eiger for the two youths. They helped others to bring the bodies back down to Grindelwald, then gave the necessary depositions to the police as to the cause of the accident. They promptly abandoned their plans for the Eiger and went back home. There were no further attempts on the Nordwand that summer. It had been three years since the last successful climb.

The summer of 1957 opened with the first serious Italian attempt on the Nordwand since Sandri and Menti's climb in 1938. Twenty-nine-year-old Claudio Corti, a truck driver, came from the little town of Olginate in the province of Como. Weighing 155 pounds, barely five feet seven inches tall, Claudio didn't look like much of a mountain climber until one noticed his hands and arms. The fingers were long and had broad spatulate tips, and his forearms moved in ropy sheaths of muscles. Claudio had been climbing in his native Grigna range of the Bregaglia since he was seventeen and had accomplished many Grade-VI ascents. Not without a price, though. Once, on the notorious wall of Piz Badile, his partner Felice Battaglia was struck by lightning and killed; the strike actually cut the climbing rope in two and dropped Battaglia a thousand feet down the wall. He was dead before Corti could rope down to him.

Corti had immense natural climbing talents and often relied on his phenomenal strength and skill to get himself out of jams he should never have gotten into in the first place. He had his flaws as a climber. Cocksure of his ability, he would frequently do without protection in places where more cautious climbers would bang in a piton. Then too, Claudio didn't read mountain faces very well. He would bull ahead up some crack, only to find himself stymied and then have to retreat and eventually to find a better line. Several years after Battaglia's death, Corti was on a rope with two other climbers, Carlo Mauri and Carlo Rusconi, when the latter, who was leading the pitch, came off his stance and fell past Corti to his death. Climbers soon began to mutter that Corti was an unlucky partner to go climbing with. That reputation wasn't helped when, in 1956, with Annibale Zucchi, he tried the west face of the Dru, a route that ranks with the Walker Spur of the Grandes Jorasses as one of the hardest climbs in the Alps. He was a thousand feet up the ridge and leading the pitch when he was hit in the face by a falling block of ice. He peeled off, pulling Zucchi with him, and both slid hundreds of feet down the icefield to its base. Corti is supposed to have immediately jumped to his feet and angrily demanded of Zucchi whether he was prepared to go straight back up again. But Zucchi was too badly hurt, and indeed Corti had to carry him on his back to the nearest village. Both men were hospitalized, and Corti was in and out of the hospital for the next five months before he was completely healed. After that incident he found it difficult to get climbing partners, but now, a year later, he arrived in Grindelwald with a new rope mate to do the Eigernordwand.

Stefano Longhi, a factory worker, was a fellow member of the "Ragni," the climbing club of Lecco to which Corti belonged. But Longhi was an occasional climber only, who had no Grade-VI routes to his credit. He was a large man who weighed over 200 pounds. His agility wasn't great, his experience was limited, and he had never before climbed a 10,000-foot peak. (The Eiger is over 13,000 feet.) At forty-four years of age he was probably past his physical prime and was, to date, the oldest man to have attempted the Eigernordwand. But Longhi was agreeable to climbing with Corti (their names, meaning "long" and "short" in Italian, closely fitted their dimensions), and Corti was having too much trouble finding partners, especially for a wall like the Eiger's north face, to turn anyone down.

They arrived at Kleine Scheidegg on August 1, walked up to the small hotel, the Eigergletscher, which sits just under a shoulder on the Eiger's west flank, and there took a room for the night. The next afternoon they hiked across to the base of the great wall, where Corti tried to "scope" out a route for their climb. His only knowledge of the face came from a small postcard that had a hazy approximation of the route laddered in from base to peak in short white bars. There were plenty of detailed maps of the Eigernordwand that he could have purchased in Grindelwald, or even at Kleine Scheidegg, but that sort of planning was not Corti's strong point. Longhi naturally preferred to let the more experienced Corti do all the route finding. After all, Corti had been on the Dru and had climbed the Piz Badile.

And so Corti made his rough plans. Then both men trudged back across the draws and ravines to the Eigergletscher. That evening they readied their equipment one last time. They took tea, sugar, coffee, ham, biscuits, and an assortment of dried fruit—enough food to last a minimum of four days. They also had along a small spirit cooker with fuel, medicine, and a pint of cognac. In addition they carried some 400 feet of rope, three-dozen carabiners, two-dozen rock pitons, and a dozen or so ice pitons. They had crampons, bivouac sacks, ice axes, and sundry other pieces of equipment.

Early the next morning they left their hotel, hiked across to the foot of the cliffs, and started up. Corti soon ran across a couple of rusty pitons and found a broken ice axe, convincing evidence that he was on the right track. Actually the pitons had been hammered in by Sedlmayer and Mehringer back in 1935, and Corti's approach was the "direct" line followed by the doomed pair of German climbers twenty-two years before. It was a line requiring great skill to follow, and the pair of Italian climbers went as high as they could go, but then found further progress blocked by smooth vertical rock faces that were simply beyond their ability to climb. By now it was late afternoon, so they bivouacked on the face. The next morning they retraced their route. In the meantime Corti had spotted another approach line and worked his way westward on the lower ledges of the mountain. He started up once again, this time assured that he had found the right approach by the appearance of several bright new pitons.

They spent the rest of the day working their way up to a suitable ledge less than a rope length from the start of the Hinterstoisser. Here the pair of climbers settled down to their second bivouac.

Monday morning, August 3, they woke to find a rope of two steadily approaching their bivouac ledge. They decided to wait and find out who the newcomers were before continuing with their climb. The climbers turned out to be a pair of twenty-two-year-old German youths who, despite their ages, were highly experienced. Günter Nothdurft was a textile-engineering student who had made some brilliant climbs in Austria, in the Dolomites, and in and around Mont Blanc. He had soloed the northeast face of Piz Badile, an achievement done only once before, by the great Hermann Buhl, and Nothdurft had climbed it a full hour faster than Buhl had, in three and a half hours as opposed to four and a half. Nothdurft's partner, Franz Mayer, a plasterer, was almost as good and had been on several tough climbs with Nothdurft during the preceding winter.

This was not Nothdurft's first time up on the Eigernordwand. Two months before, in early June, he had climbed solo to the upper rim of the Second Icefield, where he had bivouacked for the night. The next morning he was almost brained by a rock that shattered the thermos bottle in his hand as he was taking a drink of tea. Shaken by the incident, he retreated to the base of the mountain, finishing the climb in the dark with the aid of a miner's headlamp. The next day he left the meadows of Alpiglen and returned home, telling friends that the north face was too dangerous to solo. "There's death on that wall," he is reported to have said.

But something changed Nothdurft's mind, and here he was, in early August, back for another round of Russian roulette on the Mordwand, the Murder Wall. The two teams greeted each other and attempted to communicate in a mixture of Italian, German, and *Schweizerdeutsch*. The ragged introductions over, the men started to climb on two separate ropes, the Italians in the lead, they having been first to reach the bivouac ledge. The Hinterstoisser was negotiated rather slowly but without any particular difficulty, and Corti left his pitons and traversing rope in place for the use of the German pair behind him.

The climbers made slow and erratic progress up a seventy-foot crack,

across the First Icefield, and up the slabby band and difficult Ice Hose that joined the First and Second icefields. At this point the Italian pair decided to bivouac again, presumably not wanting to chance crossing the Second Icefield in late afternoon. The two teams found suitable ledges close to one another, roped themselves in, ate some food, and settled down for the night in their sleeping sacks.

People were later to wonder why Nothdurft and Mayer did not climb past the Italian pair and forge ahead at their own speed. Being much better climbers, the young Germans were probably being held back by the slower Italian pair. Several factors no doubt entered into play. The Italians were first on the mountain, and it might have seemed discourteous to overtake and then leave them behind. Also Corti and Longhi were much older men than the German pair, indeed Longhi was old enough to be their father. Age all too often exacts a sort of priority, warranted or not. An attempt to climb past by Nothdurft and Mayer might have been interpreted by the Italian climbers as an attempt to take over the lead, thus an implied criticism of their ability. Then too, Nothdurft and Mayer might not have wanted to make it appear that they were in a race with the Italian couple. They may even have sensed that the Italian climbers would get into trouble and need experienced help. And, finally, the lack of a common language hindered communication.

Early the next morning the climbers woke up and set about preparing breakfast. The Italians ate, then noticed that Nothdurft and Mayer were not having any breakfast. In a jumble of mixed languages, with Nothdurft miming what had happened, it was established that the German youths had lost their food rucksack, the bag having slid off their ledge sometime during the night and gone bounding down the mountain face.

"*Ecco, mange!*" ("Here, eat!") Corti said, handing over honey and biscuits and coffee to the young German climbers. Later it was wondered why the German pair did not turn back at this point. Nothdurft had a reputation for methodical calculation of all the odds, as witness that retreat from the Second Icefield earlier in the season. Why then did he decide to go on without food? Did he think he and Mayer could make it to the summit before the day was out? Even so, he knew enough of the Eiger to fear the unpredictability of its weather, or the possibilities of their being marooned somewhere on the wall by rockfall, injuries, or weather too vicious to allow any further climbing. Had the Italians perhaps told the German pair that they had enough food along for both parties?

Günter Nothdurft on the Totenkirchl in the Kaisergebirge.
W. SEEGER PHOTO

Again Corti and Longhi set out in the lead on one rope, the German pair following. This was now the Italians' fourth day on the face, and the exertion must have been taking a toll on Longhi. He kept enlarging the pigeon-toe steps that Corti, in the lead, was cutting. Longhi picked his way across the traverse with painstaking caution. Corti, in his turn, was surprised that the Germans behind him were climbing so slowly. After all, they were much younger and, having spent only one night on the face, presumably much fresher. The problem soon came to light. Miming a man in the grip of some awful anguish, Mayer communicated the fact that Nothdurft had both a terrible headache and a racking stomachache. Once again one wonders why Nothdurft and Mayer didn't turn back. The Eiger rarely allows second chances, yet here were the German youths without food, and one of them was seriously ill. And they were not halfway up the face, still far short of the head of the Ramp, the farthest point from which retreat was generally considered feasible. In fact they were at about the same height that Nothdurft had reached in his solo climb earlier in the summer. Yet the German climbers kept on going.

The Italians slowed their pace somewhat, presumably not wanting to get too far ahead of the German pair. It took most of that day to traverse the Second Icefield, incredibly slow going. Most climbers are able to front point it on their crampons in well under two hours.

Corti, who later gave out many conflicting reports of the climb to reporters and various officials delegated to obtain evidence, claimed that the German pair had lost their crampons along with their food on their first bivouac. That would explain the slow progress up the Second Icefield, but it seems incredible that men with the ice-climbing experience of Nothdurft and Mayer would continue the climb without crampons, knowing they had half a dozen icefields still ahead of them.

A report later issued by the Grindelwald guides strongly criticized both parties for cutting huge steps in the ice, in effect duplicating each other's efforts, wasting time and energy needed for more difficult parts of the ascent. Telescope watchers at Kleine Scheidegg said that both parties acted as though they were enemies, climbing separately, each rope cutting its own steps. Whatever the truth, it was almost evening by the time the four men got across the Second Icefield and negotiated the three or four vertical pitches that led up and over the prow of the Flatiron and on to Death Bivouac, where they were to spend the night.

Nothdurft was still sick, but Corti gave him some medicine, a heart stimulant. Food was shared, coffee brewed, and everyone hoped that the ailing climber would feel better in the morning. Once again it's to be wondered why the German pair, at least, did not make plans to turn back. Corti and Longhi may not have fully appreciated the difficulty of the final third of the Nordwand. But Nothdurft knew the Eiger, had been halfway up it, and had talked to several men, including Hermann Buhl, who had climbed it.

The next morning Nothdurft must have been feeling somewhat better as the four climbers pressed on with their goal, made the slight descent to the Third Icefield, crossed over it, and started up the Ramp. At first, according to Corti's later reports, Nothdurft felt fine. But the German climber's stomach pains returned as the two ropes made their way up the angled cleft. Corti claims that all four men were on one rope—he leading, the German pair in the middle, and the 200-pound Longhi bringing up the rear. Yet the telescope watchers down in the valley insisted that the men did not clip into a single rope until they were on the traverse above the Ramp Snowfield, much higher on the route.

To compound the difficulties, Longhi now began to complain of exhaustion. It was the older Italian's fifth day on the mountain. In addition to his strenuous work enlarging those steps on the Second Icefield, Longhi was probably also feeling the psychological demoralization of the tremendous exposures ("exposure" is the depth of sheer space beneath a climber's feet) he was constantly facing. He was evidently on the verge of what the French call *épuisement,* a state of physical and psychological trauma brought on by exhaustion and aggravated by the effects of constant adrenaline rushes through the system. At any event, when Corti reached the Waterfall Crack, a decision was made to call it a day, giving everyone a chance to get some much needed rest.

By now, of course, the shortage of food must have been sapping everyone's endurance. It was not a very good bivouac, either. It rained that night, and by morning all four climbers were wet, cold, and miserable. Not only that, but Nothdurft's illness was worse. He appeared feverish and in great pain. Yet inexplicably the climb continued in the morning. Somehow the four climbers made it up the Waterfall Crack and over the Ice Bulge, getting drenched in the process. They were able to take a breather and change into dry underclothing before they tackled the Ramp Snowfield.

Corti's inexperience now led to another route mistake that Nothdurft, had he been in good shape, would probably have corrected. Corti led the climbers too high up the Ramp Snowfield before taking the traverse line across to the Spider. He had missed the ledge that led to the Brittle Band, up which ran the route that gave onto the Traverse of the Gods.

The higher traverse was a broken line with crumbling intermittent ledges that slopped downwards at seventy- and eighty-degree angles. It called for the most exquisite sort of climbing. Here the four men hooked into a single rope—Corti in the lead, followed by Mayer, then Nothdurft, then Longhi. Banging in pitons where the rotten rock would hold them, Corti skillfully worked the four-man rope across the traverse almost to the upper edge of the Spider Snowfield.

Here he banged in a piton, anchored himself, and then ran the rope over his shoulder in order to belay the other three men. He called to Longhi to unclip from his belay piton, knock it loose, and clip it into a sling, then start moving up to the next piton placement, where Nothdurft was waiting. Corti couldn't see Longhi; the German climbers were in between. Anyway Longhi was around a corner on the ledge, but Corti could judge his partner's progress by the slack in the climbing rope that he kept taking in and looping at his feet as Longhi made his way along the ledge to the next piton. Corti kept the rope as taut as possible and was waiting for Longhi to call out that he had reached Nothdurft's stance when he heard an anguished cry.

"Volo! Tienimi!" ("Falling! Hold me!")

Suddenly the rope went smoking through Corti's gloves as he desperately tried to brake his partner's fall.

12
Coraggio, Stefano, sempre coraggio

Fritz von Almen was the owner of the hotel complex at Kleine Scheidegg, jumping-off place for most Eigernordwand climbs. He was the unofficial historian of the Eiger, and no one who had not actually climbed the face itself knew as much about the mountain and its weather as von Almen did. As time went on, more and more climbers sought his advice and help. Before the age of two-way radios, Nordwand climbers would arrange to exchange flashlight signals with Almen at specific times to indicate that the climbers were in good shape and not in need of any assistance. If a climber failed to signal, then Almen would raise the alarm.

There's no doubt the Eiger candidates made Almen's hotel famous and his family wealthy. All the publicity, especially when tragedy was in the making on the face, kept his hotel complex booming. Not only did the press of Europe besiege his facilities during a noteworthy climb, but there were those who always crowded around the scene of a possible Eiger fatality (Eiger ghouls, they were called), who paid good prices for accommodations, ordered lavish meals, and ran up hefty bar bills. Yet Almen often put up Eiger climbers and fed them free of charge, or at greatly reduced rates, and his generosity was appreciated by most climbers, nearly all of whom were chronically strapped for funds.

But the four climbers on the wall had not been in touch with Almen before they had started up. By now, the Italians' fifth day on the wall, Almen sensed that another Eiger catastrophe was in the making. He also knew that the local guides either could not, or would not, go to the rescue of the climbers. Willi Balmer, the head of the Grindelwald Rescue Service, had already confirmed that the local guides could do nothing. The climbers were too high up on the face for the guides to reach them. Nor could the guides rope down from the top, unless the four got well up into the Exit Cracks.

Fritz von Almen tried another tack. He got on the phone and called an old friend, Robert Seiler, who lived near Interlaken. Seiler had been part of the four-man Swiss team that, in 1950, had made the fifth ascent of the Eigernordwand. Seiler agreed to help and began to round up his climbing friends. He also called the Swiss Air Rescue Service at Thun, and the latter agreed to provide a trained crew of rescue experts.

Meanwhile another person was concerned about the events on the north wall of the Eiger. Ludwig Gramminger, of the Munich Mountain Guard section of the German Red Cross, had been listening to radio reports of climbers in difficulty on the Eiger. Gramminger and his crew had the reputation of being the best mountain-rescue team in Europe. Gramminger himself had invented half a dozen pieces of mountain-rescue equipment, including the Gramminger-Sitz, a back harness by means of which an injured climber could be carried to safety on the back of a rescue worker. The fifty-one-year-old Gramminger had been to the Eiger before, had been there when Sedlmayer and Mehringer were marooned at Death Bivouac in 1935. But any rescue efforts then had been futile in the face of the raging snowstorm that sealed the doom of the young Munich climbers.

Gramminger, no mean climber himself and a frequent rope mate of Anderl Heckmair in the late 1920s and early 1930s, and his mountain guards had since 1935 rescued hundreds of climbers, hikers, and skiers who had gotten into trouble in the Bavarian Alps. He had also worked out a plan to pluck men from the faces of sheer walls by lowering a rescuer on a long steel cable from the summit. He now called Willi Balmer in Grindelwald for the latest developments, and Balmer told him that the local guides were helpless to offer any aid to the climbers on the face. Gramminger asked whether he and his crew might go to Grindelwald immediately to see what could be done. Balmer agreed to the suggestion. Gramminger began to round up his men and arrange transportation to the Bernese Oberland.

In the meantime Lionel Terray, the famed Chamonix guide who, along with Louis Lachenal, had formed the second team to climb the Eiger ten years before, was camping out in Grindelwald with two Dutch

clients while they did a few climbs on nearby peaks. Terray learned that
a rope of four was in trouble on the face and with his clients, Tom de
Booy and Kees Egeler, took the cog railway from Grindelwald up to
Kleine Scheidegg. He had a feeling that his services might be needed. At
Kleine Scheidegg he met Robert Seiler and his half-dozen climbing
friends who had just arrived from Interlaken. Terray and his clients
offered to help, an offer that Seiler immediately accepted. At about the
same time Dr. Jerzy Hajdukiewicz, leader of a twelve-man Polish climbing team that was training in the Bernese Alps for a later Himalayan
expedition, arrived at Kleine Scheidegg to offer the services of his team
for any rescue attempts. It looked now as though there were far too
many rescuers on hand. Yet all would be needed.

By now practically everyone knew the identity of the two German
climbers on the face—Nothdurft and Mayer—but who were the other
two, the pair of red jackets? The smaller of the two was now leading the
way across a horizontal line above the Traverse of the Gods, while the
other red jacket brought up the rear, indicating that the two in the middle of the rope, Nothdurft and Mayer, were in trouble. And yet Nothdurft and Mayer were first-class Alpinists. All in all it was a strange
procedure that puzzled everyone who knew anything about mountaineering. The red jacket leading the rope seemed unsure of the route and
frequently had to backtrack and try new lines, a sure sign of someone
whose ability to read a face was suspect. And the other red jacket in the
rear seemed painfully slow in getting on and off his belays, in removing
pitons. It was as though the proper way to climb had been reversed, the
worst climbers doing the most important work, leading and bringing up
the rear, while the best climbers did the least, safe in the middle of the
rope. Could it be possible that Nothdurft and Mayer were both hurt?
Yet they seemed to be moving along at a proper pace, making the right
moves—neither too fast, which might presage panic, nor too slow, which
would indicate failing strength.

By midnight on Saturday, Robert Seiler and his half-dozen fellow
members of the climbing club, Les Bouquetins (Ibexes), plus a twenty-one-
man team from the Swiss Air Rescue Service, were all camped out at the
Jungfraujoch railway station, the highest in Europe, located in the saddle between the Jungfrau and the Mönch. They were a couple of miles
to the west, and a couple of thousand feet below the Eiger's summit.
They had chosen to take the train to the Jungfraujoch Station instead of
going straight up the west flank, because the recent heavy rains had left
the snow cover very unstable and heavy wet snowslides were coming
down the west flank with unpredictable frequency. The higher the party
got, the less danger from avalanches. Also, the higher the rescue workers were transported by mechanical means, the less effort it would take

to carry steel cables, winches, and other heavy pieces of equipment.

When Seiler and his fellow climbers left the safety of the Jungfrau-joch Station early the next morning, they found that the weather had drastically changed. It was well below freezing, and fifty-mile-an-hour winds lashed the men as they struggled out into the frigid air. The sudden cold snap had left the west flank the obvious route to go, as the frost now set the loose rocks and snow masses into concrete-hard stability. But the men were now up in the saddle and had to go on from there. Seiler and his Bouquetin comrades, being all Grade-VI climbers, started to break trail for the twenty-one-man team of mountain rescuers who would be portering the gear to the summit.

Meanwhile down at Kleine Scheidegg, Lionel Terray and Tom de Booy started up the west flank at daybreak. The evening before they had missed the last train up to the Jungfraujoch, where they were to join Seiler and his comrades. Terray decided to wait until morning, then take the first train up. But when morning brought a sharp change in the weather, he realized that he would reach the Eiger's summit much sooner by going straight up the west flank. After a hurried breakfast, the two men started off. While Terray was climbing up the west flank, he and de Booy discussed the north-wall climbers' chances. They didn't look promising. The rope of four had been on the face now for six straight nights. The heavy rains of the preceding day must have soaked the unfortunate climbers to the bone. And the killing frost that followed had, no doubt, frozen their garments into suits of ice armor.

When they got halfway up the west flank, Terray and de Booy edged out on a projecting knob to look in on the north face. They shouted into the void on the off chance that the climbers would hear them and answer back. But the fierce winds seemed to whip their cries right out of their mouths and hurl them away in the opposite direction. Still they went on with their shouting, to be finally rewarded when unintelligible faint cries came back to them out of the black void of that grim wall. They were alive! Or at least one of them was still alive.

Heartened by the response, Terray and de Booy redoubled their efforts to reach the summit. When they got there, they found no trace of the Swiss team they had earlier seen traversing across the north face of the Mönch. Knowing that a large, stable platform would be required, the two men started to hack at the ice cap on the summit, intending to level off an area big enough to anchor the winches and pulleys that the Swiss rescue team would be bringing along.

That same morning two Italian climbers had arrived in Grindelwald for a try at the Eigernordwand. The great wall had been climbed by the dean of German-speaking climbers, Hermann Buhl, and by the best of the French climbers, Lachenal, Terray and Rébuffat. Now it was the

turn of Riccardo Cassin, who, along with Walter Bonatti, was considered
to stand at the apex of the Italian climbing fraternity. At forty-four Cassin could look back on a brilliant career. He was the first to climb the
Walker Spur on the Grandes Jorasses in Chamonix, now rated with the
north faces of the Matterhorn and Eiger as the three hardest face climbs
in the Alps. He was the first to do the north face of the western Zinne,
and the first to climb the northeast, 3,000-foot face of the Piz Badile in
Switzerland's Ticino district, where he was one of five climbers to reach
the summit after two bivouacs. Two of the climbers died of exhaustion
on the descent. But there was one wall that Cassin had still not climbed—
the Eigernordwand. Cassin and his partner Carlo Mauri had been to
Grindelwald earlier in the summer, doing practice climbs on the Jungfrau, but it was clear then that the snow masses on the Eiger were still
too unstable for them to attempt climbing the Nordwand. The wall
needed at least another month of weathering. So Cassin and Mauri went
back to Italy, with plans to return later in the summer.

Twenty-seven-year-old Carlo Mauri was also a veteran mountaineer,
who had not only been Cassin's partner on many of his climbs, but had
also been on Italian expeditions to the Himalayas and the Andes. He
had also been Corti's rope mate on several difficult climbs. Both men,
Mauri and Cassin, were as fit as fiddles, as merry as grigs, and ready for
the great face. But the first thing they noticed the morning after they
arrived in Grindelwald was a Volkswagen bus with the insignia of the
German Red Cross, parked across from the railroad station. Cassin and
Mauri, who had heard reports of climbers in trouble on the Eiger, went
over and met Gramminger and Max Eiselin, a noted Swiss Alpinist who
had joined forces with the Munich rescue unit. When Cassin and Mauri
learned that two of the climbers might be Italian, they immediately
offered to help. It would be useful to have someone along who spoke
the language. The Italian pair and the Germans caught the next cogwheel train going up the valley to Kleine Scheidegg. Here they learned
that Terray and de Booy were almost at the summit, while eight of the
Swiss rescue party were traversing across the Mönch to join the two
Frenchmen. The others in the Swiss unit had had to turn back and come
down because of the severity of the weather and the weight of their
loads. Almen also passed on a report that someone had spotted two
climbers on the summit a little after midnight, just when the weather
had cleared and turned cold, but whether the climbers were Polish or
Swiss or German, no one seemed to know. Had they been two of the
climbers on the north wall, they would certainly have shown up at Kleine
Scheidegg by now.

After taking the train to Eigergletscher Station, Max Eiselin, Cassin,
and Mauri started up the west flank to break trail and mark the route

for the men from the Munich Mountain Guard. They soon ran across the tracks of Terray and de Booy, and, like the earlier pair, they climbed out on the same projecting bulge to look into the vast hollow of the north face. Perhaps the French climber and his companion had spotted someone on the upper reaches of the wall. But the Italian climbers could see nothing. However, at one point they thought they heard a thin, high voice wailing in the distance. Of course, it could also have been the wind shrieking through a cleft of rock. Without thinking, Mauri instinctively yelled into that vast bowl, using the high quivering yodel cry of *Ragniiii* that was used by the Lecco mountaineering club, of which Cassin was the current president. The Italian pair waited, though not with much hope of an answer.

To Mauri's astonishment, back came the familiar yodeling cry *Ragniii.*

"*Chi sei?*" ("Who is it?") Mauri cried.

"Stefano Longhi!" the voice cried back.

When Longhi fell from his stance, last on the rope of four that was edging its way across on the high traverse to the Spider, the line whistled through the nearest piton and then through the snap-link runners that Nothdurft and Mayer were also clipped into. The German climbers were not on a secure belay stance and could do nothing to slow the rope without being pulled from the wall. They could only hope that Corti would hold his partner's fall until they themselves reached a secure position and could lend a hand.

The full shock therefore hit Corti, who was almost pulled from his stance with the dead weight of the 200-pound Longhi's falling body. Still, Corti managed to brake the fall. Grabbing the rope with both hands, he saw smoke rise from the gloves he had on. The friction of the rope burned right through the gloves and into the skin of Corti's palms, burned to such a depth that his hands would bear the grooved scars for months afterwards. Yet somehow he slowed the smoking rope, then held his falling partner.

He now shouted down the face to Longhi, who, hanging in free air, asked to be lowered another six feet to where there was a crumbling ledge just wide enough to stand on. Corti lowered the doubled rope until he felt it slacken, then anchored his end to a pair of solidly placed pitons, thus providing a secure hold. He then edged over to the German climbers and had them belay him as he started down the nearly vertical slope to see how his partner was faring. Using Longhi's rope both as a guide and an aid, he descended about fifty feet but was then stopped by a bulging overhang. He peered over the lip and spotted Longhi on his ledge some forty feet below. Corti had the ability to climb down to his partner on the rope, and there is little doubt that the two Germans, by now in a secure belay stance, would have been able to hold him. But what good would that accomplish? Longhi didn't seem to be hurt, and there was little or nothing that Corti could do for him should he descend. And were he to go down, then what? He would have to climb back up the forty feet of free-hanging rope, a tiring job for a climber even in the best of condition. Shouting down over the edge, Corti tried to talk Longhi into climbing up the rope. He, Corti, would pull if Stefano would climb. But Longhi shouted back that his frozen hands were useless; there was no feeling in them any more; that was why he had fallen off the wall in the first place. Anyway, given the overhang, how could he climb when he couldn't even reach into the rock face with his feet? It would have to be hand over hand, impossible in his weakened condition.

Corti explained that he wasn't strong enough to haul Longhi up by himself. He tried several times, then got Mayer on the belay above to also pull on the rope. But Mayer's pulling didn't help. Because of the sloping nature of the face between Mayer and Corti, when the former pulled, he succeeded only in robbing Corti of half his pulling power. It was unfortunate that neither Longhi nor Corti was evidently aware of prusiking, a technique for climbing rope that had been invented by a Dr. Karl Prusik in 1931. This is a method of tying short foothold loops of cord to a hanging rope by means of a special knot that ensures that the loop can be freely moved upward on the rope, but will tighten and jam when any downward pressure is applied. By means of prusik loops Longhi could have climbed the rope, assuming he could have held onto it with his frozen hands, up and over the bulge in half an hour at the most. He could even, in a pinch, have pulled down enough slack rope to tie loops into the rope every couple of feet for handholds and footholds. Nothdurft must have known of these techniques, and it must be wondered why he didn't go down to Corti's stance and try to instruct Longhi in the use of prusik knots. But there was the language problem—Nothdurft spoke no Italian, and Longhi no German. In addition, as Corti later reported, Nothdurft was so weak that he sometimes had to have help just to force open his own carabiners.

Corti now gave his climbing partner another six feet or so of slack on the rope in case Longhi wanted to move around a bit on the ledge. Then he drove in a pair of pitons on top of the bulge to provide a solid anchor for the rope. He now lowered, on a separate rope, the rucksack with its food and medicine for Longhi. If he, Corti, couldn't make it up to the summit that day, he would never get off the wall alive and wouldn't need food anyway. The idea that he, too, could become stranded on the wall never dawned on him. Standing on the lip of the overhang, Corti shouted down a few last encouraging words to his marooned companion, *"Coraggio, Stefano, coraggio.* I am going to get help. Tomorrow we'll be back to pull you up."

"Yes, pull me up," Longhi repeated, evidently still not aware that Corti was leaving him.

"Addio, Stefano, sempre coraggio."

"Addio, Claudio," Longhi said, now fully realizing that he had to stay behind. He sat down wearily on the rounded ledge, letting his feet hang down. At least he was firmly anchored to the wall.

Corti climbed back up to the two Germans and once more resumed leadership of the rope. The trio finished the traverse and emerged high up on the Spider. They had spent three hours with Longhi, and it was now noon. A freezing rain was falling. Fortunately their traverse line brought them to the head of the Spider, and they were soon up and into the Exit Cracks. Nothdurft was still having trouble, and Mayer had to constantly help his climbing partner while Corti searched out the best line. They were now only some 800 feet below the easy Exit Snowfield, but the climbing was slow and Corti was weakening. He had been cutting steps and banging in pitons all day, in addition to his strenuous work in trying to pull up Longhi from his ledge.

At three in the afternoon, when the climbers were about a third of the way up the Exit Cracks, a rock the size of a soccer ball came bouncing and clattering down the gully in which Corti was leading the pitch. He tried to dodge the projectile, but it took a contrary bounce off a projecting nubbin and hit him a glancing blow on top of the head. He was instantly knocked from his holds and went flying down the gully headfirst, bounding off rocks and ice as his feet and hands vainly tried to grab anything to arrest his fall. After sixty feet he was brought up short with brutal force on the rope as Mayer's belay held firm. However, he was hanging head downward. Corti dimly was aware of red drops of blood staining the snow-clad rocks beneath him, then he started to lose consciousness. Mayer realized what was happening and gave the rope a swift yank that brought Corti to an upright position once more. One of Corti's hands grabbed the rope, then the other caught hold. He was finally right side up.

Belayed by Mayer above, Corti managed to climb back up the thirty feet to where the German climbers were waiting. Here Mayer packed snow into the wound to stop the bleeding, then wrapped muslin bandages around Corti's head. Mayer knew now that he and Nothdurft would have to climb out and go for help. Clearly Corti was in no shape to continue the ascent. His knees were buckling and his mind seemed to be wandering, though for lack of a common language it was hard to tell. But it was certainly possible, even likely, that the Italian had a concussion of some sort. Mayer guided Corti to a nearby ledge and made him sit down. Then he gave him their yellow bivouac sack with enough cords and pitons to anchor it to the rock. Finally, in a mixture of Italian and German, he tried to get Corti to understand that they would return for him at five o'clock the following afternoon. Mayer assumed it would be nightfall before they reached the summit, and the following morning by the time they got back down to Kleine Scheidegg. Rescuers could hardly reach Corti before afternoon at the earliest.

"Domani, fünf Uhr," Mayer said. *"Domani, cinque Uhr."* Mayer rested one cheek against his clasped hands to mimic sleep and the passing of a night. *"Domani, morgen am Nachmittag. Verstehe?"* He held up one hand, spreading wide the fingers, ticking each one off. *"Ein, zwei, drei, vier, fünf! Fünf Uhr, verstehe?"*

Corti caught the meaning of the conversation and smiled at the German youths. They would come back for him tomorrow; they were really good lads. Well that was all right; surely he could last another night, he and Longhi. *"Bene, gut, bene,"* he said to Mayer. *"Wiedersehen. Addio, addio, domani?"*

"Domani," Mayer repeated. He checked Nothdurft's rope, then took over the lead. It was up to him now; he was the only one who could get them out of the desperate situation they were all in.

Sitting on his ledge, Corti watched the German climbers make their way up the gully down which he had fallen. They moved very slowly, and it seemed like hours before he saw the bottom of Nothdurft's boots disappear into the mists above. Then the only sound was the clink and clatter of an occasional stone bouncing down the crack, or the ringing peals of hammer on piton. Fortunately his ledge did not seem in the path of any avalanches. Corti got busy and anchored his bivvy sack with pitons and cords. Then he crawled inside and took off his wet wool shirt, hoping it would dry in the air of the tent so that he could put it back on later. Not long after, he heard the drone of an airplane and wormed out of the sack. A small airplane flew past the face, a couple of hundred feet distant. Corti waved his arms and shouted, but the plane banked away and was soon lost to view. Surely they had seen him?

Feeling somewhat better now, Corti took a close look at his immediate surroundings. He was situated under a bulging prow, which meant that avalanches coming down from the Exit Snowfield, or the summit, would be parted to each side of his ledge. His view to either side was restricted by rock bulges. He could look down a couple of hundred feet to the Spider, but he could not see Longhi's perch. He called his partner's name a couple of times but then desisted. It would be better if Longhi, who was depending on the younger Italian to bring back help to get him off the face, did not know that his climbing partner was also marooned. That could hardly be welcome news.

Corti went back inside the tent and noted that his head wound was bleeding again. He unwrapped the bandage and went outside for snow to pack into the jagged laceration. Then he rewound the bandage around his skull and sat down inside the tent sack to wait out the seemingly interminable hours of the night.

13
Fame! Freddo!

When Terray and de Booy arrived that morning on the summit of the Eiger, the first thing they did was to hack out a platform for the placement of the rescue equipment. Two hours later, eight men of the Swiss rescue team, led by Robert Seiler, arrived after the traverse from the Jungfraujoch. The other dozen members of the Swiss team found the frozen snow and ice too hazardous and, after several falls, returned to the Jungfraujoch Station and there took the first train back down to the Eigergletscher Hotel. From the hotel the rescue team would go straight up the west flank, a considerably safer ascent route now that the frigid temperatures had greatly lessened the likelihood of avalanches.

Up on the summit Erich Friedli and Walter Stähli, of the Swiss rescue team, enlarged the platform started by Terray and de Booy. After hours of work they succeeded in anchoring one end of a steel cable around a rocky bulge just below the summit ridge. It was no easy job to find a safe anchor. The summit rock, like nearly all the rock on the top part of the Eiger, was so loose and friable that pitons driven into a crack would often just crumble the stone and split it into fragments. For that reason it took almost 200 feet of cable and a lot of scratching around before a rock anchor was found sufficiently secure to bear the weight of at least two men and 1,000 feet of steel cable. The Swiss now had about 300 feet of wire left, far from enough to reach either marooned climber. Telescope watchers at Kleine Scheidegg, with whom the Swiss were in radio contact, estimated the distance down to Corti's ledge at 700 feet, with a further 200 feet at least to the other red jacket on the lower ledge. Nevertheless, Friedli and Stähli decided to lower someone down for a reconnaissance and to find out how far to the right or left of the ledge the cable would come when fully extended.

Robert Seiler immediately volunteered. Perhaps the local guides in the valley would have nothing to do with the rescue, but Seiler would prove that Swiss climbers of the extremist school were more than willing to go to the help of their *Bergkameraden* of whatever nationality. Seiler strapped himself into the harness at the end of the cable. After getting a few last instructions from Friedli, he began to walk backward down the Summit Snowfield. Friedli was in continuous contact with Kleine Scheidegg, where telescope watchers had a clear view of the marooned climbers, the whole north wall, and the descending Seiler.

With a last breath intake of apprehension, Seiler stepped off the bottom of the Summit Snowfield and into space. He was now hanging free, slowly spinning on the end of the cable. He kept peering down past his crampons at the snow-plastered rocky slabs and blocks, trying to pick out a line that would not jam the cable in some narrow crack in the limestone face. He also had to be careful that his boots, kicking here and there against the face as he tried to guide the descent, did not knock a block loose and start a rockslide that would wipe out the men below him.

Slowly he kept descending, his body now bouncing, now twisting on the end of the cable. He forced himself not to think of the anchor, of the couplings that joined two lengths of cable together, of the clamp that held his harness to the cable. There were half a dozen places where the cable could suddenly part because of a faulty connection. If he fell now, he would plummet over a mile before slamming into the earth.

Then, between his legs, Seiler spotted the tent, a couple of hundred feet below him. He got on the radio to Friedli and discovered that he was at the end of the cable's length and could go no farther. Bracing his boots against the face, he shouted down. There was no movement at the yellow tent sack, no response to his calls. For ten minutes he kept shouting down the face, but to no avail. Were the climbers already dead? Unconscious? Sleeping? He had no way of knowing. He radioed the summit, explained that the cable was well off-center and would have to be repositioned farther towards the west, and asked to be taken back up. At this point atmospheric conditions began to plague radio reception, and he was able to talk to the summit only in short, frustrating snatches that tended to garble the messages. Because the cable was now hauling him up, it had a great tendency to dig into the rock face and wear grooves in the limestone, thereby increasing the friction and the strain on the steel strands of the wire. Again and again Seiler had to stand on a lip of rock, or stick his toes in a narrow crack, for what seemed like hours as some cable snarl above him was unkinked or untangled. The haul up took two or three times as long as the drop down, and when the cable jerked him up the last few feet of snowfield, Seiler was convinced that his toes were frostbitten. Friedli and Stähli, taking no chances,

---

Rescuers going up the West Flank to set up winches and cables for the Corti rescue.

LUDWIG GRAMMINGER PHOTO

ordered him down the west flank to get medical attention. Seiler took off.

Friedli now began the task of repositioning the cable a couple of hundred feet to the west. It was slow and laborious work, although more volunteers were now on the scene. Cassin and Mauri arrived in mid-afternoon. The rest of the Swiss rescue team came up with the remainder of the sorely needed equipment. Then Gramminger and his Munich Mountain Guards came trudging up the west flank with *their* equipment. Next to appear were the Polish mountain climbers, also bringing extra gear. Ludwig Gramminger now found himself in a delicate spot. He was the acknowledged master of mountain-rescue techniques. In fact Friedli had taken several courses under him in the methods and skills of mountain rescue. Yet the Swiss were the first to arrive on the scene, it was their country, and Gramminger and his men necessarily had to play second fiddle, at least for the moment.

The cable respotted, Friedli now announced that he would go down himself. Radio contact with Kleine Scheidegg had improved, there would be daylight for at least another three hours, and telescope watchers and planes buzzing the face had reported a man on a ledge, a couple of hundred feet below the yellow tent, waving his jacket back and forth. At least one person was still alive on the face. With any kind of luck they could get him off that evening.

Thus Friedli became the second man to make that chilling and lonely descent into the white hell of the Cobra's flaring hood. He went down the full length of the cable and spotted the tent. Again there was no sign of life, despite his repeated shouts. At this point it was planned to attach another section of cable, but Friedli discovered that they would have to reposition the line once more. They had overcompensated and were too far to the west. He called the summit, explained the situation, and asked to be taken up. While waiting for those on the summit to start bringing him up, Friedli kept shouting down the face, hoping to get a response from whoever was inside the yellow tent. At one point a thin, weak voice came floating up from the lower depths. Friedli couldn't make out what the man was saying, but at least the climber on the lower ledge was still alive.

During all this time Corti must have been unconscious in his tent. Otherwise he would surely have heard either Seiler or Friedli. If Longhi could hear them, then surely Corti also should have. Yet Corti had no recollection of having lost consciousness at any time. Perhaps the walls

---

Erich Friedli on the summit, directing operations for the rescue of Corti.

A. SKOCZYLOS PHOTO

of the bivouac tent were sufficiently thick to muffle the sound. Or perhaps Corti's head, wrapped in muslin bandages and covered with a woolen stocking cap, blocked outside noise. In any event, Corti missed the appearance of both men.

When Friedli reached the summit, he found that Gramminger, tired of standing around and doing nothing, had put his men to work in setting up the German winch, rollers, and brake clamps. Following the advice of Terray, who knew the face from his previous climb, they had picked a spot that should drop the cable directly down to the tent ledge. Gramminger diplomatically explained that there was no harm in having a backup system available in case anything went wrong with the Swiss equipment. The German cable, of quarter-inch steel, was actually stronger than the Swiss one. Friedli now announced that he would try another descent later that night, this one by moonlight. But the weather turned sharply colder, and the temperature in the thin air of 13,000 feet soon dropped abruptly. The equipment began to freeze, the cables turned kinky and jammed in the rollers, feeling fled from exposed fingers, and it was reluctantly decided to postpone any further rescue attempts. However, most of the rescuers agreed, despite the cold and lack of hot food, to bivouac for the night just below the summit. It would give them that much of a head start in the morning.

Never before had so many men spent a night on the Eiger's summit, and it hasn't happened again since. There were at least thirty men up there, speaking half a dozen languages—Poles, Dutchmen, Frenchmen, Germans, Italians, and Austrians, among others. One of the last to arrive had been Walter Seeger, a climbing partner of Nothdurft's from his hometown of Pfullingen. Hearing that a pair of German climbers was in trouble on the Eigernordwand, he had guessed that Nothdurft might be involved. When he was unable to locate his friend in any of his usual haunts, Seeger took off for Grindelwald on his motorbike. He caught the cog railway up to Kleine Scheidegg, then climbed the west flank in the moonlight, a route unknown to him, determined to do what he could for his rope mate.

In the morning a plan of action was quickly formulated. It was decided to use the German equipment, which was already in place and had a long enough cable to descend the thousand feet to where the lowest climber—and the last one reported to be alive—was to be found. They would try and reach this lower climber first, if at all possible, then bring him up to the other three climbers at the yellow tent. All four would be injected with heart stimulants, then winched to the surface, the weakest going up first. That, at least, was the plan.

There was some discussion as to who would do down on the cable. Ideally it should be someone who spoke both Italian and German. But it was even more important to use someone who was thoroughly familiar with cable descents. Alfred Hellepart, a burly 200 pounder from Munich, was Gramminger's most experienced man on cable rescues and was finally chosen to make the third descent. The rescuer might be called on to carry one of the marooned climbers piggyback up the face, a task requiring great strength, agility, and a cool nerve. Alfred Hellepart had proved himself on many other rescues and indeed was to prove himself once again.

In the meantime Friedli was having doubts about the hauling capacity of the big circular winch on the summit. If anything happened to it, it might be a good idea to have an alternate system available, one that relied on manual power. After all, they had plenty of men up there as a backup if they needed them. He ordered his workers to cut a firm path through the snow and back along the ridge line, so that a score of volunteers, with haul ropes and roller guides, could pull the steel cable up and through a system of direction-changing rollers.

Hellepart was now buckled into a Gramminger-Sitz, in which a wounded or exhausted man could be carried papoose style. He also carried a rucksack with food and medicine, wore a radio strapped to his back and had on a plastic crash helmet. Meanwhile the weather, though intermittently sunny, looked as though it might be changing. Ominous black clouds were quietly building up on the horizon line. A thunderstorm, of course, would put a stop to rescue operations. A man hanging on the end of a steel cable would become a lightning rod for any strikes. Then too, there were the many men crowding the summit, the most dangerous part of a mountain during a lightning storm. They would have to retreat.

Hellepart, the third man to make the cable descent, began walking backward on his crampons as the steel line slowly paid out. He reached the lower edge of the Summit Snowfield and, while waiting for a new length of cable to be added to a coupling, tested his radio. Communication with the summit was excellent. He spoke to both Gramminger and Friedli. The cable was ready again, and Hellepart stepped backward. He was now spinning down into the black void that fell away below him for almost 6,000 feet. Above him the cable, looking thinner and thinner the lower he descended, stretched away and disappeared into the milky whiteness of the snowfield. Hellepart looked down. In his own words, part of a report he later made, Hellepart said, "The glimpse took my breath away. I stifled an exclamation. This grim, menacing blackness, broken only by snow ledges, falling away into interminable depths. . . ."

The cable continued to lower in jerks and bounces, and his body spun slowly in the air. He tried to keep his legs stiffened out in front of him in order to cushion any swings into the wall. In fits and starts he descended another 300 feet, then halted once more while, up on the summit, a new 300-foot section of cable was tied in with a coupling. Again he tested his radio reception, and again it was loud and clear. However, disturbing news came from the telescope watchers that there was no sign of life in the climber on the lower ledge. The figure appeared motionless, slumped back on his rope, as though asleep or passed out. Nor was any movement evident at the ledge of the yellow tent sack. The news was indeed grim. Was Hellepart risking his life for nothing?

The cable was once again ready, and the Munich man began to kick and brace his way down the crumbling black face of the mountain. Each time his crampons knocked rubble loose from a ledge or gully, he winced, knowing that the rockfall could well strike the marooned survivors below. Yet there was no way that he could control such rockfall. Even the cable, sawing through a crust of ice, frequently started small trains of snow or flaking rock that went winging or clattering down the face.

Still Hellepart descended. Now and again he caught glimpses of the pastures of Alpiglen, an impossible mile below. Then he came in view of the Spider's upper rim. Another halt, another cable change, again the familiar jerking, twisting descent. He kept peering downward between his legs, hoping to spot a flash of yellow. At one momentary stop he thought he heard a voice. He shouted down into the abyss, and this time was positive that someone was calling back. But still he could see no one. He traversed to where the sound seemed to be coming from, rounded a bulge of rock, then suddenly saw the ledge and its yellow tent. There was someone sitting there, a figure that weakly lifted an arm in salute. Hellepart immediately reported on his radio that he had found one of the survivors. He edged over as close as he could. The cable was now jamming badly because he was dragging it sideways across the face and around the bulge of rock. Finally he could go no farther. He called to the seated man. *"Deutscher?* Nothdurft? Mayer?"

"Soi Claudio, Claudio Corti, *Italiano,"* the man answered.

"Wo ist Nothdurft? Mayer?" Hellepart asked.

In a melange of German and Italian, Hellepart was given to understand that the two German climbers had left Corti a couple of days before. Then Corti asked, *"Sigaretta?"*

Hellepart shook his head. Although he smoked, he had no cigarettes with him.

Alfred Hellepart (white helmet) preparing to go down the face on the cable and look for Corti. Above, Ludwig Gramminger (left) and Erich Friedli.

LUDWIG GRAMMINGER PHOTO

"*Mangiare?*" Corti's partially cupped hand beckoned to his mouth in that timeless Italian gesture to indicate hunger.

Hellepart fished a bar of chocolate out of his pack and tossed it across the seven-foot gap separating him from the Italian. Corti caught the bar and was so famished that he rammed the chocolate into his mouth without stopping to remove the paper wrapping.

Hellepart now decided that he would have to be taken partway up again. He might conceivably make it across to Corti's ledge, but the cable would have been pulled so far out of the vertical as to be useless in hauling anyone up, especially the weight of two men. He got on the radio and explained what he wanted to do, then traversed back to where the cable ran directly upward. Using the radio, he gave instructions to bring him up for a new approach.

Kicking against the rock face, Hellepart ascended almost 200 feet before he found the head of a gully that he had earlier picked out. He was sure it was a line that would lead him directly down to the Italian. He gave instructions to Gramminger, and once again the cable unreeled and lowered him through space. Suddenly he was dropping down to the ledge in a clatter of loose rock. He shouted a warning to Corti, then called triumphantly over the radio, "*Ich habe ihn!*" ("I have him!") He was standing on the ledge. Corti attempted to get to his feet, but Hellepart restrained him.

"Nothdurft? Mayer?" he asked again to make sure.

Corti, using scraps of Italian and German and sign language, told him that the German pair had climbed on several days before and that his own partner, Stefano Longhi, was stranded on a ledge farther down.

Hellepart looked down the face, then began to call Longhi's name. Corti joined in. They heard nothing except the shrill keen of the wind blowing in and through the fluted rock ramparts around them. At this point Hellepart must have thought of giving Corti a heart stimulant, then leaving him on the ledge while he descended on the cable to look for the other Italian. But several factors persuaded him to change his mind. There was no evidence that Longhi was still alive. In fact, the last word from Kleine Scheidegg seemed to indicate that he wasn't. Also, it looked as though Corti needed to be brought up right away. Hellepart got on the radio and asked Friedli to bring Cassin to the mike to try and find out whether Corti was fit enough to tie into the cable ahead of him. Cassin came on and began to talk to Corti. Hellepart now realized that Corti would be in no shape to make it up if he were to be tied in separately on the cable. There was that bad head wound for one thing, and how could he hold onto the cable with those deep rope burns in his palms? Hellepart noticed, too, that Corti's crampon straps were all torn off. The Italian, in his hunger, had obviously eaten the leather straps.

Hellepart now broke into the conversation and said that Corti would have to go up piggyback. Friedli and Cassin agreed.

For Riccardo Cassin the situation was not without irony. A partisan during World War II, he had been wounded in a firefight with a fascist armored car in the closing days of World War II. His old climbing partner, Vittorio Ratti, had been killed in the same action. Yet here he was, working right alongside his old enemies, including men of the Munich Mountain Guard who might, for all he knew, have been soldiers of the German Mountain Regiment that had hunted him and other partisans during the final months of the war. Terray, too, for that matter, had been in the French Maquis during the war and had engaged in several hit-and-run attacks on German troops in the Chamonix region. Yet this time, at least, they were all working together to save lives, not waste them.

Cassin now explained to Corti exactly what Hellepart wanted him to do. But Corti had trouble understanding the instructions and sometimes pushed the wrong button on the radio, cutting off communication until Hellepart was able to get the channel open again. While Corti was talking to Cassin, Hellepart looked around at the bivouac ledge. There wasn't a trace of snow or ice anywhere within reach. In his desperate hunger and thirst, Corti had eaten and licked all the ice off all the rocks, as high as he could reach, all around his bivouac place. In fact the Italian's lips were blackened and split from frost and dehydration, and half a dozen of his teeth were splintered or broken from having bitten at the ice to get it free of the rock.

Hellepart now made Corti drink some coffee from a thermos that Polish rescuers had hastily thrust on him at the start of the descent. Then he buckled his rucksack onto Corti's back and showed the Italian how to place himself in the Gramminger-Sitz, the backpack sling. Then Hellepart had to kneel down to allow Corti to place his legs, piggyback style, in the sling. With an effort Hellepart stood up, checked his cable connection, then radioed the summit that he was ready. Because Corti was on his back, Hellepart had to transfer the radio to his chest, where it now hampered his breathing.

In the meantime changes had been made on the summit. Noting that the winch had barely been able to haul up Hellepart when he asked to be repositioned for another drop down to Corti, Friedli and Gramminger decided to switch over to manpower for the cable pull. Haul ropes were attached to the cable every six feet or so, and a line of men was spotted along the ridge haul way that had previously been dug out and aligned by rescue workers. As a safety precaution a couple of antireverse clamps were attached to the cable so that no slippage would occur. In groups of four and five, a score of men now took up positions on the haul ropes. An order was given, and the men strained on the ropes. The cable tautened to a singing pitch but still refused to budge. Another half-dozen volunteers added themselves to the hauling crews. Another try, but still no gain. Then it was discovered that the cable had jammed in one of the roller guides. The wire was freed, and this time the men felt the cable give. They dug in and gained three feet, then slid the haul ropes forward on the cable. Another haul, another three-foot gain.

Down on the face, Hellepart was having his troubles. The weight of Corti on his back made any kind of maneuvering difficult. With the added weight the cable had an increasing tendency to jam in clefts. Sometimes, hanging free, Hellepart and Corti were spun around. Several times Hellepart swayed into the rock face with his side, unable to cushion the blow with his legs. When he did embrace the wall face on, Corti would lean over his shoulder and try to eat the ice and snow within reach, muttering, *"Fame, fame"* ("Hungry, hungry"). Several times Hellepart had to speak sharply to the half-demented Italian. Often the cable twanged and crackled with tension as it went up over a rocky edge, and it was all too easy to visualize its suddenly parting in a final horrendous pink! Then there were the seemingly interminable delays, stops to rest the men on the summit, delays that found Hellepart and his burden now hanging free of the rock face, now with crampons dug in on the verglas of a tiny knob, now half kneeling, half crouching on a tiny ledge. To make matters worse, Hellepart had lost a pair of gloves on the descent, and his fingers were stiffening with cold and possible frostbite. But despite the delays, the two men reached the fifty-degree sloping Summit Snowfield, where the weight of Corti, no longer borne by the vertical strength of the cable, seemed at times unbearable for Hellepart. Crawling up in a crouch, as the cable sawed into the snowfield, as Corti tried to snatch handfulls of snow and threatened to overbalance, as the radio dug into his chest and face, Hellepart found the last couple of hundred feet to be a nightmare. Once, when a shaft of sunshine lit up the snowfield, Corti calmly remarked, as though he were out for a Sunday stroll, *"Que bello il sole"* ("How beautiful the sun is").

Finally the pair reached the summit, and Hellepart, exhausted, collapsed full-length in the snow. Rescuers lifted Corti out of the sling and unbuckled the harness from Hellepart's back. Hellepart looked up, unable to believe that he had actually made it up out of that white abyss of swirling snow and ice-clad rock. He smiled at the men around him. "A cigarette, please," he said.

Rescuers on the summit during the Corti rescue.

LUDWIG GRAMMINGER PHOTO

Friends led him away to a bivouac hole for a smoke and a hot drink. Meanwhile Corti was examined by Dr. Hajdukiewicz of the Polish team, who injected the Italian with a heart-stimulant drug. Soon Corti began to act manic. Catching sight of Mauri, he boasted, "This time the wall won, but next time I'll beat it. Will you climb it with me, Bigio? I know the way now." (*Bigio*—"grey"—was a Lecco nickname for Mauri, who had grey eyes.)

Later there was criticism of Corti's remark, and others of a similar nature that he made on the summit, but in the Italian's defense, it must be pointed out that he had all but come back from the dead. Corti remembered lying down on the ledge at one point and saying aloud to himself, "I am not going to make it. What a strange place for me to die." In addition to the psychological trauma of finding himself alive after he had given himself up for dead, the heart-stimulant drug and a cup of tea heavily laced with cognac no doubt contributed to Corti's manic mood.

By now the clouds had rolled in over the summit, and another difficult decision was in the making. Should they look for Longhi? Or was it a waste of time and perhaps an unwarranted risk of other men's lives? Lionel Terray argued strongly for another attempt, offering to go down on the cable himself. After all, he knew the face quite well, having climbed it in 1947 with Louis Lachenal. If the storm caught him while he was going down or if lightning strikes were observed, he would insist on being brought right up again, but for now let them try once more at least.

So Terray was strapped into the Gramminger-Sitz, and a radio was fixed to his chest. Meanwhile Cassin was trying to find out from Corti exactly where his rope mate was located. However, Corti was vague as to Longhi's position and seemed to be more interested in learning whether he would now be recognized as the first Italian to have climbed the Eigernordwand. "But how can that be, Claudio?" Cassin is supposed to have answered. "You were brought up here on the back of another man."

The Polish doctor gave Terray a hypodermic needle and instructions on how to inject the drug. Then Terray was lowered jerkily down into the clouds on the face. The French climber must have wondered at the twist of fate that brought him back to the Eigernordwand in such dramatic circumstances. After the 1947 ascent, both he and Lachenal had

---

Lionel Terray carrying Claudio Corti on his back after the retrieval of the latter from the face.

LUDWIG GRAMMINGER PHOTO

vowed never to try the Eiger again—once was enough. And poor Lachenal was gone now, having been killed the preceding November when
he skied into a 200-foot crevasse after a snowbridge had broken on the
Glacier du Géant outside his native Chamonix.

That trip down must have been a searingly lonely one for Lionel
Terray. He later said he relived the 1947 climb with amazing intensity,
accompanied by the ghost of Lachenal. He was even able to pick out the
spot where he had hammered in the last rock piton in the Exit Cracks
before he and Lachenal had emerged on the Exit Snowfield, still arguing
furiously and happily with each other. Yes, Lachenal was gone, and so
was the great Herman Buhl, who had perished but a couple of months
before in the Karakorum. Gone, two of the greatest climbers since the
war, both killed in the mountains. And his own end? Better not to think
of that; he had a job to do, and he did it, searching every nook and
cranny in that final rock face above the Spider, looking for a body
pinned to the wall or lying motionless on a ledge or sprawled on a snowfield. But despite his searching, he found no sign of any climbers, dead
or alive. The great question still unanswered was—what had happened
to Nothdurft and Mayer? Corti stated that they had gone ahead up the
Exit Cracks to bring back help. But where were they? There was no sign
whatsoever that they had reached the summit. Perhaps they had done
so, and then fallen on the descent. But a veritable army of men had been
up and down the west flank in the past two days—surely someone would
have spotted the bodies. All of which seemed to leave only one solution,
that they had fallen from the Exit Cracks, all the way to the base and
into one of the crevasses of the bergschrund. But even that explanation
was suspect. It was unlikely that *both* bodies would have fallen into a
crevasse. And why was none of their equipment found? Climbers falling
down the face generally shed their rucksacks, ropes, slings, ice axes, rock
hammers, crampons, helmets, and even parts of their bodies. And yet
not a single piece of equipment that could be traced to either of the two
men had so far been found at the base of the mountain.

Terray continued to descend and was now coming into view of the
Spider. But then the cable halted. He opened his radio link in an attempt
to find out what was happening. He could hear bursts of conversation as
the men at the summit tried to contact him, but evidently they were not
receiving him in return. He flicked the mike with his fingers, again and
again pressed the "send" button, kept calling into the open mike, but got
no indication that anyone could hear him. The radio's batteries had
evidently weakened. To occupy his time, Terray resumed his search of
the rock face. He even swung back and forth in a pendulum move to
increase his field of vision, but the rasping cable dislodged so much
rock that he was forced to stop. Periodically he would shout down the

face, at first with no result. But later, after another bout of shouting, he was electrified to hear a faint voice crying in Italian, *"Venite! Venite!"* ("Come! Come!")

Terray shouted down into the grey curling mists below him, calling the one word he had earlier heard Cassin say over and over again when he had been talking to Corti on the radio, *"Coraggio! Coraggio!"* It was little comfort, he supposed, for the stranded Longhi. *"Il faut avoir du courage."* How many times had he muttered that phrase to himself when he had been in a tight spot—on Annapurna with Herzog and Rébuffat, in Chamonix with Marc Martinetti, even on this very wall ten years before with Lachenal. Yes, of course, it was necessary to have courage, but it was hardly necessary to tell Longhi that. Men didn't tackle the Eigernordwand if they were at all short of that particular commodity.

And now the dirty, pewter-colored sky was beginning to leak snow-flakes. Tatters of cloud wreathed in and out of the channels and crannies on the face. If a storm was coming, there was little chance of their bringing Longhi up that day. The stranded climber would have to hold out until tomorrow. Terray now began to wonder what was happening on the summit. He had been hanging for more than an hour. Lightly he tapped his crampons against the rock face, trying to move his toes. There seemed to be no feeling in them. Then, without warning, the steel cable went rigid with a crackle of tension static. A jerk, and he felt himself being lifted. No doubt the men on the summit, feeling that a blind descent without radio communication was too dangerous, had decided to bring him back up. It was a rough ascent—he had no way of telling them when the cable was temporarily jammed in a crack. Sometimes the upward pull would come so abruptly as to jerk him into the rock. He learned to protect his face by holding the cable with both hands, his forearms winged out wide to act as buffers. Even so, he was covered with bruises when he finally reached the Summit Snowfield.

As soon as he was out of the harness, he learned that Gramminger and Hellepart were repositioning the cable for another attempt to drop down to Longhi, this time with a new radio. Although it looked as though a storm was on the way, it was only 3 P.M., and there was still plenty of daylight left. Terray, noticing that Corti was still in the snow cave in which he had been placed earlier in the day, promptly began to organize a team to carry the Italian climber down to Kleine Scheidegg. There was a good chance that he might not survive another night on the mountain. Terray hoisted Corti up on his back and carried him a couple of hundred yards along the summit ridge, to a narrow defile that led downward to the west-flank route. Here the Italian was strapped into an affair—half stretcher, half sled—that the Germans employed to work injured men down off steep mountain slopes. Every hundred feet or so

Corti's stretcher had to be belayed with rock or ice pitons. It was, of necessity, a slow, cautious crawl down the west flank. After a while the storm broke, and freezing rain began to pour down from the heavens. Soon everyone was drenched, including the unfortunate Corti in his aluminum cot. The ropes stiffened with cold, and even the spring-loaded gates on the carabiners froze and had to be tapped open with another carabiner or piton. After three members of the Polish rescue team lost their footing and nearly fell to their deaths, it was decided to call a halt and to bivouac for the night. The freezing rain was turning to snow, leaving the footing extremely precarious. Meanwhile, the men on the summit decided to suspend operations. It was 4:30 P.M. They would withdraw and bivouac lower down on the west flank, then resume their rescue work in the morning.

Down at Kleine Scheidegg, telescope watchers caught a glimpse of Longhi when the clouds parted briefly and revealed his ledge. The red-jacketed figure was standing upright, arms raised wide as though in appeal to everyone down in the valley. The word was relayed to Gramminger and others on the summit. The second Italian was still alive!

At about the same time Cassin and Mauri, on their way down the west flank, reached the projecting platform where they had previously hailed Longhi on their climb up the mountain. Heads ducked into the wind, they shouted into that swirling bowl of snow-whipped air currents and shreds of fog. "Stefano! Stefano!"

Incredibly, they heard an answer which, by some fluke of wind currents, came loud and clear, *"Bigio! Venite! Venite!"*

The two Italians shouted back to their Ragni club mate, telling him to hold on—help would surely reach him in the morning.

Back from that vast, cold, dark amphitheater came two short and simple words, shattering in their brevity and what they revealed of the unfortunate climber's plight.

"Fame! Freddo!" ("Hungry! Cold!")

14

I Hate That Wall!

The rescuers spent a harrowing night in their bivouac site high on the west flank. They were soaked through and had been without hot

Corti shortly after his rescue.

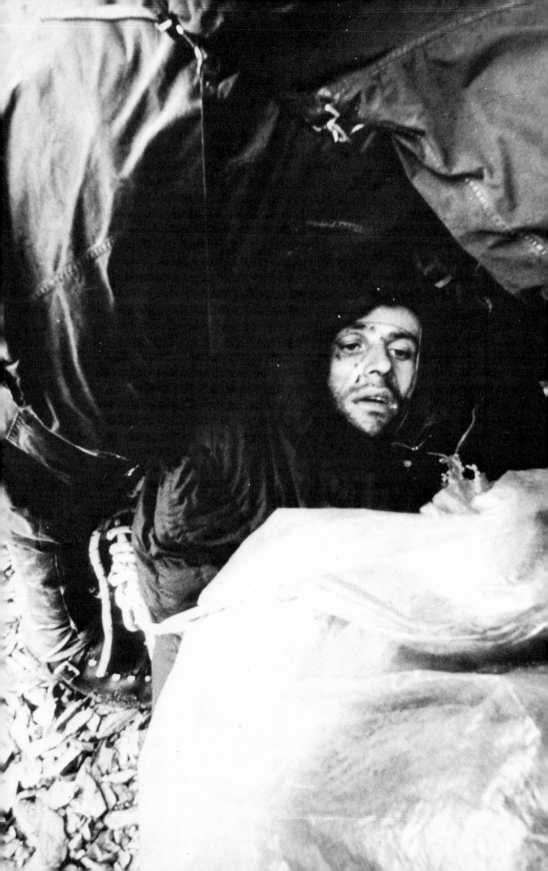

meals for two full days. The temperature was well below freezing and, as if that weren't enough to contend with, the hapless Corti kept everyone awake with his shouting. Half-delirious, he thought his rescuers had abandoned him. At other times he imagined himself back on the face, still marooned on the ledge.

In the early hours of the morning, the storm moved away after having dumped six inches of snow on the upper reaches of the mountain. Terray, Cassin, and the other members of the group started off once again, conveying Corti down the west flank. A thousand feet or so above the Eigergletscher Station they were met by a group of Swiss guides who were bringing food, hot chocolate, and coffee with them to the summit. The famished rescuers fell to and were soon wolfing down breakfast. Then, before the Swiss guides could resume their leisurely climb to the summit, more people arrived from Kleine Scheidegg with the news that sometime during Longhi's ninth night on the mountain, he had either fallen or been swept from his perch by the storm winds and now hung in his ropes, a dozen feet or so below the ledge. A light plane flew past the face and confirmed that the Italian was dead, his body hanging legs downward, his forward-tilting head already married to the rock face by a thin casque of ice. Longhi's long gallant struggle was finally over, ended by those two implacable foes that he had so despairingly named the night before—*Fame* and *Freddo*.

A new rescue team was formed to search the other approaches to the Eiger in case Nothdurft and Mayer, confused by darkness, had tried to descend the south or east face. A thorough combing of the summit and the Lauper Route down to the Mittellegi hut failed to turn up any trace of the two climbers. Another search was conducted of the mountain's base by Max Eiselin, and it too was fruitless. It was now conceded that the German pair must have fallen from the Exit Cracks and that their bodies were to be found either in a crevasse or on one of the Nordwand's snowfields. And that effectively ended the whole rescue effort.

The men returned to their homes and their usual pursuits: Gramminger, Hellepart, and the other members of the mountain guard went to Munich, de Booy back to Holland, Terray to Chamonix, Robert Seiler and his Bouquetins to Interlaken, and Cassin and Mauri to Lecco. Cassin later said of the rescue effort, "We did everything we could for Longhi. I doubt if he could have been saved after that hellish storm broke that night. Neither he nor Corti should have been on the Eiger." Cassin continued climbing, and eight years after the Corti rescue he was part of a team that climbed Mount McKinley in Alaska, North America's highest mountain. He was fifty-two at the time. At the age of sixty-two he made his third ascent of the northeast face of Piz Badile, possibly thinking, as he finished the climb, "There's music in the old bones yet," as a poet once wrote.

To Seeger, Nothdurft's old rope mate, was left the job of consoling Nothdurft's father and mother, who had just arrived in Grindelwald to await news of their son. Nothdurft senior was a particularly tragic figure. He himself had been blinded during World War II. His two older boys had been killed in the same war, and now Günter, his youngest and last living son, was missing and presumed dead.

Max Eiselin had one final chore to do before he returned to his home in Lucerne. He went to the Grindelwald-Grund railway station on the cog railway, found a red Puch motorbike in the parking lot, and from it removed a hastily penciled note that he had placed there almost a week before. The motorbike was Nothdurft's, and the note had congratulated the young climber, who was a personal friend of Eiselin's, on successfully doing the Eigernordwand. Eiselin, one week before, had recognized the bike at the station and, hearing that German climbers were on the wall, guessed that Nothdurft was one of them. With binoculars he had watched the four climbers move across the Third Icefield and onto the Ramp. Their progress was such that he was sure that the climb would be successful. Because he was going off to climb the Engelhörner, he knew he would miss the climbers on their return and thus left a congratulatory note on Nothdurft's bike. When he got back from the Engelhörner, he learned that rescue efforts were underway to bring down a rope of four in trouble on the face. He now sadly removed the note and crumpled it up. He had lost another good friend to the mountains.

The tragic loss of the three climbers recalled the earlier loss of Hinterstoisser, Kurz, Rainer, and Angerer. And, as on that occasion, controversy immediately ignited. The questions were endless. Why had the local guides played such a small part in the rescue, coming in only at the last moment, when the Eiger had already been swarming with fifty volunteers from all over Europe? Why hadn't rescue attempts been mounted sooner? Why hadn't Longhi been rescued first? What really happened to Nothdurft and Mayer? And, the most chilling question of all, had Corti abandoned his rope mate, then somehow contrived to lose the German climbers in order to assure his own survival? There was lots of fuel for that last question. A news photographer, flying past Corti's ledge in a small plane on the Saturday before the rescue, two days *after* the German pair had supposedly left him, had taken a photograph that seemed to show at least two figures, and possibly a third, on the ledge with the yellow tent.

Corti himself, far from clearing matters up, only made them worse by issuing conflicting stories to different newspapers and various climb-

ing authorities. It was clear, despite his climb, that his knowledge of the
face was sadly lacking. There was his two-day false start for one thing,
and for another his penchant for tacking Hinterstoisser's name onto any
and every difficult part of the climb, now referring to the Hinterstoisser
Pitch, the Hinterstoisser Icefield, the Hinterstoisser Chimney, and so on.
In one version Nothdurft was so sick and weak that Mayer had to open
his partner's carabiners. And yet Nothdurft had been strong enough to
climb up the Exit Cracks. In one version Nothdurft had lost all his climbing gear and food on his first bivouac night, in a second version only his
crampons. At one point Nothdurft and Mayer had left him on the ledge
early on the morning of Friday the ninth, in another story late afternoon
on Thursday the eighth. According to one report Corti gave, he and his
partner had roped up with the Germans almost at the start of the climb,
just below the Difficult Crack. According to another version they hadn't
roped up until the Second Icefield. Yet observers down in the valley
were convinced that the two teams climbed on separate ropes until the
Ramp was reached. Corti claimed that neither of the Germans had had
crampons, which would explain their slow progress on the icefields, but
would climbers with Nothdurft's and Mayer's experience have continued the climb after the first bivouac without those essential aids? After
all, at that point they still had five icefields ahead of them. And Nothdurft knew how long and steep those icefields were. He had climbed to
beyond the Second Icefield and back again in his previous attempt on
the Nordwand. And lacking food and water, as well as crampons, they
still went ahead?

Had Corti truthfully conveyed Longhi's actual predicament on the
ledge to the two Germans? If so, it would seem odd that Nothdurft or
Mayer would not have attempted to either lower prusik slings to Longhi
and instruct him in their use, or demonstrate them to Corti and have
Corti relay the information. Even a climber who had never prusiked
before should easily have been able to get up the forty feet of rope from
the ledge to Corti's position at the overhang. It might have been argued
that Longhi was too weak to prusik up the rope, but he was strong
enough to live five more days on his exposed stance. And prusiking is
not all that strenuous, certainly not anywhere near as difficult as climbing a rope hand over hand, which Corti had earlier wanted his partner
to try.

Newspapers, of course, had a field day with the inexplicable disap-
pearance of the German climbers, and speculation ranged widely—so
widely that Corti brought a libel suit against an Italian newspaper, an
action that he withdrew when the paper allowed him to present his side
of the story. There were hints of foul play in some accounts, conjectures
that Longhi and Corti had refused to let the more skilled German pair

climb on past, or that there had been an argument or fight over rescuing Longhi, and that Corti had hurled the German climbers from the face, or cut their ropes. German newspapers, in particular, kept raising the question of Corti's credibility. Even Walter Seeger, who had helped in the rescue, believed that Corti might be hiding something. Nothdurft was known to take copious notes of each climb, even when he was in bivouac. Find his notebook, people said, and the mystery will be solved. Adding fuel to the controversy was the clearly visible body of Longhi hanging in its ropes all of that summer, all of the following winter, and into the next summer.

Despite the tragedy, the whole affair had a certain grandeur to it. The Eiger rescue had called for volunteers, and men had stepped forward—fifty of them, speaking a babel of tongues, from seven nations (Germany, Austria, Switzerland, Poland, France, Italy, and the Netherlands). Men like Seiler, Friedli, Terray, and Hellepart, who went down that grim face on the thread of a cable. Hellepart was so affected by the experience that he smoked thirty cigarettes practically nonstop after the rescue, then never smoked again. Men like Cassin and Mauri, who nursed the demented Corti back down the west flank; de Booy, whose knowledge of five languages made him indispensable in facilitating communication between the various groups; Dr. Hajdukiewicz with his special skills in mountain medicine; the Polish team and the Bouquetins, so willing to do all the dirty work, such as carrying supplies, digging bivouac caves, and hauling on the cable; the technical experts like Gramminger, Stähli, and Friedli, who worked under the constant pressure of knowing that men's lives depended on their skills; and the mountaineering friends of Nothdurft like Eiselin and Seeger—all covered themselves with honor.

The year 1957 closed without a successful Eiger climb. The last climb of the face had been the twelfth, Hirschbichler and Riedl's, in August of 1953. The thirteenth ascent was indeed proving to be an unlucky one. Söhnel and Moosmüller, trying to make the thirteenth climb in 1956, fell to their deaths, while the other rope of Brandler and Buschmann was forced to withdraw. In 1957 three of the four climbers who attempted the thirteenth ascent were killed. Two Austrian climbers that summer, Wolfgang Stefan and Götz Mayr, got as far as the First Icefield but had to withdraw when the weather broke and a bad storm moved in.

In 1958 rumors were swirling that Corti intended to come back to Grindelwald in order to climb the Eiger and to cut free Longi's body, which, with the advent of summer, had broken its icy bonds to the wall and was once again hanging free in its ropes, turning slowly to the caprices of the wind.

Whatever Corti's intentions, in late July of 1958 two Austrian guides, Hias Noichl and Herbert Raditschnig, and a young Saxon climber, Lothar Brandler, arrived in Alpiglen with the double goal of finding the bodies of Nothdurft and Mayer and making the thirteenth ascent of the face. Lothar Brandler, at twenty-two the youngest of the climbers, had seen Söhnel and Moosmüller fall to their deaths from the Difficult Crack in the summer of 1956. This was Brandler's third attempt to climb the Eigernordwand. Accompanying the three climbers, and acting as their adviser, was Heinrich Harrer. He had been a member of the German-Austrian team that had made the first successful climb of the face in 1938. The four men hoped to clear up the mystery of what had happened to Nothdurft and Mayer the summer before.

Starting soon after midnight, the three climbed swiftly and made excellent progress. The north wall was in fine shape, with little or no verglas on the rocks. When daybreak came there wasn't a cloud in the sky, and the forecast called for more of the same for the next three or four days. There was one problem, however. The brilliantly sunny weather melted much of the ice that held the upper rocks in place, with the result that rockfall was heavier than usual.

By midafternoon the men were almost at the top of the Second Icefield. It was here that the first near-fatality occurred when Brandler lost his grip on the ice face. Sliding and sprawling helplessly, he fell sixty feet before his protection ice screw broke his plunge. He was able to recover, then climb up to rejoin the others. For Brandler, though, it must have been a harrowing moment, all too reminiscent of the fall of Söhnel and Moosmüller two years before.

By 5 P.M. the men were making their way up the Flatiron, hoping to reach Death Bivouac before stopping for the day. But in late afternoon the Flatiron is particularly exposed to rockfall from the Spider directly above it. The three were on a vertical rock pitch when they heard a low rumbling sound from above and knew that the Spider was laying down another artillery barrage. "Rock!" someone shouted, and the men flattened themselves into the wall, hunching their shoulders, the round curve of their helmets butting into the limestone.

A large stone cracked the top of Noichl's helmet, momentarily stunning him and nearly knocking him loose from his stance. As he hung there from one point (a hand gripping his embedded ice axe), another large stone smashed the hand. Fortunately his grip still held, and his rope mates were able to maneuver him onto a protected ledge, where they tried to deal with the wound. Noichl was losing a lot of blood, but Raditschnig and Brandler managed to stanch the flow by means of a tourniquet, and to bind the mashed hand and make a shoulder sling for the whole arm. Then they made their way to Death Bivouac, where they could spend the night in relative comfort. There was enough room to stretch full length, and the projecting roof of the ledge gave adequate protection against snow and further rockfall. Actually, at that point they were within 700 feet of Longhi's ledge.

At first light in the morning, they started back down the face, safeguarding the injured Noichl, who, with one arm in a sling, was severely handicapped. Nevertheless, he was brought down by the other two in masterly fashion. They made the long traverse across and down the Second Icefield, rappelling down the band of cliffs to the First Icefield, and then made their way down and over the Hinterstoisser Traverse. By noon they were coming down the Difficult Crack, the last dangerous pitch on the descent.

Meanwhile, Heinrich Harrer, knowing his friends were in trouble, went up to meet the retreating climbers. He used the *Stollenloch* opening and climbed out with the intention of bringing the trio back in through the Gallery Window. With Harrer came a party of Swiss guides, who were supposedly attempting to "rescue" the descending climbers.

The local guides had been stung by all the criticism that they had made no real effort to help the Italians stranded on the face the summer before. In this instance they couldn't be criticized. They were there to effect a rescue, even if the climbers didn't need or want to be rescued. Raditschnig, the last climber on the rope, had only a few feet to descend when the guides arrived. The three climbers were escorted in through the Gallery Window, put on a train, then driven by car to Interlaken for medical treatment. On the way to the hospital, weakened by the loss of blood, Noichl lost consciousness. He also lost two fingers of the injured hand but gained a whopping bill from the guides, who charged him for the services of eleven men, when only six had been present, who charged for railway transportation for all the guides, even though the guides had free passes, and who charged for bandages that they not only had never furnished, but had forgotten to bring to the scene of the supposed rescue in the first place!

Fritz von Almen of Kleine Scheidegg later said that the guides went to meet the climbers, not in order to rescue them, but rather to vent their feelings of resentment against the climbers for trying to find Nothdurft and Mayer, for trying to retrieve Longhi's body—jobs that most people felt should already have been done by the local corps of guides.

It seemed that every Eiger climb gave rise to controversy. After Corti had been rescued, the Swiss Alpine Club submitted a bill of $1,500 to cover the out-of-pocket expenses of their members involved in the operation. This accounting caused a furor among the other Alpine clubs, one Italian member pointing out that of the seven nationalities involved in the rescue, only the Swiss had sent in a bill. There were unfair comments made that the Swiss would always find a way to profit from the misfortune of others, a not so veiled allusion to Switzerland's role in World War II, when, it was widely and perhaps erroneously believed, the Swiss had made money trading and trafficking with both sides in the conflict. This supposed ability of the Swiss to turn a profit out of even the worst circumstances, had given rise to the saying, "Let a Swiss eat a nail and a screw will come out." That old aphorism was now being widely quoted.

Whatever the merits of the controversy, the thirteenth ascent was proving very elusive indeed. It proved too much for Brandler, who, after Noichl had his fingers amputated, stated bitterly, "I hate that wall!" Less than a week later, though, he was on the summit.

In late July two Austrian climbers, Kurt Diemberger and Wolfgang Stefan, arrived in Grindelwald where they spent a couple of days in a carpenter's shop and garden, getting their equipment ready for an attack on that "monstrous slab of stone with its grey riven icefields and its crumbling bastions, its polished steps of rock," as Diemberger was later to describe it in an account of the climb. Though still a young man, Diemberger had already made a name for himself in mountaineering circles. He had already done many severe Grade-VI routes and first ascents in the Alps, and he had climbed Broad Peak with Hermann Buhl.

Diemberger and Stefan next moved their tent and equipment to a steep, grassy slope right under the face itself. For a few days they were there able to follow the Noichl, Brandler, and Raditschnig climb and subsequent retreat. On the evening of August 4, the Viennese climbers noticed a policeman trudging up the slopes from the railway line a thousand feet below them. When the Grindelwald policeman arrived, sweaty and out of breath, he politely requested to see their passports. When the documents were handed over, the policeman put them in his pocket with the explanation that the climbers would get their passports back when the climb was finished. This was a new procedure, he explained, that would help to identify the bodies that were so often unrecognizable after having fallen a mile down the face. He wished them good luck and departed.

With that vote of confidence, Diemberger and Stefan started up the face at one in the morning of August 4, picking their steps in the predawn darkness with the aid of a miner's headlamp and a flashlight. The summer before, Stefan had been forced to retreat from the First Icefield because of bad weather. But this time the weather was excellent, and they reached the Hinterstoisser by 7 A.M. The rock face, as Diemberger wrote, was scored and absolutely white from the innumerable falling stones that grooved its surface on their way down from the upper parts of the face. The good weather was a mixed blessing. While the rocks were dry, the ice on the snowfields was treacherously soft and mushy, making for difficult climbing and poor belay stances. Then too, the mushy ice released many of the rocks that had previously managed to knife through the crust and find lodgment there, adding to the already high incidence of rockfall.

Mayer had no sooner started across the Hinterstoisser than a rattle of rocks came tearing down. "We're moving into a hostile district," he called back to Diemberger. The pair put on their crampons at the Swallow's Nest, where they took a break, then started up the First Icefield.

On the Second Icefield, they decided to make the long right to left traverse as high as possible, on the sound theory that rockfall, striking the ramparts on the upper rim, would arch out harmlessly over the higher part of the snowfield. They hoped to move within that clear curve of arch. Notwithstanding general theories, at one point Diemberger looked up to see a flight of small black birds come swooping down. At the last moment he recognized the flight as a scattering of black stones. One of the "birds" pinged his helmet while another hit him on the bridge of the nose. A shell burst of pain rocked his senses and for several moments he was stunned. He finally came to, got the bleeding stopped, and continued to climb. The traverse was nerve-wracking. A host of tiny pebbles and ice fragments would come racing down the slope, increasing in size as they drew closer, getting bigger and bigger until one realized that the "pebbles" ranged in size from golf balls to soccer balls. Thick plaques of ice the size of garbage-can lids, rolling on edge, would go bounding by at a speed sufficient to decapitate anyone in the way. These trains of debris would go clattering by on either side, and after they had gone, one resumed breathing and thought about the next move.

Finally the long traverse was over, and they scaled several tricky pitches to the top of the Flatiron, where they took a hot-drink break. Then it was out into another shooting gallery, the 300-foot traverse of the Third Icefield, and again they dodged rocks all the way. But they reached the Ramp safely, and, at the end of the first rope length on that great cleft, they cleared a small platform, drove in anchor pitons, and got out their spirit cooker. They consumed mouthfuls of "gorp," cornflakes, sugar, nuts and raisins, and some smoked bacon, and then melted ice to make hot fruit-juice drinks on their cooker. Fed and rested, they looked down the mountain face at the lights of Grindelwald twinkling up at them from 8,000 feet below.

That night the weather changed, and several times Diemberger woke up to hear rubble go thundering and clattering down the face, bursts of stones coming irregularly, followed by short gaps of silence, then a positive barrage, silence again, followed by a deep, booming series of thumps as a block the size of a room came down in ponderous but pulverizing wallops. The rockfall meant that the usual night frost had not occurred, that they couldn't look forward to a quiet morning climb with the rocks well anchored to the face. That bivouac night depressed Diemberger. "There is no place where one is so utterly alone. Even our friends had ceased to exist for us," he wrote.

In the morning the men woke to find a dead, grey world with fog everywhere. Water dripped down all the walls, and the Waterfall Chimney at the head of the Ramp was in full spate. Still, they managed to force it, then to climb the now rotten ice of the overhanging Ice Bulge to emerge on the lower rim of the Ramp Icefield. Here they had some difficulty finding the right approach to the Traverse of the Gods, but with the help of a large photograph they had along with them, and on which they measured rope lengths with their fingers, they were able to guess at the correct vertical pitch that led up to the traverse. Somewhere not too far above them, perhaps 200 feet, hung the body of Longhi in its ropes. It will be remembered that Corti had climbed far up on the Ramp Snowfield before making a chancy high traverse across to the head of the Spider, instead of taking the lower, and easier, Traverse of the Gods.

Still, if Longhi's body had been only twenty feet above them, it's doubtful whether Diemberger or Stefan would have spotted the corpse. The fog was now mixed with rain and wet snow. To add to their discomfort, the men were soaked from their climb through the Waterfall Pitch. But for once the Spider wasn't in bad shape. The rain and wet snow made for few avalanches. However, they lost two hours when they took a wrong couloir at the start of the Exit Cracks and were forced to retreat and pick another line. Diemberger took a short fall when a piton failed, but Mayer held him. At 7 P.M. they were subjected to a fierce hailstorm, and the rocks streamed with loose hail that piled up on the ledges. The light began to fail, but the pair couldn't stand the thought of another wet bivouac in their soaking clothes. They climbed on and several hours later heard shouts above them. They shouted back, scrambled up the last rock gully, and found themselves on the Exit Snowfield. Soon they could dimly make out figures on the ridge. Raditschnig and Brandler and a Swiss friend had come up the west flank to the summit to be on hand to greet the climbers and lend aid if needed. The men shook hands all around, then withdrew a little ways down the west flank and bivouacked for the night. With typical Eiger consistency the weather turned frigid again, the temperature dropped to ten below freezing, and the men's wet clothing froze so that anytime anyone moved it set off a fusillade of crackling noises. Dehydrated from their climb, Diemberger and Stefan spent the night brewing countless cups of tea. Earlier Raditschnig and Brandler, manning telescopes during a short break in the weather, had spotted the climbers on the Traverse of the Gods. When the hailstorm swept in, they guessed that Diemberger and Stefan were in trouble and immediately started up the west flank, prepared to lower a rope or to help in any way they could.

Needless to say the two Austrians were delighted with their achievement. It was twenty years since the first ascent on the Heckmair Route in 1938, and five years since the last successful climb of the Eigerwand. Like almost all other climbers on that face, they brought back souvenirs—Diemberger a tender nose and cheekbone from that stone on the Second Icefield, and Stefan a huge dent in his helmet from another rocky projectile. When pictures of Stefan's helmet appeared in several newspapers in Germany and Austria, sales of climbing helmets immediately shot up.

Diemberger was later to admit that he never wanted to climb the Eigernordwand again, claiming it was a once-in-a-lifetime event, "enough of a good thing," as he put it. He later went on to further exploits, climbing in the Himalayas, Greenland, Ethiopia, and the Andes. His *Summits and Secrets*, published in 1971 and based on his experiences as a mountaineer, was hailed as a mountaineering classic. Its chapter about being caught in a ring of lightning along with a girl who was actually struck by a bolt, which entered the palms of her hands, leaving black circles behind, and which exited through one ankle, is guaranteed to raise the hair on anyone's head. Miraculously, the girl survived!

And so the jinx of the thirteenth ascent of the Eigernordwand was finally broken, a fact that was duly noted in the mountaineering journals. Except that it actually turned out to be the fifteenth ascent, not the thirteenth, but that is still another story.

15
The Flying Overcoat

The Diemberger-Stefan climb marked the end of one era in the history of the Eiger. Years ago, Leslie Stephen, a Victorian literary critic cum mountaineer (and father of Virginia Woolf), a writer who did much to popularize the sport of Alpine climbing, pointed out that most notable Alpine peaks go through a progression of three stages, from "inaccessible," to "hardest climb in the Alps," to "easy day for a lady." The Eigernordwand had certainly gone through the first two categories, and if it wasn't yet an easy day for a lady, it certainly had lost much of its terror as far as experienced climbers were concerned. After all, with Diemberger and Stefan, thirty-nine men had now climbed the Eiger's north wall safely, as against eighteen who perished. The odds on surviving a climb were better than two to one.

Mountain climbing, like any sport or art, doesn't stand still. Front points on crampons led to a great advance in ice climbing. No longer did one have to laboriously carve out steps up an icefield; one could practically ladder climb up on front points, using a pair of ice axes. Other items of direct-aid equipment were invented, evolved, and improved. Lighter, stronger, virtually kink-free synthetic ropes made their appearance. Rope handling also improved, as did the knowledge of rope belays, rappels, rope slings, and the like. Better waist and chest harnesses were made. Even the carabiner was improved with a locking gate that couldn't be forced open by bulging or twisting ropes. Improved ice pitons and ice screws were designed. All the new techniques and equipment led to climbers' tackling harder and harder mountain faces, to greater skills, and to a downgrading of what had once been considered "problem" climbs. In 1925 the mountaineering writer Wilhelm Lehner, in his book *Die Eroberung der Alpen* (*The Conquest of the Alps*), acclaimed the 1921 ascent of the Mittellegi Ridge on the Eiger for having solved the last great Alpine problem.

In the early 1930s Willo Welzenbach, a great German climber who perished along with Willy Merkl on Nanga Parbat in 1934, did five first ascents in the Bernese Oberland, a series of brilliant climbs that jumped the standards to new levels, so that in 1938 Heckmair could write a book about the "last three great Alpine problems," the north face of the Eiger, the north face of the Matterhorn, and the Walker Spur on the Grandes Jorasses. *Plus ça change, plus c'est la même chose.* Last great Alpine problems had a notorious tendency to be soon replaced by newer last great problems. And so it was with the Eiger.

If one wanted to make a name as a daring climber, a straightforward climb up the 1938 route was no longer sufficient. After all, it had, depending on whom you talked to, only one or two pitches of Grade-VI severity. Then too, the route meandered back and forth across the face, taking 10,000 feet of climbing to achieve 6,000 feet of height. Surely some new way could be found to make the Eigernordwand exciting again. For one thing, there were still the national "firsts" to be achieved. Surprisingly, no Italians had yet climbed the Eigernordwand, though three had died trying. Nor had any English or American climbers mastered the White Spider. No Yugoslavs, no Poles, no Czechs, no Japanese for that matter, had scaled the north face. So far the climbers had all been Swiss, Austrian, German, or French.

Then too, the Eigernordwand had been climbed only in summer; no winter climb had yet been attempted. Nor had anyone climbed it solo.

No one had climbed it "direct," about which more later. No woman had yet climbed the Eiger. No one had climbed *down* the face of the Eiger, from peak to base. No one had climbed up *and* down. No one had made the ascent in less than eighteen hours, although speed records are generally frowned on by serious mountaineers.

As the 1960s opened, the three main variations being talked about were the first solo ascent, the first winter climb, and the first *direttissima.* The *direttissima,* or direct, was a concept developed in the mid-1930s by Emilio Comici, a brilliant Italian climber from the Dolomites. His idea was to climb up a great face following a plumb-bob line that led from peak down to foot. Or as Comici once put it, "Let a drop of water fall from peak to base and that's the line I want to follow."

The earliest *direttissime* were done in the Dolomites, then in the eastern Alps and the Mont Blanc Massif of Chamonix. Now climbers were talking of an Eigernordwand direct. There already was the start of one, because Sedlmayer and Mehringer had climbed directly from the base up to the top of the Flatiron in a vertical line. And from the evidence, instead of trying to cross to the Third Icefield and then the Ramp, they had tackled the band of cliffs separating the Flatiron from the Spider, putting in at least one rope length on a continuation of the direct line. Then too, going straight up would not only be following a more aesthetic line, but it would eliminate having to climb the Third Icefield, the Ramp, the Ramp Snowfield, and the Traverse of the Gods.

In the meantime the body of Longhi was still hanging in its ropes high on the north wall, while sightseers and tourists were lining up to pay twenty centimes for a glimpse of the corpse through the pay telescopes at Kleine Scheidegg. In the winter of 1958, rumors reached Grindelwald that the now fully recovered Corti was planning to return in the summer with a group of his friends from the Ragni Club in Lecco. Their stated purpose was to bring down Longhi's body. Another Italian party, over eighty strong, was also rumored to be making preparations to retrieve Longhi. And the German Mountain Guard of Munich, in the winter of 1958, informed the Grindelwald guides of their desire to search for the bodies of Nothdurft and Mayer and to bring down Longhi. Even the members of the Polish climbing team wanted to have a crack at recovering Longhi's body. Recovering Longhi was swiftly becoming another Alpine "problem" to be solved.

All of this put the local guides on the defensive. After all, they had been widely criticized for having taken no part in the great rescue attempt of the year before. It must have seemed to the local guides that every time a person looked through the pay telescopes at Longhi's body, it was an implied criticism of the guides' conduct and attitudes.

At all events, for whatever reason, a group of local guides decided to attempt to bring down Longhi's body. The local guides had been sharply critical of the "amateurs'" attempts at mountain rescue the previous summer. This time the professionals would do it right. The only problem was money, but then a financial backer was found, a Dutch journalist who was prepared to sell exclusive rights to the recovery story to a syndicate of European papers. Contracts were duly drawn up and signed between the guides and the Dutch journalist, Jaap Giltay.

In late May of 1959 Corti, with some climbing friends, was back in Grindelwald. The party went up the west flank to get a closer look at Longhi's body, discussed various recovery strategies, then came down the mountain again and informed the press that they would return later in the summer in order to bring their comrade down for a proper burial.

A week or two later the local guides had all the necessary equipment—cables, winches, and the like—airlifted to a small snowfield near the Eiger's summit. More than a score of guides were alerted, but then the weather turned unfavorable, as it so often does on the Eiger, and storm followed storm across the mountain's face. It was another month before the recovery got underway. Finally, on July 9, all was ready. The winches were carried up to the anchorage spot high on the northeast ridge, where four of the local guides, Fritz Jaun, the brothers Ferdinand and Oskar Gertsch, and Alfred Fuchs, prepared to descend. Fuchs and Ferdinand Gertsch would position one set of rollers partway down the line, while Oskar Gertsch and Fritz Jaun would anchor a second set of rollers farther down the face and directly above Longhi's ledge. As Gertsch safeguarded the second set of rollers, Jaun would continue the descent to Longhi's body. The whole recovery operation was under the supervision of Werner Stäger, one of the top guides in the Lauterbrunnen Valley. All four men going down the face had radios and were in contact with Stäger on the ridge. As an added precaution, Fritz Jaun wore a parachute.

Jaun stepped off and out over a hundred-foot cliff. Slowly he was lowered. Now and again he was able to rest briefly on footholds on the cliff face. A final heart-stopping lunge, and he was down on the tiny ledge, fifteen feet below which the body of Longhi was hanging. The ropes belaying Longhi were still intact and Jaun used them as a guide for the last few feet down over the ledge. Originally it was thought that Longhi's body would have dried out over the past two years and would therefore be relatively easy to place in a large body bag that Jaun had brought along. But the body seemed to have lost little if any weight, and Jaun found it impossible to work the corpse into the bag, especially as he himself was hanging free in space, not the best situation in which to maneuver something as heavy as a human body. He therefore tied the body to the cable a few feet below him, cut the ropes that had previously held Longhi, and radioed Stäger to haul up. As soon as he reached the ledge again, he halted to examine Longhi's rucksack, then radioed an inventory of its contents up to the ridge. There was nothing in the sack to give any clue as to what might have happened during the climb. People had speculated that Longhi, at some point during his ten days on the face, might have jotted down notes, but nothing like that was found in the rucksack, and the mystery was no closer to being solved. Because of the weight of the two men on the cable, it was decided to leave the rucksack, with its load of hammers, pitons, snap links, and so forth, behind on the ledge.

The trip back turned into a searing ordeal for Jaun, testing his nerve and courage to the limit. The cable kept kinking in the rollers, and Longhi's heavy body kept jamming in cracks and gullies. At one point the cable jammed in a deep groove, and Jaun tried to free it by pulling it out of the crack, an almost superhuman task, given the weight of the two bodies on the wire line. Whipping this way and that on the cable, he struggled for over an hour, but in vain. Finally, Fuchs was sent down the face from the lower set of rollers, and, belayed from above, he tied a short length of rope to the cable. The other end of the rope he dropped to Jaun with instructions to pull hard. As Jaun thus eased the tension, Fuchs managed to jerk the wire out of the groove. The ascent continued, with still further problems between the second and first sets of rollers. By the time Jaun got Longhi's body up to the top of the ridge and divested himself of all his gear, he had spent a total of nine hours in the cable harness. All in all, it was a magnificent achievement on the part of the guides, although it didn't quite prove that they could handle the cable rescue equipment as competently as the "amateurs" on the 1957 rescue had done. Much of the kinking of the line, and the subsequent spinning of Jaun like a top, could have been avoided, had they known of the antiswiveling devices used by Gramminger on his cable.

Leaving most of their equipment on the ridge, the guides conveyed Longhi's body down to the snowfield landing place, where it was put in a ski-equipped airplane and flown to the Jungfraujoch. There all entrained for the Eigergletscher Station, where they were met by a party of Italian railway workers who placed rhododendron blooms on the body of their dead compatriot. The tired guides then dispersed to their various homes, feeling, at the very least, that their honor had been vindicated.

At Longhi's inquest it was found that one leg had been broken in two places. Swelling and hemorrhaging around the breaks led to the determination that the leg had been fractured while Longhi had still been alive. Inasmuch as Corti claimed that Longhi had said nothing about any injuries, and that Kleine Scheidegg telescope watchers had several times seen Longhi standing upright on the ledge, it was surmised that some-time during his last night he had either stumbled off the ledge or been blown off by the high winds of the snowstorm, to break his leg against the rock when he had been pulled up short at the end of the slack in the rope. It was a horrifying thought, and he must therefore have spent hours in his final agony, hanging in the rope with a broken leg, an end all too reminiscent of Kurz's. It is even possible that, had it not been for the broken leg, he might have survived another day or two suspended on the rope before exposure and starvation finally killed him. Even so, it is unlikely that he could have been rescued, given the weather condi-tions over the next few days.

If there was one disappointment in the recovery, it was that no fur-ther light had been shed on the two great questions that remained to be answered. Had everything possible been done for Longhi before he had been abandoned on his perch? And what had happened to Nothdurft and Mayer?

To both questions Corti again responded that he and the German pair had spent three hours trying to haul Longhi up from his perch, not only exhausting themselves to the point where their own survival had been in jeopardy, but fraying the rope on the jagged edge of the over-hang to such an extent that he had feared it would break if handled much longer. As for Nothdurft and Mayer, he had last seen them climb-ing up the Exit Cracks on their way to the summit. As for the criticism that he had taken the wrong traverse across to the Spider because he was so ill-prepared that he didn't know the correct route, Corti said that he had thought it safer, considering everything he had heard about avalanches on the Spider, to avoid as much of the danger as possible by traversing across to it on a line that would bring him out at the head of the snowfield—an answer not without logic.

There were some who said that the truth would never be determined until the bodies of Nothdurft and Mayer were recovered. Perhaps Noth-durft's notebooks would provide some answers.

Despite the impressive achievement of the guides, they came under fire from many quarters, primarily because they had been paid for the operation. The foremost Alpine journal in Germany, *Der Bergkamerad,* charged that Longhi's body would still be hanging in its ropes if someone hadn't paid for the recovery. The guides, of course, could respond by saying that they were working men, and why should they lose a day's pay, why should they risk their lives and the welfare of their families, for men who had never hired guides in their lives? As it was, the expenses outran the money they had received, and each of the twenty-three guides was supposedly out of pocket to the tune of almost 200 Swiss francs apiece. A short time later the deficit was more than cleared twice over when the Swiss Foundation for Alpine Research paid off the debt, and then a group of four Swiss banks also paid the full deficit. This time the nail had turned into a pair of screws.

The Dutch journalist meanwhile had trouble meeting his side of the bargain and came out of the whole operation barely breaking even. Ironically enough, and this was to prove important later, the guides left nearly all their rescue equipment up on the summit, to rust and rot where it lay, scattered about where they had last used it. They intended to retrieve it later, and they did—much later as it turned out.

And later that summer two Swiss stonemasons from the Grisons, Adolf Derungs and Lukas Albrecht, both in their twenties and on holiday from working at their trade in Zurich, pitched their tent in the meadows of Alpiglen. They started up the face early in the morning of August 10. They were young and tough but still unknown among the mountain-climbing fraternity and were an unlikely-looking pair to be tackling the Eigernordwand. Inexperienced climbers, they were even ignorant of the Alpine decimal system for grading pitches. They wore old motorcycle helmets instead of the newer plastic ones. Working men, they couldn't afford the expensive down parkas used by modern climbers; so instead Derungs wore four or five cotton and wool shirts, one on top of another. Instead of modern sleeping bags for their bivouacs, Albrecht brought along an old overcoat to spread over themselves at night. They planned to do the wall with only one overnight stop, and thus brought food for only two days, cutting a very fine margin indeed.

While on the way up, the Swiss climbers met Lothar Brandler and Toni Hiebeler, who were being filmed on the lower reaches of the wall by a German camera crew that was doing a documentary on the Eigernordwand. Brandler, of course, was no stranger to the Eiger. Hiebeler, too, was a skilled climber and later was to figure in several stirring Eiger "epics." The climbers exchanged greetings, then Derungs and Albrecht moved swiftly upwards. They bivouacked their first night on the Ramp. The weather now turned bad, and the telescope watchers expected the climbers to retreat in the morning. But the pair climbed on the next day. Although they didn't know it, the young Swiss were actually being filmed by the German film crew that had taken up position high on the West flank and, with telephoto lens, was getting some spectacular footage, despite the trailing scarves and veils of fog.

Somewhere at the head of the Spider, the climbers, deciding that they would not have to bivouac again, decided to jettison the bulky overcoat. They flung it away, and it spread out and slid down the Spider snowfield, to launch out into space, a small dark shadow with sleeves flying. Cries of horror came from the telescope watchers down in the valley—someone had fallen!

But how could that be? others asked. Two distinct shapes were visible in the Exit Cracks. Could it be Nothdurft's or Mayer's body, perhaps dislodged by rockfall caused by Derungs or Albrecht? Could it even be a third solo climber whom no one knew to be on the wall? After all, visibility had been poor for the past few days. The mystery wasn't solved until the Swiss pair came down from the summit and told of their unique garbage-disposal method.

The last few hours they climbed up through a typical Eiger storm. Lothar Brandler and a friend, having learned how poorly equipped the climbers were, went to the summit up the west flank, carrying extra food and clothing. They missed the pair of Swiss climbers because Derungs and Albrecht came down the west flank in a couloir that nobody ever used, because it was subject to frequent avalanching. By some miracle they weren't swept away and reached Kleine Scheidegg in time to stop a rescue attempt that was being organized by Brandler, who brought back the news that the climbers hadn't yet reached the top and were nowhere to be seen. Whatever the trials and tribulations they had suffered, the Eiger certainly didn't faze one of them, because Derungs would be back to figure in a return engagement that was to become the third solo attempt.

In September another Swiss pair, Ernst Forrer and Peter Diener, were to make the fifteenth successful ascent. It was a straightforward climb, with one bivouac at the Ramp. They were both hindered and helped by cold weather that sapped their strength, but kept the face relatively free of rockfall. Both were experienced mountaineers, for whom the Eiger was in the nature of a training climb, and both were the following year to take part, along with Max Eiselin and Dr. Jerzy Hajdukiewicz, in the Swiss expedition's successful climb of Dhaulagiri in the Himalayas, the first ascent of the world's sixth-highest mountain (26,795 feet).

There were no further attempts on the Eiger in 1959, but in February of 1960 three Eiger tigers came to Kleine Scheidegg with the intention of making the first winter climb. One was Lothar Brandler, who, as we've seen, had had ill fortune dog him on his previous attempts. He had been up on the Nordwand at least four times, once as high as the Flatiron, and had climbed the west flank at least twice. Another was Jörg Lehne, and the third was Siegfried Löw, who was to perish two years later when he fell on a descent from the summit of Nanga Parbat in the Himalayas. Once again Toni Hiebeler was part of a German camera crew brought along to film the climb. But the Eiger was too heavily snowed up, and, despite the best efforts of the three climbers, they could get no higher than the Gallery Window below the Rote Fluh. The constantly avalanching snow on the lower slopes forced them to give up, but the climb gave Toni Hiebeler an idea for another winter attempt on the Eigernordwand.

There were no successful climbs for the rest of 1960, but 1961 was to furnish high excitement indeed for Eiger watchers.

16
Nothdurft and Mayer Found

Early in 1961 four climbers arrived at Kleine Scheidegg to attempt a winter ascent of the Eigernordwand. Organizer of the group was Toni Hiebeler, editor of *Der Bergkamerad,* Germany's foremost Alpine journal. He had been part of the camera crew filming the previous year's abortive attempt by Lothar Brandler, Jörg Lehne, and Siegi Löw. The other three climbers were Toni Kinshofer, twenty-seven, a carpenter; Anderl Mannhardt, twenty, a sawmill worker; and Walter Almberger, twenty-seven, a miner. Hiebeler was thirty-one. Almberger was Austrian, the other three German.

They began their climb on February 27 and got about a thousand feet up the face to bivouac close to the Gallery Window. The lower slopes of the mountain were blanketed in soft, loose snow in which the men often found themselves wading waist deep. It was slow and laborious going, and it took a lot of time to get all their equipment up and onto the face proper.

A winter climb of the Eiger is not as foolhardy as it might seem and indeed offers certain advantages over a summer climb. For one thing, the freezing conditions mean an almost complete absence of rockfall on the face. Then too, a thick coating of snow can sometimes make certain passages, say in gullies, easier to negotiate. Against those advantages are the colder temperatures that can swiftly lead to exhaustion, frostbite, and hypothermia. Another disadvantage is that the snow covers many of the crux pitons from previous climbs, makes it difficult to find good holds, and in general leaves the footing a lot less secure. One might say that a climber will fall more frequently in winter, and be hit by rocks more often in summer.

After the first bivouac the weather turned stormy, and the men cached all their equipment at the bivouac site, retreated through the Gallery Window, and took the railway back to Kleine Scheidegg and the hospitality of Almen. They intended to return as soon as the skies cleared. The weather stayed foul for almost a week but finally brightened on March 6. The men left their wallets and passports with Almen, then walked up the railway tunnel to almost the Eigerwand Station before they realized that they had passed the *Stollenloch*.

They retraced their steps, reached the lower opening, then found that the huge wooden doors were jammed shut by a heavy cushion of snow on the outside. After some trouble, they forced the doors open and proceeded to their bivouac site. There they loaded their rucksacks on their backs, looped their slings and hardware around their shoulders, and roped up. Each man carried fifty-five to sixty pounds, a heavy load indeed for a sustained climb like the Eiger. In addition to the usual food-stuffs, the men carried a thousand feet of rope, movie and still cameras, an SOS rocket, four miners' headlamps, four regular flashlights with extra batteries, almost a hundred ice and rock pitons of various sizes and shapes, thirty carabiners, an altimeter, hammers, ice axes, crampons, a small snow shovel for the preparation of bivouacs and digging out of snow caves, a spirit cooker, and appropriate medical supplies, including Ronicol tablets to combat frostbite. They also had a pocket radio that proved almost useless in the freakish atmospheric conditions on the north face. Voices that static slurred into gibberish seemed to be all they could get, and when for tantalizingly brief periods reception was in the clear, they were favored with bursts of Arabic, Latvian, and Danish to mull over at their leisure.

That night they bivouacked just short of the Hinterstoisser Traverse. The next morning the pitch, which can be negotiated in fifteen minutes if the rock is dry, took them two hours. Hacking with ice axes was a delicate business, because too deep a bite could cause a large slab of ice to crack free of the rock. This happened to Kinshofer, who was leading and fixing a rope for the others when a shield of ice gave way and he fell fifteen feet. His protection piton held.

Their second bivouac was at the head of the First Icefield and their third one on the Flatiron, a few hundred feet below Death Bivouac, their scheduled stop for the night. Their fourth bivouac was on the Ramp, and their fifth on the start of the Traverse of the Gods. That night a storm blew up, the temperature went on a glissade, and the climbers had recourse to their antifrostbite tablets. The next day, on the traverse, a piece of ice gave way under Hiebeler's foot, and he fell twenty feet. His warning cry alerted the others, and Almberger and Mannhardt man-aged to hold and then to recover him.

Halfway up the Exit Cracks, Hiebeler was hit by a rock on the nape of the neck, a blow that temporarily paralyzed him. For long moments he could not move his head, but eventually mobility came back and he was able to resume climbing. There was some difficulty with the Quartz Crack, a band of white quartz that had also given Heckmair and Buhl trouble, but they eventually surmounted it and passed Corti's bivouac ledge before stopping for the night. The weather was appallingly cold, they were now forty-eight hours without hot food or drink, and they got little sleep that night because of the constant shivering of their bodies.

The next morning they reached the summit, having spent six nights on the face. It was one of the Eiger's great climbs, carried out with courage, tenacity, and style, under difficult and extremely cold conditions. Another Eiger first, a winter ascent of the Nordwand, had been accomplished, once again by German and Austrian climbers.

However, no sooner had the climbers accepted their plaudits than controversy boiled over. Critics charged that Hiebeler tried to cover up the fact that the final assault started from the Gallery Window and not from the foot of the mountain. Approximately 1,200 feet of the climb had been left out. This charge, of course, was false. The men had climbed that portion of the face six days before starting out on the rest of the climb.

Hiebeler himself was to blame for some of the controversy. In his account of the climb in the April 13 issue of *Der Bergkamerad,* he reported nothing about having resumed the climb from the Gallery Window and summed up the first day's effort in these words: *"Vom Einsteig bis nahe zum Hinterstoisser Quergang"* ("From the beginning to near the Hinterstoisser Traverse"). This left the clear impression that the climb had started from the base of the mountain. Perhaps Hiebeler downplayed the use of the Gallery Window fearing that the team might not get recognition for the climb, because they didn't do it nonstop, from base to summit. It was a silly and needless controversy—no one would have questioned their actions in interrupting the climb because of bad weather and then resuming it from the point at which the climb had been aborted. Hiebeler's book *North Face in Winter* gives a full account of the exploit.

Despite the controversy, it was an epic climb and ushered in a notable year on the Eiger. Now that the first winter ascent had been made, people began to wonder when the first solo climb would be achieved. Günter Nothdurft was evidently the first to make a serious attempt to climb the Eigernordwand alone when he got as high as the top of the Second Icefield and then retreated. He had earlier told Buhl that he thought the best way to do the Eigernordwand was a solo climb. Perhaps he later decided to climb with Mayer in the belief that a regular climb on the face, with a companion, would give him a better idea of what he might need in the way of equipment and technique to go it alone. Much honor would, of course, accrue to the first one to climb the Eigernordwand solo.

The summer of 1961 opened badly. The weather was stormy and didn't really clear until mid-August. Late that month, twenty-three-year-old Adolf Mayr, a young Austrian born in Bad Hall but resident in

Innsbruck, came to Grindelwald alone to try the north wall. He was a man with a passion for solo climbing and had lots of big-wall experience in both eastern and western Alps, as well as in Norway, where he had put up a series of redoubtable solo "firsts." On the evening of August 26, he phoned his fiancée, Hilde, and told her he would soon be with her again, after "just this last climb." Then he wrote a close Swiss climbing friend telling him not to go up on the wall after him should anything happen, pointing out that his friend had prior responsibilities: *"Du hast Frau und Kinder"* ("You have a wife and children").

On the morning of August 27, he started up the face, climbing swiftly to the start of the Difficult Crack. Up to that point the climbing is generally considered "hard hiking," and most parties don't rope up until this pitch is reached. The sun came up on a lovely day, clear weather and practically unlimited visibility. Telescope watchers at Kleine Scheidegg soon picked up the young climber working on the Difficult Crack. He seemed to be moving surely and strongly. He reached the Hinterstoisser, where there were still plenty of fixed ropes on the traverse, and moved swiftly across it, then climbed up the First Icefield to the Ice Hose. Here Mayr took to the rocks on the left-hand side and duly reached the Second Icefield. Several French climbers down in the meadows commented that his climbing up to that point had been quite fast, as fast as a rope of two would have traveled, which implied that he climbed the First Icefield without belaying himself. There are several techniques that a solo climber can use to protect himself against a fall, but they are cumbersome and time consuming. In any event, using ice axe and crampons, Mayr moved diagonally up and across the snowfield, reached the rock band of the Flatiron, and from there tic-tac-toed up several pitches to Death Bivouac. Here he decided to stop for the night. It was early afternoon, not yet three o'clock. Death Bivouac, despite its macabre name, is well protected and relatively comfortable. Anyway, he had seen and heard the rocks starting to pockmark the Second Icefield just as he was getting off it. In midafternoon of a sunny day the Third Icefield would be a shooting gallery, he knew, catching everything funneling down from the Spider.

Mayr ate some food, brewed tea, and, in early evening, with his electric torch, flashed the agreed-upon signal that all was well down to Almen at Kleine Scheidegg. The next morning he started early, negotiated the Third Icefield, and reached the Ramp. To Eiger watchers he seemed to be moving slowly and erratically, but that may have been due to the normal stiffness of arms and legs after a day's strenuous climbing and a long night's bivouac. Fortunately, the day was clear, and most thought that, with any luck, Mayr might even reach the summit before darkness.

He halted at the waterfall at the head of the Ramp, a pitch that many considered to be the hardest of the whole climb. It was 8 A.M. Watchers now saw him start up the ice-clad rocks at the bottom of the pitch. They saw him reach his leg out to the left for a hold. It wouldn't go. He drew back and tried again. Still no go. Then he hacked at the hold with his ice axe, presumably enlarging it. Once more he stretched. An extra effort this time would surely do it. Then a dark bundle slowly detached itself from the rock and tumbled down, turning over and over, to bounce off the left edge of the Third Icefield, go sliding down that white granulated slope, and launch out into space again, falling and bounding 4,000 feet down the long channel to the left of the Central Pillar until it finally came to rest at the base of the mountain. The Eiger had claimed its nineteenth victim.

Adi Mayr's body was recovered on August 30 and taken to Bad Hall. At the funeral his climbing companions served as pall bearers, and his casket was draped with the flag of his climbing club. A year later a group of friends honored him by placing a small commemorative plaque at the foot of the Eiger.

Despite the fatality and the lateness of the season, another half-dozen climbs followed before the end of September. On 30 August, Czech climbers Radovan Kuchar and Zdeno Zibrin, two thirty-year-olds who had already done the Walker Spur on the Grandes Jorasses and the Matterhorn's north face, got their gear ready for an Eigernordwand climb. They had plenty of experience in the Elbsandstein and Tatra ranges of their native country. While examining the face, they were approached by Kurt Schwendener, chief of police in Grindelwald, who tried to dissuade them from climbing. When they insisted on going ahead, he demanded a deposit of 1,000 francs against the expenses of conducting a rescue operation, should they get in trouble. Perhaps because they came from behind the Iron Curtain and were unnecessarily awed by anyone in uniform, they turned over the keys of their car in lieu of the 1,000 Swiss francs—quite a large sum of money for two impoverished climbers to be carrying around. Schwendener took the keys, and the two Czechs started off on their climb. Hours later, while spiking their way up and across the Second Icefield, they looked down and saw a group of guides at the base of the mountain, searching for Mayr's body.

One of the climbers lost his axe on the Second Icefield, which slowed their progress somewhat. That night they bivouacked on a rock ledge at the front of the Flatiron. They reached Death Bivouac at 10:30 the next morning and here found evidence that Adi Mayr had suffered violently from diarrhea his last night on the mountain. He had no doubt been weakened by the attack, which might explain his slowness on the Ramp the next morning. The Czechs noted that his cut-out steps on the Third Icefield were huge, much larger than necessary, further evidence that he was feeling shaky and unsure of himself.

The pair bivouacked the next night at the head of the Ramp. They found nothing to indicate why Mayr had fallen, beyond noticing that the downslope rock shelves forming the Ramp were badly iced up, which would partially explain Mayr's slow progress on the Ramp pitches. After a supper of honey and Hungarian sausage, chocolate, and cheese, they settled down for the night. After a supper like that, you and I might not settle down very well, but *chacun à son gout*.

They reached the Spider at eleven the next morning and then surprised the telescope voyeurs by going directly up the rocks on the left-hand edge of the Spider rather than venturing out onto the snowfield, a variant no doubt dictated by that missing ice axe.

They stopped for the night well up in the Exit Cracks, at the Corti Bivouac, and reached the summit at 10:30 the next morning. Then they hurried down the west flank to reclaim their car keys from the Grindelwald police. Kuchar and Zibrin were the first Czech climbers, indeed the first climbers from anywhere behind the Iron Curtain, to complete an Eigernordwand ascent. They were fortunate in that the weather had been exceptionally good for the whole duration of the climb, a circumstance explained by Kuchar as being due to the fact that the team had its own weather expert along—Zibrin was a meteorologist.

Later on the same day, two Polish climbers, Jan Mostowski and Stanislaw Biel, trudged up the Summit Snowfield, took the obligatory photographs, and congratulated each other on being the first Polish climbers to do the Eigernordwand. The Poles were followed by a trio of Swiss climbers, Alois Strickler, Kurt Grüter, and Sepp Inwyler, and an Austrian mountain pilot, Leo Schlömmer, who climbed for relaxation from his job of flying in and out of narrow precipitous mountain valleys. Altogether eight men reached the summit that same day, recalling the combined Austrian-French rope led by Buhl and Rébuffat, when nine had reached the top on July 28, 1952.

Actually, the Poles, the Swiss, and the Austrian met on the Ramp and climbed on as a single rope. They were subjected to some bad rockfall on the upper reaches of the Spider. At the start of the Exit Cracks, they split into three separate ropes but rejoined each other on the summit. It was another example of what happened on the Eigernordwand—climbers of three nationalities speaking three different languages, meeting up on the face, and climbing on as a separate "European" rope. While the men were actually on the peak, a light plane flew past, taking photographs of the culmination of the climb. The plane carried a writer-photographer team of Anneliese Lüthy, twenty-four, and Gerold Zust, thirty-two. The pilot was Johann Zumstein, and all hailed from Lucerne. It was Anneliese's first airplane flight—and her last. Caught in a turbulent downdraft, the plane crashed on the Eiger glacier between the west flank and the Mönch. All were dead when a rescue team reached the crash site.

Meanwhile, the six climbers were 1,500 feet down the west flank when it began to snow. They prudently bivouacked for the night in a couple of hastily dug-out snow caves and made it down the next morning.

The weather held good right through September, which meant more climbers on the face. On September 22 a rope of four, the Austrians Karl Frehsner and Helmut Wagner and the Bavarians George Huber and Gerhard Mayer, stood on the summit after three bivouacs on the face.

Huber, twenty-two, and Mayer, nineteen, had arrived in Grindelwald with very little money and were preparing to sleep out in a field in their bivouac sacks when they met a fourteen-year-old apprentice carpenter who had a passion for mountains and mountaineers. The youngster said that he had a room for them where he worked. Cautioning quiet, he led them on tiptoe up a flight of stairs to a second-story loft. In the morning, when Huber and Mayer woke up, they found themselves in a storeroom full of finished coffins. Hearing the sounds of men working on the floor below and not wanting to get the apprentice lad in trouble, they tiptoed up to the attic, where they discovered a balcony from which they rappelled down to ground level without being noticed. Anderl Heckmair, leader of the first successful ascent of the Eigernordwand, had had a similar experience when, in the days of his youthful vagabondage through the Alps, he and a companion had been arrested by Swiss police in a small mountain village over a prior altercation with a local farmer. They had been escorted to a small fourth floor room in a turret for "questioning" and locked inside. Heckmair and his friend had promptly found an anchor for their ropes and rappelled out a small window, then speedily taken to the hills, all of which proves that if you're going to lock up a mountaineer, better make sure you take his rope first.

Huber and Mayer had one further adventure on the face itself, when a small plane flew by as they were climbing. The pilot cut the motor and in the ensuing silence shouted, "Good weather to continue," surely the most unorthodox weather report ever received by climbers on the Eiger.

Several months later Huber, with the English climber Brian Nally, was involved in a winter climb of the Matterhorn's north face in which he lost eight fingers and toes to frostbite. Despite these injuries he continued climbing, only to lose his life in 1964, when he died of exposure on Cho Oyu in the Himalayas.

The climbing season of 1961 closed out with yet another successful climb, when two Austrians from Innsbruck, Erich Streng and Robert Troier, fought almost continuous snowstorms all the way up the face to finally emerge on the summit after bivouacs at the Swallow's Nest, the Ramp, and the Exit Cracks. The date was September 29 and it was either the twenty-first, twenty-second, or twenty-third ascent, a confusion that will be discussed shortly.

There was one other noteworthy occurrence that September. On the twenty-first, while Mayer, Frehsner, Huber, and Wagner were on the face, actually making their way up the Spider, Lauterbrunnen guide Werner Stäger, who had overseen the recovery of Longhi's body, went with a few guides up to the summit to see what they could salvage of the rescue equipment they had abandoned on the peak after the recovery attempt two years earlier. One of the guides, rolling a tightly coiled bundle of rope ahead of him, let it get away, and it bounced down the southwestern side of the summit ridge a couple of hundred feet and came to rest in a couloir. The guide went down to retrieve the bundle and came across the remains of two human bodies, curled around each other. All that was left were two skeletons inside their clothing, but from a string of pitons around the neck bones of one body and from an ice hammer hanging from the wrist bones of another, it was obvious that the two had been climbers. The guides marked the location of the bodies with the intention of later coming back to retrieve them. On their descent they found yet a third body, this one identified as the remains of Engelbert Titl, a Viennese climber who had been observed in 1958 coming down the west flank after a summit traverse from the Mittellegi Ridge. He had never been seen again.

When the other two bodies were taken down to the mortuary, it was discovered that the climbing hardware and rucksacks, indeed all of the equipment, was German. The only German climbers known to be missing were Nothdurft and Mayer. Relatives of the climbers, including Nothdurft senior and Walter Seeger, came and identified the bodies. One part of the 1957 mystery was thus solved. The German climbers had obviously reached the summit Friday night. (There had been that report, passed along to Fritz von Almen, that a pair of climbers had been sighted on the summit late Friday night—a report that was discounted.) Nothdurft and Mayer, no doubt driven by the urgency of Corti and Longhi's plight on the face, had despite the snowstorm tried to descend the west flank in the dark and had lost their way and been forced to hole up temporarily in a snow cave because of the ferocity of the storm, then had found themselves too exhausted to continue. Either that, or they had been caught in an avalanche. It had been a gallant attempt on the part of the young Germans, and it laid to rest any speculation that there had been some sort of altercation between the German and Italian ropes on the Nordwand. Nothdurft must have known the high risks that he and Mayer were running in trying to descend the west flank in the dark during a snowstorm. He would hardly have taken those risks had there been bad blood between the two ropes. Nothdurft's little notebook was found, but it was blank. Whatever writing it may have contained had been washed away by weather over the previous four years, and not even ultraviolet light could bring it back. Indeed there was no evidence that Nothdurft had taken any notes on the climb.

Especially tragic was the thought that starting at 6 A.M. on the day following the arrival of Nothdurft and Mayer on the summit, on Saturday, fifty men had been tramping around within a few yards of the Germans' position. The speculation could go on forever as to whether Saturday would have been too late had they been found. Too late, obviously, if Nothdurft and Mayer had been trapped in an avalanche, not too late, perhaps, if they were lying in some snow hole, comatose from exhaustion.

The finding of Nothdurft and Mayer vindicated Corti's account of the climb. "Corti Not a Criminal," blared one headline in an Italian paper. He had been telling the truth when he said he saw them going up the Exit Cracks. He hadn't cut their ropes or somehow contrived to hurl them off the face. There were still some questions to be answered, of course. Had everything possible been done for Longhi? Why hadn't the two German climbers, with their greater experience, taken a more direct role in getting Longhi off his ledge? And why, above all, had they roped up and stayed with a slower and less experienced pair of climbers, men with whom they could hardly communicate because of language problems? These questions, of course, will never be answered to everyone's satisfaction. However, one thing was clear: Nothdurft and Mayer had earned their place on the roll of Eiger conquerors. Their selflessness in leaving Corti their bivouac tent and the rest of their provisions, their forcing of the Exit Cracks, and their decision to go straight down the west flank for help, despite exhaustion and snowstorm, were the actions of men serving the highest principles of mountaineering and of humanity. They did everything possible to bring help to the Italian climbers, at the price of their own lives.

Swiss Alpine historians had by now belatedly recognized Uli Wyss and Karl Gonda's climb in August 1953 as a true ascent. The pair had been swept away in an avalanche on the Summit Snowfield, and it was felt that on account of a few yards of easy snow hiking, they should not be deprived of recognition for the ascent. There also was the possibility that the climbers had already reached the summit and were coming back down toward the Mittellegi Ridge with the intention of bivouacking in the Mittellegi Hut, when the avalanche caught them. At all events, Wyss and Gonda's climb was now recognized as the twelfth ascent, which meant that the thirteenth ascent went to Hirschbichler and Riedl, who had climbed the face a few days after Gonda and Wyss had. (Hirschbichler was to die, four years later, in an expedition to the Karakorum.) To Nothdurft and Mayer then went the credit for the fourteenth ascent, the most puzzling and poignant climb yet of the Eigernordwand.

Following a year that saw no ascents at all, 1961 could be classified a banner year on the Eigernordwand. True, Adolf Mayr had died, but twenty others had successfully taken and passed their final exam, and 1961 equaled 1952 for putting the highest number yet on the Eiger's summit in a single year.

The year 1962, however, was to reverse this auspicious pattern.

17
The Dangle-and-Whack Lads

By 1962 no English or American climber had yet done the Eigernordwand. But a number of excellent American climbers like Gary Hemming, Tom Frost, Royal Robbins, and John Harlin were now appearing in the Alps, eager to prove themselves in the home of mountaineering, lured by the snow and ice climbing, by the challenge of big faces involving long, mixed climbs. Most of the American climbers had learned their skills on the sheer rock walls of El Capitan, Lost Arrow, Half Dome, Sentinel, and a dozen other spires and cliffs in the Yosemite Valley of the Sierra Nevada Range east of San Francisco, or on the many and varied peaks of the Colorado Rockies, where fifty-four summits are over 14,000 feet. Until the early 1960s, American climbing bore little relation to Alpine climbing, and American mountaineering progressed at its own pace and in its own direction. It's no surprise that American climbers improved, adapted, and devised their own equipment for the technically very difficult grade of rock climbing they were mainly engaged in. Some American "Alpine" climbing was being done, of course, as far back as Victorian times, and again between World Wars I and II. There were ascents of Mount Rainier in Washington State, of peaks in the Canadian Rockies, of Longs Peak in Colorado, of Mount McKinley in Alaska, and of various Himalayan peaks, but the great majority of American climbing prior to 1962 was done on sheer rock faces innocent of snow or ice.

Yvon Chouinard, a young California climber, actually began to forge his own pitons and carabiners from a chrome-and-molybdenum alloy that was not only lighter than the steel used in standard pitons, but that had the advantage of being practically immune to metal fatigue. He also developed a knife-blade-thin piton that needed penetration of only a quarter of an inch to hold a man's weight. These new thin pegs he called realized ultimate-reality pitons, or rurps. Another new development was the Logan or sky hook, the hook end of which could, like the point of a grapnel, be engaged over the lip of a tiny flake or knob of rock, places that wouldn't take a piton. The eye in the lower end of the piece, at the other end of the shank, would then take a sling, which would take a carabiner, which would take a stirrup or *étrier*, which would take a climber up the wall, if everything went according to plan.

In the British Isles mountaineering had also taken a new direction. In contrast to the old purist approach of the British Alpine Club, where many thought that placing a piton in rock was an abomination on the level of eating the fox that the dogs had killed after a hunt, a wave of young climbers were coming along to open up new free and direct-aid routes on the mountains and cliffs of England, Wales, and Scotland. Referred to scornfully by the older generation of gentleman Alpinists as dangle-and-whack lads, because of their dangling half-sitting stances in slings while they hammered and whacked pitons into cracks, the hard men, as they often called themselves, dangled and whacked to such great effect in hair-raising direct-aid climbs all over the British Isles that they almost eclipsed the older generation as a serious force in British mountaineering. Though some of the younger climbers were university students, many, if not most, came out of working-class and lower-middle-class backgrounds and had little reverence for what they saw as the stuffy establishment of the British Alpine Club. The new climbers mostly belonged to small local clubs of "rock hoppers" or "scramblers" and had nothing to do with Alpine climbing.

British climbers, too, brought advances in techniques and equipment. They were the first to use chocks, wedge-shaped chunks of metal on rope, nylon, or wire slings that, when placed in a crack, jammed tighter and held better the greater the weight that was applied to them. The original chocks had been mechanical metal nuts of various sizes whose inside threads were filed down so as not to abrade a sling or rope. Chocks had the advantages of not requiring the use of a hammer, because they could easily be placed in a crack and often as easily dislodged, when no longer needed, by a sharp upward jerk on the attached sling. Then too, chocks could be used in cracks too wide to take a piton.

Chris Bonington (left) and Don Whillans setting out from England for Grindel-wald and the Eiger.

Nor did they deface the rock, the way pegs often did. With a dozen chocks of various sizes and shapes, climbers often found it no longer necessary to employ pitons. Chocks had their origin in the practice of some British climbers of filling their pockets at the start of a climb with stones of various sizes. When protection was needed, they would slot a stone into a wide crack, then thread a sling behind the stone. A carabiner would then be clipped into the loop end of the sling. Some climbers would keep specially shaped chockstones and remove them when no longer needed. Tales are told of climbers distraught at losing favorite chockstones that they dropped or that were wedged too tight to be retrieved.

Instead of just tying the climbing rope around one's waist, climbers now began to use waist and/or chest harnesses designed to be put on and taken off in a matter of moments. Not only did a harness hold one more securely, it also helped to spread the shock of a fall much better and thus to reduce the chances of a blackout after a sudden arrest.

In the early 1960s such British climbers as Don Whillans, Nick Estcourt, Ian Clough, Chris Bonington, Tom Patey, Joe Brown, Bev Clark, Dougal Haston, Mick Burke, Brian Nally, Tom Bourdillon, and Stew Fulton were looking more and more to Europe to expand their climbing horizons. Mention must also be made of a group of climbers in Scotland who, working out on the glaciers and snowfields of Ben Nevis and the other Highland peaks of Glencoe, advanced the art of ice and snow climbing to newer and more rarified heights. Dougal Haston, Tom Patey, and Stew Fulton were typical of these climbers from north of the border.

The austerity years of Britain's recovery from World War II were almost over, money was more plentiful, and the Alps were only a few hours and a few quid away across the Channel. British climbers like Joe Brown and Tom Patey, having picked their teeth on the Aiguilles of Chamonix, were now casting their eye on the Eigernordwand.

The climbing season of 1962 turned out to be one of the busiest yet in Grindelwald. A record number of ascents took place, including the first British and American attempts, but death stalked the face all that summer. The season did start out on a bright note with a successful, straightforward ascent by four Swiss mountaineers, Bernard Meyer, Michel Zuckschwert, André Meyer, and Jean Braun. The four climbed swiftly, the conditions and weather were decent, and they all reached the summit after bivouacs at the Swallow's Nest and the start of the Traverse of the Gods. While the Swiss team was in its last bivouac, a pair of British climbers, Brian Nally and Barry Brewster, moved up and occupied the Swallow's Nest in their attempt to be the first British climbers to do the Eiger's north face. The Swallow's Nest had by now become the favorite first bivouac of Eiger aspirants, replacing the cave at the head of the Shattered Pillar. It was a protected, roomy perch, and it got the climbers farther up on the face, thereby assuring them of a good head start in getting through the First and Second icefields early in the morning, while low temperatures and ice still held the loose rock.

Brian Nally was, at twenty-five, the older and more experienced of the pair. A house decorator and a member of a London climbing club, he had a year earlier climbed the north face of the Matterhorn with Tom Carruthers, a Scot. He had also tried a winter climb of the Matterhorn's north face with Georg Huber, a Bavarian, and had accomplished other Alpine climbs of a comparable difficulty. His companion, Barry Brewster, a university student, was twenty-two and a member of a Welsh climbing club. He was known for having done many of the hardest routes in Wales and in the Lake District of England. If not quite as much at home on ice as Brewster was, Nally was probably the better rock climber; so together they made a well-balanced team and had agreed, before they started up, that Nally was to lead on ice and Brewster on rock.

They left the Swallow's Nest at 5 A.M. and, relying on Harrer's route guide in his book *The White Spider,* tackled the First Icefield and the rock band leading to the Ice Hose. Here, either Harrer's guide was in error or Nally and Brewster lost the route. In any event, they followed a false line that took two hours to correct, thereby resulting in a two-hour delay in their starting on the Second Icefield. To complicate matters, the night before had been warm and rocks had continually fallen down the face. They now started on the Second Icefield, with Nally in the lead, and ran into further trouble. The ice was treacherously mushy, and Nally had to patiently cut a stitch run of foothold steps in order to safeguard his less experienced ice-climbing partner. Nally was making a diagonal right-to-left climbing traverse of the Icefield with the intent of finishing up on the lower reaches of the Flatiron. Another pair of British climbers, Don Whillans and Chris Bonington, watching Nally and Brewster through a telescope (unaware they were compatriots) remarked on the long period of time the traverse across the Second Icefield was taking. More experienced climbers, in order to complete the traverse as quickly as possible and thereby shorten the time they would be exposed to rockfall, would have front pointed with their crampons straight up to the top of the icefield, then traversed over to the base of the Flatiron on the shrunken-back crack where the ice separated from the rock at the head of the field. Here fairly speedy progress could be made with the feet finding purchase on the leading lip of the ice and the hands, sometimes using an undercling grip, following along on the rock face above. They would now also be within the comparative safety of the clear arch of rockfall coming down the face, most of which would strike the icefield below them. Front pointing would have gotten the climbers off the icefield in one quarter of the time it took to cut out steps in traversing across to the Flatiron. Front points can't be efficiently used in diagonal traverses.

At all events, the pair, dodging stonefall the whole way, had just gotten off the icefield when Brewster took over the lead on the rock buttresses and pillars of the Flatiron. On belay, Nally clipped himself into a ring piton that still hung there from one of the earlier ascents. Above him Brewster climbed, banging in one piton and threading his rope through it; another piton and he was out of Nally's sight. Down at Kleine Scheidegg, watchers saw stone fall come bounding down the rock face that Brewster was trying to climb. Nally watched the rope pay out, stop, pay out another few feet. Then he heard the cry "Stones!" as, above him, Brewster was knocked from his holds. He screamed, "Brian!" as he flew past his partner. The descent was arrested for a split second as the first piton took the shock of the fall. But it ripped out, as did the second piton, and Brewster resumed his plunge to the icefield below. He had fallen almost a hundred feet when the shock hit Nally at his belay piton. This final peg held, and Nally looked down. Brewster now hung head downward on the Second Icefield. He appeared motionless, which did not surprise Nally, who had seen his partner's body strike projecting rocks with terrible force on the way down. Because of Brewster's upside-down position, the fact that he seemed unconscious, and the near impossibility of hauling an inert body a hundred feet up a fifty-five-degree slope, Nally drove in a fresh piton, secured the rope to it, and gave the belay piton a couple of whacks of his hammer to make sure it was securely anchored. He drove in a fresh piton for added insurance, then climbed down the rope to his friend's aid. Brewster was still unconscious.

Nally spent the few remaining hours of daylight laboriously hacking a flat platform out of the ice on which to place his rope mate for protection, all this while dodging the occasional stone that came aiming at their position. It must be remembered that Nally had already cut steps up the whole thousand-foot-plus traverse of the Second Icefield and clearly had to be very tired. Watchers at Kleine Scheidegg noted that his movements were the painfully slow ones of an exhausted man. Nevertheless, he managed to drag the unconscious Brewster up to the ice-platform stance. Next, using nearby rocks and a rucksack, he built a rampart on the upper side of the ice platform to protect Brewster from falling rocks. Nally now took off his partner's climbing boots, then put on his regular ones, and over them a thick, heavy pair of down bootees for use in frigid weather. He put gloves on his friend's hands, a wool cap over his head, and wrestled him into a down jacket. He placed his own helmet on Brewster's head, then got him into a bivouac sack and secured the sack with a couple of extra loops of rope. Slight movements were observed in

Brewster's body from time to time by telescope watchers, but whether he was conscious or not, no one could determine. Darkness fell, and Nally planted himself beside his partner to wait out the long hours of a night during which unseen rocks came whirring and thumping down the icefield. Nally, never knowing when one of these projectiles would strike him or Barry, slept little, if at all. When dawn came, he climbed up to his rucksack at the anchor piton and retrieved a small stove. Bringing it back down, he got it going and made a tin of soup. Brewster appeared to regain consciousness, and Nally held him in his arms, getting ready to spoon some hot soup into him. Then, according to Nally's account, he "seemed to know where he was and who I was and he said, 'I'm sorry Brian' and he died. And everything went dark and it really was the end of everything."

Nally now climbed back up to the rock belay above to get his knapsack and some ice pitons. Retreating once again to Brewster's position, he drove in several ice pitons and attached the dead man to them with carabiners clipped into his harness, securing everything with several knots of the rope around the pitons and through the carabiners. Convinced that his partner was now fully secured, he cut the climbing rope about ten feet above his position. Positive that he could do no more for his partner, Nally climbed up to the belay stance at the rock band just above the head of the Second Icefield, where he was protected from falling stones and could await the arrival of the rescue party that he was sure was on the way. Nally later said that his first thought, early in the morning, had been to descend and get help but that he had decided against it because he hadn't been able to stand the thought of Brewster's coming to and finding himself abandoned.

In the meantime, completely unaware of the drama being enacted just above them, British climbers Don Whillans and Chris Bonington were just getting up after having bivouacked for the night at the Swallow's Nest.

Also on the lower part of the face was a rescue party of half a dozen local guides, led by Karl Schlunegger, who, with his brother Hans, had taken part in the third ascent of the face back in 1947. Also part of the rescue party were two other climbers who had previously done the Eigernordwand, Swiss guide Hilti von Allmen who had made the climb the year before, and Sepp Larch, who, with Karl Winter, had made the seventh ascent of the face ten years before. The rescue party left the Gallery Window at 4 A.M., and thanks to this head start, and driven by the urgency and precarious position of Brewster on the Second Icefield, soon began to catch up to Whillans and Bonington, who were climbing at their own steady pace, completely unaware of the plight of Nally and Brewster. The pair of British climbers had lost one of their ice axes the

evening before and, in view of the now chancy weather and the steady
rockfall, were on the verge of turning back when they were hailed by
members of the rescue party, who shouted up to them that two compatriots of theirs, one of whom was hurt badly, were in trouble on the
Second Icefield. Sensing that the guides would not climb that high to
effect a rescue, Whillans and Bonington immediately said they would go
to the aid of the injured man. The pair of guides turned back. The
English climbers emerged from the Ice Hose and moved onto the bottom of the Second Icefield, where they caught a glimpse of a tiny red
bundle near the base of the Flatiron. Was that the injured climber?
When they saw the body move, they called out, telling the climber to stay
where he was until they reached him. The figure paid no attention and
moved another thirty feet across the head of the icefield to finally stop
at a knob and either sit or lie down—at a distance of a thousand feet it
was hard to tell which. In any event, if he was hurt, he was at least still
able to function.

Then Whillans and Bonington heard another sound, a booming that
seemed to fill the whole wall. Suddenly they saw the tiny figure of a man
shoot down the ice, the wind tearing and flapping at his clothes, then
launch out into space from the bottom of the icefield. Both climbers
were immobilized with shock and instinctively hugged the ice themselves. When they recovered, they checked to see whether the falling
climber was the one they had hailed just moments before. He wasn't.
That figure was still at the head of the icefield. Their mouths dry with
fear and shock, Bonington and Whillans resumed climbing.

Beneath Bonington and Whillans the rescue party saw an avalanche
of rock and snow come thudding and sluicing down the face. Amid the
rubble was a human body. Horrified, the members of the rescue team
watched the body bounce off rocks, carom off buttresses, turn slow and
awful somersaults in its 3,000-foot death journey to the foot of the wall.
Hours later, at Kleine Scheidegg, that experienced Alpinist Sepp Larch
was still in shock over what he had witnessed.

Exactly what happened to Brewster no one seems to know. Nally says
that at one point he saw a huge rock avalanche come bounding down
from above. He barely had time to shelter beneath a rock bulge before
the avalanche hit. When the danger was past, he looked down and was
no longer able to see Brewster's body. From the local guides' evidence,
it would seem that Brewster was swept free from his ice platform by a
snow and rock avalanche, confirming Nally's account. But anything as
large as a body falling down the face will often be accompanied by ice
and rocks set in motion by the falling object itself. There were some
telescope watchers who were convinced they saw Brewster stand up and
begin, in a sudden frenzy, to pull at the ropes binding him to the ice

pegs in his stance. Coming out of a concussion, perhaps, half-delirious with pain and shock, might Brewster not have imagined himself to be trapped in some way by the ropes and irrationally have tried to unclip from his harness? Others thought that, realizing he was mortally injured and not wanting to endanger the lives of Nally and other rescuers, he simply unclipped himself from the ropes and allowed his body to slide the rest of the way down and over the 3,000-foot precipice at the bottom of the icefield. Nally, however, was convinced that Brewster had died earlier in the morning.

When Bonington and Whillans recovered from the shock of seeing that body go shooting helplessly down the ice, they again shouted up to Nally to stay put—they were coming to get him. They cut careful, good-sized holds in the ice, knowing they would have to escort back a man in a state of physical and mental exhaustion. It had begun to rain by now, and the icefield was streaming with runnels of water that tended to dis-integrate the carefully cut steps. Nevertheless, Bonington, in the lead, reached Nally, whose first question, "Are you going to the top? Can I tie in?" indicated how poorly his mind was functioning under the strain of Brewster's fall and death.

Bonington, his own nerves on edge from the whole experience, told him not to be a bloody fool, that his friend was dead and that they had come to bring him, Nally, back down. Nally objected and asked why they didn't continue their climb? After all, they had come this far. By now Bonington realized that Nally was out of it, was in fact acting and talking like an automaton, incapable of thinking for himself. He gently undid the ninety-foot tangle of rope around Nally's neck, unclipped himself from the climbing rope, and tied Nally in. Whillans was waiting at the other end of the rope, 150 feet down the icefield, at an ice-piton belay, anxiously watching rocks go thudding and smashing down the grey ice-field.

Bonington now tied into the end of Nally's rope and motioned to Nally to start down, making the survivor the middle man in a three-man rope, belayed from both ends. Just then a stone, coming from above, hit Nally on the bare head. He swayed backward, but Bonington grabbed him before he could fall. Even this didn't seem to faze the robotlike Nally. After a moment or two, he started numbly down the rope toward Whillans. The trio had just reached the bottom of the icefield when a furious thunderstorm broke over their heads. Lightning bounced all around them, and they were soon drenched to the skin by sudden teems

Ian Clough on the Hinterstoisser Traverse.
CHRIS BONINGTON PHOTO

of rain. They made it back to the Ice Hose, to find a waterfall streaming not only with slushy ice but a new Eiger devil—mud. Every step down they were in imminent peril of peeling off.

All three were hurt by falling debris, and at one point Nally, hit on the head with a stone for the second time that day, would have fallen but for Bonington's quickness in pinning and holding him to the wall. They followed the waterfall to where it plunged over the cliff face, instead of continuing down the First Icefield, and here Whillans, in an inspired bit of reverse route finding, decided that if they rappelled down at that point, they would arrive at the start of the Hinterstoisser. He had, on the ascent, spotted a stream of water coming down from above at the start of the traverse. (Unknown to the climbers, the Hinterstoisser Traverse had already been prepared for them with fixed ropes by the guides' rescue party.) Whillans banged in a belay piton and disappeared down the wall, anxiously watched by Bonington. Moments later a cheery call came floating up, and the other two took their turn. Had Kurz and his party known, or guessed at the rappel route, they could easily have saved their lives.

The three made it back down and in through the Gallery Window. Here they were met by a special train and the flashbulbs of photographers and the questions of journalists. For some reason the train delayed a full hour while the journalists peppered the British trio with questions, despite their exhausted and drenched condition. The unnerved Nally contradicted himself on several points—contradictions that the newspapers made much of in their articles. Cynics say that the railway authorities delayed the train so that the Swiss journalists would have free rein to question Nally, who, in a state of psychological trauma after a twenty-four-hour-long nightmare, could hardly be expected to give a detailed, crisp report of the catastrophe.

The British climbers finally reached Kleine Scheidegg, where they were told that what was left of Brewster's body, clad in an orange windbreaker, had been spotted at the foot of the wall. Guides had already gone out to retrieve the corpse.

Barry Brewster, "in that rich earth a richer dust concealed," was buried in the small, immaculate cemetery of Grindelwald. His grave faces a trio of peaks across the valley—the Wetterhorn, the Schreckhorn, and the Eiger. The grave marker is of the same local limestone as the Eiger,

---

Brian Nally on the Second Icefield just before his rescue by Chris Bonington and Don Whillans. Note missing helmet, tangle of rope coils around neck, possible rope snarl around left forearm.

CHRIS BONINGTON PHOTO

and it reads, "In loving memory of Barry Brewster. 1940–1962. Eiger-nordwand. Shattered my glass ere half the sands had run. I hold the heights, I hold the heights I won." (From Geoffrey Winthrop Young, an English mountaineer-poet.) On top of the grave someone placed an old-fashioned wooden-handled ice axe and a coil of old manila rope that today, eighteen years later, are still there, though looking as though they would crumble to dust at a touch.

Like all Eiger tragedies, this one sparked off its own share of controversy. Many said the two climbers had simply not been experienced enough for the Eiger, look how long it had taken them—six hours—to negotiate the Second Icefield. Others said that Nally should somehow have contrived to haul Brewster up and off the Second Icefield, out of the path of rockfall, though how that was to have been accomplished by a physically exhausted man in a state of psychological shock was not explained. Nally was criticized for having left Brewster that morning and having climbed back up to the head of the Second Icefield. Yet had he stayed, it is likely that he, too, would have been swept away by the avalanche that doomed his rope mate.

Adding to the controversy was the hefty bill, 2,000 Swiss francs, that Nally received the next day, covering the services of fourteen guides, the hire of the special train, and the supposed loss of or damage to the guides' equipment, including laundry bills for clothing dirtied on the rescue attempt. And all this despite the fact that only two guides had climbed as far as the bottom of the First Icefield. On seeing that Bonington and Whillans were going to the rescue of Nally, the guides had quickly rejoined their companions at the *Stollenloch,* instead of sending a party to the bottom of the Second Icefield in case they were needed to support the Bonington-Whillans rescue attempt. Once again the local guides had covered themselves, if not with honor, at least with lucre.

There was no controversy, however, over the heroism of Whillans and Bonington in bringing the demoralized Nally down off the wall. Nally himself later said that he owed his life to their efforts; he would never had gotten down on his own. Whillans was later to call the time he spent bringing Nally down as his most frightening experience on an Alpine wall.

The controversy over Brewster's death was soon eclipsed by two attempted climbs that came a week later. One was an all-Swiss rope of four—two men, Michel Vaucher and Michel Darbellay, and two women, Yvette Attinger and Loulou Boulaz, the first rope of their sex to try a Nordwand ascent. Michel Vaucher, from Geneva, was one of the Swiss team that, in 1960, made the first ascent of Dhaulagiri in the Himalayas, the world's sixth-highest mountain (26,795 feet). Later he was to marry his lovely climbing companion Yvette, some say to keep her from outclassing him on big climbs. A rather daring young lady, Yvette's other hobby was sport parachuting, in which she had over a hundred jumps to her credit. Michel Darbellay, a guide from the ski resort of Martigny, had long been fascinated by the Eiger's north face. The fourth member of the group, Loulou Boulaz, had not only been the first woman to tackle

Barry Brewster's grave in Grindelwald.   A. ROTH PHOTO

In loving
memory
of

BARRY
BREWSTER

1940–1962

Eigernordwand

Shattered my glass ere
half the sands had run—
I hold the heights, I hold
the heights I won

the Eigernordwand, back in 1936, but she was probably the world's foremost lady mountaineer. At over fifty years of age, she was the oldest climber, male or female, ever to try the north wall. She had already climbed both the Croz and Walker Spurs on the Grandes Jorasses, and in 1969 she and Yvette were to do the first all-woman climb of the Cassin Route on the Piz Badile.

The four started up the face on July 28 and stopped at the Bivouac Cave at the head of the Shattered Pillar. The next morning the weather was chancy. Mists and clouds rolled across the face, and it looked as though a typical Eiger storm were brewing. Despite the weather the decision was made to continue, and the two ropes of Vaucher and Attinger and of Darbellay and Boulaz, climbed both icefields and reached the foot of the Flatiron, where they found Brewster's crampons and ice axe. After a short break at Death Bivouac, they crossed the Third Icefield and reached the traditional bivouac spot on the Ramp by midafternoon, a remarkable bit of climbing considering that they had gotten a late start that morning and that the rainy weather meant frequent stone fall on the icefields and difficult climbing conditions in general.

During their second night they bivouacked on the Ramp. Down below Eiger watchers were speculating. Should the weather get worse, the four would probably have to retreat in the morning. There might even be another Eiger rescue operation in the making, though it was hard to tell, because the weather had blocked any view of the climbers from the Second Icefield on. In fact, watchers assumed that the four were at Death Bivouac.

The next morning the weather got even worse, and waterfalls everywhere poured down the rock faces. The Ramp was a torrent, and visibility was down to feet. The four climbers reluctantly decided to turn back and began their retreat across the Third Icefield. Despite the stormy weather and drenching torrents, they reversed their climb of the previous day and, moving steadily but safely, made it to the shelter of the Bivouac Cave at the Shattered Pillar. Here they settled down for the night and managed to dry out their sodden clothes. By noon the following day they were back once again at Kleine Scheidegg; there they learned, somewhat to their surprise, that two Austrian climbers, having passed their bivouac site early that morning before they were awake, were already up and on the First Icefield. There were also rumors flying around that another solo climb was in the making. Michel Darbellay, in particular, was to remember that solo climb. He was also to have a return engagement with the Eigernordwand the following year.

Meanwhile, the Austrian pair, Helmuth Drachsler, a student, and Walter Gstrein, a cabinetmaker, pushed ahead and, despite the bad weather that made a shower bath of the whole face, got as far as Death

Bivouac on their first day. Their intention was to do a "direct" climb from Death Bivouac straight up to the Spider. Indeed, they had followed the Sedlmayer-Mehringer line up the cliffs between the First and Second icefields instead of taking the Ice Hose.

The next morning they started up the cliff face leading directly to the Spider. Others, including Sedlmayer and Mehringer, had tried this line, but all had been forced to retreat. Because of the bad weather the telescope watchers caught only occasional glimpses of the pair. But the Austrians kept putting away pitch after pitch. Finally, they were halted by a combination of factors: poor visibility, ice-annealed rocks from melting water on the higher snowfields, a sheer buttress that seemed to offer no continuation of the line, and rockfall from the Spider's launching chute.

The decision was made to retreat, and they abseiled down to Death Bivouac. There were still some hours of daylight left, so they decided to chance the dangerous traverse across the Third Icefield. No stones hit them, and they settled down for the night at the usual Ramp bivouac site. At least they had the consolation of knowing that they had pushed the direct line up from Death Bivouac higher than anyone else had. Though they gave up on the direct, they did not give up on the climb, and the next morning saw them moving on up the Ramp. The weather was still poor, rain mixed with sleet, the Ramp was clogged with ice, and the Waterfall Pitch and Ice Bulge, that Scylla and Charybdis guarding the entrance to the final third of the face, were more difficult than usual to surmount. In fact, they had to take the Terray Variant in order to turn the Waterfall Pitch. Then they were over the Ice Bulge and on the Ramp Snowfield. They moved up the Brittle Crack and across the Traverse of the Gods to the Spider. It was now midafternoon, and the icefield was alive with bounding rocks and snow avalanches. Drachsler and Gstrein were faced with a tough choice, either venture out on the ice shooting range or rope themselves to the wall until morning. They found another alternative and went up the rock pillars and cracks on the left-hand side of the Spider, a variant used before by the Czech climbers Kuchar and Zibrin. When they reached the top of the icefield, they traversed across to the right-hand branch of the inverted Y that marks the start of the line up the Exit Cracks.

When darkness fell, they were forced to bivouac on a minuscule ledge and attach themselves to the face with slings and pegs. To add to their woes, the weather got even worse, the temperature dropped below the freezing mark, and snow began to fall. As though that weren't enough, a thunderstorm gathered on the peak, and soon the men were being shaken like rats time and again by nearby lightning strikes and shattering brattles of thunder. Their ironmongery danced and sparked

with static electricity, and the air was full of the sulfurous smell of limestone riven by lightning strikes. Mercifully, the thunderstorm didn't last,
but the men got little sleep that night on their airy perch.

The next morning when they resumed climbing, it was still snowing
and blowing. They moved up slowly, breasting snow avalanches all the
way. The new snow made it very difficult to find handholds or footholds,
and they constantly had to sweep and brush away loose snow to locate
tiny knobs and cracks and wrinkles that were covered with ice that now
had to be chipped away with the ice axe. The difficulties of the last dozen
pitches can be gauged by the fact that it took the Austrian pair about
twelve hours to master a section of the wall that can be climbed in normal
conditions in little more than three hours.

The Viennese climbers finally reached the peak at 5 P.M., their
fourth day on the face. They immediately took the west flank down to
Kleine Scheidegg.

Unknown to the Austrian pair, another climber was on the face. He
was Adolf Derungs, the Grisons bricklayer who had discarded an old
overcoat on the Spider in his previous ascent with Lukas Albrecht in
1959. This time Derungs was attempting a solo ascent—the third, if one
counted Nothdurft's attempt when he had reached Death Bivouac and
then turned back.

Now thirty-two, Derungs had been drawn back to the Eiger. He had,
since climbing the wall with Albrecht in 1959, obtained his professional
guide's license and had stated his intention of changing his profession
from stonemason to bergführer. But the field was overcrowded, and
Derungs had started late in trying to build up a list of clients. However,
were he to do a new spectacular climb, he might draw rich patrons;
someone might even put him in a movie that would make him famous.

Early that summer a German film-making crew under Wolfgang
Gorter, and including the well-known Austrian Olympic skier Toni
Sailer, had taken up residence at Kleine Scheidegg with the intention of
filming ascents of the Eigernordwand. They shot footage of some climbers on the lower part of the wall, as far as the Difficult Crack and the
Hinterstoisser, then filmed other climbers higher on the face by lugging
their cameras halfway up the west flank and taking shots from there.
There were those who said that the presence of the camera crews all that
summer brought out publicity-seeking climbers whose skills were not up
to the demands of the Eiger north face. There were those who charged
that Derungs hoped to become famous for being the first to climb the
Eigernordwand solo. He was reported to have said that the talk of the
Nordwand's being a wall of death was nonsense. He had been up there,
and he knew. He could even climb it solo—and would, as soon as he was
ready. There were those who claimed that Derungs was being paid by

the film company to make the attempt, so that their crews could shoot spectacular footage of that lone climber making his slow and perilous way up that immense face. Opposed to that theory is the fact that Derungs started up the face in mainly foggy weather, which greatly reduced the chances of getting decent pictures of him. Then too, Gorter accompanied Derungs to the base of the wall and there pleaded with him not to make the attempt, or at least to wait for better weather. But Derungs was not to be daunted and handed over his wallet and some papers, including his guide's license, to Gorter to hold for him. Then he started up the stepping stone ledges at the right of the First Pillar, around noon on August 31, the same day that Drachsler and Gstrein started their climb and that the descending rope of Darbellay, Vaucher, Attinger, and Boulaz were in their final bivouac at the head of the Shattered Pillar.

No one saw Derungs, who hoped to bivouac that night at the Swallow's Nest. At nine o'clock no flashlight signal came from the Swallow's Nest. Ten o'clock came and went—still no signal. Surely nothing had gone wrong? It was too early in the climb. Perhaps Derungs had dropped the flashlight, or perhaps the batteries were dead.

The next morning, telescope watchers could spot no sign of life at the Swallow's Nest; nor did any tiny figure show up in their scopes, climbing the First or Second icefield. The weather now turned bad, visibility swiftly narrowing down to zero. Gorter and his camera crew, high on the west flank, came back down to Kleine Scheidegg. Perhaps Derungs had turned back because of the bad weather? But, no, he didn't show up at Kleine Scheidegg either. The next day, telescopes scanned the bottom of the wall and picked up a patch of red. Guides went out to investigate but found nothing except a piece of loose cloth.

On Sunday, August 5, a dozen guides went out to conduct a thorough search of the base of the mountain. They finally found Derung's crumpled body, half-hidden by snow in a corner of angled rock. There was no clue as to why, or whence, the Swiss climber had fallen. Somewhere on the lower side of the Hinterstoisser Traverse, probably at the Difficult Crack, something happened and he peeled off the face to plummet to his death. Heinrich Harrer speculates that he probably lost his footing on the easy, but iced-up, rocks leading to the Hinterstoisser. It is a fact that many climbers are killed on easy terrain, lulled by the seeming innocence of Grade-III and Grade-IV pitches—lulled to the point that they sometimes ignore elementary safety practices, such as roping up to one's partner or being careful of one's footing. Whatever happened to him, Derungs became the twenty-first fatality on the Eigernordwand and the second to die while attempting a solo climb.

On August 11, half a dozen Italian climbers met up on the face.

Romano Perego, Andrea Mellano, and Gildo Airoldi were in one rope when they met up with Armando Aste, Franco Solina, and Pierlorenzo Acquistapace at the bottom of the First Icefield. The six promptly decided to join together in one rope, hoping to notch the first Italian climb of the Nordwand.

A week or so previously two other Italian climbers, Roberto Sorgato and Giorgio Redaelli, had been as far as the Second Icefield when bad weather forced them to retreat. While they were on the Ice Hose, the climbing rope joining the pair somehow came loose and fell down to Redaelli, leaving Sorgato unprotected and in the position of having to down climb unroped. Redaelli could climb up to him with the end of the rope, but he would be climbing unbelayed on a very difficult and slippery pitch. Fortunately, Sorgato spotted a loop of rope sticking up out of the ice a few yards away. He reached the loop and jerked hard on it. The rope held. He used the hanging part of the rope as a rappel to get down to his partner, where he roped up again. The iced-in rope had been left behind, several weeks earlier, by Brian Nally in his retreat with Bonington and Whillans after the death of Barry Brewster.

But now it looked as though, at long last, an Italian rope would finally master the Nordwand. On the Second Icefield, the six Italians were passed by a rope of four Austrians led by Walter Almberger. For a while there were ten men on the Second Icefield at the same time, reminiscent of Buhl and Rébuffat's climb when nine men had followed each other up and across that long ice climb to the Flatiron.

The Austrian team of Almberger, Klaus Hoi, Hugo Stelzig, and Adolf Weissensteiner made a more or less routine climb, bivouacking at the Flatiron and the Traverse of the Gods before topping out on the summit. It was a straightforward climb—for the Eiger—that is to say, there were the usual weather difficulties, chancy bivouac stances, pitons that wouldn't hold in friable rock, plenty of stone coming down the face, and avalanches roaring down the Spider like express trains. However, for Almberger, a mountain guide in his native Styria, the climb was something special. He achieved a double first on the Eigernordwand—becoming the first man to climb the wall twice, and the first to climb it in both summer and winter. (He had been part of the Toni Hiebeler winter climb the year before.)

Three days later the Italian team reached the summit after a total of seven days and six bivouacs on the face. Their relatively slow pace can be largely attributed to their unfamiliarity with long mixed climbs on ice and snowfields, and to the size of their party. Perego and Mellano led the ice pitches and Aste the rock sections of the climb. They became the first Italians to climb the Nordwand, twenty-four years after Sandri and Menti had fallen to their deaths from just below the Difficult Crack.

In an article that he later wrote for an Italian journal, Armando Aste downgraded the climb, saying that it wasn't very difficult—just dangerous. They hadn't used even one *étrier* on the ascent, or planted a single piton. (Undoubtedly, though, they made good use of pitons planted by previous parties on the face.) Aste did admit that the weather, the snow, the ice, and the constant rockfall made the climb something to be remembered. He claimed that the Italians climbed in complete security, moving only during the morning hours when rockfall was negligible. Still, there's a defensive tone to the whole piece, especially regarding the length of time it took, and in Aste's statement that Italian mountaineers certainly didn't need an Eiger victory to save their honor as climbers.

Be that as it may, the first Italian ascent was also the twenty-seventh climb of the face. And 1962 was still not over.

18
Blond God from the Valley

At midnight on August 19, one day after the six Italians came down from the summit, a blond, good-looking American crawled out of a tent in the meadows of Alpiglen. John Harlin, born in 1935, a scant two months before Sedlmayer and Mehringer perished at Death Bivouac, had been to the Eiger before, as far back as 1954 when he had gone a thousand feet or so up the face with Tenzing Norkay. Tenzing, after his Everest triumph of the year before, had been visiting Grindelwald as a guest of the Swiss Alpine Club. While staying in the area, he met a brash Stanford freshman on his summer vacation, the nineteen-year-old John Harlin, who had ideas of becoming the first English-speaking climber to do the Eigernordwand. He promptly latched onto Tenzing and with the famed Sherpa mountaineer and several Swiss companions climbed the Jungfrau. Then Harlin and Tenzing climbed halfway up the west flank of the Eiger to get a good look in at the middle and upper reaches of the Nordwand. This wildly ambitious American teenager now conceived an added dimension to his dream, not only would he be the first English-speaking climber to do the Eiger's north face, but he would do it in the company of the coconqueror of Mount Everest. And evidently Harlin did talk Tenzing into some exploratory scrambling on the lower reaches of the face, perhaps getting as high as the top of the Shattered Pillar. But the forty-year-old Sherpa was not an extremist and lacked experience in the more esoteric areas of direct-aid, technical climbing. His skills lay in high altitude, 26,000-foot-plus, ice and snow climbing in the Himalayas. For whatever reason, Tenzing regretfully shook his head and said to the hero-worshiping American teenager, of a possible attempt on the Eigernordwand, "Too difficult, too dangerous." Tenzing went on with the rest of his triumphal tour of Europe, and Harlin went home, back to Stanford. His dream was dead, perhaps, but at least he would have an amusing story to tell his children one day.

But now Harlin was back, considerably matured and with a lot more climbing experience on his rack. (A rack is a shoulder sling with its accompanying pitons, carabiners, slings, chocks, and the like.) Harlin had originally begun climbing as a member of the Stanford University Alpine Club, served his apprenticeship on the local cliffs of Tahquitz and Suicide Rocks, on the university buildings after dark, and gone on to the sheer-rock walls of Yosemite Valley. He had also climbed Mount Rainier in Washington State, in the Canadian Rockies, and had done some notably difficult routes on the Mont Blanc range outside Chamonix. An exceptionally strong climber, with a well-muscled body and blond good looks, he was sometimes called, half satirically, half fondly, the Greek God by his climbing companions. Right now he was a fighter pilot in the U.S. Air Force, stationed at Bernkastel in Germany. Married, he and his wife, Marilyn, were the parents of two—a boy, John Jr., and a girl, Andrea.

John reached into his tent and shook awake his climbing companion, a young German named Konrad Kirch. Harlin and Kirch had climbed together many times, in the Kaisergebirge outside Innsbruck, where they had done the difficult Totenkirchl (Death Chapel), the direct on the south face of the Scharnitzspitz in the Wetterstein, in the Dolomites (Piccolo di Vael and the Cima Grande di Lavaredo), as well as two unsuccessful attempts, one in summer and one in winter, on the Walker Spur of the Grandes Jorasses. Whereas Harlin was self-assured to the point of arrogance, strong willed, and endowed with tremendous desire to excel once embarked on a project, Kirch was quiet, cautious, conservative, low-key, and physically slight compared to Harlin, though equal to him in mountaineering skills. A law student, Kirch was also something of a linguist, speaking French and English almost as well as his native German. Because of their complementary temperaments, they made an excellent climbing team.

It was just after midnight when, by the light of the moon, Harlin and Kirch began their long climb up the steep-ridged meadows of Alpiglen, up the shifting rock screes to finally cross the bergschrund and come to the broken ledges of the wall itself. The night was clear and cold, the sky riddled with stars. They now found, as the Italians and Austrians had before them, that the rock was often clad with ice and that it required extreme caution and frequent clearing of holds with the axe, even on the fairly easy Grade-III and Grade-IV pitches on the lower part of the face. Before they reached the Difficult Crack, they heard the sound of voices somewhere below them on the wall—Austrian voices, Kirch said, recognizing the accent. Climbing steadily, they reached the Hinterstoisser at 7 A.M. and were halfway across the traverse on the fixed ropes when a large ice boulder, winging its way down the Rote Fluh, shattered on the face just above Harlin, fragments cannonading against his helmet and shoulders. The mountain artillery had opened up. After a two- or three-minute rest to regain his composure, Harlin continued to lead the traverse, then climbed up the crack to the Swallow's Nest, where both he and Kirch took another brief rest. Then it was out onto the first of the icefields. Harlin had barely edged out to the First Icefield when he was struck on the lower part of the jaw by a small stone that he had not seen coming. The blow was severe enough to cause him to black out for a moment or two. Again shaken, he moved to Kirch's belay to recuperate and get over this second shellshock, as he termed it. Two hits, and they were still only at the bottom of the First Icefield. At the head of the icefield, Kirch led on the rock pitch that went up to and through the Ice Hose. In his account of the climb, Harlin described the rock on this part of the face as "utterly rotten, without a substantial hold in it anywhere."

The Second Icefield proved no easier, with constant rockfall, and the climbing was even riskier because Harlin had forgotten to sharpen the points of his crampons, and they kept skidding off the hard blue ice. As a result he had to cut steps a thousand feet up and across the ice shield instead of front pointing straight up and traversing left on the upper rock hem of the ice. To make matters worse, he lost hold of his ice hammer, lunged for it, and nearly came off. The hammer went bounding and clattering away down the icefield and out into the void below. Kirch now took over the lead, Harlin following on his blunt crampons and using an ice piton to stab balance holds for his hands on the ice wall. The pair eventually reached the bottom of the Flatiron, where they decided it would be too dangerous to climb the buttress at that time of day because of the rockfall from the Spider. They found a small sheltered ledge and waited for the Austrian rope, Nikolaus Rafanowitsch and Hans Hauer, to catch up with them. When they did, all four settled down to have some supper, brew tea, and bivouac for the night.

The next morning, Harlin and Kirch, getting an early start, left the Austrian pair behind and made it to the top of the Flatiron. As they were crossing the Third Icefield, they looked down to the Second Icefield and spotted six climbers coming up the steps that Harlin and Kirch had cut in the ice the day before. Four of the six were Swiss and the other two Austrian; counting Nick and Hans, that now made ten men on the face at the same time. Unknown to Harlin and Kirch, there were yet another six men below the six who were visible, making a total of sixteen on the face on that same day, August 20. The Eigernordwand was threatening to turn into the Hörnli Route on the Matterhorn. However, the last six climbers, including the first Spanish pair to attempt the Nordwand, were forced to withdraw. All six made it safely back down to the foot of the mountain.

Harlin and Kirch reached the Ramp, where, at the head of that cleft, they found the Waterfall Crack completely frozen. Harlin decided to remove his dull crampons rather than trust them to hold on the ice. Then he attacked the ice wall with his hammer and chipped away until he uncovered a piton. He clipped in his rope, used his *étriers* to gain height, then dug out two more spaced pitons into which he again clipped *étriers* and his climbing rope. *Étriers* or stirrups are four-step rope ladders made from nylon tape and used in direct-aid climbing. The ends of two *étriers* are clipped into a piton; then the climber uses each step in the *étrier* to gain sufficient height to let him place a higher piton on the rock. He can now unhook the *étriers,* one at a time, from the lower piton, transfer them to the higher piton, and repeat the process. They are, in effect, short and flexible ladders that enable climbers to ascend sheer rock faces and overhangs not otherwise negotiable.

At the final overhanging bulge of the Waterfall Crack, Harlin managed to nest three pitons into a wide hole, then wedge them in with shards of pointed ice that he broke off the frozen waterfall. Hanging a sling tight into the face and hard over the nest of pitons, he trusted this rather catch-as-catch-can arrangement and clipped his rope into the low end of the sling. Then, belayed by Kirch below him, he managed to surmount the overhang without pulling out the clump of pitons. Soon both men were over the Ice Bulge and moving up the right-hand edge of the Ramp Icefield.

After their long hours of physical effort and mental concentration, and looking ahead at the rocks bounding down across the Traverse of the Gods, they decided to call it a day. They found a tiny ledge at the head of the Brittle Crack and tied themselves into it by looping ropes around a loose limestone block. There was no place to drive in pitons, and with this chancy belay they settled down, ate a supper of sorts, and got into their sleeping bags.

Around midnight they were treated to a spectacular display, a thunderstorm that was approaching the mountain from across the lowlands. Lightning flashes miles away sporadically lit up a rolling and billowing line of clouds. They watched the storm obliterate the lights of Berne, then those of Thun, then the necklace of lights from the chalets ringing Lake Thun. Next Interlaken went dark, and the lights of Grindelwald gradually winked out under the leading edge of clouds. While the storm brought snow, it had fortunately lost much of its intensity by the time it finally reached the Eiger, and the men experienced none of the usual unpleasant side effects of a thunderstorm.

Toward dawn the snow ceased, and the two men left their bivouac and, with Kirch leading, made their way across the Traverse of the Gods. Kirch reached the edge of the Spider and stopped. Behind him Harlin moved up and looked over his rope mate's shoulder. "I was speechless," he said. The left couloir of the Spider was alive with tons of swiftly moving snow. "Does it ever stop?" Harlin asked. Kirch shook his head. Several minutes later the snow dwindled to light periodic washes that a man could stand up against if he had to. Two minutes later another heavy avalanche came roaring down. They timed the heavier ones and found that they seemed to arrive on a two-minute schedule. Harlin looked ahead to a rock rib, a sort of central spine, that ran almost the full length of the Spider. This rib parted the snow into two streams. If they could reach that rocky spine without being peeled off, they should be able to follow it up to the head of the icefield and into the Exit Cracks. The only alternative was to climb the rock bands and chimneys on the left-hand border of the Spider. It had been done twice before, but now the rock was glazed with ice and coated with inches of snow.

Finally Harlin decided to chance it across to the center rib. Borrowing Kirch's ice axe, he ventured out on the icefield, knowing that he had only two minutes to scuttle across to that central spine. The light snow coming down the left couloir was parted by his body, flowing to each side. The fine spindrift rising from the snowslide threatened to suffocate him. He felt he was swimming in the stuff and had to duck his head back and down under his arm to draw a decent breath. Despite these difficulties he kept cutting pigeon-toe steps like mad and reached the rib just as the next heavy avalanche started boiling down. He just had time to bang in a hasty ice piton and snap in a carabiner and his rope. Then Kirch was shouting to him to hold the rope up high. Harlin did so, while Kirch did the same at his stance, trying to keep the tumbling masses of snow from dragging the rope down the couloir and perhaps peeling them both off the face. Some of the snow caught the rope, but they were able to keep it out of the main flow. As soon as the slide dwindled to a trickle, Harlin managed to get the piton placed more securely and yelled at Kirch to come up and across. Despite the lack of an ice axe, Kirch stepped out while Harlin kept the rope taut until Kirch reached him. Kirch now leapfrogged, leading the next pitch up the rib. He was about eighty feet above Harlin when a huge avalanche, the biggest one they'd seen yet, came pouring in a white wave down the Exit Cracks, hit the top of the Spider, and creamed down in a waist-high wall that broke over the central spine. Kirch managed to bang in a shaky ice piton before the snow wall swept over him. Down below, Harlin braced. The torrent of snow hit him, and he held his breath to keep from getting snow in his lungs while he waited for a second shock, Kirch torn from his belay and falling directly down on top of him. The intensity of the snow slackened, there was suddenly clear air to breathe again, and miraculously there was no falling body. Kirch immediately took off, trying to gain as much height as he could before the next avalanche came down. Three rope lengths later they reached the Exit Cracks, iced-up funnels down which compressed plumes of snow were pouring with the regularity of waves breaking on a beach.

Harlin picked a gully and started to lead the next pitch. He reached a ledge, then heard voices below, speaking German. He and Konrad waited to see who the newcomers were. Soon they were joined by the Austrians Felix Kuen and Dieter Wörndl, and a rope of four Swiss— Franz and Josef Jauch, Franz Gnos, and Josef Zurfluh. The six were the same rope Harlin and Kirch had noted the day before, coming up the Second Icefield. Kirch asked about Rafanowitsch and Hauer, the other Austrian pair they had last seen at the foot of the Flatiron, and learned that the newcomers had passed them on the Ramp. The men now decided to try to reach the summit as one party, an international rope of eight—Austrian, Swiss, German, and American. The Austrian pair led off, the four Swiss followed, while Harlin and Kirch brought up the rear.

At the overhang above the Quartz Crack, a pitch that had given Buhl, and Heckmair before him, so much trouble, the climbers ran into difficulties. The Austrians and one of the Swiss got up over the bulge, but the rope was now untied and pulled out of the intermediate runners in order to haul up a sack. The rope hung free, out of reach, and was of little or no use to the next climber, who, however, managed to reach the bulge. Just when it appeared he was going to make it, he came off and fell thirty feet. Although shaken, he immediately tackled the overhang again, and again fell off. He rushed at the pitch a third time. Half-hysterical by now, he once more reached the crux of the overhang and, with water and snow pouring into his face from the lip of the bulge, cried out, "Zug! zug!" ("Pull!"), even though the rope could not be used to help him. Then he fell once more and this time collapsed on the rocks below, moaning that he couldn't climb any more, that his ankle was broken.

The climbers still below the bulge held a conference. There was no way the injured climber could be hauled by the others up to the summit. They would be lucky to make it up by themselves. The only thing to do was to secure the Swiss climber to a stance, leave him with extra clothing and food, then climb up to the peak and seek the help of rescuers in

Left to right: John Harlin, Nikolaus Rafanowitsch, Hans Hauer, and Konrad Kirch after their 1962 climb. Hauer's feet are still swollen from frostbite.

HANS LORENZ PHOTO

lowering a cable down the face, much as had been done for Corti. In fact, they were close to the Corti Bivouac at that point. The Swiss climber now announced, tentatively, that his ankle felt better. Perhaps it wasn't broken after all, perhaps it was only a bad sprain. He tested it and said that perhaps he could get by on it.

Harlin later wrote that he thought the climber had become "exposure crazy," an ailment sometimes marked by incoherence, hysteria, and irrational behavior. It is brought on, some experts feel, by the body's providing too much adrenaline for too long a period of time. The condition is also known as survival madness, or *épuisement* in French. Evidently the Swiss climber and his two companions below the overhang were beginning to fear they would never make it up and off the face.

Hours were lost, and it was midafternoon before Kirch finally took over the lead, surmounted the overhang, and brought Harlin up to his stance. Then the other three, with the aid of a rope that Kirch had fixed back into the runners on his way up, were hauled up to the bulge, one by one. The delay now meant that it would be necessary to spend another night on the face, in weather that had turned sharply colder.

The eight climbers endured a frigid and largely sleepless night, roped and anchored to tiny ledges in the Exit Cracks. Harlin and Kirch, their feet hanging in space, were afraid to go to sleep for fear of frostbite and kept each other awake through the long hours until dawn. To keep the circulation going, they moved their toes inside their boots to a rhythmic chant. In the morning, shivering with cold, they resumed the climb. Kirch took a short fall nearing the head of the Exit Cracks but was unhurt. The Austrian pair, in the lead, unroped from the other six when they reached the Exit Snowfield. The four Swiss, with Harlin and Kirch, reached the summit together a short time later. The sun was shining on the peak, though a thousand feet lower down the clouds covered the whole valley. Harlin felt ecstatic and found beauty in everything he looked at. Even the chips of ice flying from the head of an ice axe looked like diamonds, he later reported in an article he wrote for the *American Alpine Journal*. For John Harlin it was a particularly gratifying climb. The Eiger had loomed in his thoughts ever since he had first begun scrambling over rocks and reading about Alpine faces. And now he was the first American, indeed the first English-speaking climber, to do the dreaded Eigernordwand. He grinned at his German friend. *"Bergheil, Konrad,"* he said. *"Bergheil, John,"* Konrad answered.

Hauer and Rafanowitsch, the other Austrian pair, reached the summit the following evening, but they were suffering from exhaustion and frostbite, and were both hospitalized as a result of their injuries. Harlin and Kirch were also frostbitten, though much less than the others, and Harlin spent several days recuperating in an air-force hospital. At that he was more fortunate than the six other climbers who accompanied him and Kirch to the summit. All had varying degrees of frostbite, and all lost either fingers or toes, with two of the Swiss climbers losing both.

John Harlin snatched the honor of being the first English-speaking climber to do the Nordwand just in time. A week later three English climbers were on the face.

19
Triumph of the Hard Men

Five days after John Harlin and his climbing companions had reached the summit, a Viennese mountaineer, twenty-year-old Diether Marchart, started up the face on the fourth solo attempt. Despite his youth he was one of the best climbers in Austria, and most Eiger experts felt that of all the ones to have so far attempted a solo Eiger climb, he had the best chance of succeeding. Marchart had done the usual variety

of difficult faces, many of them solo, in the eastern Alps, including a
winter climb of the south wall of the Dachstein. He had also been part
of the team to make the first successful ascent of Distaghil Sar, a 21,000-
foot peak in the Himalayas. Perhaps his most impressive achievement
was a solo climb of the north face of the Matterhorn—at the age of nineteen!

Marchart was very modest about his climbing and indeed told no one
back in Austria about his Matterhorn venture until word of the exploit
filtered through the climbing grapevine from Switzerland. At Kleine
Scheidegg he registered under an assumed name, possibly from a natural modesty allied to a fear of being besieged by the press, should reporters get wind of his attempt. The name he signed in the hotel register
was Georg Winkler. Winkler, a fellow Austrian, had been a noted solo
climber in the 1880s, one of the first to prefer climbing alone. Winkler
had started climbing at age thirteen and had over the next few years
made many high standard climbs. Stopped by an unscalable pitch, he
would twirl a grapnellike metal claw around his head and let fly. When
it hooked onto something, he would give a good testing jerk, then start
to climb. He was only seventeen when he fell and was killed on a solo
climb of the Weisshorn in 1887.

Marchart started at first light and overtook a pair of German climbers, Anderl Enzinger and Otto Huber, on the First Icefield. Surprised
by a lone climber, the Bavarians asked Marchart whether he wanted to
tie in on their rope. He thanked them for the offer and said that later
he might, when the climb got a little more difficult. The German pair
wondered who this young solo climber could be. Did he know what he
was attempting? They asked who he was, and where he was from. Ignoring the first question, he said, "Vienna," then climbed on, effectively
ending the conversation. He swiftly moved ahead. Minutes later he was
on the Ice Hose between the First and Second icefields, when something
happened and he fell. His plummeting body knocked Enzinger from his
holds, and the latter fell thirty feet before a piton held him. But there
was no protection for Marchart, and he fell all the way to the base of the
wall. When Enzinger and Huber finally got over the shock, they pulled
themselves together and roped down to report the accident. Diether
Marchart was the third solo climber in a row to be killed on the face, and
the Eiger's twenty-second fatality in all. His body was so badly battered in
the fall that it could be positively identified only because of the twisted

OVERLEAF: (*Left*) *Martin Epp on the face. Note piton placement* (*where rope
changes direction*). (*Right*) *Epp in bivouac on the Traverse of the Gods.*

PAUL ETTER PHOTOS

fingers of his right hand, previously crippled from frostbite on his ascent of Distaghil Sar. He was buried in Grindelwald, just a few plots away from Barry Brewster, who had preceded him in death by only a month. His headstone, bare of any embellishments and compatible with his innate modesty, contains only this simple information: "Diether Marchart. 11–11–39—Wien—27–8–62—Eigernordwand."

Two days later a pair of young Swiss guides, Martin Epp and Paul Etter, started up the regular route, bivouacked at the Traverse of the Gods, and, helped by excellent conditions, reached the top by noon of the following day, August 30. It was another one of those "lightning" climbs that the new generation of Swiss guides were now making on the Eigernordwand and other difficult faces. Etter would be heard from again on the Eiger.

Later in the afternoon on the same day that the Swiss pair started up, a British rope of two, Chris Bonington and Ian Clough, also began climbing the face. They had heard that good weather conditions were to prevail on the Eiger for the next four days. Bonington, it will be recalled, had been on the face a month earlier when he and Don Whillans had abandoned their climb in order to bring Nally back down from the Second Icefield. In fact, Bonington had been on the Eiger as far back as 1957 with a Scottish friend, though they had gone only a few hundred feet up the wall before they turned back. Several years later Bonington had gotten as far as the start of the Hinterstoisser with Don Whillans before bad weather forced them down again. They subsequently both took off for Chamonix, did some climbing, and came back to the Eiger for another go. This time they got as far as the Swallow's Nest and bivouacked for the night. However, the weather was exceptionally warm—too warm, for the Second Icefield was hopping and whizzing with projectiles the next morning. They peered up at it, shook their heads and roped down. In the meadows they were approached by an excited tourist who was convinced that he had seen a climber fall. They followed the man and discovered the near naked body of a climber whose clothes had been shredded off in a long fall, apparently from the northeast ridge, 5,000 feet above. They covered the body and pitifully mangled limbs with a blanket, and swiftly took their leave of Grindelwald.

And now in 1962 Bonington was back, fresh from the first British ascent of the northeast face of the Piz Badile and from a climb of the Walker Spur on the Grandes Jorasses. The morning of their arrival,

Epp leading on the Traverse of the Gods.
PAUL ETTER PHOTO

Bonington and Clough had scurried around in Grindelwald, buying food for the climb and copying the pitch-by-pitch description of the classic route from the back of Heinrich Harrer's book *The White Spider* in a bookstore, while a concerned salesgirl regaled them with horror stories of recent fatalities on the Eigernordwand. They were too poor to buy a copy of the book. Next they found a blacksmith who agreed to sharpen the points of their crampons, lugubriously shaking his head and eyeing them with pity when he heard of their intended destination. After all that it was a relief to get up to the meadows of Alpiglen and have a final brew in the Hotel des Alpes and then head for the wall.

On the way up the lower ledges, Bonington noticed a trail of bloodstains and then a piece of flesh adhering to a rock, grim reminders of Marchart's fall several days previously. He said nothing to Ian Clough, not wanting to upset him. After the climb he found out that Clough had also noticed the bloodstains and had remained silent out of consideration for Bonington's feelings. Despite all these grim omens (bookstore clerk, blacksmith, bloodstains), they climbed to the Bivouac Cave at the top of the Shattered Pillar and there settled down to eat supper, brew some tea, and catch a night's sleep. Soon they heard voices, then saw the rounded helmets and bulging rucksacks of two climbers coming up the broken ledges. The first to arrive was an Austrian, Egon Moderegger. Bonington and Clough were surprised to hear English as the second climber appeared. He was Tom Carruthers, a Scot from Glasgow. Carruthers had been Nally's partner in their successful climb of the Matterhorn's north face the summer before. He had been unable to find another English-speaking partner to try the Eigernordwand with him, but then had been introduced to a young Austrian who was staying in the Hotel des Alpes and who said he had done his climbing in the eastern Alps and in the Caucasus. Despite the language difficulties—Carruthers spoke no German, and Moderegger no English—the two men decided to team up for a try at the Nordwand. Clough and Bonington were dubious about the idea of taking a partner whose climbing skills were unknown, and especially one with whom communication would be difficult because of the language barrier.

Later there were those who wondered why Carruthers hadn't paired up with his old partner Nally on the latter's attempt with Brewster a month earlier. But then climbing partners are always splitting up and recombining. Partnerships like those of Harlin and Kirch and of Terray and Lachenal are unusual. Nor is this seeking of new partners necessarily a bad thing. Climbers learn their skills not only on rocks and ice, but also from other climbers, and the greater the range of partners one can team up with, the greater the number of potential teachers one can learn from.

At five the next morning Clough and Bonington started off from the Bivouac Cave. There was no talk of roping up with Carruthers and Moderegger, who had bivouacked nearby. If the latter pair climbed with the same skill and at the same pace as Clough and Bonington, then perhaps all four could form a single rope at the Flatiron or on the Ramp. But it was better to first determine the relative skills of the climbers.

And indeed Carruthers and Moderegger soon fell behind the more experienced British pair, who now began to tackle the first real difficulties on "the frightening cruel vastness of this notorious wall," as Clough was later to write. Fortunately, the night before, the weather had been quite cold, which meant little or no rockfall until midafternoon at the earliest.

Bonington and Clough put away the Difficult Crack with ease and found the Hinterstoisser free of ice. They were able to climb the sloping slabs of rock on the edge of the First Icefield, because the ice had receded and it was a matter of scrambling up on ribs and shoulders of bare rock sticking up through the ice. Even the Ice Hose was free of ice and presented a straightforward rock climb. The Second Icefield, however, posed problems. The old blue ice forming the subfloor of the icefield was as tough as cement, and their crampons had a tendency to skid off as they tried to cut steps.

They decided to go directly up the icefield on front points, employing ice axe and ice dagger. They kept the pitches short, to rest their aching calves and the better to hold a possible fall. So far the Spider was still quiescent—there was only a negligible amount of rockfall to contend with—and they reached the top of the Second Icefield before midmorning. They traversed across the top of the Second Icefield to the stance where Nally had held Brewster's fall. Here a piton was brutally twisted and bent out of shape, evidence of the tremendous shock it had taken. A brief rest, and they both agreed that they should try and reach the Ramp before the Spider began belching and coughing debris down from the heights. They reached the top of the Flatiron, moved up to Death Bivouac, and then looked back and down to see what progress Carruthers and Moderegger were making. At first they couldn't find them, but they finally picked up two tiny dots just venturing out onto the Second Icefield. They were so small and moving so slowly as to be almost indistinguishable from rocks embedded in the ice. It was clear that, instead of front pointing straight up, they were going to cut steps across the long diagonal traverse. Bonington and Clough shouted and waved at them to cut straight up the icefield, but they were too far away to hear. At the rate they were going, they would be caught out in the middle of the icefield, or on the Flatiron, during the period of heaviest rockfall. But there was nothing the British pair could do, and, after a short rest, they regretfully moved on. They saved some time by doing a tension traverse across the head of the Third Icefield, then started up the Ramp. As usual the Eiger began brewing up its own weather, independently of Zurich meteorologists. Wisps of fog began trailing across the face, hiding the climbers from the telescope watchers below. Anyway, the Eiger voyeurs had a much more interesting situation to follow in the agonizingly slow progress of Moderegger and Carruthers on the Second Icefield.

The Waterfall Crack turned out to belie its name, for no water came down, although the rocks were all covered with verglas. Bonington and Clough got up it—"one of the hardest pitches on the climb," Clough was to call it—then mastered the Ice Bulge above. Emerging on the Ramp Snowfield, they were surprised to hear voices on the rocks above. They had been unaware that anyone else was on the face ahead of them. At the top of the Brittle Band, they caught up with two young Swiss climbers, Werner Hausheer and Paul Jenny. One of them had been hit by a stone, although the injury wasn't too serious. Because of that and the fact that it was almost five o'clock, the Swiss pair had decided to bivouac for the night. In a brief conversation, conducted in broken English, Bonington discovered that the two were rather inexperienced. One claimed to have trained for the Eiger by cycling to work every day during the winter! After ascertaining that the Swiss didn't want to go any farther that day, Bonington and Clough decided to push on. They even considered the idea of reaching the summit before dark. But now the sun was shining on the upper part of the mountain, although thick, billowing clouds covered the whole bottom part of the face and the valley below. The huge walls, incarnadined by the late-afternoon sun, rearing above and plunging down into cloud below, exhilarated both climbers. Clough was to say that he understood why the Traverse of the Gods had earned its name, because he had felt like a veritable god himself, picking his airy way across the downward-sloping slabs of loose scree on the traverse.

They reached the Spider without mishap. Bonington had barely edged out onto the icefield and had cut only a couple of steps on his way across to the central rib that John Harlin had used to such good effect, when a roar above caused him to look up. An avalanche of rockfall came bounding down the Exit Cracks. He skipped back to Clough at his belay stance on the traverse. A dozen huge blocks went bucketing by, like a string of London buses heading for the garage. The blocks and the attendant train of debris shot down over the lower rim of the Spider and

Chris Bonington leading out on the Spider.

IAN CLOUGH PHOTO

whirred out into the void. Considerably shaken, both climbers listened to the dull, whumping thud and rumble of the rocks striking the face, the Flatiron, then the Second Icefield. Bonington looked at his watch. It was approximately 5:15. They were to remember that particular rockfall later.

Then and there they decided to wait until morning before going out on the Spider again. The late-afternoon sun was obviously playing hob with the rotten rock on the upper third of the face. At the other end of the traverse, they could see two red dots that they knew were the anoraks of their Swiss friends. They found a tiny, somewhat protected ledge, banged in anchoring pitons, and scratched around for some snow to melt down for tea. They managed a good supper and were even able to catch a catnap now and again in between long conversations about various climbs they had done in the British Isles and the Alps. The Eiger night went by on its usual leaden feet, but dawn brought a welcome surprise, clear skies and perfect climbing weather.

The Spider was as quiet as a lamb as they worked the clumsiness and cold out of their bodies by a bout of sustained step cutting across to the central rib, then up to the start of the Exit Cracks, five full rope lengths, or about 750 feet. The English pair were now the focus of early-morning Eiger watchers down in the valley. At first Bonington and Clough took the wrong gully upward and, unintentionally, caused great excitement at Kleine Scheidegg, where the rumor quickly spread that the British team was putting up a new direct line to the summit.

By now Hausheer and Jenny had caught up with Bonington and Clough, and Bonington pulled the two Swiss up to his stance. However, he could now clearly see that he and Clough had taken the wrong line and would have to rope back down. They should have followed an ice-choked gully to their left. He explained this to the Swiss climbers and told them that he and his partner were going to abseil down and start up the proper gully. The young Swiss dumbfounded the English pair when they confessed not knowing how to abseil. They were shown the technique by Clough, who wanted to know what they thought they were doing on the Eiger if they didn't know how to rappel. One of the Swiss excused himself by saying that he had been climbing for less than a year. Clough and Bonington later agreed that the Exit Cracks on the Eiger's north wall was hardly the place to teach, or learn for that matter, one of

---

Werner Hausheer and Paul Jenny on the Second Icefield. Photo taken from the Flatiron.

PAUL ETTER PHOTO

the most elementary of rock-climbing techniques—the rappel. Somehow the Swiss climbers "rapped" down, and this time Bonington and Clough led up the right gully, the Swiss following on a separate rope. Gradually the snow and ice ran out, and the route turned into a straightforward rock climb. The British climbers were surprised. Could this have been the section that had caused Heckmair, and later Buhl, so much trouble? But they realized, too, that conditions were everything on the Eiger, and the conditions for their climb had been excellent; there had not even been an afternoon storm. "We were lucky to have it so easy," Clough wrote, with typical English understatement, in an article in the British *Alpine Journal.* "Chris Bonington and I had a smooth uneventful climb in perfect weather and conditions." Despite this, Bonington said, he had never been on a climb with such a grim atmosphere.

They reached the summit in early afternoon, carved out a nice broad step, and sat down to munch dried fruit and enjoy the view, delighted with themselves. When they saw the Swiss pair reach the head of the Exit Snowfield, they decided that Hausheer and Jenny were clear of danger and that they themselves could take off down the west flank. About the time they reached Kleine Scheidegg, Hausheer and Jenny reached the summit, marking the thirty-second ascent.

The pair of English climbers were soon seated at a good dinner in a Kleine Scheidegg dining room, sharing a bottle of wine in honor of their triumph, the first British climbers to do the Eigernordwand. Indeed their achievement, plus the exploits of Joe Brown and Tom Patey who were climbing half a dozen other Grade-VI Alpine peaks that same summer, gave notice that British climbers had suddenly shouldered their way into the top rank of Alpine mountaineers, thus recovering a prestige that British climbing had not enjoyed since the turn of the century. The "dangle-and-whack" boys had arrived.

Bonington and Clough had little time to share that triumph, however, because Fritz von Almen came over to them and said that two bodies had been spotted at the bottom of the wall. Did the British pair by any chance know who they were? Surely it couldn't be Jenny and Hausheer, they thought, and then remembered Carruthers and Moderegger on the Second Icefield.

"We were shattered, sick with pity," Clough wrote. "Tom Carruthers and his Austrian partner were dead." Bonington said, "Even in those seemingly perfect conditions, the Eiger had made its claim."

Moderegger and Carruthers had been lost to the telescope watchers by the mist and cloudlets that had come racing across the face the preceding afternoon. When last spotted, they were not yet halfway across the Second Icefield and climbing very slowly. It was estimated that it would have taken them eight hours to cut steps the whole way across and up to the base of the Flatiron, as opposed to the two hours or less that it had taken Clough and Bonington to front point straight up and then to traverse across. Moreover, Carruthers and Moderegger were on the Second Icefield during what some climbers called rush hour—i.e., the period of heaviest stone fall. When the bodies were recovered, Clough learned that Carruthers's watch had stopped at 5:15, and he remembered the heavy rock slide that he and Bonington had watched, with awe, come thundering down the Spider at just about that time the preceding afternoon. More than likely that same rock avalanche had swept Carruthers and Moderegger off the ice and to their deaths.

Clough was later critical of both Carruthers's and Nally's attempts to climb the wall, saying that both teams had lacked the necessary skill and experience for the Eiger. "The cause of both accidents was the same (rockfall on the Second Icefield). It wasn't just bad luck. Both parties were slow, mainly on account of errors in route finding and judgment." He went on to claim that both pairs lacked enough experience of big-mountain climbs. He noted that the Eiger, vast and complex, was a rigorous test of judgment and skill, for the Alpinist a logical progression, a sort of graduate school, the mountaineer's Ph.D. But he also blamed the press for turning the Eiger into a media circus, an arena bathed in spotlights where young men, blinded by the glare and glamour of publicity and TV cameras, tried to make a name for themselves by premature attempts on the Ogre. "Some get up, but the roll of honor is long," he wrote.

When Hausheer got down off the summit, he was met by the police, who had been contacted by telephone by the young climber's parents, in Davos, with the news that their son had left behind a note saying that he intended to climb the Eiger—a note that bothered them very much because, you see, Werner was not a mountain climber. The indignant Hausheer insisted that he *was* a climber. Had he not just conquered the infamous Eigernordwand? What other climbs had he accomplished? the police wanted to know. "I did a wall near Davos," he said. "It was good training for the Eiger." The police asked for the name of the wall. "Oh, it was too small to have a name," Hausheer airily replied. Hausheer's climb, too, set some sort of a record, an Eigernordwand climb by the youth with the least amount of climbing experience.

There was also that film crew parked at Kleine Scheidegg. What role did it play in encouraging attempts on the Nordwand? Whatever the role of the media, before the 1962 season was over, another five ascents were made. On one of those climbs a pair of Swiss climbers, Claude Asper and Bernard Voltolini, found the desiccated remains of Karl Mehringer on the Second Icefield, twenty-seven years after his death.

Altogether, 1962 saw forty-four climbers who stood in the bright light of the Eigergipfel (Eiger summit), including the first Italians, the first American, and the first Britons to do the climb. However, there were also five casualties—five who fell into permanent darkness.

20
The Eiger Solo

On July 30, 1963, three separate ropes were on the face at the same time. Two Austrians from Salzburg, Max Friedwanger and Friedl Schicker, had started up the day before, as had Douglas Haston of Scotland and Robert (Rusty) Baillie of Rhodesia. While both pairs were climbing separately, but in long-range sight of each other, a third pair of climbers, who had started up the face when it was yet dark that morning, were climbing with great speed and assurance. The last team to start and the first to finish consisted of two young Swiss bergsteigers, Arnold Heinen and Erich Friedli. The latter was the son of the Erich Friedli who had been in charge of the Thun Swiss rescue team on the summit at the time of the Longhi disaster, and who had been one of the four men lowered down the face on a steel cable. Heinen and Friedli opened a new variant at the head of the Flatiron. Instead of dropping down to bridge across to the Ramp via the Third Icefield, they did a rock traverse above the icefield itself, a route that called for exquisite Grade-VI+skills in rock climbing. They reached the Ramp, then moved quickly through the other Eiger way stations—the Waterfall Pitch, the Ice Bulge, the Brittle Ledge. They now moved across the *Götterquergang,* to give that godly traverse its German name, then bivouacked for the night. They reached the summit the following morning, making the thirty-eighth ascent and another lightning climb by Swiss guides.

Meanwhile Dougal Haston and Rusty Baillie were trying to become the second British team to do the Eiger north face. Haston, a dropout philosophy student from the University of Edinburgh, had started his climbing while still a teenager, on local stonework railway bridges. He graduated to rock cliffs, reinvented pitons (six-inch nails) and climbing ropes (clothesline), then joined a climbing club and eventually became one of the best snow and ice climbers in a school of Scottish mountaineers who were probably the top all-around ice climbers in Europe.

Haston had been to the Eiger in the summer of 1960 when he and his partner Jim (Eley) Moriarty, having just done the west face of Cima Ovest in the Dolomites, decided to try the Eigernordwand. They climbed to just under the Difficult Crack before they ran into a thunderstorm, got thoroughly drenched, bivouacked, and found everything snow covered in the morning. They turned back. In 1962 Haston returned to Grindelwald after he and his partner, Andy Wightman, had been harried off the north face of the Matterhorn by bad weather. They bivouacked below the Difficult Crack and got as far as the head of the Flatiron the following day. Ahead of them, dotted along the Ramp, was a party of six Italians, in the process of making the first Italian ascent of the face. That night a hailstorm deluged their bivouac, and the two climbers, facing bad weather and knowing they would have trouble passing the slow-moving Italian rope of six, regretfully decided to retreat. Soaked to the skin, they made it back down both icefields and across the Hinterstoisser with no more than the usual slips and frights. They rappelled down the Difficult Crack and, thus being unroped, decided to stay that way for the last thousand feet of broken ledges. They hadn't progressed more than a hundred feet when Wightman fell. For a moment it looked as though his unbelayed body would go all the way to the bottom of the face. Scrabbling with hands and feet, however, Wightman managed to stop his fall on a ledge 150 feet below his partner. When Haston reached him, Wightman had a deep cut on his face, and then discovered that he had a broken ankle. Two Italian climbers, Nando Nusdeo and Luigi Alippi from Lecco, appeared from a nearby site where they were preparing to bivouac, and helped Haston get Wightman back up the wall to the Gallery Window. The Italian pair fixed a double rope in the *Stollenloch* opening for Haston and Wightman. The last pitch was accomplished by climbing up the rope, as Wightman, seated on Haston's shoulders, provided the hand power and Haston the leg power—a sort of two-man mountain climber. Once inside the tunnel, Haston and the two Italians took turns carrying Wightman back up to the Eigerwand Station, where they all spent the night and took the first train down in the morning. Wightman duly recovered in the hospital in Interlaken, and Haston returned to Scotland.

Now, in 1963, after several strenuous weeks of climbing in the Dolomites, he was back paying court to the Ogre. He and Rusty Baillie started up the face on the afternoon of August 29 and bivouacked close to the Gallery Window. The next morning they were passed by the Salzburg pair, Friedwanger and Schicker, who took over the lead on the iced-over slabs of the First Icefield. They startled Haston and Baillie by going the full runout of their rope without putting in any intermediate pitons, which meant a potential fall of more than 200 feet if the leader came off. In truth, pitons were almost impossible to place on the slabs, and Haston and Baillie soon found this out. However, they also made it up without incident and on the way met a lone Italian climber who had evidently changed his mind about doing a solo and was on his way down. The climber said hello and passed on. Haston and Baillie crossed the Second Icefield in two hours and climbed the Flatiron, where they found the Austrians already in residence. The British pair bivouacked nearby and, next morning, climbed along with the Austrian pair. All four moved up the Ramp, and Haston and Baillie tackled the Waterfall Crack while Friedwanger and Schicker, to save time, took to the Terray Variant. The British climbers, after a slight bit of trouble, surmounted the pitch. Then they heard Friedwanger calling for help. Although he stood on Schicker's shoulders, Friedwanger was still six feet short of finishing the variant. Haston dropped a rope, which the Austrians gratefully used to get them up the last few feet. The Ice Bulge, the Ramp Snowfield, and the Brittle Band were duly put away and the quartet gingerly crossed the protection-poor Traverse of the Gods. "What a ledge this is!" Haston was to write. "Only Grade III but 4,000 sobering feet on your right keeps the delight within bounds. Orgies of phototaking ensued."

When they reached the Spider, the snowfield was alive with debris; so the four decided to bivouac for the night at the end of the traverse. A meal was prepared, tea brewed up, and three of the climbers kept highly amused by the antics of Max Friedwanger trying to fertilize the Second Icefield below while hanging from the end of a rope. The next morning was frigid cold, the Spider still asleep, and the Exit Cracks armed with verglas. They had just started up when they were overtaken by Heinen and Friedli, who sportingly thanked them for the ladder of cut-out steps on the Spider. The Swiss pair pushed on ahead. Haston and Baillie had a little trouble at the Quartz Crack, but they finally came out on the Exit Snowfield and found the ice, now warmed by sunlight, treacherously soft and mushy. But, climbing cautiously, they reached the summit by midafternoon and speedily made their way down the west flank to the delights of Kleine Scheidegg.

Haston would return to the Eiger a couple of years later, to take part in one of its most famous climbs. However, Erich Friedli, who with Heinen had made the thirty-eighth ascent, was not so fortunate. The following year he was killed while doing a winter climb on the north face of the Gletscherhorn in his native Bernese Alps.

The day before Haston and Baillie started their climb, one of Italy's best climbers, indeed one of the world's best, had come to the Eiger. Walter Bonatti had been everywhere and done everything in mountaineering circles, including participating in the 1954 Italian expedition that had made the first successful ascent of K-2, the world's second-highest mountain. In 1958 he climbed Gasherbrum IV, a 26,000-foot peak in the Karakorum. On K-2 he and his Pakistani porter survived what had been up to then the world's highest bivouac (26,200 feet). It was a record later eclipsed by an American bivouac at 28,000 feet on Mount Everest. Bonatti's list of credits was a yard long, with a score of first ascents, including the first winter ascents of the Brenva Face of Mont Blanc, and the Tre Cime di Lavaredo. When only nineteen he did the second ascent of the northwest face of Piz Badile. In a four-day climb with Luciano Ghigo, he did the first ascent of the east face of the Grand Capuchin in Chamonix. He did the first ascent of the Red Pillar of Brouillard on Mont Blanc, and a new route on the Furggen Ridge of the Matterhorn. Oddly enough, his most famous climb was a failure, a week-long, storm-bound attempt on the Freney Pillar of Mont Blanc, along with his climbing partners Andrea Oggioni and Roberto Galleni. The Italians joined with a four-man French rope of Pierre Mazeaud, Antoine Vielle, Roberto Guillarme, and Pierre Kohlman. They were all storm bound on three tiny ledges well up on the face by a six-day snowstorm. Kohlman was struck by lightning and temporarily paralyzed. They eventually retreated, rappelling down the face in nightmare conditions. At one point Bonatti, at the end of a 300-foot rappel, barely made it to a small knob under an overhang, only to have the rappel rope snatched out of his hands, leaving him alone without a rope on a cliff with no possibility of retreat. Fortunately the next man down on the rappel was able to get him off. Crossing a glacier to the Gamba hut, Oggioni, nearly dead from exhaustion, went into a trance and seemed unable to move. Next Vielle died in his steps. Kohlman wept at his friend's death, then a short time later became violent, attacking Galleni and Bonatti in turn. The latter two, stumbling and falling repeatedly in the waist-deep snow, finally made it to the Gamba hut late that night. Bonatti told the climbers who were overnighting in the hut to go out and search for his comrades. They found only Mazeaud alive—Oggioni, Vielle, and Kohlman having died from exhaustion.

And now, two years later, the press and the Eiger watchers had something to look forward to, the great Walter Bonatti doing the first solo climb of the Eigernordwand. It was to be the fifth attempt at a solo, and if anyone could succeed, it would surely be Bonatti. On August 28 he started up and bivouacked that night at the Swallow's Nest, where he found a stack of pitons and a rucksack full of food and equipment, probably belonging to the Austrians Friedwanger and Schicker who were to start their climb the following day.

The next morning Bonatti had no sooner set out on the First Icefield than a thundering salvo of boulders chased him back to the Swallow's Nest. Unfortunately the night had been warm, which meant that loose rock hadn't been frozen in place overnight. He started out again, successfully negotiated the icefield, then the Ice Hose, and was soon cutting steps across the Second Icefield. He was on a particularly delicate rock rib sticking through the ice when he felt the rock underneath his hands and feet start to vibrate, and a loud humming sound fill the air. He thought first of an airplane and looked up the icefield, veiled here and there with trailing wisps of fog. The throb grew louder, the vibration worse, then an incredible sight filled his field of vision. A huge black mass was blotting out the icefield, growing larger and larger, seeming to explode just before it reached him. There was no way he could dodge to either side, there was just too much rock coming down, some boulders being the size of automobiles. He flattened himself against the rib as huge blocks and smaller shards of rock and ice went thundering and chittering and screaming past him. The acrid smell of burst limestone filled his nostrils as he waited for the inevitable rock that would smash him loose from his stance. It came, a rock that struck his back and drove the breath from his body. "An intolerable pain spread through my chest, a horrible sensation as though my thorax were melting," he later wrote in *The Great Days,* a book about his climbing experiences.

Yet somehow he was still alive, still clinging to the rock rib, and the rock slide had ceased. He brushed pebbles and sand away from in front of his face, then cautiously moved his legs upward. With every movement pain seared his back. He now noticed that his climbing rope was cut halfway through. He retrieved his rucksack from the rope. One of his arms began to hurt intolerably as he tried to move off the icefield and out of the line of fire. The fog grew heavier and it began to rain. Very slowly, in great pain, he made his way to a boulder behind which he hoped to shelter. When he reached the place, he scraped out a sit-down platform with his ice axe and collapsed, still half-dazed from pain and shock. He realized, of course, that he would have to retreat. Even if his injuries turned out to be less serious than he thought, he was in no psychological state to continue on a wall like the Eiger, where a climber needed every bit of self-control he possessed. The afternoon wore on, and still he rested there, wondering what to do. He could visualize the headlines: "Bonatti Plucked from Eiger by Local Guides." He didn't want that. But could he continue his retreat unaided? The whole face was streaming with water, and there was still plenty of rockfall coming down. He finally decided to bivouac where he was for that night and hope for better conditions and renewed strength in the morning.

The next day was brilliantly clear and sufficiently cold to reduce rockfall to a negligible factor. The air in the valley below him was crystal clear. The woods shimmered in the sunlight, and the people were already sitting out and sunning themselves in the terraces around Kleine Scheidegg. Wet slate roofs gave off gauzy vapors as they dried in the sun. The clanging of those enormous brass bells worn by the local cows rose up to him. The crackety-clackety sound was the rack railway train creeping up from Grindelwald, and the high peremptory whistle, just short of a scream, he knew to be a rock marmot's alarm.

He got his ropes ready for a series of rappels. At first the pain in his back was almost unbearable. But gradually he got used to it, and by the time he met Haston and Baillie, at the bottom of the First Icefield, he knew he could get down off the face unaided and therefore said nothing about his ordeal of the day before. It would hardly serve as a warning. Compared to how it had behaved yesterday, the mountain today seemed in a deep sleep; everything—ice, water, rock—frozen into place.

Below the Rote Fluh he saw some bleached-out bones deep in a crack and wondered what unfortunate climber had lost his life there. Then he was down off the face and talking to reporters, one of whom quoted Bonatti as saying of his ordeal, "No mountain is worth a man's life."

When Bonatti got to a doctor and had his chest and back x-rayed, he was found to have a broken rib, in addition to a number of deep bruises and contusions. Because Bonatti made so little of his ordeal on the face, there were whispers that he had lost his nerve for solo climbing. The Eiger, combined with the tragic Freney Pillar climb of two years before, had taken the heart out of him, or so it was said.

Bonatti answered these critics when, two years later, on the hundredth anniversary of the first ascent of the Matterhorn, he did the first direct of the mountain's north face—solo—in the dead of winter, on February 22! He spent a total of ninety-four hours on the wall, in temperatures down to thirty below zero. In effect, he climbed the face three times, using a self-belay system that meant two ascents and one descent of the route.

Whatever the disappointment in Italy, and among Bonatti fans everywhere, over his failure to solo the Eiger, one young Swiss climber was relieved. Michel Darbellay, a twenty-nine-year-old guide from the Swiss ski resort of Martigny, not too far over the border from Chamonix, had arrived at Kleine Scheidegg with his own plans for a solo climb of the Nordwand. He told no one—press or friends—of his resolve, except the hotel proprietor Fritz von Almen and his wife. It was to be the sixth attempt to do a solo of the Nordwand. Three of those earlier solo aspirants had died on the wall (Mayr, Derungs, Marchart), and one, Nothdurft, who had turned back, had perished after a successful Eiger climb with his partner. Of the five contenders to date, only Bonatti remained alive, and he had only gone as far as the Second Icefield.

Darbellay had been to the Eiger before, the previous summer, with his partner Loulou Boulaz, when both had gotten as high as the Ramp before being forced back by bad weather. But now he had come to the Eiger alone, and, in the waning hours of August 1, he readied his equipment: a hundred feet of rope, eight rock and three ice pitons, a thermos of lemon tea, packets of dried fruit and meat, an ice hammer and ice axe, crampons, and a helmet, but, strangely enough, no bivouac sack.

He evidently hoped to do the climb nonstop. He left Kleine Scheidegg in the early hours of August 2 and hiked across the meadows and screes at the foot of the wall. A full moon was casting plenty of light, which helped him on the broken rocks and scree-covered ledges of the lower part of the face. He climbed steadily, did the Difficult Crack and several pitches above it, then heard voices that kept getting louder. At the start of the Hinterstoisser he overtook two German climbers, Eckert Gundelach from Wasserburg and Dieter Zelnhefer from Nürnberg. They asked whether he was alone, and Darbellay answered yes. Then they asked where he was from, and he told them. They asked whether he wanted to tie in with them, and he declined. "Alone, then?" they asked.

"Yes."

"To the summit?"

"Yes."

"Well, then, good luck," they called after Darbellay as he climbed on

Michel Darbellay.

past. At that point he no doubt recalled that the solo climber Diether Marchart had met and passed two climbers not far away, on the First Icefield, moments before he had come off and fallen to his death.

In midmorning Fritz von Almen looked for Michel through his telescope. There was no one on the Hinterstoisser. He moved his circular field of view up a hair. Perhaps the First Icefield? No, but then, yes, there was someone climbing the Ice Hose between the First and Second icefields. That had to be Michel, except that there was a rope hanging down from the man's waist, running through his legs to a second climber. It was Gundelach and Zelnhefer moving at their own slow but steady pace. Again Almen moved the telescope, traversing his instrument slowly back and forth across the Second Icefield. No one. Could Michel have reached the Flatiron already? But there was no one on the Flatiron. He made a careful pitch-by-pitch search of the Flatiron's top and flanks. Against the dark rocks, it would be easy to miss the tiny figure of a human. But there was no sign of the Swiss climber. Surely he hadn't reached the Third Icefield already? In swinging the telescope up and over to that section, Almen caught movement on the lower end of the Ramp. Yes, there was a lone climber there, and it had to be Michel.

The small black figure was climbing down, obviously on a self-belay move, then climbing back up again. A solo climber, on difficult pitches, has to cover the distance three times, twice ascending and once descending. At the start of such a pitch, he will bang in a solid piton into which he ties the end of his climbing rope, the rest of the rope being looped over his shoulders. He then pays out rope as he climbs, knocking in intermediate pitons for protection. When he has gone the length of the pitch, he ties off his rope to a piton and then descends the fixed rope to his original position. Here he unties the beginning of the rope, knots it to his harness, and collects all the intermediate pitons, slings, and carabiners as he either prusiks, jumars, or climbs up to his new stance. It's a time-consuming but necessary series of maneuvers if one hopes to survive a fall.

Darbellay was slowed somewhat at the Waterfall Crack, where he took the Terray Variant up the dry rocks and onto the Ramp Snowfield. Soon he was spotted balancing his way across the Traverse of the Gods. He reached the Spider by midafternoon. The Eiger experts were consumed with curiosity. Would he, knowing that the Spider was supposedly at its worst in late afternoon, bivouac where he was for the night? If he ventured out on that steep shooting gallery and got knocked from his holds, he would have no belay partner to arrest his fall. And even self-belay with ice pitons was poor protection compared to a piton driven into rock.

Incredulous watchers saw a black dot move out onto the icefield and front point swiftly upward, covering 700 feet in half an hour! Once in a while a stream of white smoke would plume out from the top of the Spider, a snow avalanche going down the chute, but fortunately there was little rockfall. The black dot kept moving upward and then was off the icefield and into the security, however doubtful, of the overhanging bulges and fissured ribs of the Exit Cracks. There were still some hours of daylight left, and the big question at Kleine Scheidegg was whether the young Swiss guide would attempt to reach the summit before dark, perhaps to bivouac up there and come down the west flank in the morning.

But Darbellay was tired, and tired men make mistakes. He had no intention of becoming another victim of the White Spider. He stopped at a ledge just above the Corti platform, tied himself in securely to an anchor piton, and ate his prepared food. It was 7:30. At 9:30 he began to signal Fritz von Almen with his flashlight that all was well. Almen's torch winked back, almost eagerly, it seemed. The hotel proprietor had been waiting, with growing anxiety, for the signal that was supposed to come from the wall at 9:00 P.M. Darbellay's watch, it turned out, was half an hour slow.

Alternately dozing and waking, humming and singing snatches of song to keep his spirits up, Darbellay got through the long night. Below him the two Germans were ensconced at Death Bivouac.

At first light in the morning Darbellay stood up, working some agility back into his cramped legs, then rappelled down thirty feet to rejoin the original line from which he had departed to reach his ledge. Climbing slowly to work out the kinks, he started up an ice gully. Several hours later he climbed the Summit Snowfield and stood on top of the Eiger. It was 8 A.M. The sun was shining, and down at the Kleine Scheidegg two minuscule dots were waving a white sheet back and forth to signal him and share his triumph. Not only was Darbellay the first to do a solo of the Eigernordwand, he had climbed it in eighteen hours (excluding the hours spent in the bivouac), the same length of time it had taken Waschak and Forstenlechner. It was a remarkable achievement for a solo climber, one of the most brilliant climbs yet on the Eiger's north wall.

Darbellay took off his helmet and set it on the snow at his feet, then lifted his tired face to the early morning sun. At that altitude it felt quite strong, seeming to warm even his bones. He moved one foot, then watched, with tired surprise, his helmet go rolling down the Summit Snowfield to finally lose itself in the abyssal depths below, a final tribute, a symbolic sacrifice to the wall. He stared after the helmet a long moment, then turned and started down the west flank.

Hailed all over Europe for his feat, Darbellay was especially acclaimed in his native Switzerland. The days of stolid, cautious Swiss guides leading "ladies and lords" with their picnic hampers, were evidently gone for good. The Swiss guides now were at least equal to, if not better than, mountaineers anywhere in Europe, or the world for that matter. Darbellay had set the standard of achievement for a series of skillful, swift climbs of the Eiger and other Alpine and Himalayan routes by a new generation of Swiss guides.

Darbellay later reported that he had found the head of the Ramp the most difficult pitch, and the Ice Hose the next hardest. He was not hit by any rocks; nor did he suffer any falls. He reported no ill effects from the climb, beyond being extremely tired the next day.

On the same day that Darbellay came down from the summit, a German rope of two from Munich, Helmut Salger and Horst Wels, were at the bottom of the Second Icefield after an overnight bivouac at the Swallow's Nest. Here they met Gundelach and Zelnhefer, who had turned back, not liking the changed weather conditions. The Munich pair, however, climbed on, through a bad thunderstorm that brought hail and snow, and reached the summit at 7 P.M. Then they climbed back down the Mittellegi Ridge to the Mittellegi hut, where they took shelter for the night. This may have been what Uli Wyss and Karl Gonda had started to do when they had been carried away by a Summit Snowfield avalanche ten years before. The next day Wels and Salger were back down in Grindelwald. It was the forty-second climb of the Eigernordwand.

The same day that Darbellay started his climb, two Spaniards set up their tent at the foot of the wall. A week later they embarked on a climb that was to be all too reminiscent of Mehringer and Sedlmayer's tragic attempt.

21
An Excess of Courage

On August 11, 1963, a pair of Spanish climbers, Alberto Rabada, twenty-nine, and Ernesto Navarro, twenty-eight, both from the province of Aragon, men whose climbing experience had been largely confined to the Spanish and French Pyrenees, began to climb up the broken ledges at the bottom of the wall. Since the 1930s, Catalonia had been the home and main base of Spanish mountaineering, its Barcelona club, *El Grupo de Alta Montaña*, the most prestigious climbing club in Spain. The area to the north of Barcelona was generously supplied with the mountains of the eastern Pyrenees, and the Alps were but a moderate rail journey from the Spanish-French border.

In the late 1950s and early 1960s another climbing group came to prominence in Aragon, that region of hard, tenacious peasants. Foremost among the Aragonese climbers were Rabada and Navarro, who put up many impressive new routes in the Pyrenees. They had come to Grindelwald in the beginning of August, determined to snatch for Aragon the distinction of supplying the climbers who would make the first Spanish ascent of the Eigernordwand. In fact the climbers' own club, *Los Montañeros de Aragón,* had underwritten most of the expenses of their trip. Regional loyalty seems to be fiercer in Spain than anywhere else, witness the Catalans, the Basques, the Castilians. The Aragonese are equally proud of their province and have a reputation for being stubbornly cocksure of themselves, even arrogant. A Spanish wit once said of the Aragonese that they practiced "all things in excess, except moderation."

Rabada and Navarro soon met two other teams, a Japanese pair, Daihachi Okura and Mitsuhiko Yoshin, both from Yokohama and both trying to be the first of their nationality to scale the face, and another pair of exceptionally strong Italian climbers, Roberto Sorgato and Ignazio Piussi, who had their eye on doing the first direct of the Eiger's north face.

Watching the three parties from his tent in the Alpiglen meadows was John Harlin, who had returned to the scene of his earlier triumph with the idea of adding another Eiger first, the direct, to his record. But John had only one climbing partner with him, Stew Fulton, and he felt it would take at least three to do a direct. He had been hoping for the arrival of Tom Frost or Gary Hemming. Konrad Kirch, his old partner, had other business that summer. Harlin was about to suggest to the two Italians that they team up with him and Fulton for a try at a direct when, during a temporary break in the weather, the Italian pair took off up the wall, unbeknownst to Harlin.

That morning he watched the three teams work their zigzag way up the lower reaches of the wall. The Spanish and Japanese pairs following the normal route were of less interest to him. It was the Italian rope he was most concerned about. He had no desire to see them claim the honor of being the first to do an Eiger direct.

The three teams, on separate ropes, climbed steadily that day, then bivouacked for the night, the Japanese at the Swallow's Nest and the Spaniards at the bottom of the Second Icefield. The Italians were bivouacked well over to the east, near the direct line of Sedlmayer and Mehringer. The next morning the three teams resumed their climbs. Despite the forecast of four days of good weather when they started, a storm began to move in that afternoon. The Eiger, as usual, was making its own weather.

Harlin, using the telescope at Kleine Scheidegg, noted that the Spanish team was higher than the other two. However, they were taking a long time on the Second Icefield and nearly came to grief when Rabada took a fifty-foot glissade down the ice. Fortunately Navarro was able to hold him. More problems began to pile up. The weather grew steadily worse as a storm dumped pouring rain on the lower reaches and snow in the higher elevations. Harlin was just able to catch a glimpse of the Italians and Japanese turning back before the face was completely curtained off with clouds.

Later, for just a moment, through a rift in the clouds, he spotted the Spanish team at the head of the Second Icefield, still climbing. Perhaps they meant to stay overnight at Death Bivouac, then retreat in the morning, which would make sense. It would be a lot safer to go back down the Second Icefield when there was less chance of rockfall. During the night the storm continued to rage. There was little question now as to what the Spanish pair would do in the morning. It made no sense to continue in the face of such violent weather. In any case, it was known that they had only a three-day supply of food, not enough now to carry them through to the summit. Despite the storm the Japanese and Italian teams effected a safe retreat.

At midmorning of the next day, during a break in the weather, when capricious winds opened a brief window on the face, the watchers scanned the Second Icefield, expecting to see the Spanish pair in retreat. But there was no sign of them. Finally they were spotted at the start of the Ramp. They were going on! However, they still had time to turn back. The Ramp was considered the point of no return. Once past the Waterfall Crack, it was generally considered safer to climb up and out. This side of the Ramp, prudence called for a retreat in bad weather. At that point, storm clouds closed off all observation of the wall. When last seen, late in the evening, they were at the start of the Waterfall Crack. It had taken them all day to climb the Third Icefield and then the Ramp. That same evening there was talk of possibly having to mount a rescue effort. The local chief of guides, Fritz Gertsch, telephoned to Spain, to officials of *Los Montañeros de Aragón*. Gertsch was assured that all the expenses of a rescue attempt, should one prove necessary, would be met by *Los Montañeros*.

There was still a possibility that the two climbers would turn back the next day. Surely they would have to. To climb on would be suicidal, yet climbers in a state of exhaustion were sometimes known to act irrationally.

The weather cleared that night, and visibility the next morning was excellent. The wall wore a coat of new snow down as far as Death Bivouac. The Spanish pair, still moving very slowly, with Navarro in the lead, got about three-quarters of the way across the Traverse of the Gods before they bivouacked for the night on a tiny stance. But the good weather was at an end, and another storm visited the Eiger that night, the climbers' fourth on the face. It was a typical Eiger performance—some rain, some hail, some sleet changing to snow, accompanied by rapidly falling temperatures. By now Rabada and Navarro had to be out of food so it must have been a cold, hungry bivouac for the pair. The next day the storm persisted, and the climbers were hidden from view all day. Various rescue operations were being discussed. Two Spanish climbers arrived from Chamonix in order to lend a hand should they be needed. Together with Toni Hiebeler of winter-climb fame, and Roberto Sorgato, the Spaniards hiked up the west flank to see if they could establish communication with Rabada and Navarro. However, the wind was blowing too strongly for their cries to be heard. They stayed on the flank all that day and bivouacked there for the night.

The next day Harlin, who had been following the climb all along, knew that the climbers had to be in great difficulty, probably on the edge of complete exhaustion. Together with Ignazio Piussi, who, with Sorgato, had come down off the face a few days before, he hiked up the west flank to join Hiebeler and the others. The hastily improvised plan was for Hiebeler and Sorgato to climb the upper shoulder of the west flank and, from a pulpit projection, shout into the Spider Snowfield and upper reaches of the face with the hope of determining the exact location of the Spanish pair. Once that was established, Harlin and Piussi would rope down from the summit with food and whatever other aid they could bring the exhausted climbers. In the meantime a full-scale summit rescue effort would be launched, complete with rollers, winches, and steel cables.

But when Harlin and Piussi reached Hiebeler and the others, the news was discouraging. Repeated shouting into the flared hood of the upper part of the wall produced no response. They climbed higher to another vantage point, but again there was no sight or sound of the Spaniards. Early the next morning Harlin contacted Kleine Scheidegg by radio and learned that on the upper part of the Spider an inert body was visible through the telescopes. It had not moved the whole time it was being observed. From the body a rope led upward to where a second climber, though hidden from view, was also presumed to be dead from exposure. Visibility, however, was not particularly good and an airplane flypast was being arranged to either confirm or deny the telescope observations. At noon a helicopter flew back and forth across the face and reported that there was no movement in either of the bodies, one of which was at the head of the icefield and the other lower down. The lower body simply lay on the ice of the Spider; it was already half covered with snow.

The would-be rescue teams retreated. The Eiger had claimed its twenty-fifth and twenty-sixth victims. All that remained now was the melancholy task of bringing down the dead.

As a result of the west flank rescue efforts, Harlin got to know Sorgato and Piussi and was very impressed with the Italian team's climbing ability. Sorgato was a student at Milan University and Piussi a giant of a man of peasant background from an Italian village near the Yugoslav border. Harlin later said that Piussi went up the west flank in leaps and bounds, as though it were a mountain pasture. Harlin now proposed to the two Italians that they consider joining him in a winter direct. The Italians, too, were primarily interested in doing a direct, which was, after all, an Italian specialty to begin with. Piussi and Sorgato promised to keep in touch and to let Harlin know when they might be free for another attempt.

As for Alberto Rabada and Ernesto Navarro and their desire to be the first Spanish team to climb the Eigernordwand, they came very close indeed and might have succeeded, had they had more experience in big wall climbing. They probably didn't realize how much the altitude and cold would sap their strength, that every night's bivouac would inexorably eat away at their physical reserves, that the proper food and equipment, especially clothing, were absolutely essential on the Eiger, on whose upper reaches men have frozen to death in the height of summer. Their courage was unquestioned. They climbed on and, after the second day, were periodically visible to watchers below in the valley. They had to be aware of that fact, for in those clear spells they could look down and see the Hotel des Alpes on the rack railway, and the larger complex of hotels and stores at Kleine Scheidegg. Yet at no time did they give any indication that they were in trouble; at no time did they signal for help. They simply climbed until they could climb no more, then died in place. The wonder is that, in their exhausted state, nearly dead from cold and hunger, they were yet able to manage the Traverse of the Gods and then climb almost the full length of the Spider. "An excess of courage kept betraying them until they died," one of the Italian climbers later said.

The two bodies were retrieved four months later, in the dead of winter, in a spectacular achievement by three young Swiss guides. Paul Etter (who had taken part in the thirtieth ascent the year before), Ueli Gantenbein, and Sepp Henkel (the latter two but twenty years old) went up the west flank to the summit on December 27. They bivouacked on the peak in weather that was unsettled. The next morning, they heard on their transistor radio a weather report that forecast clear skies for the following four or five days. They immediately began readying their equipment. Each man carried a loaded rucksack, a 300 foot coil of rope, and the usual ice axes, ice hammers, and climbing hardware.

They started off down the Mittellegi Ridge until they reached the Exit Snowfield, and here they had to be careful about avalanches. From the Exit Snowfield they roped down the Exit Cracks in a series of rappels. Down at Kleine Scheidegg their appearance caused a sensation. No one knew who they were, or what they were doing on the wall. The three guides had bypassed Kleine Scheidegg in their ascent, not wanting to draw attention to their plans.

Despite the descending nature of the route, it took the trio until early afternoon to reach the head of the Spider. Here one of the younger guides hacked out a level, sheltered place for a bivouac. The other guide belayed Etter as he kicked across and down on his crampons, to where he found Navarro high up on the right edge of the Spider. The standing Spaniard was anchored to a solidly placed rock piton, his ice hammer hanging from his right wrist. His crampons, Etter noticed, had no front points. His climbing rope ran from his waist harness, between his legs and down, through two intermediate ice pitons, almost the full runout of the rope, to his partner, Rabada. The latter lay face down on the ice, his ice axe pressed to his chest. He was almost totally encased in ice. He had taken off his crampons, also lacking front points, and stuck them into the ice just above his head. Neither climber seemed to have been hit by falling rock. From the evidence of the secure and workmanlike placement of the rock belay piton, of the two ice piton runners, of the taut climbing rope still connecting the partners, it was obvious that neither of them had fallen or been hit by rock. They looked as though they had decided to rest for a moment, then simply passed into a coma, followed by death. What is remarkable is that both men seemingly reached their limits of exhaustion at about the same time. Perhaps one called vainly down, or up, the rope to the other for a while before unconsciousness mercifully set in. But if Rabada, who was a big, strong man, had been even a little less exhausted, he would surely have climbed up the taut rope to his companion's stance, if for nothing more than to share his friend's company as they waited for the inevitable end. Similarly, if Navarro had had any reserve strength, he would surely have climbed down to his partner.

Also remarkable is the fact that Rabada's body had stayed on the snowfield for four months without being torn loose in one of the innumerable Spider snow avalanches or rockfalls. Of course, with the onset of cold weather, the rockfall had practically ceased, but snow avalanches must have increased in both size and frequency. Undoubtedly the ice in which the body was slowly encased built up to a smooth rounded boss that easily parted the avalanches into twin streams on either side. And those crampons, stuck in the ice in front of Rabada, posed a mystery.

Certain acts, normal in the context of everyday life, take on poignancy and mystery because death hovers in the wings. (That apple, with a fresh bite taken out of it, on a suicide's night table.) Why did Rabada remove his crampons? Had the framework of the metal overshoes been conducting cold to his feet, to the point where he took them off temporarily in the hope that some warmth would return to his frigid toes? Or was it a simple act of finality. Did he think, "No point in wearing these any more, the climb is over"? One thing we do know, the men from Aragon died hard.

The Swiss guides got Navarro's body wrapped and roped for a descent, but the light was failing and they had to stop and bivouac for the night. The next day it took three hours of hard and heavy work to hack Rabada free from his icy cocoon. But they finally managed to loose him from his bonds and lash him to his dead comrade. They lowered their funereal burden down to the lip of the Spider, where they hammered in a number of rock pitons. Etter now abseiled to a stance below. The other two lowered the corpses on ropes, down almost 800 feet of cliff face that had never been negotiated before, either up or down. The guides maneuvered themselves and the two bodies down to the Flatiron, where they again prepared to bivouac, their third night on the mountain. They roped the pair of corpses to a rock piton driven into the face, then hunted around until they found a suitable bivouac site a short distance away.

Despite their fatigue and the intense cold, the three guides managed to get some sleep. When they broke camp the next morning, they were startled to find that the bodies of Navarro and Rabada had disappeared. From the evidence a snow avalanche had swept down sometime in the night, ripped out the anchor piton from the rock, and carried the bodies away. The guides now continued their descent, made another bivouac just before the Hinterstoisser, and finally got off the face on December 31, just in time, appropriately enough, to close out the year 1963.

It was a demanding and highly dangerous descent, one that taxed to the utmost the courage, ingenuity, and skills of the three guides. They were the first to make a complete descent of the Eigernordwand, from tip to base, and they did it in wintertime, though rockfall would probably have made it even chancier an exploit in summer. But that wasn't their only reward. "We were happy having made the first descent of the wall, but happier still to have spared the rescue group a job that they had been regarding for some time with anxious eyes," Paul Etter wrote, perhaps tongue in cheek.

The local guides went out and retrieved the bodies from the foot of the wall, no doubt happy that the two Spaniards were no longer frozen into the Spider Snowfield, where their corpses could supply a cheap sensation for the tourists queueing up at the telescopes of Kleine Scheidegg in the following summer.

22
Suicide or Fall?

The 1964 climbing season got off to an early start on the Eiger. Everyone knew that a *direttissima* was in the offing. The technique was there, the climbers were there, it was only a question of matching up the right men with the right weather and of a little bit of benevolence on the part of the Eigernordwand.

The astounding descent from peak to base by the three young Swiss guides in the closing days of 1963, supposedly to take down the bodies of Rabada and Navarro, was viewed by many climbers and Eiger watchers as a reconnaissance venture for a possible direct. They would be back, those young Swiss, doing a *direttissima*, people were saying.

All of which lent a sense of urgency to a dozen or more climbers who had their eye on being the first to do a direct of the north face. The Swiss, by now, were among the best climbers in Europe. How long would they wait before they tried? And the Germans and Austrians would like to bag the prize too. After all, it was a mixed German-Austrian team that had done the very first ascent of the Nordwand. And there were Italian climbers who, so far, had been spectacularly unsuccessful on the Eiger. A direct would retrieve their reputations. Then there was a Scot, Dougal Haston, talking of an Eiger direct, as well as several Polish climbers who thought it was high time that climbers from Poland proved they were the equal of any in Europe.

And then there was John Harlin, who had dreamed of doing an Eiger direct for years. Now discharged from the air force, he had taken a post as a physical-education director at the American School in Leysin, Switzerland. He had been at the Eiger the summer before, 1963, with enough climbing companions to make a good Eiger direct team—Stew Fulton, Tom Frost, Gary Hemming, Konrad Kirch, Pierre Mazeaud, and the Italian pair of Sorgato and Piussi—but they had never been there at the same time, and when they briefly had, conditions on the face, or bad weather, had ruled out a climb. Gary Hemming had left, some say because he was jealous of all the attention being paid to Harlin. Pierre Mazeaud had left to keep some climbing dates in Chamonix, and Konrad Kirch had had business to attend to in Austria.

But early in 1964 Harlin wrote to Sorgato and Piussi suggesting a winter try at the Eiger. However, neither of the Italians was able to get away from his job at that point. Harlin now wrote Konrad Kirch, who was also tied up, but who suggested that a good friend of his—a physicist, ski instructor, and mountain climber named Hans Albert Mayer—might be interested in some winter climbing.

Early in January Harlin met Mayer in Grindelwald and together the two decided on a reconnaissance climb of the normal route. Harlin had neither the manpower nor the equipment for a try at the direct, for which he planned to use a minimum of four climbers, on a ten-day ascent, employing siege or Himalayan tactics. However, a reconnaissance should give him a good idea of what climbing on the face would be like under winter conditions.

And he soon found out that the face was not in very good shape. The snow was deep and had a tendency to avalanche off at the slightest movement. Still, he and Mayer climbed up as far as the start of the Hinterstoisser, where they dug out a cave from a heavy snow bulge adhering to the face. At least the weather was decent. However, that night Mayer came down with stomach cramps and in the morning was too weak with nausea to continue. For his part, Harlin was just as happy to call off the attempt. His feet were on the verge of frostbite, and he realized that he would need much warmer clothing if he were to try a winter direct. One of the first things he did when he got back to Leysin was to start designing a double snow boot especially for the Eiger.

Before he returned to Leysin, however, Harlin fell in with a local Oberland guide, Martin Epp, who suggested that they both do a winter climb of the north face of the Mönch, a climb that had been done only once before. The Mönch, being the Eiger's neighbor, would make a good practice climb. Epp was one of the young Swiss guides who had, with Paul Etter, already made a "lightning" one-bivouac climb of the Eigernordwand in the summer of 1962.

Epp and Harlin spent a night in a mountain hut at the foot of the Mönch, then started off at four in the morning. The weather was clear and snow conditions excellent. They reached the summit at 3:30 P.M., having spent less than twelve hours on a route that had taken four days by the only other team to have made the ascent. It was hardly a rehearsal for the Eigernordwand, though, and Harlin knew it. The Mönch, though higher than the Eiger, is not nearly as difficult. Still, it was an impressive climb and sent Harlin back to Leysin in a happy frame of mind, full of ambition and plans for an Eiger direct.

In mid-January a German team of four arrived at Kleine Scheidegg with their own plans for doing a direct. Peter Siegert, Reiner Kauschke, Werner Bittner, and Gerd Uhner spent two days attacking the wall but got only 1,200 feet up the face. Bad weather forced them to spend the whole of the third day in a snow cave, and they retreated the next day by climbing in through the *Stollenloch* and taking the railway down to Kleine Scheidegg. They said they would be back, and indeed Bittner and Uhner, on two separate ropes with other companions, climbed the normal route that summer.

In mid-February Harlin was back in Grindelwald to meet Sorgato and Piussi and two other Italian climbers, Marcello Bonafede and Natalino Menegus, for yet another try at an Eiger direct. The team picked out a route that started well to the east of the Central Pillar, a direct that more or less followed the original Sedlmayer-Mehringer route. This line, however, called for a whole new map of the face, and would miss such well-known sections as the Hinterstoisser, the Ice Bulge, the Ramp, the Traverse of the Gods, and the Exit Cracks. It would involve climbing several bands of cliffs instead of icefields. The new route called for new stations, and they soon acquired names: Foot of Fixed Ropes (approximately level with the middle of the First Pillar), First Ice Cave (level with Hinterstoisser), First Band (level with First Icefield), Second Band (level with Second Icefield), Central Pillar (just above the Flatiron), and finally the Fly, a small snowfield to the right of and above the Spider. The direct line crossed the normal route only at the Flatiron and came together again with the normal line at the bottom of the Spider—except that, on leaving the Spider, the normal route went to the left and up the Exit Cracks, while the direct line went to the right and up to the Fly. In terms of distance traveled, the direct was naturally much shorter. The normal line made so many traverses back and forth that it involved 10,000 feet of actual climbing on a 6,000-foot face. The direct avoided all these traverses and went straight up from base to summit in as reasonably direct a line as could be plotted.

After several days of waiting, a good weather front was forecast, and the five men started up the face on February 22. Their intention was to place fixed ropes as they progressed. Because the climb was estimated to last ten days, it would involve at least two team members ferrying supplies up to each new bivouac as it was established. After a day of climbing up and down, that team would lead the route the next day and the other team would now take over the supply duties. These "siege" tactics, as they were called, were the ones commonly employed in Himalayan expeditions on which a string of supply camps were set up and maintained at various levels on the mountain, with the intention of ensuring that at least one pair of fresh climbers would eventually reach the summit.

The Italian-American team launched its attack from the top of the crumbling ledges that marked the end of the tough-hiking section of the climb. Ahead of them soared a jumble of cliffs topped by overhangs and

split by couloirs, a band that rose to the level of the Hinterstoisser Traverse, but a good thousand feet to the left of that feature. It took the
five climbers the whole day to negotiate the broken cliffs. Every handhold and foothold, every piton placement, had to be cleared of snow.
Once, looking down and across into a crack, Harlin spotted a reminder
of other climbs, other men, on the Eigernordwand. Sticking up out of
the snow, the hand in a supplicating gesture, was a blackened dismembered arm of a climber long since dead. There was nothing Harlin could
do, so he ignored the grim memento mori and climbed on. At the end
of the first day, they found the snow cave that the four German climbers
had used on their attempt the preceding month, and gratefully took
possession of it.

The next day, the weather holding fair, they crossed the relatively
narrow icefield, here not too steep, and tackled the 600-foot precipice
called the First Band. Harlin had not climbed far up it when he ran
across another gruesome reminder of previous attempts on the north
wall, this time a dismembered leg that, from its still fresh state of pres-
ervation, he guessed had come from one of the two Spaniards whose
bodies had been swept from the Flatiron just months before.

Again he ignored his find and continued to climb. After hours of
hard nailing and hanging from the wall in *étriers,* the climbers were
stopped when their way up was barred by a huge overhang. Finding a
handy wide ledge just beneath the bulge, they decided to bivouac right
where they were. There were still a couple of hours of daylight left, so
Harlin and Sorgato, climbing several hundred feet, reconnoitered both
sides of the bulge and found a line to take in the morning. In the meantime the other three Italian climbers went down the fixed ropes to the
snow cave and humped up several loads of fresh supplies to the new
bivouac.

That evening Radio Geneva predicted an approaching storm front.
The forecast was repeated the following morning, but despite this, the
weather was still good on the Eiger itself; so the decision was made to
continue climbing. Piussi and another climber took over the lead while
Harlin and Sorgato roped down to the ice cave to haul up fresh food,
ropes, and supplies. That afternoon Piussi and the others returned to
the bivouac and announced that they had reached the top of the First
Band, fixing ropes all the way. Everything was going fine except for that
weather forecast. The next morning the weather was so dirty, the clouds
so low and menacingly heavy, that even Piussi, who would climb in any
kind of weather, dolefully shook his head and agreed to retreat from the
face. Perhaps the skies would clear in a day or two.

They came in off the Nordwand through the Eigerwand Station windows, and there Harlin reported, to a station guard, the grisly discover-

ies he had made earlier in the climb. The guard telephoned the news to the Grindelwald police who requested Harlin to recover the dismembered parts, because they were important evidence in helping to establish legal proof of a climber's death. Harlin agreed to retrieve the leg, which wasn't too far below the Eigerwand windows, but refused to go for the arm because it was too distant. Rappelling down from the platform windows, he found the leg, strapped it to his rucksack and returned to the Eigerwand Station, where he took the next train down to Grindelwald and there delivered his macabre find to the police. (He missed a good opportunity to bill the local authorities for a day's pay, perhaps for new ropes, and even for pitons and carabiners, because he had definitely been requested to go back out on the face. One can imagine the howls of anguish, however, had such a bill been rendered.)

The weather didn't clear in the next day or two, and neither Harlin nor the Italians had the necessary resources to wait long. Reluctantly they broke camp and headed for home. It had been a good try; they had gotten almost halfway up the route. Perhaps the next time.

The following April two Polish climbers, Jan Mostowski and Crestan Momatiuk arrived at Kleine Scheidegg to try a direct. They had gotten about 2,000 feet up the face when Mostowski took a spectacular fall and plunged over 1,000 feet—to his certain death, as his partner thought, but Mostowski landed in a snowbank and, incredibly enough, suffered nothing worse than a sprained knee. While it did put an end to the climb, Mostowski's plunge also set some sort of free-fall-and-still-survive record for the Eiger.

In early July Harlin, still driven by the possibility of doing a direct, came back with two top-class French climbers, René Desmaison and André Bertrand. They took the route that Harlin had worked the preceding winter and, despite the heavy and continual stonefall on the route, got as high as the top of the Second Band, roughly equivalent to the top of the Second Icefield. Good weather had brought forth other teams, including Sorgato and Piussi, and had the weather not turned unfavorable, there would probably have been a joining of forces. But a storm front moved in, and the climbers retreated, waited a few days, then split up, the Italians returning to Milan, the French to Chamonix, and Harlin to Leysin.

The summer of 1964 saw ten successful ascents of the face by German, French, Swiss, and Spanish climbers. Noteworthy was the first Spanish climb of the route by José Anglada and Jordi Pons, two Barcelona climbers who had made their first bivouac at the Swallow's Nest, their second on the Flatiron, and their third at the end of the Traverse of the Gods. The next morning the weather turned bad, and it took the whole day to battle their way through heavy snow up the Spider and the

Exit Cracks to the summit. While on the Spider, they retrieved and took with them an ice axe belonging to their Spanish compatriots, Navarro and Rabada, who had perished of exposure the year before. On their descent of the west flank, they were forced by the severity of the storm to bivouac for yet another night. Their exploit was widely acclaimed in Spain, where the memory of Rabada and Navarro was still fresh.

On July 30, two Swiss brothers, Kurt and Rolf Güngerich, started climbing the face. They bivouacked twice and then were hit by a terrible snowstorm in the Exit Cracks. They reached the Corti Ledge and briefly considered a third bivouac, but a weather report picked up on their transistor radio forecast even worse conditions; so, by the light of miners' headlamps, they continued the climb and eventually reached the summit at 3 A.M.! It was the latest, or earliest, arrival time ever at the summit. As soon as day broke, they went down the west flank.

On September 1, Werner Bittner, a twenty-six-year-old electrician from Munich, and his climbing companion started up the face. The pair bivouacked at the Swallow's Nest and at the head of the Ramp. On their third morning they lost a few hours by getting off the Ramp Snowfield too soon to pick up the Brittle Crack. Despite the delay they managed to reach the summit late in the day. Rather than chance a descent in the dark, they bivouacked on the peak and went down the next morning. It was the fifty-first ascent of the face, and the first by a woman. Bittner's rope mate was a secretary from Munich, Daisy Voog. Her success had one sour, but comic, note. Daisy had claimed to be twenty-seven years old, but as a result of all the publicity, her true age was revealed to be thirty-two. Actually this was her second attempt on the face. Earlier in the summer she had teamed up with Sorgato and Piussi, but after an overnight bivouac at the Swallow's Nest, the trio had been forced down by bad weather.

After Daisy's climb there were critics who said that the Eiger had finally become an easy day for a lady. It was far from that, as subsequent events were to prove, but certainly the normal route had now lost many of its terrors. The route was firmly fixed; often there were ropes hanging down the Difficult Crack, or fixed across the Hinterstoisser. There were pitons already in place in strategic areas like the base of the Flatiron, the head of the Ramp and in the Exit Cracks. The climbers now knew that they could and should avoid the icefields, the Flatiron, and the Traverse of the Gods during late afternoon, the hours of heaviest rockfall. If the Eiger had not yet been tamed, it had at least been considerably gentled in comparison to its earlier days. The Eigernordwand was still far from being a simple matter, however, as 1965 and 1966 were to demonstrate very graphically. Both years were to be distressingly similar—only one successful climb each year, and each climb claimed a life.

On August 19, 1965 two Japanese climbers, Tsuneaki Watabe, twenty-nine, and Mitsumasa Takada, thirty-one, members of a group of Japanese who were in Europe for a summer's climbing, started up the wall. The summer of 1965 had been so bad that no one had yet notched up a successful climb. The Japanese, who had come a long way via Russia and the Trans-Siberian Railway, were fearful that they would never get a chance at the Eiger if they didn't start soon. They carried enough food for seven days and made their first bivouac at the Swallow's Nest. Their second bivouac was on the Ramp, and, despite the bad weather, both climbers made it across the Traverse of the Gods, up the Spider, and into the Exit Cracks. They passed the Corti Ledge, no doubt reminding themselves of the story of the Corti-Longhi climb, and continued, rope length after rope length. They were within a couple of hundred feet of the Exit Snowfield and an easy route from there up to the summit, when Watabe, leading the pitch, fell from his stance and went tumbling a hundred feet down an ice gully. Takada was able to hold his partner, then climbed up to his position and managed to pull him on to a tiny ledge, where he discovered that Watabe had a broken leg. Takada now drove in a pair of pitons to anchor his friend to the wall, then told him that he was climbing on out to get help. He left Watabe his rucksack and some food and started off up the gully. It was 5 P.M.

Takada, climbing alone reached the summit that evening. Despite the fact that it was dark and still snowing, he started down the west flank to arrive at Kleine Scheidegg at 4 A.M. For some reason he didn't stop and wake someone at the hotel; instead he continued down the trail to his compatriots at Alpiglen. He arrived there half an hour later, and the alarm was raised. Kurt Schwendener, head of the Grindelwald Rescue service, and Hermann Steuri, head of the local guides, seemed dubious about a rescue attempt. How could they retrieve Watabe when they didn't even know where he was? Nevertheless they alerted a score of guides, who got the necessary equipment ready. But first the rescuers wanted an aerial reconnaissance of the face in order to determine the exact whereabouts of Watabe. The Japanese were evidently too polite to protest—to ask why three or four guides couldn't immediately make a forced march to the summit, go down the summit ridge to the Exit Snowfield, then rope down the couple of hundred feet to the marooned climber. The Japanese offered to go with the guides. Takada knew exactly where Watabe was; in fact he was closer to the summit than Corti had been. The Japanese offer was declined. Later in the day half a dozen Japanese climbers started up the west flank on their own.

John Harlin on the Eiger.
JOHN HARLIN PHOTO

At 11 A.M. a helicopter arrived at Kleine Scheidegg, but the weather was too unpredictable to chance flying back and forth across the turbulence on the face. A more powerful craft was needed. At 4 P.M. a heavier helicopter arrived. Meanwhile the six Japanese were halfway up the west flank, leveling out a bivouac spot and preparing to spend the night there. That same afternoon four German climbers, all familiar with the Nordwand, offered their services to the rescue team. They were ignored. The helicopter, with two guides, finally took off for the summit, flew around for a while and then came back, reporting no sign of anyone in the Exit Cracks.

At 5:45 Toni Hiebeler, who had just arrived at the scene, called Kleine Scheidegg from the Eigergletscher Hotel and asked them to survey the bottom of the face through their telescopes. A few minutes later someone spotted a red crumpled bundle near the foot of the mountain. At 7:30 P.M. the helicopter went out and retrieved the body of Tsuneaki Watabe.

What happened? Some say Watabe committed suicide, a report that gained credence because Takada was positive that he had firmly tied and anchored his partner to the wall. Had Watabe, suffering from hypothermia, perhaps hallucinating, in the irrational grip of "survival madness," reached the conclusion that no one was coming for him and, remembering Longhi's horrifying end, decided that he might as well get it over with right away? The Japanese don't have quite the same moral strictures against suicide as Westerners do. Or had Watabe, in some attempt to put his broken leg in a less painful position on the ledge, inadvertently unclipped himself from the anchor piton and then fallen off?

Some say it was another comedy of errors on the part of the local rescue service and local guides. Had they heeded the climbers who knew the wall—Takada and the Germans who volunteered to help—they could have reached Watabe by noon at the latest. Even two climbers, one of whom knew the wall, could have been lifted up to the Exit Snowfield with enough rope to get to Watabe within an hour or so. Winches, rollers, and a steel cable weren't necessary.

Whatever the truth, Watabe was the Eiger's twenty-seventh fatality and, some people said, the most needless.

23

The Direttissima

John Harlin spent the summer of 1965 chomping at the bit. He still had his dream of doing an Eiger direct, but all that summer the clouds seemed to pack the Alpine valleys tighter than cotton wool in a medicine bottle, and the Eiger was out of the question. He did get in one decent climb, a direct on the west face of the Petit Dru with old Yosemite hand Royal Robbins. Anyway, he still thought winter the best time to do an Eiger direct. The summer of 1965 was memorable not only for bad weather but also for the death of Lionel Terray in a climbing accident. The preceding year, 1964, Terray had climbed Mount Huntington in Alaska with a shoulder so badly injured in a near-fatal accident that he had had to climb practically one-handed. Then, in September of 1965, Terray and Marc Martinetti, roped together, fell 1,200 feet on a climb in the Vercors, an area of limestone cliffs near Grenoble. It was never determined why the pair had fallen on what was, for men of their exceptional ability, a comparatively easy climb.

With Buhl and Lachenal and now Terray gone, the old Eiger hands were passing from the scene. There was still Heckmair, of course, now leading wealthy clients on relatively easy climbs, and Rébuffat and the seemingly invicible Bonatti, but fortunately, or unfortunately, depending on the point of view, there was always room at the top for new mountaineering superstars. And John Harlin was rapidly building a name for himself—this man who, as another climber once said, "flamed up a mountain." He was thirty, and an Eiger direct would surely boost him into the ranks of Europe's top half-dozen climbers. And after that? Perhaps Everest, the unscaled south wall. Harlin, a big man, had big dreams, and he had the ability to make outlandish projects come to fruition.

By his own estimates, Harlin had been up on the Eiger a dozen times by early 1966, with only one ascent to show for it. Most of these attempts had been rush trips to Grindelwald to climb with whoever was available and as long as the weather held. He knew a direct, especially one in winter, would require the kind of planning needed for a minor Himalayan expedition. Already he had decided on the nucleus of his team. To lead snow and ice pitches he had Dougal Haston, a twenty-five-year-old Scot who had first met Harlin in the Bar National, in Chamonix, a favorite hangout for English-speaking mountain climbers. Harlin had climbed with Haston on several big walls, including the murderously steep ice of the Shroud on the Grandes Jorasses, where he had carefully noted Haston's skill with ice axe and dagger and with ice screws and crampons. Haston had already done the Eiger, and Harlin considered him one of the best ice men he had ever seen in action.

For rock climbing, Harlin had Layton Kor. A bricklayer, originally from Boulder, Colorado, Kor generally worked six months of the year at his trade and spent the other six months climbing. Along with Tom Frost, Royal Robbins, and Gary Hemming, he was one of the top rock climbers in America and, at this period, must have been one of the three or four most highly skilled, all-around rock (free and aid) climbers in the world, if such a judgment could or should be made. Kor had started climbing as a teenager after having seen a movie on mountaineering. Fired up, he headed for one of the many canyons around Boulder and attacked a cliff wall with a mason's hammer, trying to chop steps up the face. After hours of hard work and twelve feet of elevation, he retreated—sweaty, disillusioned, exhausted. It was one of the few walls that Kor ever backed away from. Someone told him about the Colorado Mountain Club, where short courses in rock climbing were periodically offered. Kor joined, took to climbing like a lizard to rock, and within days was outperforming his instructors.

Six feet four inches tall and endowed with huge, sure hands, Kor seemed to dominate mountains by his size and strength alone. He had only one fault as a climber. On Grade-VI pitches, because of his long reach, he sometimes placed pitons too far apart for the next man on the rope to handle, or to take out when it was the second man's job to clean the route. One good thing about Kor was that, despite the very difficult rock climbs he had accomplished on virgin faces and routes all over the Rockies, he had never lost a rope mate. Kor was lucky, other climbers said, and as a result he rarely lacked for partners. His rallying cry, on difficult climbs, was a cheery, "Come on, the worst that can happen is you'll fall and get killed. Then all your worries will be over."

Harlin had also secured the services of Chris Bonington, who, along with Ian Clough, had made the first successful British ascent of the Eiger's north face. A graduate of Sandhurst and one of the best British mountaineers, Bonington had climbed everywhere—in Britain, the Alps, the Himalayas, and the Andes. He was also an excellent photographer and had arranged to shoot pictures of the climb for London's *Weekend Telegraph,* a paper that had already agreed to underwrite much of the expenses of the proposed direct.

In mid-January Haston arrived in Leysin, at Harlin's house, where Kor was already in residence. Harlin promptly put Haston in charge of all the ice equipment that would be needed, and Kor in charge of all rock equipment. Among the many special items were the Eiger boots that Harlin had designed, and a French manufacturer had made. They were composed of a double boot, a felt-and-suede inner boot within an outer boot of hard leather. Harlin and Haston had tested them in winter conditions on the Walker Spur of the Grandes Jorasses, and the boots had worked extremely well. They were to wear only one pair of socks— more than one pair tends to restrict circulation and thus increase the chances of frostbite. Over their footwear they wore zippered gaiters designed to keep snow from working inside their boots. They wore long underwear (Harlin wore two pairs, one of silk and one of wool), wool trousers, and overtrousers of polyurethane and nylon. For the upper half of their bodies they had a wool undershirt, a regular wool shirt, a light wool sweater, and a heavy wool sweater over that. Over these four layers of clothing, they wore a down jacket, and over the jacket, a waterproof parka. For their hands they had thin silk gloves within a pair of woolen mittens for use while climbing, as well as a pair of waterproof down mittens they put on in bivouacs or any long inactive periods on belay. In addition, Harlin worked barehanded whenever possible, believing that the more one's hands grew accustomed to the cold, the less likely they were to freeze. In the winter he often went for ten-mile training runs in the hills around Leysin, wearing a minimum of clothing, carrying snowballs in his bare hands to acclimate his body to frigid conditions.

Harlin and Haston, after a lot of searching around, finally found a Swiss rope, "Mammut," that wouldn't freeze up and kink under winter conditions. They ordered 500 feet of seven millimeter perlon for prusiking and hauling rucksacks, and 600 feet of heavier, eleven millimeter perlon for climbing rope. Kor picked out the rock hardware—some sixty pitons of varying lengths and shapes, all made of chrome molybdenum steel, the high-strength, lightweight alloy developed by the American climber Yvon Chouinard. Chrome-moly pitons were not only lighter than steel ones, but their shape held better and they could be removed and used over and over again. In addition new ice axes and ice hammers were purchased, along with three dozen ice screws and pitons. Each man had his own pair of crampons, a plastic crash helmet, a down sleeping bag, a tent sack to draw over himself at night, a rucksack, and a waist harness. They also purchased a pair of walkie-talkies. Some of the material, such as the ropes and boots, was donated by manufacturers. The *Weekend Telegraph* paid for most of the balance of the equipment.

Harlin hired a helicopter to fly back and forth across the face while he took still and moving pictures of different features of the Nordwand. The direct line would be over virgin territory for much of its length, and Harlin wanted as good a picture as he could get of what he and the other climbers would be up against. The helicopter, piloted by the famous Swiss mountain pilot Hermann Geiger, who was known as the glacier pilot, because of his many daring rescues of people in trouble in the Alps, flew as close as possible to the wall, making ten back-and-forth runs at different levels before Harlin was satisfied. It was this attention to detail that made Harlin such a good leader on climbs. Tragically, the pilot, Geiger, was to be killed later in the year when his plane collided with another just after a routine takeoff from Sion airport in Switzerland.

The three men "scoped out" the photographs for days; Kor picked out possible lines on the rock bands, while Harlin and Haston traced ice gullies and couloirs to see if and how they would go.

On February 3 the three men left for the Oberland and that evening were bunked in at Villa Maria, a special annex of the Kleine Scheidegg complex that the proprietor Fritz von Almen had set aside for them at a special climbers' rate. Eiger aspirants, especially for a direct, always drew the press and sightseers and were good for Almen's business.

For several days the trio pored over the photographs and examined the face, foot by foot, pitch by potential pitch, through Almen's telescopes. Then Chris Bonington arrived from London, and the team was finally ready to start. But the Eiger wasn't, and while they waited for a good forecast, it snowed and stormed for over a week.

When they were able to, the four skied. When they couldn't ski, they argued over the route or the supplies or the equipment. But it was friendly debate and part of the process of learning to get along together, despite diverse backgrounds. Both Harlin and Haston were intellectuals. Harlin not only sketched very well (for a while he had toyed with the idea of becoming a fashion designer), but he also wrote poems, short stories, and accounts of his more noteworthy climbs. (His report of his 1962 climb of the Eiger, in the *American Alpine Journal,* makes excellent, vivid reading.) Haston, like Harlin, was a prima donna, moody, somewhat of a dandy, and a man whose thoughts were frequently as rarified as the air he climbed in. He, too, was a writer who was to produce several excellent books about his climbing experiences.

The ex-soldier Chris Bonington, despite his penchant for getting high up in the air on mountain faces, was refreshingly down-to-earth, a shrewd judge of character, a no-nonsense practical fellow who loved climbing, but not to the point of obsession. Kor was sui generis, a bundle of nervous energy, a man who never seemed truly at ease except on a mountain face, a man capable of carrying tremendous loads, a man of great stamina, yet oddly enough not driven in the way that Harlin was. One got the feeling that Kor derived more pleasure from solving the problems of each pitch on the route than he would ever get from standing on the summit. Instead of George Leigh Mallory's reason for climbing Everest, "Because it's there," Kor might have preferred, "Because I'm here," an appreciation of the journey more than the destination.

In mid-February, still waiting for the weather to clear, they debated the ethics of taking their supplies up by train to the Eigerwand Station, which would be very close to the direct route. They could haul them out through a window and stash them in a snow hole. They themselves, of course, would climb up from the bottom, but it would certainly be a help not to have to haul all that stuff up through the waist-deep loose snow and up over those ledges and split arêtes on the lower part of the face.

After all, isn't that what Hiebeler had done? Well, not quite, but why press the point? They spent one whole day taking the loads up by train to the Eigerwand Station windows, and then safely stowed them in a convenient snow hole a short distance away.

The next day Harlin, out skiing, tried a fancy one-legged turn, fell, and dislocated his shoulder. He went to a local doctor who eased it back into place but warned the young American that climbing was out of the question for at least a couple of weeks. Meanwhile the weather was still bad, so Harlin returned to his wife, Marilyn, and the children in Leysin to give the shoulder a chance to heal. He took Haston with him, leaving behind Kor and Bonington to prepare the First Band with fixed ropes if and when the weather cleared.

In the meantime, Peter Gillman, a writer for the *Weekend Telegraph* and also a climber, arrived at Kleine Scheidegg to cover the direct attempt for his paper. Hearing that the project was postponed for a couple of weeks because of Harlin's injury, Gillman turned right around and took the next plane back to London.

Several days later Marilyn Harlin received a phone call from Grindelwald. She took the message, then interrupted Harlin and Haston in the basement, where they were working on some equipment, with the startling news that a German rope of eight had started up the Eigernordwand on a direct.

Harlin was bowled over. He had so long been accustomed to the idea that he would lead the team to do the first direct on the Eigernordwand that the news came as a bombshell. Hastily he and Haston gathered up their equipment and left Leysin early the next morning in a van. They arrived in Grindelwald that afternoon just in time to see the German climbers come down off the face, the first 1,500 feet of which they had already prepared with fixed ropes. That evening a council of war was held in Villa Maria in which it was decided that Kor and Haston should start up the face first thing in the morning. Harlin's shoulder would still not allow him to climb, though it did seem to be healing rapidly.

Early the next morning, February 20, Haston and Kor, with Bonington accompanying them to get photographs, reached the foot of the wall. They started up, while Bonington took pictures of them as they followed the fixed ropes the Germans had placed. On Friday he had, from the same position, tried to get photographs of the German team in action but several of the climbers had pelted him with snowballs until he was forced to put away his camera.

Haston and Kor used the German fixed ropes at first, but after several pitches decided to climb free. By afternoon they had reached the supply cache just beneath the Eigerwand Station windows. Here they stamped a platform out of the snow for a bivouac site, then brewed something hot to drink. With still some daylight left, they decided to tackle the First Band, a 600-foot-high cliff of almost sheer rock, with few handholds or footholds and almost no cracks to take a piton. It was Kor, the rock expert, who now took over the lead, Haston having led the ice pitches up to that point. Somehow Layton was able to place knife-blade pitons, often sunk only half an inch into the crack. Kor had a reputation for finding piton placements where no one else could. He increased the piton's effectiveness by using "hero loops," short slings tied off on the piton shank right up against the rock face, a practice that considerably reduced the torque on the piton's eye and lessened the chances of its pulling out. The climbing *étriers* and climbing rope were now clipped into the carabiner on the end of the hero-loop sling.

Hours later they had managed to get only ninety feet up the First Band. Here Kor drove an expansion bolt (a sort of molly bolt) into the rock as a solid anchor for a rappel. He and Haston abseiled down to their bivouac site, cooked a couple of steaks, and pulled the bivouac sacks over their heads. Just in time, too, because it began to snow. The wind rose and the powder snow invaded their sleep sacks, piling up behind their backs and trying to nudge them off the ledge. The temperature dropped to zero, and down at Kleine Scheidegg wind gusts of up to a hundred miles an hour were recorded.

Harlin and Bonington grew increasingly worried about the chances of Kor and Haston coming through what now seemed to be the worst winter storm in years. They were so worried that at first light in the morning they hired a special train to take them up to the Eigerwand Station. From there they intended to go out on the face, find their comrades, and bring them back in to safety. Before they arrived, however, Kor and Haston had already decided to retreat and had followed the fixed ropes down to the foot of the wall. By noon everyone was back together again at Villa Maria. Two days had passed since they had launched their attack. Progress so far—ninety feet. At that rate it would be May or June before they reached the summit.

For the next several days no climbing was done, and the German team and the British-American team, unavoidably thrown together by weather and circumstances, gradually became acquainted. What had been a faint feeling of hostility soon turned into a grudging mutual respect. None of the Germans, who were all from the Stuttgart area, had ever climbed the north face of the Eiger, though four of them had traversed the peak, from the Mittellegi Ridge to the summit and down the west flank, as a reconnaissance climb the previous month. All were first-class climbers who had done many of the Grade-VI routes in the Alps and Dolomites. The team had two coleaders—Jörg Lehne, thirty, who worked for a Stuttgart publishing company, and Peter Haag, twenty-eight, an engineering student. The other six were Günter Schnaidt, thirty-three, a carpenter; Karl Golikow, thirty-one, a mechanic; Siegfried Hupfauer, twenty-five, a toolmaker; Rolf Rosenzopf, twenty-six, an engineer; Günther Strobel, twenty-four, a carpenter; and the youngest member, Roland Votteler, twenty-four, a mechanic.

Harlin and Haston met with Lehne and Haag to discuss the climb. The press, the European radio and TV stations, already had reporters and cameramen on the scene and were now pulling out all the stops, "pumping" the climb up into an epic battle between the two teams, almost making it into a replay of World War II. *Blick,* a Swiss publication, ran photos of Harlin, Haston, and Kor with the caption, "Against the Germans."

The climbers bemoaned this media attitude of melodrama, of sensationalizing and personalizing the climb into a struggle between the two teams. As the English climber Don Whillans, who had just arrived from Leysin, put it, "Well if it's a race, it's the slowest race in the world."

And yet there was a certain hypocrisy in the climbers' patronizing attitude toward the writers and cameramen. For it *was* a race. Harlin was fiercely determined to be the first to do an Eiger direct. And the German climbers were equally determined to bag the prize for themselves. Mountain climbers tend to be intensely competitive, and these men were no exception. Then too, Harlin had an instinct for publicity and used the press whenever he could. After all, a newspaper, the *Weekend Telegraph,* was financially backing the expedition. One of the climbers, Bonington, was taking photos for the same paper. Harlin, it was well known, had ambitions to lead an American expedition to climb the virgin south face of Everest. A successful Eiger direct, with all its attendant publicity, would vault him into prominence in mountaineering circles and be a giant step in attracting support. The more a competition, a race, seemed to be in the making, the more publicity would be given to the event, and the more Harlin's name would become known in that periphery of the mountain world where grants were dispensed, loans arranged, equipment donated, and backing found for big Himalayan expeditions. The truth is that once the news media arrived to cover the climb, the event became a competition, and the climbers, consciously or unconsciously, played up to it. Publicity created competition, which in turn created more publicity, which created more competition, *und so weiter.*

Although there was some talk of the two groups' joining forces—in that way everyone could share credit for the direct, for solving the last great Alpine problem, as some people were now calling the route—the psychological climate was not yet ready for that. Anyway, joining forces would create problems—a team of twelve climbers? Even eight seemed too many to Harlin. The German plan was to have four climbers out in

front, route finding and fixing ropes, while the other four would ferry loads up to the various bivouacs as they were established, "bringing up the rear and the gear," as American climbers called it. The front four would also be responsible for digging out snow bivouac caves and general housekeeping. From day to day climbers would change places, alternating between climbing or load hauling, or even at times retreating to Kleine Scheidegg for a day's rest and recuperation.

The German method meant that four men theoretically could climb and prepare the route twice as fast as a two-man team. Actually, of course, this wasn't true. Only one man at a time could effectively lead a pitch, and while four climbers were able to save some time in placing pitons and fixing ropes, the time saving was offset by the British-American team's greater knowledge of the face and its ability to climb lighter and faster. The Germans planned an eighteen-day climb, the Harlin team a ten-day climb.

The leaders of the German and the Anglo-American teams came to an impromptu agreement. Although both groups had fixed their own ropes up the first third of the face, they would now use each other's ropes wherever it was handy to do so, at least on the lower part of the wall. After that they would handle each problem as it came up. Undoubtedly each side was convinced that it would win the race. The Germans, with their planned string of half a dozen bivouac snow caves, with their constant shuffle of food and ropes moving inexorably up from one bivouac to the next, were confident of ultimate success.

Harlin, on the other hand, had a somewhat different concept. He, too, would use the shuttle system and two or three snow caves as far as Death Bivouac on the Flatiron, or perhaps even to the bottom of the Spider, but from there, carrying all their provisions and equipment with them, his team would make a nonstop dash for the summit. And his plan had every chance of succeeding; Haston, with years of ice climbing behind him, in his native Scotland as well as in the Alps, was one of the world's best ice climbers. The same could be said of Kor on rock. And for mixed climbing Harlin belonged to an equally elite group of mountaineers. It would be hard to put together three men better qualified for the attempt. And for a backup climber they had the ever dependable Bonington.

1966 JOHN HARLIN DIRECT

1. Foot of Fixed Ropes	*5. Death Bivouac*	*9. Fly*
2. First Ice Cave	*6. Central Pillar*	*10. Summit Snowfield*
3. First Band	*7. Where rope broke*	*11. Summit*
4. Second Band	*8. Spider*	

Meanwhile Peter Gillman had returned to Grindelwald to cover the climb for the *Daily Telegraph* and to man a walkie-talkie as liaison between the climbers on the face and Kleine Scheidegg. Also at Grindelwald was the English climber Don Whillans, who had wangled two weeks off from his job as a physical training instructor at the American School in Leysin. Whillans had climbed many times with Bonington and Harlin. He now took over the matter of food, supplies, and equipment, meeting each radioed request from the mountain and seeing to it that the necessary material was ferried up to the climbers. Where necessary he himself humped loads up the fixed ropes to the first snow cave. Wendy Bonington, Chris's wife, was also at Kleine Scheidegg, acting as courier to speed her husband's films on their way to Geneva and London.

On February 25, the weather still somewhat overcast, the German team returned to the face. They climbed the fixed ropes to their huge snow cave, their *Eispalast* (Ice Palace), as they called it.

Worried that the Germans would steal a march on them, Kor, Haston, and Bonington also started for the face but later in the day found conditions impassable as avalanches were constantly streaming down. They were forced to retreat to Kleine Scheidegg. The next day snow conditions had improved, and the climbers were soon up the face and visiting with the Germans in their Ice Palace.

Leaving Bonington to hack out a snow cave, Kor and Haston prusiked to the head of the rope they had fixed almost a week before. Several Germans were working a parallel line some fifty feet to their right. After greetings were exchanged, Kor went to work leading the pitch.

With on-and-off weather it took several days to master the first series of cliffs. Another bivouac cave was established, and the slow tedious work of hauling up ropes and other supplies was carried on by Bonington and Whillans. By now Harlin, his shoulder almost healed, had joined the climbers and in fact led the way up an ice gully on the second band of cliffs. Above this band the Flatiron loomed. The Germans had taken a different line and were soon in difficulties when one of their climbers, Karl Golikow, peeled off the wall. Fortunately he fell only twenty-five feet or so, his protection held, and he was uninjured.

Indeed falls were to be expected on the climb. Already Haston had been flipped upside down on an abseil when an extra rope caught in his waist harness. He hung there for twenty minutes before Bonington got a knife up to him and he was able to cut the jammed rope and right himself. On another occasion, Bonington, using only one jumar because the angle of the fixed rope had eased off on a snow slide, had the jumar jump the track, and it was only by a lightning grab of the rope with his free hand that he stopped himself from toppling backwards into a possibly lethal fall.

In the meantime there was a lot of visiting back and forth between the two camps. Haston and Kor and Harlin would frequently pop into the Germans' snow cave to be offered a cup of coffee by whatever climber was in residence at the time. Often they were greeted by Golikow, whose one sentence of English was the doleful comment, "It's a hard life." That phrase, and the lugubriously good-natured grin that accompanied it, never failed to cheer the British and American climbers. "A delightful and friendly character," Bonington called him in his account of the Eiger climb. Grudging respect was giving way to affection.

On March 9 the Anglo-American team reached Death Bivouac on the Flatiron. It was almost evening when Haston, leading the pitch and fighting a snowstorm, reached the bivouac ledge. He dug a rudimentary cave out of a bank of firm snow, then called for the others to come up and across the traverse rope. By now it was dark, and Bonington, unable to see where he was placing his crampons, slipped and had to grab the rope. He hung from one hand, sweating, knowing that the rope was pegged with only one thin chromalloy piton in a crack, and one ice piton that was far from being firmly embedded. However, he managed to right himself and finished the traverse in a fine sweat. Soon Harlin and Kor came up, and all four climbers were together. They worked on enlarging the snow hole until all were able to fit inside. Then they got a gas cylinder started to brew some tea, but something went wrong and the cylinder caught fire. Fearing an explosion, Haston tried to throw the cylinder out of their snow cave. It hit the edge of the exit hole and bounded back inside to land near Bonington, who promptly dove for the doorway, forgetting that just beyond the threshhold there was a 4,000-foot drop to Grindelwald. He managed to stop his forward progress in time by elbow jamming himself in the entrance hole. At that point a blazing gas cylinder went flying past his right ear to light up the black void outside with the orange trailing glow of a Verey light, or the fall of a dying rocket. Harlin had hurled the container over Bonington's shoulder and out into the night. Bonington wriggled himself back into the snow hole, some sheepish apologies were made all around, then everyone collapsed with laughter. It took a while to settle things back to normal, but as any Englishman will tell you, tea works wonders, and after innumerable cups, the men drifted off to sleep.

In the morning they discovered that their cave had been hollowed out of a jutting cornice of old frozen snow. The walls of the cornice were so thin that the daylight was able to penetrate inside. Not only that, but if one were to make a hole in the floor of the cave, one could see straight down to Grindelwald. It was not exactly the sort of place to inspire confidence and deep, restful sleep.

The weather had moderated somewhat from the near blizzard conditions of the preceding night, and Bonington now announced that he was going back down to Kleine Scheidegg. He had taken all the photographs he needed for the moment and was eager to get the rolls of film on their way to the *Weekend Telegraph*. Actually he hadn't planned on being a full-fledged member of the climbing team but had, like Whillans, agreed to help in the establishing of bivouacs and ferrying of supplies. He said good-bye to the others and took off down the rope.

Haston, Harlin, and Kor spent most of the morning organizing their gear and making the snow hole more habitable. At noon it was decided that Harlin, whose shoulder was still sore, would finish up the housekeeping and prepare an evening meal while the other two climbers went on ahead to reconnoiter the route.

Above Death Bivouac there loomed a sort of second Flatiron, a prow-shaped arête that the climbers had named the Central Pillar. After climbing straight up a couple of pitches of mixed ice and rock slabs, Haston and Kor came to a bulging overhang below the pillar, where they met Peter Haag and Günther Strobel. The German pair said they were going to take the prominent chimney on the right-hand side of the Central Pillar and were confident that it would go.

Haston was not so sure. There were huge snow blocks at the head of the chimney that, his experience of snow and ice climbing told him, were often highly unstable. Meanwhile Kor spotted what he thought was a feasible line. This was a traverse of an eighty-degree rock cliff running up and beneath the bottom of the bulge to a likely-looking line of ice gullies and rock cracks that seemed to end near the top of the Central Pillar.

The pair now "rapped" down to the snow cave at Death Bivouac, where Harlin already had dinner going on their tiny portable stove. Afterward all three went over the route possibilities again, and they decided to try the rock traverse, which Kor would lead. They agreed that it was important to reach the top of the Central Pillar before the Germans did, because the first group to make the Spider would probably lead all the way to the summit. Of course, they weren't in a race, but, still, it's always nice to be first.

That night, however, it snowed, and it continued snowing all the next day. Climbing was out. Not only that, but the Geneva weather report, relayed to them via walkie-talkie by Gillman down at the Kleine Scheidegg, called for at least another couple of days of intermittent storms. At this point Kor decided to retreat down to civilization. There were some pieces of equipment the climbers needed that he could bring back, along with fresh food, at the first sign of any break in the weather. Harlin and Haston decided to wait it out. Should the weather unexpectedly clear, they would be ready to climb right away, thereby ensuring that the German team, which also had left two of its members in a snow cave, wouldn't steal a march, or even a pitch, on them.

Meanwhile, cracks were opening here and there in the precariously thin walls of their snow cave that jutted out from the rock face, cracks that offered awe-inspiring but queasy views of Alpine meadows far below. The rents were quickly plugged with snow, and cave keeping went on. A day passed, a night, another day, and still no sign of clearing weather. Harlin and Haston sealed up the mouth of their snow cave with a bivouac sack in order to keep out the spindrift and to conserve heat. Then they stuffed some spare socks and gloves anywhere a crack showed at the back of the wall where the snow met the rock face. There were other problems to occupy them, including a lack of snow to melt down for drinking water. The walls of their snow hole were already too thin to tamper with; and they did not want to open the mouth of their cave again. Not only did it let out the heat that had built up inside, but it also let in clouds of spindrift that, on melting, got everything wet. They finally managed to get some ice chipped loose from the rock face at the back of the cave.

To make matters worse, their food was fast running out, and no one had been able to get up to them with fresh supplies. Then, on their sixth straight day in the snow cave, Harlin came down with a high fever and a racking cough.

24
It's a Hard Life

Maintaining good health inside the snow hole was becoming a problem. The humid air and the lack of even normal exercise gave rise to respiratory problems. The night-time temperatures frequently got as low as twenty below zero, and the men had trouble keeping warm. To combat the cold, they took antifrostbite tablets before going to sleep, which kept their extremities warm for at least four hours. Then it was either move around or take more tablets. Despite these efforts Harlin's condition seemed to be deteriorating. Finally he called Kleine Scheidegg on the walkie-talkie and asked Gillman to look around for a doctor who might advise him over the radio link. Gillman did better than that, he rounded up five of them, four women and a man, who were all in the same party of French doctors, traveling together on a holiday. The doctors fired questions at Harlin over the radio. His pulse? Temperature? Urinating normally? Diarrhea? After a conference, the team of doctors diagnosed his condition as probably bronchitis. It was all right to stay up there for the day, but if there wasn't some improvement by the following morning, Harlin should make plans to come down. He thanked them and agreed to follow their advice. Perhaps he and Haston would have to go down anyway, because they were practically out of food. There was still another factor that favored withdrawal. Even if the weather cleared that night, it would be at least another two days before the face would be fit for them to climb. It would take that long for the new snow to either plume off in avalanches or compact itself to the underlying snow in those areas not subject to snowslides. However, the next day Harlin felt much better, and his pulse rate had dropped thirty beats. Once again he got in touch with the group of doctors at Kleine Scheidegg; they agreed that he could probably stay up on the face for at least one more day. As for food, perhaps Bonington and Kor could hike in to the bottom of the face and then start up with supplies? Unfortunately the slopes at the foot of the Eiger were six feet deep in loose snow, and avalanches posed an ever threatening danger. As an alternative they discussed taking the railroad up to the Eigerwand Station, then going out on a rope and up to the bivouac site. But that alternative also posed problems.

Finally, on the morning of March 16, after a weather report indicating at least two more days of unsettled weather, Harlin and Haston decided to come down. Harlin's cough had come back. He also felt that he needed at least a few days rest before he would be fit to climb again. The two men roped down and soon were in the snowy meadows of Alpiglen, being met by Bonington and Gillman. At the Alpiglen Station the four men, along with two German climbers who had also come down off the face, took the next train to Kleine Scheidegg, where the press was waiting for them.

Harlin and Haston had spent the last six days in Death Bivouac and a total of thirteen consecutive days on the face, three days longer than Harlin had planned for the entire climb! If nothing else, they had proved that men could stay on the face in the dead of winter for a couple of weeks at least.

Paradoxically enough, as soon as they were down off the wall, the weather began to clear. Bonington and Kor now decided to ferry supplies back up to the first ice cave at least, and on to Death Bivouac if possible. They would stay overnight and, if the following day held fair, would make a start on preparing a route up the Central Pillar above Death Bivouac. They knew the Germans would already be climbing and didn't want them to get so far ahead that there would be no chance for the Anglo-Americans to reach the summit at least with their competitors, if not before them.

On their way up, Chris had noticed that some of the fixed ropes were beginning to show signs of wear. They had been in place for almost a month, and the wind had started to abrade them, especially in those places where they ran over the rock edges of overhangs. The constant slapping of the wind caused a sawing effect on the outer sheath of the ropes, and thin threads had begun to peel away. Still, the ropes had a breaking strength of over a thousand pounds, and up to Death Bivouac at least, there was a double rope.

It took all day to reach the bivouac site, which by now was showing considerable evidence of the previous tenants' occupation. The entrance to the snow cave was rimmed with frozen excrement, and inside they found a score of yellow urine bore holes drilled into the snow walls of the cave. Haston, a day or so before he and Harlin had come down after their six-day stay in the Death Bivouac snow hole, had blithely announced over the walkie-talkie that he and John were covered "in a

Dougal Haston and John Harlin just after coming down off the face after a week spent in an ice-cave bivouac.   CHRIS BONINGTON PHOTO

mixture of Scots-American excrement," a report that caused great hilarity among the journalists, but it was a piece of "hard" news they had great difficulty in working into their dispatches.

Bonington and Kor spent a not uncomfortable night in the bivouac, but the next day, with typical Eiger consistency, the weather turned soft again and avalanches went cascading down the face. Climbing was out. But at least the Germans were also held up. The following day, however, dawned crisp and clear, and the two climbers laid their plans. Kor especially, with his tremendous stores of nervous energy, hated being cooped up in the snow hole and eagerly got his gear sorted out. They climbed up the ropes that Harlin and Haston had earlier fixed in place, and found Jörg Lehne belaying Karl Golikow, who was out in front, leading the next pitch.

"It's a hard life!" Golikow shouted down with his typical mournful grin. The German pair was going up the snow couloir that the Anglo-American team had already rejected as too problematical because of the overhanging snow blocks. Kor now proposed to traverse right under the base of the Central Pillar to an ice gully, then follow that up toward the head of the pillar. The Germans thought the traverse couldn't be made, and even Bonington had his doubts. But those vertical slabs of rock were meat and drink to Kor, and he started out, driving a piton, clipping his *étriers* into the higher of two carabiners tied on a sling to the piton. His climbing rope, belayed on the lower end by Bonington, went through the second snap link. Stepping up in the *étriers,* he surveyed the rock landscape ahead of him. The traverse was not a strictly horizontal one but ran left to right across the rock at a rising angle. Half a dozen whacks of the hammer and Kor had another piton tapped into place. Step up two rungs in both *étriers,* then loosen the foot in the lowest one, unclip the *étrier* from the lower piton, and clip it into the higher one. Then the climbing rope was threaded through the new snap link and a cow tail (or "cheater") clipped into the piton. This aid, a sling tied into a carabiner to the waist harness and the other end clipped into an anchored piton, allowed the climber to lean back and take a moment's breath, both hands free to sort through his hardware, scratch himself, or join together in a swift prayer if so inclined. (And, at those inclinations, the climber frequently was.)

Kor simply swarmed up and across the traverse in a superb display of direct-aid climbing, leaving a line of well-planned runners for the

---

Layton Kor leading on a difficult rock pitch across the foot of the pillar above the Flatiron—one of the key pitches of the climb.

climbing rope and Bonington coming behind. Though Kor couldn't know it, of course, he was adding to the history and legends of the Eiger. That traverse was ever after known as the Kor Traverse. "He was a craftsman, superbly adapted to this highly specialized form of climbing. He climbed with a speed and precision unequaled by any European climber," Bonington was later to write of him. Jörg Lehne was to write that this "amiable American giant," as he called Kor, moved over the rock so securely that it was as though there were some sort of "magnetic attraction between Layton and rock."

Kor chopped a level stance out of an ice bulge and belayed Bonington up to his position. From there a steep ice gully led to an equally steep icefield. Bonington, being much more experienced on ice than Kor was, now took over the lead. He started off, knowing he was climbing far higher than he had ever intended to go, climbing on ice that was frequently too thin to take ice-screw placements. Often, when he chipped away at the inch-thick crust of ice to the rock underneath, he found the rock as smooth as "a baby's ass," as Lionel Terray once described the rock face of the Eiger, offering little more adhesion to the boots and hands than the ice itself. He was aware all the time of the danger of coming off, aware that Kor's ice belay stance below him wasn't very secure, that if he did come off, he could well peel his partner off with him. One slip, and "it was all the way to Grindelwald," as he put it. It was dicey climbing, and as the rope fell away below him in a long, lazy curve, he kept constantly thinking of that 150-foot length with no protection in between, all the way to Kor's stance. One slip now, and after sliding 150 feet, he would go shooting past his partner at forty miles per hour. And while Kor gave the impression of being able to stop a runaway train if he had to, Bonington had no illusions as to the outcome of such a fall. Thinking such gut-warming thoughts, he made his way, slowly and cautiously, up to the bottom fringe of an icefield, where the danger eased off somewhat. After another twenty feet or so, he found that the smooth rock had a welcome cleft, and he managed to get a solid rock piton in for a belay anchor. Above him stretched the snowfield, and he could now see the top of the pillar. The rest of the way was a piece of plum duff. He listened carefully for the sound of German voices, heard nothing, and guessed that their friends were having trouble with those overhanging blocks of snow in their couloir, which meant that he and Layton would beat them to the top of the pillar.

Sitting back in his stance, shouting, "On belay," to let Kor know that

Bonington on the Third Icefield.

IAN CLOUGH PHOTO

he could start up, Bonington felt a wave of pure joy sweep over him as he paid in the rope for his partner climbing to meet him. "It had been the hardest and most spectacular ice pitch I had ever climbed," he wrote later. In fact both pitches, the Kor Traverse and the Bonington Ice Gully, were superbly led by highly skilled climbers working at the top of their powers on what proved to be the crucial pitches on the direct, at least so far as the Anglo-American team was concerned.

When Kor reached him, it was nearly dark and they hammered in some extra rock pitons for added protection, then decided to rappel back to the bivouac, leaving a fixed rope behind them. The way to the

Kor in a snow-cave bivouac.   CHRIS BONINGTON PHOTO

top of the Central Pillar was clear now, the gate to the Spider finally open.

They abseiled down the ice gully, and Kor led across the fixed rope of the traverse. Bonington followed. Impressed with the American technique of using a snap link on the rope to act as a brake, he clipped one on. Then looking down at the 3,000-foot drop below him, he added another. He was halfway across the traverse when he got hung up in a snarl of knots and carabiners. Everything he tried seemed to make the tangle worse. In the meantime Kor, complaining of cold feet and thinking Bonington was merely checking his gear, took off down the next pitch, leaving his rope mate all alone with his problem.

Bonington could move neither backward nor forward, his hands were stiffening with cold, and the light was fast failing. He hung at the middle of the traverse, the rope now stretched taut in a deep V with the weight of his body. He spent a full hour fumbling around, trying to sort things out, all the time aware that his life depended on eight clumsy fingers coiled around the traverse rope, that a 3,000-foot drop awaited him if those fingers failed. He checked and rechecked his knots and carabiners to make sure he wasn't unclipping himself from the rope. Finally he got the snarl untangled and made it back across the traverse and down to the bivouac.

At Death Bivouac he met Lehne and Golikow (the Germans had their cave hole close by), who admitted that their approach had failed because of those overhanging snow blocks. Lehne asked whether he and Golikow could use the fixed ropes put up by Bonington and Kor. They agreed, with the proviso that the Germans wait and follow them up in the morning. He had no intention of letting them get ahead on a lead he and Kor had won so dearly. Lehne now put forward the suggestion that they all climb together on a combined team, and Bonington called it a good one but said they would first have to talk the whole thing over with Harlin, the nominal leader on the climb. They would soon be in touch with him on the walkie-talkie. Lehne agreed to wait for their decision.

In the meantime, down at Kleine Scheidegg, Harlin was making good use of his mini-vacation. The first thing he did was call Leysin and have a long talk with Marilyn. He got all the latest news, including the fact that his son, John Jr., had done well in a children's Mickey Mouse (Topolino) ski meet in Italy. The next morning he went to the funeral of Hilti von Allmen, an old climbing friend and Eiger hand (Allmen and Ueli Hürlemann had made the twenty-second ascent in 1961), who had been killed by an avalanche while skiing.

That afternoon Harlin went to the hospital in Interlaken for a check-up, at which he received the welcome news that the only thing wrong with him was a lingering case of bronchitis that should soon clear up. Feeling rejuvenated, he caught the next train back to Kleine Scheidegg, where someone showed him a Swiss newspaper report that he had been admitted to the hospital with pneumonia, a story that must have highly amused him. That evening Harlin spoke via walkie-talkie with Bonington at Death Bivouac. Bonington reported that Kor and he had solved the Central Pillar line and were within a pitch or two of one of the trailing legs of the Spider snowfield. Once they got a toehold on the Spider's leg, it would be straightforward ice climbing to the head of that pivotal icefield. Harlin and Haston were elated with the news, but not too happy with Lehne's request that they join forces with the German team. Harlin did not want four, or perhaps even six, German climbers to reach the summit first, then appear to be bringing up the Anglo-American team last. They had the advantage now, why give it up? However, he agreed to a mixed rope of Kor and Golikow for the following day's climbing. After that they would see.

The next morning Kor and Golikow (now affectionately known as Charley by the members of the Anglo-American team) set off together to finish the line to the bottom of the Spider. They would fix ropes to serve both teams equally. Bonington, in the meantime, had begun to feel guilty about his role on the climb. He had promised his wife, Wendy, that he wouldn't do any high climbing on the Eiger, and yet he had already led one of the most difficult and dangerous pitches on the face. He was also supposed to be taking pictures for the *Weekend Telegraph*. If Kor climbed with "it's-a-hard-life Charley," it would free him to get on with his photography, a task that he had somewhat neglected in the excitement and enthusiasm of such challenging pitches.

Down in the valley, Whillans had to return to his post at the American School in Leysin, but his place was taken by Mick Burke, another one of the "hard" men of British mountaineering. He and Bonington had often climbed together, and he had many Grade-VI+ Alpine routes to his credit. Burke made an excellent replacement for Whillans and served as a "Sherpa" in humping supplies up the fixed ropes to the lower snow cave and then to Death Bivouac.

While Bonington was taking photographs, Kor and Golikow were reaching the top of the Central Pillar. There they banged in a secure anchor for the fixed ropes, and for rappels. Then they tackled the 300-foot rock band that led to the Spider's leg. The climbing was all artificial, with one bad bulge, but Kor got his six-foot-four frame folded over the overhang enough to hammer in a rock piton, secure the climbing rope, then abseil down to the top of the Central Pillar. The way was now open to the Spider.

At Death Bivouac Kor found that Bonington had decamped to get his rolls of film back to Kleine Scheidegg and on their way to London. But good news awaited Kor. Harlin reported that the weather forecast was excellent, offering a strong likelihood of four or five clear days ahead. That meant that the push for the summit was on. He and Haston would leave Kleine Scheidegg at midnight with full loads and plan to spend the following night at Death Bivouac. The day after that they would set up another, and final, bivouac, somewhere on the Spider. Kor asked them to bring more pitons. He was running short.

Kor, the only member of the Anglo-American team now on the face, was invited to dinner in the German snow cave, the "Crystal Room." He found himself attending a party to celebrate the fact that the way to the Spider was open and the final push about to begin. It also happened to be Golikow's birthday, in honor of which a rocket was fired by the German team members down at Kleine Scheidegg. The Germans on the face answered with two firecrackers, one red and one green.

In the morning Kor had breakfast with Lehne, Golikow, Hupfauer, and Votteler before he and the Germans took off to see what the Spider had to offer.

Meanwhile Harlin and Haston left Kleine Scheidegg at one that morning and by six were sitting in the snow cave at the foot of the First Band, brewing up some badly needed hot drinks. The climb up the face on the fixed ropes had been exhausting, for each climber hauled a rucksack containing sixty pounds of supplies. Because the final push was on, they would clean out and take with them whatever supplies were left in the First Band ice cave, thereby adding to their loads. The day had brought superb weather, clear and brisk. As Haston and Harlin were prusiking up to the top of the Second Icefield, on their way to Death Bivouac, they could see Kor a thousand feet above on the face, gently swinging in a sling belay. Haston shouted up a question, and Kor's voice came floating back down to them, "Just *great,* man."

Haston and Harlin reached Death Bivouac, and then it was time for another rest and more hot drinks. Despite the cold, they were soaked with perspiration. From outside their snow cave at Death Bivouac, they could actually watch Kor and Lehne high above them, working on the ice gully that formed one of the Spider's trailing legs. The climbers were clearly making good speed, and by afternoon they were well up on the Spider itself.

That afternoon Harlin called Peter Gillman down at Kleine Scheidegg and outlined his plans. He and Haston would jumar up the fixed ropes first thing in the morning, carrying equipment and food for three days at least. Then, with Kor, they would make a determined push for the summit. If the weather held fair, there was a chance of making it all the way the next day, or at least of getting to within a few hours of the summit. In the meantime, Harlin asked, what *was* the latest weather?

Gillman had disturbing news. The weather picture had changed. The latest report from the Swiss Weather Bureau in Geneva forecast that a storm might arrive by midnight the following day. They might have one day of good weather, but they couldn't be sure of more. Harlin swore—typical Oberland weather. By tomorrow they would have less than three days of food left. Supposing they got caught in a Spider or Fly bivouac by a week-long snowstorm? Even a three-day storm would mean a five-day delay, because avalanches would make the face unclimbable for another two days afterward. Could they survive that long? For that matter, could they find a suitable snow hole in either location? Harlin told Peter that he and Haston were sticking to their plan of making the summit push the next day. Maybe the weather would change again, at least enough to give them the promise of another, climbable twenty-four hours. Give them that, and they'd do it, if they had to tunnel up the last few hundred feet to the summit.

Late that afternoon Kor came swarming down the ropes from the Spider. He, Lehne, and Golikow had gone halfway up the icefield where the Germans had established a temporary bivouac for the night. However, the band between the Spider and the Fly looked quite difficult, Kor reported. It looked as though it might well take a full day's climbing to negotiate. The Germans had even talked of going partway up one of the Exit Cracks, then traversing across to the Fly in order to outflank that crumbly band of rock.

The three climbers kept going over the alternatives. Climbing a face like the Eiger is like playing a game of chess. You pick a route, then plan your game as many moves ahead as you can. But unlike chess, you have to play the game backward as well, to safeguard your retreat. If they had to, could they make it back down the fixed ropes from the Fly to Death Bivouac in a snowstorm? Could they make it back down in the dark, or would they have to bivouac on the Fly? Would they run out of food? How about fuel? Without fuel they couldn't melt snow for water to drink. Had they enough rope? Could they endure the cold if they couldn't find a snow hole? The questions were endlessly debated that night among the three climbers before a decision was finally reached. Caution prevailed. If the weather report showed no change in the morning, they would sit tight, wait it out, and hope that the bad weather didn't last more than another day or so.

The morning call to Kleine Scheidegg clarified nothing. The cold front, and the accompanying bad weather, had been stalled by another weather front and might not arrive until the following evening. That would give them the rest of the day and perhaps a full day on the morrow. Harlin and Haston, remembering Kor's report of the seeming difficulties in reaching the Fly from the Spider, now wanted a little more than thirty-six hours of good weather for the summit push. They decided to make a climb to the Spider and establish a supply cache there, then come back to Death Bivouac and check the latest weather. Bonington now came on the radio and offered to ski in, with Mick Burke, to the foot of the fixed ropes, then climb to the first snow cave with added supplies. Perhaps Kor could make one of his lightning up-and-down climbs to pick up the stuff?

Kor, however, was somewhat disheartened. It looked as if the summit push was off for another couple of days, at least. He felt tired. The hard, concentrated climbing of the past three or four days had gotten to him. If he went down to the first snow cave, he might as well go all the way to Kleine Scheidegg and get a good night's sleep, then come back up in the morning with a rucksack of extra food. Most climbers wouldn't have considered that a rest, but Harlin and Haston knew how their friend hated to be cooped up and agreed that Kor could take off down to Kleine Scheidegg.

Later there was a report by a German observer of the climb that Kor and Harlin had had an argument over joining forces with the Germans—Kor being in favor of such a move and Harlin against it. Harlin's view is supposed to have prevailed, leading an angered Kor to take off down the face. Against this theory stands the fact that Haston mentioned nothing of such an argument in his book on the Eiger climb, and he was one of the three principals involved. Nor did Bonington say anything about such an argument in his book. According to one later written by Lehne and Haag, the Germans offered several times to join forces, both when they had the advantage and when they hadn't. Those offers hadn't been quite turned down; nor had they been accepted.

In the morning Harlin and Haston decided to make their supply climb to the Spider in the afternoon, and to spend the morning housekeeping and checking out their equipment, splitting it into rucksack loads. They would leave for the Spider right after the noonday call, which would give them more up-to-date information on the weather.

The noon radio call brought electrifying news. "John, there is a German climber on the Fly. Repeat, there is a German climber on the Fly!"

Harlin was thunderstruck. They were going to do it after all, beat him to the direct! The Germans had obviously ignored the bad-weather forecast, and on the strength of that gutsy decision alone, they probably deserved to reach the summit first.

"Are you sure?" Harlin asked.

There was no doubt about it, Bonington told him. In midmorning a telescope watcher had picked up one climber on the Spider, with a rope leading upward into the rock band above. Higher still, another black dot was seen, firmly anchored in the middle of the Fly snowfield, rope trailing down.

Harlin discussed the situation with Bonington on the radio. He and Haston could reach the Fly by nightfall, bivouac there, then join the German team in a push for the summit the following day. Maybe it wouldn't be a clear-cut victory for the Anglo-American team, but a mixed German-Anglo-American rope sounded good to him now. After all, he and Haston and Kor and Bonington had shared the mountain for the past month with the German climbers—why not share the summit also?

Harlin told Gillman to explain to Kor why they had gone on without him. Perhaps Kor could join with the second German team in its try for the summit. If there was nothing else, Harlin said, he had to get going. "Go!" Gillman said. "Go! We'll see you on the summit. Go for it!"

Harlin closed the radio link and grinned at Haston. By early afternoon they had quit Death Bivouac and were eagerly climbing up to the base of the Central Pillar. Harlin was on his way, the last leg of his greatest dream, the completion of the first Eiger direct, the solving of the last great Alpine problem. And next there was Everest. For Haston, too, it was a happy moment. They hadn't climbed far when they overtook Siegfried Hupfauer, who was ahead of them on the candy-striped seven-millimeter perlon rope. He was ferrying supplies up to his countrymen on the Spider and the Fly. Haston and Harlin now worked in unison with the German climber. When Hupfauer reached the head of an overhanging rope, he shouted down to Haston to start up. When Haston reached the top, he shouted down to Harlin to let him know it was safe to proceed. This method avoided the danger of inadvertently having the weight of two climbers on the rope at the same time.

Following each other, the three went across the Kor Traverse and up the Bonington Ice Gully to the head of the pillar. Just before the fixed rope reached the lower rim of the Spider, there was a hundred-foot, free-hanging drop from a flat slab of rock. That particular prusik pitch gave Haston some problems. The heavy weight of the rucksack resulted in two bad tendencies—one was to cause the climber to spin around on the rope while jumaring, and the other was to increase the possibility of overbalancing, being pulled over backward by the heavy rucksack. But Haston finally made it to the top of the pitch without incident, grinned at Hupfauer, then yelled down to Harlin to clip in and climb.

Then Haston joined Hupfauer on the small platform to wait for the arrival of his rope mate.

25
Somebody's Falling

Haston waited at the stance for Harlin to reach him. Normally it would take twenty minutes to jumar up that length of fixed rope. Half an hour passed, then forty-five minutes. Haston assumed that Harlin had run into some trouble with his gear. It could be any one of half a dozen things: a broken strap and a crampon may have bounced down the rocks to providentially get netted in a mantle of snow covering a ledge, necessitating a descent to retrieve the object, then jumaring back up again; or Harlin's bronchitis may have been troubling him, forcing him to halt until a bout of coughing subsided and his lungs were breathing free again; or a crampon may inexplicably have gotten caught in a snarl of jumar slings and fixed rope.

After another half hour had passed, Hupfauer told Haston he was going up to the Fly with his load of supplies. Hupfauer waved good-bye and went on ahead. Meanwhile Roland Votteler, on his way down to haul another load of supplies up the face from one of the lower snow caves, stopped to exchange greetings with Haston. Haston explained that he was waiting for Harlin, who was now an hour and a half overdue. He asked Votteler to tell him that he had decided not to wait and was going on ahead to start hacking out a cache platform on the Fly. Votteler backed off the ice stance and went rappelling down the face.

Haston clipped in his jumar slings, yanked hard on the fixed rope to test the solidity of its placement, then started moving up the Spider. He went about a hundred feet before he turned around to look down, wondering whether Harlin might now be visible. He saw a dark figure just coming up over the lip of the small ice and rock platform at the bottom rim of the Spider. A terrific elation swept over Haston. Until that moment he hadn't quite realized how strong a sense of dread had been slowly invading his mind.

Down on the terrace of the Kleine Scheidegg hotel, Gillman was planted at the telescope, checking the progress of both teams of climbers. It was three-fifteen in the afternoon. He had been watching the German climbers pack loads up from Death Bivouac for their final assault on the summit. Gillman put the slightest of finger pressure on the eyepiece end of the scope, tilting the field of vision as he followed the line of fixed ropes up to the Spider. Suddenly a small red bundle dropped down through his circular field of vision. The red figure was turning over, "slowly, gently and with awful finality," Gillman later wrote in his account of the climb.

"Somebody's falling. A man's falling!" he shouted. He tried to follow the object, but it was nearly impossible to keep the scope on a smooth enough traverse to track an object falling swiftly through space. He saw a plume of snow puff out of a couloir near Death Bivouac, but that was all.

At Death Bivouac, Rolf Rosenzopf had just left the Crystal Room to start jumaring up the rope with another load of supplies when an avalanche of snow swept down the couloir on his left. In the middle of the snow Rolf saw a human figure go cartwheeling by. Horrified, he went back to the snow cave and abruptly sat down. His first thoughts had to be of his comrades. He had seen a red jacket and caught a glimpse of blond hair. Was it Harlin? Or could it be Votteler?

Down on the terrace at Kleine Scheidegg, Guido Tonella, the mountaineering journalist of the *Tribune de Genève,* asked Gillman whether he had seen arms and legs? Might it not have been a rucksack? Or even an anorak?

Gillman said that he had seen a figure, a human figure. It was stretched out and falling.

A correspondent for a group of English papers now looked through the telescope. Minutes earlier he had followed a figure jumaring up the fixed rope just beneath the lip of the Spider. No figure was there now. Nor could he see the fixed rope itself.

Bonington and Fritz von Almen were sent for. Soon the hotel proprietor, who had an uncanny ability to spot things on the face—climbers, chamois, even ravens—picked up a flash of red at the base of the mountain, several hundred feet below the start of the fixed ropes. Around the red bundle were scattered pieces of brightly colored equipment, items ejected from a burst rucksack, or torn off a waist harness. Almen shook his head, then turned the telescope over to Bonington. He spotted the body right away and soon, a short distance from the red bundle, a familiar blue object that he guessed to be the climber's rucksack. Harlin had been carrying a blue rucksack. However, on-the-site confirmation was needed, so Bonington, carrying a radio, and Kor set off from Kleine Scheidegg and skied across the snow slopes at the foot of the Eiger. They came within a few hundred yards of the red bundle and at first were swept with a flush of relief. They thought the bundle was just a piece of equipment. Layton was sure it was a bivouac sack. But then the bundle was reached and Harlin's body was clearly recognizable, despite the horribly contorted position of the limbs. Bonington came on the air to Kleine Scheidegg, saying over and over, "It's John! He's dead!" Then he and Kor sat down in the snow, weeping, overcome with grief and shock.

Up on the Spider, Haston's relief changed to concern when the figure he had taken to be Harlin he now recognized as Votteler. He swiftly climbed down, and Votteler told him that the fixed rope had broken near the top and that Harlin was nowhere to be seen. Votteler tried to console Haston. There was still the faint possibility that Harlin had survived the fall. Confirmation of disaster was swift in coming. Hupfauer came down the fixed rope from the Fly to the head of the Spider to shout down the icefield that Harlin was dead. The Germans had just received the news through their radio contact with Kleine Scheidegg. "A broken rope and gone was my greatest friend and one of Europe's best mountaineers," Haston wrote in his account of the climb, *Direttissima,* which he coauthored with Peter Gillman.

Up on the Fly the horrified German climbers were still not sure exactly who had fallen. Then a request came over the radio that they send down the unit to Haston so that he could communicate with Gillman, Kor, and Bonington. The Anglo-American radio had gone down with Harlin.

Golikow immediately volunteered to bring down the radio, but he was in such a state of shock that he left the Fly twice without the unit, having forgotten it each time. Twice he had to return for it; finally, on his third parting, he had the radio with him. For once he didn't say, "It's a hard life," when he reached Haston and Votteler. He didn't have to. Instead he kept awkwardly patting Haston's shoulder while showing him how the radio worked.

It was almost dark by now, but rather than go back to their comrades on the Fly, Golikow and Votteler decided to stay with Haston and bivouac right where they were for the night. The instinctive first reaction by members of both teams was to call off the climb. But soon the climbers were having second thoughts. There was no doubt what Harlin would have wanted them all to do. Jörg Lehne, for the German climbers, and Haston and Kor, with Bonington, now agreed to try and finish the climb on a combined rope and, should they prove successful, to name the route the John Harlin Memorial Direct, as a tribute to their fallen ropemate. Kor decided to start up the face that evening to join Haston and the German climbers for the final attack.

The next morning Golikow went down the fixed ropes to Death Bivouac and found six places where the rope was badly frayed. Because of that, it was decided that all those above Death Bivouac would take part in the final assault, while all those at Death Bivouac and below, including Kor, who had just arrived from Kleine Scheidegg, would retreat. Golikow now agreed to climb back up to the Spider and to strip all the ropes and pitons from the Spider down to the foot of the mountain on his descent.

If any two men deserved to be with the group headed for the summit, it surely had to be Layton Kor and Karl Golikow. Fate willed otherwise, and the pair were left out of the summit assault team. At Kleine Scheidegg Burke and Bonington decided to go up to the summit via the west flank to get photographs of the climbers and to greet them when they topped out. They were able to hire a helicopter whose pilot agreed to drop them well up on the west flank. They jumped ten feet from the hovering chopper, praying their impact wouldn't start an avalanche. They checked their equipment, then headed for the summit while the helicopter slid away and back down to Kleine Scheidegg.

On the mountain itself final preparations were underway. Four German climbers were now on the upper part of the face—Lehne, Strobel, Votteler, and Hupfauer. With them was Dougal Haston, now the only surviving member of the Anglo-American team on the face.

The rest of that day Lehne and Strobel prepared several pitches above the Fly. Meanwhile Votteler was down at the Spider bivouac, housecleaning that site and making up three haul loads of equipment and supplies to ferry up to the others. Haston and Hupfauer, with a shovel and ice hammer, were hacking out two bivouacs with enough room for four men.

Later in the afternoon it began to snow, the start of that long-heralded storm. However, when darkness fell, four of the climbers were securely bivouacked on two ledges while the fifth, Votteler, was down at the Spider bivouac site, preferring to spend the night there rather than crowd the others on their narrow ledges.

The next morning the wind rose, the temperature dropped, and the men's faces were soon covered with rime. The decision was made to have two lightly laden climbers, Lehne and Haston, out front, leading and fixing ropes, while the other three followed, hauling up supplies and bivouac equipment, taking out the fixed ropes and pitons as they advanced. There was no point in leaving the fixed ropes. They were going to reach the summit—either that, or they would die there on the wall. Retreat was not only psychologically abhorrent, but practically out of the question, because the ropes were now stripped all the way to the foot of the mountain.

The climbing for Haston and Lehne was dreadful. The visibility was sometimes down to a matter of feet, the wind was an endless series of stinging slaps of snow across the face, and, though in two pairs of gloves, the men's hands were woodenly numb with cold. Haston's jumar clamps kept icing up and either slipping off the rope or not holding, threatening all the time to peel him clean off the face. Lehne, who was having the same problem, had to constantly pick the ice out of the teeth of his jumars with the point of a knife that he carried in his mouth, "like a savage on the warpath," as he wrote. The ropes themselves, after exposure to the freezing snow, soon turned into rigid and obdurate cords of ice, more like steel cables than climbing ropes.

Despite the appalling conditions, they fought their way upward through hundreds of small spindrift avalanches that seemed to have an uncanny ability to filter through the slightest opening in their clothing. The rock slabs were poor and offered few places that would take a piton. By late afternoon they had managed to gain several hundred feet and were now hopeful that they were within a pitch or two of the Summit Snowfield. Lehne, not wanting to alarm his support members down at Kleine Scheidegg into any premature rescue attempts, radioed an optimistic report that they had practically reached the Summit Snowfield and were now going to bivouac for the night and finish the climb in the morning. Then his radio weakened and went dead, the batteries having failed in the intense cold.

Actually, Burke and Bonington were waiting for the climbers up on top. They had spent the preceding night in a snow hole several hundred feet down the west flank. When they reached the summit that morning and saw no sign of the climbers, they tried to hang around and wait for them to appear, but they were forced to retreat after only half an hour because of the savage winds. Down at Kleine Scheidegg, gusts of ninety miles per hour had been clocked, with the temperature registering twenty-six below zero. The wind was even fiercer and the temperature colder up on the peak. Unable to stand the summit conditions, Burke and Bonington retreated to their snow hole, prepared to wait for radio word from Kleine Scheidegg that the climbers were actually approaching the summit before going back up to meet them.

Down on the rock bands, the five men were now bivouacked for the night, enduring the whipsawing winds and below-zero cold as best they could. They were without hot food and drinks for the second night in a row. Haston was anchored to a foot-wide ledge with slings and pitons—seated, with one leg stretched along the narrow shelf and the other dangling over but supported with a sling, with the outside arm also sling supported. He kept dozing off, only to be awakened by uncontrollable fits of shivering. Blowing spindrift snow kept working into his bivouac sack, melting on his face, then refreezing on the inside of the sack and the collar of his jacket. Fortunately he was able to remove his crampons. The metal spikes conducted the intense cold straight through to the toes. The other climbers fared no better, and all night Haston could hear the mumble of their voices around him; they, too, were unable to sleep. And all night the driving snow piled up and plastered the five bundles up against the rock face, melding their shapes slowly but surely into the shape of the wall itself.

The next morning, down at Kleine Scheidegg, Toni Hiebeler, who was covering the event for a German publication, and three of the other members of the German direct team (the fourth was sick), now proposed to climb to the summit and wait for the appearance of the five-man final-assault team. Hiebeler radioed Bonington up on the peak, who told him that it was bloody cold up there but that he and Burke would prepare for their arrival by carving out a snow cave big enough for everyone. Kor was asked to join Hiebeler and the others but had to decline because he was going to Leysin, where Harlin was being buried later in the day.

With Lehne's radio out of commission, there was no word from the climbers on the face. However, at the first sign of dawn, the five-man team got ready to continue the climb. They had been without hot food or drink for over forty-eight hours, and the wicked cold had affected everyone's stamina. It took concentrated effort to tie or untie a simple knot. A strap on one of Haston's crampons broke, and he had to jury rig a substitute strap from a piece of cord dug out of his rucksack. By the time he had finished this simple task, a full hour had gone by. Because of Haston's shaky crampon, Lehne and Strobel led the climb the next morning, with Haston following and the other two Stuttgart climbers bringing up the rear. Haston hadn't gone far when he realized that his hands were frozen. He pulled off his gloves to look at the pale-white, slightly bloated, lumps of hardened flesh and bone. Clumsily he dug out of his rucksack a bottle of Ronicol, an antifrostbite drug that speeded up the flow of blood. He took the medicine and waited. Half an hour later agonizing pains in his fingers gave evidence that the Ronicol was taking hold. He resumed climbing.

Above him Günther Strobel took a thirty-foot fall when his fifi hook, a metal S-hook used to attach a sling running from the waist harness to a piton, broke, an almost unheard of thing. Considerably shaken, Strobel nevertheless managed to get back on course and continue to climb. The rock was so rotten that he and Lehne joked about their "locomotor" pitons that would pull out of the crack after the leader had climbed above them, to join together on the rope, forming a train of five or six loose pitons that had come undone.

Haston finally reached a dark-grey, granular ice slope that he fervently hoped was the start of the Summit Snowfield. He couldn't tell, though; visibility was so poor. Nor had he any contact with the pair preceding him. He climbed on, following the fixed ropes that Lehne and Strobel had placed, Hupfauer and Votteler somewhere below him but out of sight.

And then, within shouting distance of the summit, Haston found

---

Günther Strobel and Jörg Lehne on the summit after finishing the Harlin Direct.

CHRIS BONINGTON PHOTO

himself facing his hardest pitch of the whole climb. Inexplicably there was a long gap in the fixed line that trailed on up the icefield. Lehne and Strobel, running out of rope, had decided to leave a stretch of icefield unprotected in case they ran into steeper ground ahead on which ropes would be imperative. However, the two climbers were soon in shouting contact with the men on the summit, and they now turned around and called down to Haston, telling him to wait where he was. They would finish the climb, then borrow a 300-foot rope from the climbers on the summit and lower the end to him. Haston shouted back what Lehne and Strobel took to be an affirmation. In fact, because of the wind, Haston hadn't heard a word of the instructions, merely some vague shouts to which he had responded.

With crampons, ice axe, and hammer, the sixty-degree slope in front of him would not normally have been difficult. However, he soon got off the line taken by the pair above, and now, not only had he no rope to follow, but he couldn't find any cut-out footholds or handholds. Furthermore, Haston had no axe or ice hammer. The two lead climbers were carrying them. All he had was a solid, dagger-pointed ice peg. Because of that substitute strap, one crampon had worked loose and was wildly skewed on his foot. His precarious position and deadened fingers wouldn't permit him to stop and fix the crampon. The other crampon was also loose. The fierce summit winds were packing drift snow into his face at such a rate as to build white eaves of snow out and down over his eyebrows and partially block his already poor vision. Half-blind, he had to pat and fumble around on the snow-covered ice slope in front of him, still hoping to come across a handhold or foothold previously cut by Lehne or Strobel. To add to his miseries, he knew that if he ever came off, there was a distinct possibility that Hupfauer and Votteler below him, who were on a very poor ice belay, would be unable to hold his fall and would also be plunged to their deaths.

Stopping periodically to wipe his gloved hand across the upper part of his face and crack away the ice that blocked his vision, his thighs and calves straining because of those loose crampons, his fingers now dead to all feeling, Haston somehow kept making progress. By now he was climbing blind, stabbing for purchase with his ice peg, delicately jabbing his loose crampons into the ice. He bleakly wondered if he would have to climb all the way up the Summit Icefield without protection. Every foot of height gained, he knew, would increase the velocity of his body should he fall, subsequently decreasing the chances that Hupfauer and Votteler would hold him, or even stay on the wall themselves. But then, after the buffeting slaps of a particularly fierce wind had caused him to stop and burrow in upright against the snow wall, he saw the clouds chase away up the slope, clearing the snowfield and revealing a rope dangling down, twenty feet off to his left. At that same moment, for two or three minutes, the top part of the face was clear, and down at Kleine Scheidegg watchers picked up five tiny dots toiling their way up the Summit Snowfield. A wave of jubilation swept the hotel. Barring some last minute complication, they were going to do it! Radio contact was established with the peak, where Bonington and Hiebeler were alerted to ready themselves to greet the climbers.

However, Haston was now faced with a desperate problem. His line had taken him up twenty feet to the right of the fixed rope. Somehow he had to traverse across that twenty feet. The rope lay down an ice gully, and a rock bulge separated him and the end of the rope. The rock prevented his climbing upward and bearing slightly left, so that his line would cross the rope. He had to traverse directly across to it, or risk losing it altogether.

He made a couple of tentative moves to his left but quickly drew back. His crampons were so loose now that he dared not trust them on a traverse where he couldn't cut steps. And without an axe, or at least the spike end of an ice hammer, he had no way of cutting even a tiny foothold. The only solution he could think of was a tension traverse, but on what? He still had his ice piton. He reached as high and as far to the left as he could and with his Hiebeler clamp (a small, lightweight piece of aluminum) managed to bang the peg an inch or so into the ice. It wobbled around in its groove and would easily pull out with any upward pressure, but it might yet do. To reduce the torque, he tied off a sling around the shaft of the piton and tight up against the face. Then he clipped a carabiner into the loop of the sling, threaded his climbing rope through and started his move.

He was acutely aware that three lives depended on a small piece of metal loosely placed in an inch-deep channel of ice. Held into the face by the tension of the rope, he managed to claw his way over the gap. Reaching the fixed rope, he clipped into it with the Hiebeler clamp, then hung there for a minute, all the tension drained from his body. He was beginning to believe that he just might possibly make it up the face after all. Minutes after he resumed climbing, he heard voices. Two vague figures gradually loomed up and took shape in the mist. Jörg and Günther, he thought, but the two leaders had already reached the summit and were now taking a break in the snow hole with their German comrades.

"It's a hard life!" Golikow shouted with a big grin. With him was Bonington, snapping away with his camera. Then the last two German climbers, Hupfauer and Votteler were up, and Bonington, his camera frozen, was trying to take a picture of the five-man assault team on the summit—the Eiger direct finally accomplished by men who looked as though they had survived some hellish catastrophe. They had now been

without hot food and drink for sixty straight hours. Their clothing was ripped, their equipment awry. Their eyes were sunk and bloodshot; their faces, "so low in the flesh, so high in the bone," as the song has it, were cadaverous with the strain of their ordeal. Their brows were covered with plastered snow that melted and then refroze into thin shields and plaques of ice. Icicles hung from their nostrils and the corners of their mouths. Their beards and mustaches were clotted with ice balls, and they literally tinkled when they suddenly moved their heads. Lehne reported that he tried to smile but couldn't, because his face was frozen into a gelid casque. He even had trouble talking because his lips were frozen.

They had been on the face for twenty-one days and had solved the last great Alpine problem. And they were alive. Meanwhile, that same afternoon, in the village of Leysin, the same snowstorm was dropping huge snowflakes on the people gathered to watch John Harlin's body being lowered into the grave. Marilyn was there, with the two children, John junior and Andrea. Layton Kor was there, wearing a white shirt hastily borrowed from Bonington and a black tie borrowed from Gillman. Konrad Kirch spoke and, ever the linguist, delivered his remarks in both English and French. Mourners were there from Grindelwald, Leysin, Germany, Chamonix. There were wreaths and messages of condolence from Harlin's climbing friends all over the world.

Simplest, and most touching, was a wreath from the members of the German Eiger direct team. The offering bore two plain English words: "Good-bye John."

26

A Flawed Rope?

The five climbers were forced to spend yet another night on the summit, in a snow cave, along with their friends, who kept brewing drinks of hot tea, coffee, and Ovomaltine, holding the cups up to the mouths of the climbers whose fingers were still too frozen to hold the drinks.

When they came down the west flank the next morning and arrived at Kleine Scheidegg, they found a telegram addressed to the joint Anglo-American-German team congratulating the members on their achieve-

Dougal Haston coming up the Summit Snowfield as he finishes the Harlin Direct.
CHRIS BONINGTON PHOTO

ment and thanking them for "continuing the climb in John's spirit." The telegram was signed by Marilyn Harlin, and John Harlin's parents.

There was the usual controversy after the climb, most of it centered on the team's use of Himalayan rather than Alpine tactics. It was claimed that the constant retreats to the lush surroundings of Kleine Scheidegg robbed the exploit of its spartan purity. Yet, when weather prevented continuous climbing, what else could the climbers do but come down? There was little point in staying on the face, eating up food supplies that would have to be replaced. One English publication ran the comment of a local guide who claimed that he could have dragged his grandmother up the network of ropes that festooned the face.

The sharpest controversy, though, was over John's death, and here some of the charges leveled had a certain measure of validity. There was criticism of using a fixed rope only seven millimeters thick. Yet this was the standard size of rope used for Alpine jumaring. The rope was designed to hold 2,000 pounds, eight times more than the weight of the average climber and his rucksack. It wasn't designed to bear the slamming shock of a human body being suddenly arrested after a hundred-foot fall, for example, but the seven-millimeter rope, unlike the eleven-millimeter climbing rope, rarely, if ever, faced that contingency when used on a prusik or jumar. There is little, if any, shock force on a prusik rope. Then too, using heavier ropes would have meant that much added weight for the climbers to carry up the face, a vital consideration in view of the literally miles of rope that were used by both teams.

When Golikow came down after having stripped the ropes from the face, he brought with him a thin slab of rock in the hairline cracks of which could be seen fibers of the rope where they had abraded before breaking. He also brought a small piece of rope showing the splayed-out pattern of threads where the break actually occurred. The fibers were worn rather than cut, a fact that eliminated the possibility that the sharp edge of a falling rock had struck the rope at precisely the right angle to cut it through. Golikow also reported having examined, some hundred feet below the break, a piton that was bent over double and still held a tiny patch of red fabric that must have been ripped from Harlin's anorak. The falling climber obviously struck the peg and wall with some force, probably hard enough to render him unconscious, though this, of course, is conjecture. It was obvious, when the body was found, that Harlin was dead well before he reached the base of the mountain. The list of his injuries, in the autopsy report, filled a whole page.

It was asked why that particular length of rope had broken, while similar stretches of rope on the lower face had been jumared over a hundred times without parting. As it turned out, that particular stretch of seven-millimeter perlon had not been part of the original store of

rope made by, Mammut, one of Switzerland's most highly reputed manufacturers of cordage, but had been part of several hundred meters purchased in a local shop when the original supply of seven-millimeter rope
had run out. Possibly the locally purchased rope was substandard or
contained an undetected flaw in an otherwise standard rope. One
German-language paper headlined its story, "Fall Due to Flaw in Rope."

There were two other criticisms. The first was that the climbing
ropes should have been inspected daily, especially at points of stress
where the rope ran over a piece of rock. If either Haston or Hupfauer,
both of whom preceded Harlin up the rope that afternoon, had
inspected the several inches that ran over the edge of rock, they couldn't
have failed to notice the frayed condition of the rope. Such rope inspection, taking practically no time, should have been part of the mountaineers' normal precautionary measures. When Golikow did make such an
inspection, just after Harlin's death, he found half a dozen badly frayed
spots in the fixed ropes. And Bonington, earlier in the climb, had
noticed that some of the fixed ropes were beginning to fray. On the
other hand, Haston said that he had noticed some slight abrasion in the
outer sheath of the rope here and there, but no more than normal. Also,
immediately above the break, the rope had run over a smooth, rounded
edge. The possibility of its breaking had never occurred to him, and he
had been the climber immediately preceding Harlin on that fatal length
of rope.

There was the added criticism that each climber, while jumaring,
should have been belayed by a partner. However, that was not the practice in Alpine mountaineering, would have slowed an already slow climb,
and would not have helped those who, like Kor, frequently jumared
alone with supply loads. A rope's actually breaking with a climber on
jumar clamps was practically unknown. Death in Alpine climbing came
most often from falling rock, from being swept away in avalanches, from
exhaustion and cold, from rappelling mistakes, or from falls while the
climber was unroped and hiking over "easy" sections. Even the deaths
that occurred while a climber was on a prusik, or jumaring, were usually
caused by clamps that iced up and jumped off the rope, or an exhausted
climber who, not thinking clearly, inadvertently pulled the release handle on a waist jumar, causing his body to fall backward and his foot to
slide out of the foot sling.

There were still some purists who insisted that you didn't come down
midway through a climb. When you started out, you carried what you
needed with you and climbed until the route was finished. The answer
to that charge was that the Eiger direct couldn't be done that way. Stone
fall down the face on the direct line was too heavy in the summer to be
battled through. Given that the Harlin Direct was the straightest route

from base to summit, that the safest time to climb it was in winter, and that it required a week to ten days of actual climbing time, it was still almost impossible to find a stretch of clear weather lasting that long. It was inevitable that the climbers would be forced to hole up in snow caves because of poor weather, eat up their food supplies, and then be forced down in order to replenish such supplies.

As for the charge that the success of the Harlin Direct would be followed by scores of teams trying Himalayan tactics on other Alpine faces, the truth is that there is only one Eigernordwand. There are no other Alpine faces that can compare with it in size, in difficulty, in sheer height, and in objective dangers.

As it was, the Eiger direct climbers paid a price for their achievement. Both Bonington and Haston had to be hospitalized in London for severe frostbite and were lucky not to have lost toes or fingers—particularly Haston, whose right hand was covered with huge, black frostbite blisters. Not so lucky were Votteler and Strobel. Both had all their toes amputated in the hospital in Stuttgart. Lehne lost the big toe on his right foot.

Several months later Haston took over as director of the International School of Mountaineering that Harlin had founded in Leysin. Haston's subsequent climbing career included a winter climb of the Matterhorn's north face with Mick Burke, a 1970 Annapurna south-face ascent with Don Whillans, a first ascent with Doug Scott of Changabang in the Himalayas in 1974, and an ascent of Everest with Scott in 1975. The 1975 expedion was led by Chris Bonington and succeeded in putting four men on the summit, including Peter Boardman, at twenty-one the youngest ever to have climbed Everest. On that same expedition, however, Mick Burke disappeared near the summit. His body has not yet been found.

On January 17, 1977, while skiing down a couloir above Leysin, Haston was engulfed in an avalanche and killed. He was thirty-seven years old. Haston was considered by many people to be austere and aloof. This was especially true after he was convicted of killing a pedestrian in England—"causing death by careless driving"—for which he served several months in jail. He was so affected by the death that he never drove a car again. Still, for the score of years that this brilliant climber graced the Alpine and Himalayan scene, he blazed a bright trail. On Haston's death, Peter Boardman took over as director of the ISM School in Leysin.

The German team leaders, Jörg Lehne and Peter Haag, coauthored a book on the Eiger Direct, *Eiger: Kampf um die Direttissima*. Not available in English, it was published by the Belser Verlag in Stuttgart in 1966 and is dedicated to Marilyn Harlin. The Eiger Direct, Lehne had promised his wife, would be his last major climb. A true mountaineer, however, finds it hard to stay away from the mountains. During the summer of 1970 he went to Chamonix with his friend Karl Golikow to climb the Walker Spur of the Grandes Jorasses. While in their first night's bivouac, they were caught by rockfall that mortally wounded Lehne and left Golikow with a broken thigh. Lehne's last words were typical of the man: "Thank you, Karli, for the good times we've had."

Very early in the morning, deep in shock and pain, the dead body of his comrade beside him, Golikow was reached by two British climbers attracted by cries for help. Will Barker and Dave Yates climbed to his ledge in the dark, using flashlights. When they reached the position and Golikow heard English voices, he greeted his rescuers with a pained smile and the comment, "It's a bloody hard life." Barker and Yates took care of the leg as best they could, then moved Golikow farther down the mountain to where he could be lifted off by helicopter. Golikow kept up a cheerful conversation throughout, Barker reported, faltering only when the broken bones grated, or the rescuers inadvertently bumped or jarred his body while carrying him down.

Two years later, mountain fit once more, Golikow was climbing the northeast face of the Piz Badile in Switzerland with his partner Otto Uhl. Another rope was also on the wall at the same time, old Eiger friend Siegfried Hupfauer and a partner. Golikow and Uhl had planned on a lightning climb of the face and had therefore brought no down jackets or bivouac sacks. However, a vicious storm blew up and brought plunging temperatures. Night caught them, and they were forced to bivouac without adequate clothes or protection. During the course of the night Uhl died of exposure. Golikow tried to fight his way off the face and onto the north ridge. He had almost made it to the ridge the next morning when he, too, succumbed to the cold and died, that cheerful heart now cracked forever. Hupfauer and his partner managed to complete the climb, though both were exhausted and barely made it down.

Hupfauer went on to climb in the Himalayas and in 1973 was a member of the team that put up a new route on Manaslu (26,760 feet). In 1978 he climbed Everest. Günther Strobel also climbed in the Himalayas, making ascents of Nanga Parbat and Manaslu.

Layton Kor went back to his native Colorado after the climb. A year later, along with Wayne Goss, he did the first winter ascent of the Diamond face of Longs Peak in Colorado, one of the great "big wall" climbs in America. The climb was a new route. Not long afterward Kor became active in Jehovah's Witnesses. In 1969 his nephew Kordel Kor took a fall on Longs Peak and was very seriously hurt. Whether as a result of this or of John Harlin's death or of his new-found interest in religion, Layton Kor stopped climbing. He lives today in Glenwood Springs, Colorado, and refuses to even talk about climbing. "I'm completely out of climbing," he told one writer who wanted information on the Eiger Direct. "You'll have to talk to the other survivors of the climb, if there are any left."

There are climbers in Colorado who will tell you that, despite these disclaimers, they've recently seen Layton Kor on winter climbs in isolated areas of the state. "Layton, the great un," a legend while he climbed, evidently is still a legend in his retirement.

John Harlin's son, John Harlin III, is today a skilled rock and alpine climber and guide, working mainly in Colorado. He writes frequently for climbing publications.

After the Harlin Direct it seemed that the Eiger had no challenges left. The direct probably was the last great epic climb. Although there were no Eiger "firsts" left, the mountain and its mountaineers still had a few surprises to offer.

27
A North-Wall First: The Rising Sun

There were no further climbs of the Eiger in 1966. In March of 1967 Roland Travellini, a thirty-one-year-old French climber from Montreuil, a suburb of Paris, came to Grindelwald with the announced intention of doing a solo on the Harlin Direct. He had been to the Eiger in 1965, but had withdrawn from the lower reaches of the face with the comment that he didn't like the condition of the iced-up rock, which was even worse than that on Mont Blanc. Now he was back.

He left Kleine Scheidegg for the wall early one morning and was never seen again. Nor was his body found. The general belief is that he must have fallen to the foot of the wall and into a crevasse that completely hid his body. Travellini was the Eiger's twenty-ninth fatality, and there were more to come.

On July 18, 1967, four German mountaineers, escorted by several friends, arrived in Grindelwald to do the Eigernordwand. They were Günter Warmuth, twenty-five; Kurt Richter, Thirty; Günter Kalkbrenner, thirty-two; and Fritz Eske, thirty-three. All four were experienced climbers who had just come from Zermatt, where they had climbed the Matterhorn's north face on July 16 and 17.

At 1 P.M. on July 21 they started up the easy ledges at the foot of the wall. The quartet reached the Shattered Pillar by 3 P.M. They were watched from a repair depot by several workers on the Jungfraujoch cog railway. They were also being watched by Fritz von Almen, who was surprised by the speed with which they mastered the Difficult Crack. The four climbers moved on. They were several pitches below the start of the Hinterstoisser, all four roped together, at 4:15 P.M., Kurt Richter leading the pitch. He climbed twenty feet or so, banged in a piton for protection, then moved on up. But something happened, and he peeled off his holds, fell backward, and ripped out the protection piton. Then he was tumbling and bounding down the sixty-degree slope. He shot past Fritz Eske on the belay stance, and seconds later the rope twanged as it went taut with strain. For a split second Fritz Eske held, but then he, too, was pulled off his stance. Richter was unable to right himself in time to grab something, and now two bodies were bouncing and bounding, with sickening thuds, down the face. Warmuth, next on the rope, desperately tried to halt the plunge but failed, and he too was snapped off in turn. The falling rope of three, yanking each other's bodies in brutal leapfrogging plunges off ledges and boulders, now whipped Kalkbrenner off, and the last man on the rope was tumbling helplessly after his comrades. At the top of the Shattered Pillar the rope broke between the others and Kalkbrenner.

Down below a young railway conductor, who saw every phase of the fall through binoculars, turned to two workers nearby. Ashen-faced with shock, he described what he had just witnessed. The workers immediately set off for the wall. On the way they met two friends of the climbers who had accompanied them to the foot of the face. They were unaware of the tragedy being played out above them. The railway workers told them of the accident, and the German pair turned back to help.

The next morning, guides of the Grindelwald rescue unit went out to search the screes and crevasses at the foot of the Eiger. They found three bodies, all except Kalkbrenner's. The guides later issued a report in which they stated that rockfall was not to blame for the tragedy. The climbers were just under the Rote Fluh. A handhold must have come away, and the protection piton which should have held Richter simply hadn't been driven deeply or securely enough. Because the climbers were still on the so-called easy part of the wall, the other two below Eske hadn't bothered to anchor themselves to the face, relying solely on Eske's body strength to hold a possible leader fall. Had Kalkbrenner, last on the rope, been on a solid anchor belay and using a belay plate (a simple friction device to improve the holding power of a belayer), he should have been able to stop all three falling climbers. In fact the rope should have parted before he was pulled off his anchor.

On August 1, two Czech climbers, Sylvia Kysilkova and Franz Chlumsky were climbing up between the First Pillar and the Shattered

Pillar. Sylvia hoped to become the second woman to do the Eigernord-wand. Just to the left of the Shattered Pillar the Czechs spotted a body lying crumpled on a ledge. They traversed to the ledge, and Sylvia was shattered to discover the remains of Günter Kalkbrenner, a climber she knew very well.

The four deaths were the highest number of fatalities on a single climb since the deaths of Hinterstoisser, Kurz, Rainer, and Angerer in 1936, and brought the fatality toll to thirty-three.

Less than two weeks later an Austrian pair, Hans Herzel, twenty-one, and Kurt Reichardt, twenty-three, started up the face after having waited almost two weeks to make their attempt. They bivouacked the first night at the Flatiron. The next day the weather was bad and they had trouble on the Ramp, which was heavily iced up. Fog and cloud hid them from view, but they probably bivouacked that night at the start of the Traverse of the Gods. The next day brought snow, but they fought their way up through the Spider to bivouac a final time in the Exit Cracks. They reached a summit bathed in sunshine at noon the follow-ing day. The west flank was frozen with new snow and ice, but, of course, the conditions were not nearly as severe as they were on the north face. Roped loosely together, but not belaying each other, the pair descended. Somehow one of them slipped and went sprawling down an ice slope, dragging his partner after him. The pair fell almost a thousand feet and were dead when Lauterbrunnen guides found them the following day. It was a familiar story in mountain climbing, a moment of carelessness on the descent after the climb was over, and a dearly won victory turned into the ultimate defeat of death.

Over the course of the summer of 1967, there were seven successful ascents, including the second by a woman when Christine de Colombelle and her partner Jack Sangnier from Grenoble, France, spent seven days and six bivouacs on the 1938 Heckmair Route. The other six teams were composed of thirteen climbers, of whom nine were Austrian—Otto Cud-rich, Franz Hawelka, Toni Schramm, Helmut Fiedler, Kurt Reichardt, Ignaz Gansberger, Hans Herzel, Helmut Lenes, and Karl Winkler; two German—Manfred Rogge and Hans Saler; and two Swiss—Paul Nigg and Ernst Neeracher. However, 1967 also saw seven fatalities, the largest number of climbers ever killed in a single year on the Eiger. The moun-tain was far from tamed.

The development of climbing on a big wall in the Yosemite Valley, or on a big Alpine face such as the Eiger, tends to follow the same pro-gression. First, the easiest route is climbed. Someone then finds a harder line, a *direttissima*, and that, too, is mastered. The desire to be first, to climb a line that no one has ever climbed before, to set hand and foot on a piece of rock and be practically certain that you are the first human being ever to have touched that particular part of our planet, to explore the unknown through a new route, is a powerful motivating factor, and soon there are anywhere from four to forty different lines up a particular face.

In 1968 two parties, Polish and German, were looking at a new route, a possible third on the Eigernordwand. There was the classic 1938 route, the 1966 John Harlin Direct, and now what came to be known as the North Pillar Route. This line, between the Eigerwand Station and the ridge followed by Lauper and his party in 1932, was well to the east of the 1938 route. There were three bands of broken cliffs, separated by three buttresses or pillars, and it was a classic Eiger route with a little bit of everything thrown in—a total of more than 5,000 feet of ice, snow, rotten rock, rockfall, avalanche, and waterfalls.

A Polish party of four—Krzysztof Cielecki, Tadeusz Laukajtys, Ryszard Szafirski, and Adam Zyzak—took three days doing the route. They roughly followed the Harlin Direct as far as the Eigerwand Station windows, traversed left to the foot of the Second Pillar, then climbed up and across to the Mittellegi Ridge and thence to the summit.

Back home in Poland the four talked of doing a new Eiger direct, but in Alpine circles the claim was treated with skepticism. It was a route that wandered all over and exited on the Lauper Ridge at approximately the same level as the top of the Flatiron. It wasn't direct, and at least half of the climb wasn't on the north face proper.

The day after the Polish climb, another team of four climbers, led by Toni Hiebeler, also started up a new route on the east side of the north face. Hiebeler had been a member of the successful German team that had made the first winter ascent of the north wall in 1961. Along with him were two Italians, the South Tyrolean brothers Reinhold and Günther Messner, and Fritz Maschke, a friend of Hiebeler's. The four men climbed the broken screes to the left of the First Pillar, then tackled the cliff. In late afternoon they were level with the top of the First Pillar and preparing to bivouac when they noticed the tracks of four climbers, crossing a snowfield. The trail had been made by the Polish party that had started up the face the day before and had crossed over from the Eigerwand Station that morning. The Messner brothers followed the tracks for three rope lengths and found where the party had bivouacked. They abseiled back down to where Hiebeler and Maschke were, leaving fixed ropes behind them.

It was a cold, uncomfortable bivouac that night, as water gushed down from the cliff face above them, and it wasn't long before everything and everyone was sodden. They couldn't get their stoves going and thus had nothing hot to eat or drink, but fortunately the temperature stayed relatively mild. The next morning they started up the fixed ropes and soon reached the strangers' bivouac, where they found some notes written in Polish that revealed the nationality of the other team on their route. Two pitches further on, the Polish tracks veered sharply away to the Lauper Ridge. The German-Italian party stayed true, climbing short crumbly walls separated here and there by steep ice pitches. By the end of the second day they were on a level with the Mittellegi hut and within a thousand feet or so of the summit. They spent another sodden bivouac night, the temperature much colder now because of the increased altitude.

It was snowing the next morning when they started out. After some tricky pitches on crumbling rock, the four men emerged on the Mittellegi Ridge, which they followed on up to the summit. They had established a new route on the Eigernordwand, the third. For Toni Hiebeler this third route was his second Eiger "first."

The Messner brothers went on to world-wide fame as mountain climbers. In 1970, Reinhold was near the top of Nanga Parbat, climbing alone, up the Rupal Face. Near the summit he looked down the slope and saw Günther following in his tracks. Both men were exhausted, and, as neither had a rope, they decided to go down the easier Diamir Flank. They bivouacked once, on the way down, and had put the hardest part of the retreat behind them when an avalanche evidently caught Günther and swept him away. Reinhold spent a whole day wandering pitifully around, searching for his brother, without success. He then stumbled down to the valley, where some natives found him. His feet were frostbitten, and several toes had to be amputated. Two years later he did a new route on the south face of Manaslu, once again a solo climb. He was to return to the Eiger's classic route in 1974, with his climbing partner Peter Habeler.

The year 1969 saw a wave of Japanese climbers in the Alps, and inevitably they came to the Eiger. It will be remembered that in 1965 a Japanese, Tsuneaki Watabe, took a bad fall in the Exit Cracks and broke a leg. His partner Mitsumasa Takada secured his friend and completed the climb alone, thus becoming the first Japanese mountaineer to do the classic north-face route. Unfortunately his partner Watabe fell to his death before he could be rescued. It was an unfortunate introduction to the Eigernordwand for Japanese climbers, and they didn't return for another four years. But in 1969 they were back in force.

Mountain climbing is popular sport in Japan, with an estimated three to four million adherents. One Japanese peak, Mount Tanigawadake, north of Tokyo, has already claimed the lives of over 600 climbers! Despite these mortality figures, Japanese mountains simply don't pose the same degree of difficulty as the Alps or the Himalayas, and, with the increasing prosperity of the average Japanese, it was inevitable that they would soon appear in those regions.

Like New Zealand climbers, and for much the same reasons, the Japanese wanted to climb the hardest routes once they reached the Alps. Having come halfway around the world and having gone to great expense, they wanted to show something special for their efforts. Many of the Japanese climbers took the Trans-Siberian Railway across Russia and into Eastern Europe, a tiring three-week trip that was then considerably cheaper than airfare. The Japanese had, of course, read about the Eiger in their own mountaineering publications, and a group of them arrived in Europe with the goal of doing the first summer ascent, and the second ever, of the John Harlin Direct. However, they were quickly dissuaded by several European climbers who pointed out that the Harlin Route went straight up the face in the path of the heaviest rockfall and would be murderous to climb in the summer. It was really a route for the winter, when ice kept the rocks firmly clamped to the face.

The Japanese now planned a new direct—one long advocated by Toni Hiebeler—going up the Rote Fluh. This great wall is avoided on the normal route by use of the Hinterstoisser Traverse, which swings the climber to the left and down to the start of the First Icefield. The Rote Fluh, a sheer wall, is almost a thousand feet at its highest point. The line the Japanese would follow, however, was only about six hundred feet. Because the wall was sheer, rocks coming down the face sailed harmlessly off the lip and into space, well clear of anyone working on the wall itself.

The leader of the Japanese team was twenty-five-year-old Takio Kato, one of Japan's finest climbers, who had already done the north face of the Matterhorn. Takio's brother Yasuo, a university student, was at twenty the youngest member of the six-man team. The team doctor, Michiko Imai, twenty-seven, was one of Japan's top woman climbers. She and another Japanese woman, Yosehiko Wakayama, had previously made the first all-woman ascent of the Matterhorn's north face, the first of the three major Alpine north faces to be climbed by an all-female team. The other three team members were Susumu Kubo, twenty-four, an electrician; Hirofumi Amano, twenty-two, an engineer; and Satoru Negishi, twenty-two, a railwayman.

The Japanese came with a full ton of equipment including over 200 expansion bolts, 200 pitons, 200 carabiners, and enough rope to reach from the base of the Eiger to the peak and then back down again—over 13,000 feet of cordage. In addition they had the usual number of ice axes, ice hammers, crampons, Hiebeler clamps, jumars, as well as three lightweight pulleys for load hauling. They even brought most of their own food.

The Japanese team intended to bolt their way methodically up the Rote Fluh, a face with few vertical cracks, or even cracklings, for piton placements. Although the use of bolts is frowned on by many Alpine climbers, the Japanese clearly favored them. Some bolts, fewer than a dozen, had been used on the Harlin Direct but only as belay or rappel points, where a particularly strong anchor was imperative. In bolting, one uses a hammer and hand drill to bore out a hole approximately two inches deep. Into this hole a malleable bolt that is slightly larger than the hole is tapped home. Compression causes the bolt to grip the surrounding rock tightly. The end of the bolt has a hanger into which a carabiner can be clipped. Bolts are considered much safer than pitons, but they involve mutilation of the rock itself, in a way that pitons do not. And, of course, once driven home, a bolt is very difficult to take out again and is usually left in place.

With bolts any cliff face, no matter how steep or faultless, can be climbed, given time and a sufficient number of bolts. Bolting reached its apogee, or height of absurdity, depending on one's viewpoint, when an Italian climb of Cerro Torre in South America was made possible by a gasoline-powered compressor hauled up the cliff face to power a mechanical drill for boring bolt holes. The compressor hangs on the rock of Cerro Torre to this day. On Cerro Torre normal piton placements were ignored. Bolts were placed every three feet up the wall. This sort of tactic has done much to revive enthusiasm for "clean" and "free" climbing, a reversion to the Victorian days of mountaineering when the use of pitons was not considered "sporting," or giving the mountain a fair chance, as it were.

The Japanese pitched their tents at the foot of the Eiger and were soon preparing camps on the face. This was to be a Himalayan or siege climb, not the classic Alpine straight-ahead push. Two climbers, unladen except for essential climbing tools and hardware, would go out in front, route finding and fixing ropes for the rest of the party, which would, in the interim, ferry food and equipment from one camp to another, much the same strategy used by the Harlin Direct team.

Their first camp was established just below the Difficult Crack, a place they named Hotel Eiger. Their next camp was at the base of the Rote Fluh, and it was here, at the start of the Hinterstoisser, that the line departed from the original route. Now the bolting began on the soaring, clean face of the Rote Fluh. Bolting is a slow process, it can take upward of half an hour to get one bolt properly placed. A bolt provides approximately three feet of headway. The climber advances only six feet an hour. Of course, other factors will affect the rate of progress—the hardness of the rock, the strength and skill of the bolter, the severity of the weather, even the temperature. The Japanese used up 150 of their bolts on the 550-foot line they followed on the Red Wall. As they bolted, they fixed ropes for the rest of the team to ascend on jumars. Meanwhile the other members were ferrying supplies from the meadow tents to Hotel Eiger, or from Hotel Eiger to camp II, "fortress" camp, at the foot of the Rote Fluh. The Japanese were lucky in that the valley was blessed with day after day of faultless blue skies, the longest stretch of good weather in over twenty years.

The good weather brought out many other teams trying the 1938 route, and hardly a day passed without the Japanese having drop-in guests at their "fortress" camp. The visitors would exhange greetings, wish the Oriental climbers good luck, then swing away on the Hinterstoisser while the Japanese went back to work on the cliff overhead. There was a rumor that two of the Japanese climbers, impatient with the slow progress of their direct, asked permission to leave the direct team, join two of their countrymen climbing the 1938 route, then rejoin their comrades two days later. It could actually have been done, a "classic" within a "direct," but apparently the pair couldn't be spared.

Finally the Rote Fluh was all prepared, and the teams climbed to its head and then up the right side of the Second Icefield, where they were fortunate enough to find a small cave to serve as camp III. Now the hard work began, ferrying all the equipment up the Red Crag while a pair of route-finding lead climbers went exploring on ahead from camp III. It was while route finding that Michiko Imai, the team doctor, took a violent blow on the shoulder from a large rock that came loose from the wall, fortunately not too far above her. For a while it was feared that she would have to withdraw from the climb. The injury was severe enough to force her to stop route finding or hauling. She had to spend the next week or so practically immobilized at camp III, restricting her work to such routine jobs as cooking and cleaning, chores she admittedly hated, whether at home or on the mountain. Fortunately she was still able to give medical help to the other team members as needed.

Above the Second Icefield the Japanese were cut off from the base and from Kleine Scheidegg when their radio failed. At this point they stripped the ropes from the Rote Fluh, committing themselves to finishing the climb, because they were now past the point at which an adverse weather report might cause a retreat. They had been two weeks on the route, and with the ropes stripped from the Rote Fluh, could no longer descend periodically for rest and recuperation to the relative comforts of the fortress or Eiger hotel, or the meadow tents of base camp. They took a two weeks' supply of food with them for the final effort.

The rock bands above the Second Icefield turned out to be very difficult, Grades V and VI. Lead climber Kato took one fall when the small cogwheels on his jumars froze and didn't grip the line. He slid down the rope thirty feet before one leg got hung up and he was flipped backward, to hang upside down on the rope. Fortunately he was able to right himself and climb back up.

At a place called the Center Band, roughly parallel to the Traverse of the Gods, camp IV was established on a narrow, sloping ledge. Above, the way to the summit was blocked by a huge pillar called the Sphinx. The Japanese were still wonderfully lucky with the weather, having so far experienced only one light snowfall. Several days of hard crack and chimney climbing now brought them to the top of the Sphinx, a couple of hundred feet above and to the right of the Spider. Here, a tiny ledge served as camp V. Now their luck with the weather finally ran out, as a savage storm swept in, with snow, hail, thunder and lightning—a storm that caused constant snowslides and severe icing up of the route.

The rest of the way was a grim struggle to reach the summit before their food ran out. Every foot of the wall had to be fought and the severe, Grade-VI pitches were made doubly bad by ice conditions and freezing temperatures. The worst moment came when Yasuo Kato took a twenty-foot fall, breaking his nose. He was treated by Imai, and the climb continued. Their last bivouac was just beneath the summit, on their fifteenth consecutive day on the face and exactly one month to the day since they had started the climb. Their food had run out, and they were near exhaustion.

The French mountain climber Jack Sangnier, who had two Eiger ascents to his credit, including a solo on the Lauper Route, climbed the west flank in the storm along with a client in order to meet the Japanese climbers and offer them some treats in the way of food and drink that he brought along in a rucksack. He met the snow-coated Japanese on the summit, "looking like ghosts," as he later reported, and here team leader Kato proved that he was well versed indeed in Eiger history. He refused any food or drink from Sangnier, and later, at the base of the west flank, when a railway official gallantly offered to carry Imai's knapsack, Kato stopped him and reminded Imai that their climb didn't end until they had all reached the Eigergletscher Station, still several hundred feet away. Kato wanted no press reports that the Japanese were so exhausted that they had to be assisted down from the summit, nor was he taking any chances on eventually getting a bill from the local guides for "rescue" operations.

The usual controversy sprang up afterward. The heavy reliance on bolts meant that the Japanese style of climbing was more engineering than art. Why not build scaffolding while they were at it? Thirty-one days to climb a wall! That wasn't Alpine climbing; that was a military campaign or window cleaning or whatever, but no longer a sport. Still, a normal progression in mountaineering is to have a route climbed with heavy reliance on direct aid, then to have it done again and again, each time with less aid, until someone finally climbs it free, using pitons or an occasional already-in-place bolt, solely as protection against a fall.

Whatever the criticism, a new direct had been established on the Eigernordwand, perhaps not quite as direct a line as the Harlin Route, but a new and challenging one for all that—the *Japaner Direttissima,* as it came to be known locally. Another white laddered band of steps could be printed on the Eigernordwand postcards that showed the various routes. There were now four; including two directs, something of a contradiction in terms.

One thing the Japanese proved was that they had moved into the top rank of mountaineering countries. Actually, that summer, while the Japanese were doing their direct, a total of eleven of their compatriots climbed the regular 1938 route. And Japanese teams would be back twice more on the Eiger within the next nine months.

28

The Worst Winter in a Hundred Years

The winter of 1969–70 brought something new for Eiger watchers. At one point they could follow three teams working on three different Nordwand routes at the same time.

In late November of 1969, six Japanese climbers, all in their late twenties, were at Kleine Scheidegg, intending to do a second ascent of the Harlin Direct as preparation for a later Himalayan objective. The team was led by Jiro Endo and Takao Hoshino, two of Japan's top climbers, who already had a Matterhorn north-face ascent to their credit. The others were Masatsugu Konishi, Masaru Sanba, Yukio Shimamura, and Ryoichi Fukata. Once again the Japanese brought along a full ton of equipment, including several hundred bolts. Very few bolts had been used in the original climb of the Harlin Direct, but the Japanese seemed to love bolting their way up high walls. In fact, two of the climbers were machinists.

For several weeks the Japanese, who had flown to Switzerland, hung around waiting for their equipment, which had been shipped by sea and was now held up in Marseilles by a dock strike. Their gear eventually arrived, and on the day after Christmas they began transporting everything to the base of the wall. Appropriately enough, they started the climb proper on January 1, 1970, the first day of a new decade, pushing

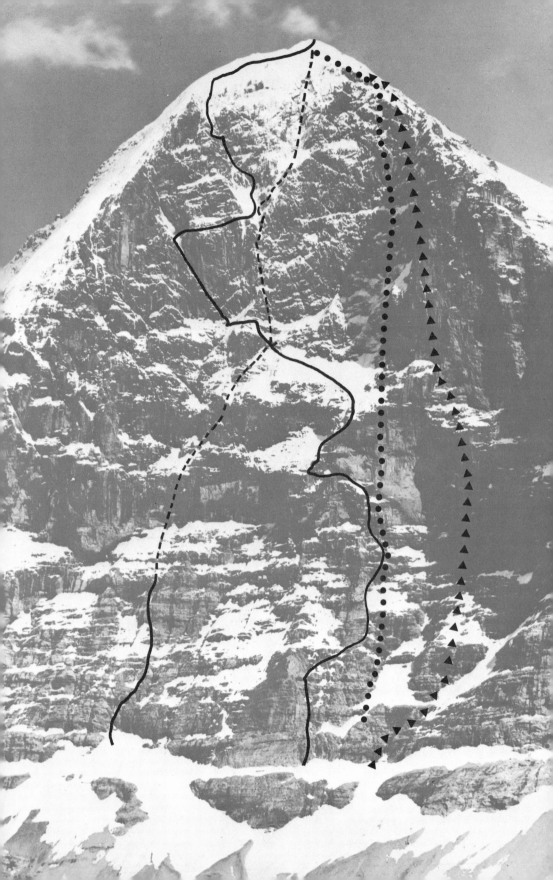

their ropes up to the foot of the First Band. The weather, however, was not favorable. As though to make up for all that good weather the earlier Japanese summer team had received, the skies lowered and churned while snowstorm chased snowstorm across the Eiger face. The Japanese spent day after day holed up in various snow caves, listening on their shortwave radios to music tapes played for them down at Kleine Scheidegg.

It was actually mid-February before they reached the snowfield between the First and Second bands. Falls were frequent, and Fukata took a twenty-foot tumble that put him out of action for several days. Even when, in brief stretches, climbing was possible, sometimes only twenty feet of headway was accomplished in a day. Because the climbing was so slow, ferrying supplies did not take as much time as expected, and the team now established a new alternating pattern—two climbers route finding and fixing ropes, two ferrying supplies up and down the ropes, and two resting back at Kleine Scheidegg.

Camp II was established at the site of the German *Eispalast* on the original 1966 climb of the route. Camp III was set up at the foot of the Flatiron, and camp IV at Death Bivouac. But it was now the end of February, and the Japanese were beginning to have serious doubts as to their ability to finish the climb. The best summer in twenty years was being followed, according to local inhabitants, by the worst winter in over a hundred years. When an occasional clear day did come along, constant snow avalanches set off by sun and settling snow pack, made climbing almost impossible. Still, by March 3 the Japanese had reached the Kor Traverse at the foot of the Central Pillar. Here, where Kor had done the traverse on thin knife-blade pitons, sometimes tied off with hero loops, the Japanese utilized bolts all the way, unable to see the tiny cracks that Kor had used. The Japanese had nothing to be ashamed of in relying on bolts. There weren't half a dozen climbers in the world with Kor's "superb piton artistry," as Dougal Haston called it, his uncanny skill in finding good piton placements.

On the traverse, Sanba took a thirty-foot fall when a bolt popped free, though fortunately he suffered no injuries. March 10 saw the Japanese on the Spider, where they established camp V halfway up the icefield. Several good climbing days brought them up to the Fly and camp

――――――――― 1938 ROUTE

― ― ― ― ― ― ― 1966 HARLIN DIRECT

● ● ● ● ● ● ● 1969 JAPANESE DIRECT

▶ ▶ ▶ ▶ ▶ 1976 CZECH DIRECT

VI. The rock bands above the Fly called for all their skills, most of the pitches being Grades V and VI. The rock was rotten, and protection often thin or nonexistent. Some days they climbed as little as forty feet. But they were now committed to reaching the summit. Jiro Endo later wrote that due to the cold, the snow, and the appalling climbing conditions, the men were all depressed and close to exhaustion, and he doubted if they would have undertaken the climb had they known of the difficulties they would face "on this horrible wall and its terrible weather," as he described the face.

On March 17 three climbers overcame the final pitch on the head wall and went up the Summit Icefield for a hundred meters. Then they abseiled down to the others and announced that they would all be on top the following day. Despite a vicious storm, so bad that the men could barely see each other as they moved up the fixed ropes, they reached the summit by noon the following day, seventy-seven days after they had started the climb. On the peak the winds were so fierce that the climbers had to hold onto each other to keep from being blown off the snowfield. To commemorate a dead climbing comrade who had wanted to do the Eiger with them, but whose life had been cut short in a climbing accident, they buried their rope mate's ice axe, which they had brought with them from Japan, in the Summit Snowfield.

Then the climbers did something incredible, an action that showed their sensitivity to criticism that the earlier Japanese team had left most of their ropes and pitons strung over the face. They turned around and went abseiling down the fixed ropes, stripping them as they went, leaving the face as clean as they had found it. That night they bivouacked at the Spider, and it took two more bivouacs before they got down to the base of the wall with all their equipment. They even brought down a red bivouac sack that had been left behind by Jörg Lehne and Günther Strobel on the 1966 Harlin Direct.

It had been an epic, three-month climb that fully matched, if not exceeded, the heroism of the 1966 Harlin Direct, a whole winter spent climbing a wall in the worst weather to hit the Bernese Oberland in over a hundred years.

That same January another Japanese team had been working on the Eigernordwand, seeking to accomplish the second winter ascent of the 1938 route in a straight-ahead Alpine push. The team leader was Kenji Kimura who, the preceding summer, had climbed the regular route, thus completing the trio of great northern faces—these of the Matterhorn, Grandes Jorasses, and Eiger. The others were Yuji Hattori, Tetsuo Komiyama, Masaru Ogawa, and Masaru Morita. They had the same vicious stormy weather to contend with as the Japanese Direct team, but they nevertheless made excellent progress, and their seventh day found them well up in the Exit Cracks. Kenji Kimura was leading on the notorious Quartz Crack, where he found and clipped into an old piton from an earlier climb. The peg ripped out, and although his fall was short, he broke an ankle. Word was relayed to Kleine Scheidegg and a rescue operation set in motion. The Swiss Air Rescue Service helicoptered guides, steel cables, and winches to a point on the Mittellegi Ridge directly above the Exit Snowfield. Guides quickly set up their equipment, and two of them, Rudolf Kaufmann of Grindelwald and Oskar Gertsch of Wengen, went down on a cable, strapped Kimura to Kaufmann's back in a Gramminger sling, and brought him back up to the Summit Snowfield. A hovering helicopter winched Kimura up into the machine, and a short time later he was in the hospital in Interlaken. It was the first helicopter rescue from the summit of the Eiger. The whole operation had taken less that twenty-four hours, a remarkable accomplishment when one considers that it took three full days to winch Corti up to safety in 1957 and another day to get him back down to Kleine Scheidegg. The rest of the team completed the climb on January 27, its ninth day on the face. Tragically, the guide Oskar Gertsch was later to lose his life in an avalanche on a Canadian mountain in January, 1979.

While two Japanese teams were notching "seconds" on the Harlin and 1938 routes, a five-man Swiss team composed of Alpinists from the Thun climbing club, *Bergfalken* (Mountain Falcons), was upholding the mountaineering reputation of its country by doing both a "second" and a "first" on the *Japaner Direttissima* Route of the previous summer. Their intention was to make a first winter ascent, as well as the second-ever climb of the route.

The team's leader, Peter Jungen, twenty-five, had already done the 1938 route the year before. The Swiss climbers started their attempt on December 21, but a snowstorm forced them to come down off the wall, and, once down, they took a few extra days for the Christmas holidays. They started back up again on the twenty-seventh and made fairly good progress. Of course, the Rote Fluh had already been bolted by the first Japanese Direct team, and their bolts, and indeed a few of their ropes, were still in place. All the Swiss had to do was to fill in the gaps. They therefore completed in half a day what had taken the Japanese climbers weeks to achieve. They reached an eighty-foot crack above the Second Icefield and were preparing the pitch when they got a forecast of very bad weather and decided to retreat off the face. Unsure as to whether they'd be able to return (some of the climbers had other commitments), they stripped the ropes from the route, thereby undoing all their hard work.

In the meantime a new member joined the team, Hans Peter Trachsel of Frutigen, who had not only climbed the 1938 route, but had also done a winter ascent of the Lauper Route. The team was now composed of Jungen; Trachsel; Max Dörfliger, a professional guide; Hans Müller, a bricklayer; Otto von Allmen, a locksmith; and Werner Asam, a German climber resident in Interlaken.

On January 5 the weather cleared, and the Swiss team decided on another try. Having already climbed the lower part of the face, they felt justified in bringing their gear by train up to the *Stollenloch* opening and resuming the climb from that point. Since the route had previously been well reconnoitered, the going was straightforward, and they were firmly established in a bivouac snow hole on the Second Icefield by early afternoon of the following day.

The next morning the lead climbers Jungen, Allmen, and Müller started while it was still dark and, with the aid of miners' headlamps, picked their way upward. They made a good day's progress and were within 300 feet of the Center Band by late afternoon. They abseiled back down to the snow cave. The next morning, in a snowstorm, Trachsel and Dörfliger started out, jumared up the fixed ropes to the previous high point, and got to work. But the snowstorm made climbing difficult, and they somehow got off the Japanese line and couldn't find any pitons. Even cracks for piton placements were difficult to locate. At the end of the day they were still 100 feet shy of the Center Band. The evening weather forecast was the standard one for that winter, another snowstorm on the way; so the team reluctantly decided to descend the ropes to the Eigergletscher Hotel and to wait out the bad weather in relative comfort.

It was ten days later, January 20, before the weather cleared again and they were able to resume the climb. The next day they managed to reach the Center Band, where they cleared an uncomfortable bivouac site on some sloping ledges. They had hammocks along, however, and were able to pin them to the wall and thus to get a night's sleep, trying not to think of the disquieting fact that falling out of bed in their position meant a drop all the way to the base of the wall.

The next day Jungen, leading a pitch, came upon a Japanese rope. Yanking sharply on it, he decided that it was well anchored and clipped in his jumars. He climbed up the rope and was near the head of it when he discovered, to his horror, that the rope wasn't attached to anything. The end of the rope was simply frozen to a nub of rock in a half-inch coating of ice. Paralyzed with fear, he hung for minutes on the rope, afraid to move. There was no handhold or foothold nearby that he could reach. Finally, afraid of completely losing his nerve, he moved the jumar upward another several feet, expecting to see the end of the rope pop free at any moment. But the rope held, and a move or two later he was able to find a handhold and a foothold, to which he clung, stunned with relief. He hadn't planned to learn the Indian rope trick in the middle of the Eigernordwand. After a minute or so he drove in a piton and a couple of bolts and brought his second up the pitch. But for the rest of the climb Jungen refused to touch any of the Japanese ropes that he ran across.

That evening they prepared the route as far as the Sphinx Pillar. The next day they surmounted the Sphinx Pillar, and the day after that their high point was within a hundred feet of the summit. They reached the peak by 4:30 on the afternoon of January 25, having spent most of the day hauling all their equipment to the peak, leaving the route clean behind them.

While the month-long, though often interrupted, climb was no doubt an impressive achievement, doubly so because of the vicious weather the Swiss team had to contend with, the route had been largely prepared by the Japanese climbers of the preceding summer. How important that preparation was can be gauged from the fact that Hans Müller came back in the summer of 1970 and, with his fellow *Bergfalke* Hans Berger, made a lightning ascent of the Japanese Direct, bivouacking but twice before reaching the summit close to midnight on July 30— three days on a direct that had originally taken a full month! They lost a rucksack with an ice axe and crampons, but otherwise had no falls or injuries. They were fresh enough at the finish to descend the west flank in the dark, arriving at the Eigergletscher Hotel at 3:30 A.M.; there they found spare bunks in a dormitory room containing six Italian climbers. The Italians were flabbergasted in the morning on discovering them, and at first wouldn't believe that the Swiss pair had come down off the Eiger after doing the Japanese Direct.

Both climbers weighed themselves before and after the climb. Over the three days Müller lost fifteen pounds and Berger twenty, and this loss from men who were in superb physical condition after strenuous training climbs on half a dozen of the local peaks earlier in the summer.

The summer of 1970 was to see yet another new climb on the north face when three Scottish climbers—twenty-year-old Ian MacEacheran, a mechanic; twenty-four-year-old "Bugs" McKeith, a town planner; and twenty-seven-year-old Ken Spence, an art student—all belonging to an Edinburgh club called the Squirrels (after the Cortina Squirrels), did a North Pillar Direct. This was an expedition climb, hampered by bad weather and the heavy amount of snowfall still on the mountain from the exceptionally severe storms of the preceding winter. The first half of the route, approximately 3,000 feet, was almost entirely rock climbing of Grades V and VI, often overhanging in slabby roofs that called for mechanical aid and the almost continuous use of *étriers*. The top half of the route was almost entirely icefields of a fifty- to sixty-degree angle.

There was little objective danger, because on the lower half, a series of cliffs, any rock coming down sailed well out past the face, while the upper half of the climb was above most of the area of heavy rockfall.

It took the team fully a month of hard climbing to reach the top of the First Pillar. There was rotten rock to contend with, as well as frequent storms that forced the men back down to the meadows. Sometimes, nailing their way along the ceiling of a roof, then up and over a bulge, it would take the whole day to gain only forty vertical feet.

Having reached the top of the First Pillar, they were now on a level with the Eigerwand Station, the windows of which were often lined with tourists watching the climbers at work, several hundred feet away. The climb up the Second Pillar went much faster, though enlivened halfway up by a lightning storm that almost terrified the three Scots out of their collective wits. Their metal hardware, piled in a heap, set off a constant menacing hum. Spence could feel minor electrical shocks dancing on his forehead, while McKeith felt and saw blue sparks jumping from his mustache. He promptly abseiled down off the exposed ridge and found an overhang beneath which he sheltered. Two hours later the storm moved off, and he climbed back up, half expecting to find his rope mates killed by lightning. But they were alive, and all three bivouacked that night on the ledge. In the morning, hearing on their radio that the weather forecast called for more snow, they roped down to their tents in the meadows and took a few days rest.

On July 23 they returned to the wall. On their way up to the bivouac site on the Second Pillar, McKeith was knocked from the fixed rope by a rock that struck his shoulder. Fortunately no bones were broken, but it was a reminder that, depsite the relatively sheltered line they were on, it was still possible to get wiped from the face by rockfall. They attacked the Third Pillar, but hadn't made much progress when yet another storm swept in, forcing them to descend the iced-up ropes, off which their jumars frequently jumped. It made for a bated-breath retreat all the way to the base.

Three days later, with clearing weather, they started off again. Coincidentally it was the same day that the Swiss pair, Berger and Müller, began their "lightning" climb of the Japanese Direct. On their way up, the Scots noticed that the fixed ropes were beginning to show signs of wear, and mindful of John Harlin's death, they all agreed that this attempt, win or lose, would have to be the last. Yet another storm broke as they reached the top of the Second Pillar, where they bivouacked. However, the morning brought moderating weather, and they started up the fixed ropes to the high point previously reached. On their way up they had a close call when one of their fixed ropes broke just as MacEacheran's jumar passed a worn spot. He was protected by a belay rope, but a recovery, hanging well clear of the face, would have been very difficult.

There was another bivouac, in yet another storm, but the next day was clear, the rocks though wet were not iced up, and they made it to the top of the Third Pillar, the last pitch being up through a hand-and-foot jam crack. From there it was ten rope lengths up a fifty-five-degree icefield to the juncture with the Lauper Route. They bivouacked once more and made the summit on the following afternoon, having opened up yet another route on the Eigernordwand, the fifth, an 8,000-foot climb. They were completely exhausted when they reached the peak. McKeith later wrote, "there was no feeling of elation. The pressures had been too great. We could only think of getting off the mountain alive."

They bivouacked once more on the descent. McKeith was to be killed in Canada in July of 1978 when a section of corniced summit ridge on Mount Assiniboine gave way.

Less than a week later, on September 5, 1970, four British climbers, Cliff Phillips, Pete Minks, Eric Jones, and Leo Dickinson, started up the 1938 route, intending to make a film of the whole climb. They were bankrolled by Yorkshire Television and a Manchester merchant who sold climbing equipment. All four were experienced Alpinists. It was a far from routine ascent, however. The cameras and cans of film added considerable weight to the rucksacks, and a route that would normally take two or three days climbing was now projected to take five or six.

The quartet actually started up the face in mid-July, filming as they went, intending to set up a cache depot as high as they could. They reached the Second Icefield and traversed over to the far-right-hand edge where the Japanese had found a bivouac cave on their direct. It was a little off the regular route but its sheltered position was worth the detour. They deposited their loads and retreated down the mountain.

A few days later Phillips was climbing unroped up a snowfield near the Shattered Pillar when he lost his footing and started sliding down the slope. Cameraman Dickinson happened to be filming him at the time. Phillips tried desperately, but without success, to break his fall with his ice hammer. Dickinson kept filming. Phillips hit a four-foot ledge below which there was a 500-foot drop to the screes. This was the same area where an Austrian climber, Martin Weiss, had slipped the preceding summer and fallen 300 feet, to die later of his injuries. By some intense scrabbling, Phillips managed to arrest his fall at the lip of the ledge. Dickinson kept filming. When Phillips got his composure back, he called up to his friend, "Did you get it all?" Dickinson said yes, and that he was sure the scene would go over big with the television viewers. Dickinson was mercilessly ribbed for the sangfroid with which he filmed his rope mate's fall to what appeared to be a sudden death. Dickinson later said, "Mesmerized, through the lens I watched his death dance down the slope, assuming he must die."

The climb went on. The next incident occurred when Dickinson, absorbed in filming Minks delicately picking his way across the Second Icefield, forgot to look after himself and got hit on the shoulder by a rock. He was knocked unconscious, but fortunately he was well anchored and didn't fall. However, the injury was serious enough to set back the filming by a couple of weeks.

Finally, on September 5, Dickinson's shoulder well on the mend, the four climbers started up again. On the Hinterstoisser a falling stone knocked the camera out of Dickinson's hands as he was reaching out to film Eric Jones leading the traverse. Fortunately the camera was attached to his waist by a cord and was none the worse for the impact, but Dickinson surely must have felt that the mountain was trying to tell him something.

They made it to the Japanese bivouac cave at the edge of the Second Icefield, where they had stashed some supplies. Here they spent the rest of the afternoon sorting out loads for the next day's climb.

They started off early in the morning, but, heavily laden, they made slow progress. They traversed across the top of the Second Icefield, often underclinging the slabs above the bergschrund separating the Second Icefield and the rock face above. That night they bivouacked on a ledge at the bottom of the Flatiron. The three Grade-V pitches up to Death Bivouac were heavily iced, which again made for slow going. While Dickinson and Eric Jones prepared a campsite at Death Bivouac and got some tea brewing, Phillips and Minks went ahead and strung ropes across the Third Icefield.

The next morning found them on the Ramp and climbing well, despite the verglassed rock. At the Waterfall Pitch they decided to try the Terray Variant, now rendered somewhat easier by half a dozen well-placed pegs left behind by previous parties. Dickinson got some spectacular footage on these pitches, and afterwards compared the variant to a minor Dolomitic wall stuck on the face of the Eiger.

Their fourth bivouac, on the brittle ledges leading to the Traverse of the Gods, was enlivened by an awesome thunder-and-lightning storm that left the party cowering at one end of their bivouac ledge. At the other end, blue sparks darted from the tips of their piled-up metal hardware. They managed to survive the storm, and next morning they negotiated the Traverse of the Gods. Dickinson was last on the rope going up the Spider, the other three already in the Exit Cracks, when he looked up and saw a huge boulder topple slowly and majestically off the face. Thinking, no doubt, that the third time was it for him, he watched the boulder strike a rock bulge and literally explode. He was showered with rocks of every size, half a dozen of which hit him and knocked him from his holds, leaving him stunned, hanging helpless on the rope. With the help of his mates he finally managed to get back into climbing position and to reach the start of the Exit Cracks and out of the line of fire.

Their fifth night on the mountain was at the Corti Ledge, well up in the Exit Cracks. Despite a forecast of poor conditions, the weather stayed reasonably fine, and they reached the summit the next afternoon, ending their six-day ordeal in a blaze of sunshine. There was a final bivouac on the west flank before they reached Kleine Scheidegg. The film subsequently won several prizes at mountain-film festivals and was widely shown on British television.

The 1970 season was not yet over. In late September a party of eight French climbers, led by René Desmaison, got into trouble in the Exit Cracks, where they were caught by a vicious snowstorm. A dozen French guides and eight locals formed a rescue party and climbed to the summit, then down to the Exit Snowfield. They established contact with the marooned men and helped bring them all up to safety. Of the eight climbers on the wall, only Desmaison escaped frostbite.

Given all the climbing in 1970, it was a miracle that there was only one fatality. On July 16 the Italian climbers Angelo Ursella and Sergio de Infanti were well up in the Exit Cracks on their fourth day of climbing and had just reached the Corti Ledge when Ursella took a hundred-foot fall. De Infanti was jerked from his stance, but the belay held. By the time de Infanti got back to his holds, however, Ursella was dead—killed by a fluke snarl of rope that looped around his neck and strangled him. The next morning Fritz von Almen, manning his telescope, noticed the climbers' predicament and sounded the alarm. A rescue operation was mounted, and a helicopter airlifted guides, winches, and cables to the summit. The shocked and heartsick de Infanti was brought up on the cable and by noon was back at Kleine Scheidegg. The body of his unfortunate rope mate was retrieved later.

There was one other exploit on the Eiger in 1970 that, though not connected with climbing, deserves mention. On March 9, 1970, the Swiss "extreme" skier Sylvain Saudan had himself dropped, with skis, on the Eigerjoch, the saddle connecting the Mönch and the Eiger. He climbed to the summit of the Eiger and then launched himself, skiing down the

---

OVERLEAF: (*Left*) *Oskar Gertsch getting ready to go down on the cable and search the Exit Cracks for Kenji Kimura.* (*Right*) *Oskar Gertsch (carrying Kenji Kimura) and guide Rudolf Kaufmann bringing Kimura up on the cable to the summit.*

RUBI PHOTOS

west flank at murderous speed, somehow contriving with great skill, and no little luck, not to break his neck before he arrived at Kleine Scheidegg.

29

Helicopter Rescues

The year 1970 ushered in a new era on the Eigernordwand, the age of helicopter recoveries. The Schweizerische Rettungsflugwacht (SRFW), the Swiss Air Rescue Service, was founded in 1952 and for many years depended on light ski-equipped planes capable of landing on glaciers and snowfields to effect recovery of injured skiers, hikers, climbers, and others. With the rapid improvement of aviation technology, helicopters were soon available that could operate in the thin air of the high Alps. Then the helicopter cable-descent technique was developed, and in September 1970 helicopters of the SRFW lowered and retrieved the local guide Rudolf Kaufmann from five different locations on the Eiger north face, including the Ramp Snowfield, the Spider, and the Flatiron, proving that helicopters could rescue an injured climber from almost anywhere on the Nordwand. This demonstration, having little to do with the actual art of mountain climbing, nevertheless came close to eliminating the possibility of a climber's being marooned on the wall. To a certain extent the Eigernordwand had been tamed. There was now an easy way off the mountain for the climber in trouble. This meant, among other things, that less-skilled climbers would be tempted to pit themselves against the Nordwand.

Partly because of helicopter recovery, partly for other reasons, since 1970 casualties have dropped sharply, while the number of climbers has increased. The trend had already started with the unusual spell of fine weather in the summer of 1969 when, appropriately enough, sixty-nine mountaineers successfully climbed the 1938 route. There was, however, one fatality. On 3 August, a young Austrian climber, Martin Weiss, was climbing an easy slope, on the lower part of the face, unroped, when he slipped and fell 300 feet to his death. He was the Eiger's thirty-sixth fatality.

By the summer of 1970, all four of the major routes on the Eigernordwand had seen at least two ascents apiece, most having now been

---

Swiss climbers on the Rote Fluh, Japanese direct route.

RUBI PHOTO

climbed in summer and winter. There were challenges left, to be sure, but the White Cobra's fangs had been drawn, and increasingly the Eiger became, if not a run-of-the-mill climb, certainly far less than a "last problem" or a "do-or-die" effort.

The 1971 season was to prove the effectiveness of helicopter recovery of climbers in trouble on the face. On September 9 two German climbers, Peter Siegert and Martin Biock, started their climb. Both were experienced mountaineers, with a number of difficult Alpine routes to their credit. While the pair was on the Difficult Crack, a rucksack that was being lifted on a haul rope somehow came loose and fell, landing on a ledge 500 feet below. When the climbers reached the ledge, they found that Biock's crampons, attached to the outside of the sack, had disappeared. For Biock to attempt to climb the half-dozen icefields yet in front of them without crampons would be foolhardy. It looked as though they would have to give up their attempt. Then Siegert had an idea. They were close to the *Stollenloch*. Suppose one of them climbed in through the opening, caught the next train down to Grindelwald, bought a new pair of crampons, caught the next train back to Eigerwand Station, hiked down inside the tunnel to the *Stollenloch,* climbed out on the wall, and rejoined his companion? Siegert volunteered to go and a couple of hours later was back with the crampons. The pair reached the start of the Hinterstoisser and found it streaming with snowmelt from above. By now it was late afternoon, and the Eiger's artillery had opened up and was sweeping the Hinterstoisser and the First and Second icefields with rockfall. The pair now decided on an interesting variant, they would climb the Rote Fluh. Because of the wall's verticality, they would be relatively safe from rockfall. Then they could rejoin the regular route at the head of the Second Icefield, thus bypassing the Hinterstoisser, the First Icefield, and the Ice Hose.

With the aid of bolts placed by the Japanese, they soon were near the head of the wall and there slung their hammocks from the rock face just above a narrow ledge. They now discovered that their portable stove, which had been inside the rucksack, was partially crushed and would no longer function. Luck, it seemed, wasn't with them. Making do with a cold supper, they crawled into their hammocks and went to sleep, considering a retreat in the morning.

But the next morning was beautifully clear, and after a cold breakfast the pair decided to continue. After all, they had come to climb, and it would be a pity to waste such a beautiful day by roping back down and then aimlessly strolling up and down the streets of Grindelwald. They finished the Rote Fluh, made the long traverse across the head of the Second Icefield, climbed the Flatiron, and settled down at Death Bivouac to their second camp on the mountain.

Around midnight a violent storm hit the mountain and left climbing conditions impossible in the morning. The pair stayed put that day, that night, and most of the following day. Toward evening they flashed signals to Kleine Scheidegg with their electric torches. Fritz von Almen responded and, assuming that the pair were in trouble because of the stormy conditions, alerted Kurt Schwendener, head of the Grindelwald Rescue Service. Schwendener in turn contacted Günther Amann of the SRFW in Interlaken. He also notified the local guides, who put a rescue party together with the intention of going out the *Stollenloch* to see whether they could meet the climbers somewhere on the Second Icefield.

The next morning visibility was patchy, but Amann took off in his helicopter with the guide Rudolf Kaufmann and made two runs past the face at the level of the Flatiron. Kaufmann hailed Siegert and Biock on a loudspeaker and asked whether they wanted to be lifted off. However, the noise of the chopper made communication a garbled static of half-heard shouts. By now Siegert and Biock had rappelled two rope lengths down the Flatiron to the head of the Second Icefield. This time the helicopter came in much closer, and the pilot determined, by interpreting various hand signals, that the German pair did indeed want to be rescued.

The helicopter drifted in as close as it could and lowered Rudolf Kaufmann on the cable to the climbers' position. Biock was hooked to the steel wire, swung away from the icefield, then reeled upward into the machine. He was disembarked at Kleine Scheidegg, and fifteen minutes later Amann was back for Kaufmann and Siegert. They too were lifted off. The whole operation took less than an hour and was the first helicopter rescue from the north face proper. It was an impressive technical achievement and finally proved that a retrieval of a climber from the face was practical. Too practical, some critics charged, claiming that had the helicopter not been available, both climbers would have made it back down under their own power. After all, neither of them had been injured. Many climbers had retreated from the Flatiron, from Death Bivouac, even from the head of the Ramp Snowfield (Schlunegger in 1946). In 1958 Raditschnig and Brandler had brought Hias Noichl, his left hand shattered and his arm in a sling, down safely from the Flatiron. In 1962 Bonington and Whillans had brought an emotionally shattered Brian Nally, whose partner Barry Brewster had just been swept to his death by rockfall, back safely through a violent storm and from the head of the Second Icefield. Haston, with the aid of two Italians, had brought Andy Wightman, with a broken ankle, in through the *Stollenloch*.

The question asked was whether it was fair to risk the lives of the pilot and guide on a rescue effort that may not have been necessary in the first place. The bowl of the north face, with its tricky contradictory winds, its erratic updrafts, its sudden storms, the fog and mist that formed suddenly out of nowhere—all this constituted far from normal operating conditions for a helicopter. The helicopter had to fly past, not over, the vast upended 1,250 acres of wall that towered more than a mile high, sometimes flying so close that the rotor blades were literally a few feet away from the face. If the helicopters were called out to rescue people who simply got tired of climbing, it was inevitable that one of the guides would be marooned or that one of the machines would crash, with loss of life. A similar situation had already occurred, when a French helicopter had crashed on a rescue mission in Chamonix.

In 1972 the SRFW was called out again, in even more questionable circumstances. In March three male Czech climbers, Jiri Smid, Zbynek Cepela, Lubos Novak, and a woman climber, Sylvia Kysilkova, started up the face intending to do the third winter ascent of the 1938 route, and the first by a woman climber. Conditions were poor and the four climbed slowly. It took three days to reach the Hinterstoisser. Here Cepela and Novak decided to retreat. The other two pressed on and, after three more days of climbing, were just short of Death Bivouac when they realized that their pace was too slow to offer any hope of success. They decided to retreat.

Meanwhile observers down at Kleine Scheidegg surmised that the pair were in trouble and called out the SRFW. A helicopter appeared just as Jiri Smid and Sylvia Kysilkova, on their way back down, were preparing to tackle the Ice Hose. The Czech climbers were induced to hook onto the cable and be airlifted off. They were winched to safety, and another helicopter rescue was chalked up. However, the Czech climbers were duly presented with a bill for 2,600 Swiss francs, covering the costs of the rescue. They protested that the charges were excessive. They had never in their lives seen that much money at one time, much less possessed it. Czechs, like other Eastern European climbers, were allowed to take very little currency, their own or foreign, with them when traveling abroad.

The Czechs furthermore protested that they had not called for rescue, that a chopper had suddenly appeared out of nowhere as they were effecting a normal retreat, and that they had been persuaded to use its services. Fritz Bühler, director of SRFW, finally waived the charges. A short time later the SRFW was reorganized under the insurance principle, by which subscribers pay a modest annual membership fee of twenty Swiss francs. SRFW's services, including air ambulance, are rendered free of charge. The service now has half a million subscribers, and the number of stranded and injured people it has rescued is in the thousands.

To backtrack for a moment, in 1971 there were twenty-seven men who did the 1938 route. Six were Czech, two French, two Austrian, two German, two Swiss, two Belgian, and eleven English and Scottish—proving that, for United Kingdom climbers at least, the Eiger was becoming just another Alpine route. Oddly enough, John Harlin was still the only American to have climbed the Eiger north face, and he had done it back in 1962.

In 1972 there were only two successful ascents, one by Dave Morris and John Yates of Great Britain, and a "lightning" climb by the Austrians Willi Prax and Richard Franzl, who did the 1938 route in eighteen hours.

At 1 P.M. on August 1 of that year, two Japanese climbers, Furukawa Masahiro and Masaru Miyagawa, started up the face. They had been climbing for only a couple of hours and were near the head of the Difficult Crack when something went wrong. Both came off their holds. Their bodies bounced down the lower ledges for almost a thousand feet before finally coming to rest near the bottom of the First Pillar. They were the Eiger's second and third Japanese deaths and the thirty-eighth and thirty-ninth fatalities overall.

1973 was fatality free, as twenty-two climbers safely did the classic Heckmair Route. One of these ascents was the third winter climb of the route by the Swiss bergsteigers Hans von Känel and Hansjörg Müller in the second week of January. They spent six nights on the face. Although there were no deaths in '73, there were several close calls.

On August 18 two Japanese climbers, Teruo Kato and Buntaro Yamazaki, were working on the Quartz Rib in the Exit Cracks, one of the hardest pitches on the climb, when Yamazaki, leading the rope, came off and fell almost fifty feet, breaking his right foot. His partner began waving a yellow storm jacket back and forth as a distress signal. Someone at Kleine Scheidegg noticed the activity and alerted SRFW in Interlaken. A helicopter took off with the pilot Günther Amann and the rescue guide Werner Bhend. After a flypast it was decided that it was too risky to try a direct winch rescue, so the helicopter flew a thousand pounds of rescue equipment, cables and winches and pulleys, to the summit. Meanwhile local guides were alerted, and early the next morning more than a score of them reached the peak. Two of the guides, Ueli Sommer and Andreas Ringgenberg, went down on the cable almost a thousand feet, and then brought Yamazaki back up to the summit. An hour later Kato was also brought up, and the rescue operation swiftly concluded with a helicopter recovery of both climbers from the summit.

The SRFW was called out again three weeks later when the Swiss bergsteigers Ulrich Kämpfer, twenty-six, and Paul Marti, twenty-five, after a bivouac at the Swallow's Nest, reached the Traverse of the Gods.

Here they were greeted by a fierce snowstorm. They tried to wait it out but finally decided to retreat. No one before had ever tried to come down from so high up on the wall. The pair made it to the Brittle Band, where they set up another bivouac. That night a bad thunderstorm was followed by heavy snowfall. Their progress the next day was through incessant powder snow avalanches. Rappelling as much as possible, they were back down the Ramp and at the Flatiron by noon. There, they doubted their ability to finish the retreat and fired off an SOS rocket. However, the weather was still too stormy for helicopter flights. They stayed that night at Death Bivouac.

The next morning, fearful that the bad weather would keep the rescue helicopters grounded too long, they tried to continue their retreat and got down the Flatiron to the Second Icefield. The weather began to clear, and a helicopter took off for the face. The Swiss pair now reclimbed the Flatiron, figuring that recovery would be easier on the top of the prow rather than on the precipitous Second Icefield.

The pilot Günther Amann brought the chopper in as close as he could, the rescue worker Adolf Rüfenacht manned the winch, and the veteran guide Hans Kaufmann dropped to the landing zone. He buckled an exhausted Paul Marti into the apparatus and watched the helicopter swing its human burden aloft and away from the face. The chopper deposited Marti at Kleine Scheidegg and was back soon for Kaufmann and Kämpfer. Another SRFW rescue had been brought off.

August of 1973 saw another interesting climb when a pair of Yugoslavs, Ivo Kotnik and Franc Verko, took the Japanese Direct up to the right of the Fly, found the going above that too difficult, traversed over to the Harlin Direct line, which they down climbed to the head of the Spider, and there took the Exit Cracks on up to the summit, neatly managing to combine three routes in one climb—the Japanese Direct, the Harlin Direct, and the normal 1938 route.

30
Hollywood Comes to the Eiger

Nineteen seventy-four was the year Hollywood came to the Eiger, when Clint Eastwood arrived with a film company to make *The Eiger Sanction*. The company hired several English climbers, including Dougal Haston, Dave Knowles, Hamish MacInnes, and John Cleare, to help pick out and set up locations, and to act as consultants on the technical climbing.

Clint Eastwood, despite his lack of climbing experience, was called on to cut his climbing rope and take a 15-foot fall over 3,000 feet of solid nothing in one scene. He was belayed by a safety rope and made the cut, displaying in the process no hysterical tendencies and a virile courage that came close to matching the courage depicted in many of his screen performances. He trained for his Eiger feats by doing a Tyrolean traverse to the tip of Lost Arrow in Yosemite Valley.

On August 13, just after a camera crew had filmed a climber being pulled up to a ledge on the west flank after supposedly having been hit by stone fall, the English climber Dave Knowles, middle man in a rope of three, was hit and killed by a large rock that came bounding down the face. A nearby cameraman was injured. Knowles, no stranger to the Eiger, had climbed the Heckmair Route in 1971 along with Allen Fyffe, Kenny Spence, and Ian Nicholson.

On the day after Knowles was killed, a thirty-year-old German-speaking Italian climber from the South Tyrol, Reinhold Messner, and a young Austrian climber, Peter Habeler, came to Grindelwald to try the Eigerwand. Earlier that summer they had climbed the north face of the Matterhorn, and back in 1966 when both were in their early twenties, they had done the Walker Spur on the Grandes Jorasses. Now only the Eiger remained for them to complete the three great Alpine north faces. Actually Messner had already done an Eiger ascent, in 1968, when he and his brother Günther, along with Toni Hiebeler and Fritz Maschke, put up a new line east of the Eigerwand Station windows, the North Pillar Route.

The pair started out from Kleine Scheidegg at 2 A.M. and reached the base of the wall while it was still dark. Here they sat down to wait for daylight and while resting noticed a flashing light high up on the face. They knew that three pairs of climbers were already up on the wall, battling what had been, up to then, steady rainfall over the preceding several days. The light winked out the Alpine distress signal. The men debated turning back and notifying someone down at Kleine Scheidegg, but they reasoned that the SOS would soon be noticed by someone, and in the meantime they were in position to reach the distressed climbers much sooner.

At dawn they started up the series of ledges that led to the First Pillar, moved past it, surmounted the Shattered Pillar, and stopped at the bottom of the Difficult Crack. Here they split up their pitons, ice screws, carabiners, and the rest, and roped up. As it happened, the Difficult Crack was liberally laced with ropes put up by climbing experts for the camera crew filming *The Eiger Sanction*, portions of which were being shot on the lower reaches of the wall.

Making good use of the ropes, Messner and Habeler climbed swiftly and soon put away the Hinterstoisser Traverse, despite the thorough drenching they got from waterfalls streaming down the face. They next disposed of the Ice Hose and, at the bottom edge of the Second Icefield, ran across the origin of the distress signals noted earlier that morning. Two Polish climbers, one of whom had broken a leg in a 130-foot fall the previous day, were awaiting the arrival of an SRFW helicopter. While Messner and Habeler were attempting to converse with the Polish climbers, the pilot Günther Amann arrived in the helicopter, lowered Hans Kaufmann on a steel cable, then slid away from the face. Kaufmann swiftly splinted Ladyslav Wozniak's broken leg, then signaled for the copter's return. The chopper came back, hovered about 70 feet up and lowered a cable. The injured climber was buckled into the end of a special wire harness, then swung up and away from the face as the chopper lifted. When the craft was well clear of the mountain, it reeled in the injured climber and set off for Kleine Scheidegg and medical help. Messner and Habeler, convinced that their aid was no longer needed, began that long traverse across the Second Icefield. They hadn't been climbing too long when the helicopter returned to retrieve the rescue technician and the other Polish climber.

Messner and Habeler reached the Flatiron, did the traverse across the Third Icefield, and were on the Ramp by 9 A.M.—phenomenal speed. Although they had been exposed to some scattered ice and rockfall on the snowfields, it was rather sparse, because the sun had not yet had enough time to loosen the ice bands that held the rock to the face. On the Ramp they caught up with an Austrian party of four, Franz Kröll, Wolfgang Lackner, Oswald Pucher, and Otto Zöttl, who had spent three days on the face! Peter Habeler knew his compatriots, exchanged greetings with them, then moved ahead to take over the lead. The pair reached the head of the Ramp and there took the obligatory shower bath (the Waterfall Crack), that gave entrance to the Ramp Snowfield.

Continuing to climb with great speed, the pair were across the Traverse of the Gods and on to the Spider by noon. Clouds had fortunately obscured the sun, which meant that the snowfield was relatively free of rockfall and avalanches. However, it also meant that the Exit Cracks were all iced up, making it difficult to find holds, and indeed this final stretch proved to be the most difficult part of the climb. However, neither man fell and neither was hit by rockfall, and they soon made their way up to the Exit Snowfield. By now the sun was shining again, but they were well above the danger of rockfall. They unroped and slogged together up to the summit, which they reached at 3 P.M. Making good use of long rappels, they were back down the west flank and at the hotel at Kleine Scheidegg by 5 P.M. By 7 P.M., after a bath and something to eat, they were on the hotel terrace watching, through a telescope, the Austrian rope of four making its way up the Exit Cracks. Also visible was a party of two, just below the Rote Fluh, preparing to bivouac for the night.

Messner and Habeler had done the climb from base to peak in ten hours, 5 A.M. to 3 P.M., seven hours faster than anyone had ever climbed the Eigernordwand before. As usual, controversy flared and the pair was criticized for trying to set "speed" records on the Eiger's north face, as though the mountain were a race track. This criticism, of course, was nonsense. All other things being equal, the quicker the climb, the safer on a face like the Eigernordwand. The less time spent exposed to the objective dangers of avalanche, rockfall, and sudden weather shifts, the less likelihood of injury or death. Then too, the speed of the climb enabled the men to get up into the Exit Cracks before the sun had had much of a chance to loosen the rocks and snow on the face. And once one is above the Spider, one is above the area of greatest rockfall.

The truth is that Messner and Habeler were a pair of beautifully conditioned climbers, superbly fit and technically brilliant, probably the best Alpine climbers to come out of the 1960s and 1970s, and certainly the best rope of two to make an appearance since Lachenal and Terray. The ten hours they spent on the ascent undoubtedly represented their natural speed in climbing; it averaged out to a thousand feet per hour, including all the footage of the back-and-forth meanders of the route. They were confronted with no emergencies or accidents (meeting the Polish pair had only held them up for ten minutes or so), had relatively good weather, and met with conditions on the face that were, at the least, no worse than average for an Eigernordwand climb.

In 1978 Messner and Habeler were the first to climb Mount Everest without oxygen. Two years later Messner became the first to solo Everest, via the North Col and Northeast Ridge. Now considered the world's foremost mountaineer, Messner has climbed five of the world's fourteen 8,000 meter peaks: Nanga Parbat (twice), Manaslu, Hidden Peak, Everest (twice), and K-2.

Later Messner was to write that for height, verticality, technical difficulty, objective dangers, mixture of snow, ice and rock climbing, and commitment once started on the climb, the Eigernordwand was one of the three great walls of world mountaineering—the other two being the Rupal Face of Nanga Parbat in the Himalayas, and the south face of Aconcagua in the Andes.

The day after the Messner-Habeler climb, two American mountaineers, John Roskelley and Chris Kopczynski, started up the face. They had stopped over in Grindelwald on their way home from a disastrous Soviet expedition in which eight Soviet women mountaineers perished on a peak in the Pamirs. The eight were storm bound on the summit. Their male colleagues, lower on the mountain, were unable to reach them, yet were still in radio contact with the desperate Russian women until, one by one, they all froze to death. The last radio message was, "Now we are two. We are very sorry. We tried but could not. We love you. Good-bye."

Roskelley and Kopczynski were well known in American climbing circles, and indeed the Eigernordwand posed no particular terrors for them. Kopczynski reported that the holds on the Hinterstoisser "were only wrinkles," while Roskelley, at the top of the Ice Hose, got pranged on top of the head by a rock that split his helmet, but other than that it was a more or less routine climb. They bivouacked twice, at the Swallow's Nest and the head of the Waterfall Crack, and finished the climb in the late afternoon of their third day. It was the first all-American ascent of the Eiger, though they were only the second and third Americans to do the face, because John Harlin had completed the regular route in 1962 as part of a mixed Swiss-Austrian-German-American rope.

In that same August two English climbers, Pete Allison and Dave Cuthbertson, reached the Swallow's Nest on an attempt to do the regular route. However, the heavily iced-up conditions of the face caused them to have second thoughts about the climb, and they decided to retreat. They started down and were near the bottom of the wall when Cuthbertson saw a gloved hand and part of an arm sticking out of a patch of snow. He and Allison reached the spot and grimly began to dig away at the snow burden. Their horror, however, soon turned to laughter as they uncovered the fully clothed and equipped dummy of a climber, undoubtedly one that had been used in the filming of *The Eiger Sanction*. Their good intentions were suitably rewarded, because much of the equipment and clothing on the dummy was in perfect condition, though they must have felt rather odd eagerly stripping the flesh-colored body of its clothing in full view of hundreds of telescopes below in the valley. In any event, they reburied the mannequin and then hurried down to the meadows with their loot.

The climbing season of 1974 was to end on a sad note when the historian and general expert on the Eiger, Fritz von Almen, proprietor of the Kleine Scheidegg complex of hotels and guesthouses, died in August—fittingly enough, the most popular month for climbing the Eiger. Almen had known most of the Eiger candidates and, at one time or another, had been of help to almost every one of them, through his hospitality and encyclopedic knowledge of the Eigernordwand and its weather. However, his feelings about Eiger climbers were ambivalent. He had, at times, tried to dissuade Eiger aspirants whose experience he thought not quite up to the north wall's demands. He once said, "When I hear a man is leading a climb on the Eiger, I wonder what is wrong with him."

31

Impossible? But So Are We!

At 5 A.M. on August 9, 1975, eight climbers crawled out the *Stollen-loch* window, split up into four separate ropes, and started climbing. On one rope was the forty-five-year-old Yvette Vaucher and her partner Stephane Schaffter, twenty-three, a law student from Geneva. Both ladies were hoping to make the first all-woman ascent of the Eigernord-wand. This was Yvette's third attempt on the Nordwand.

The second rope consisted of Michel Vaucher and Jean Juge. Michel, Yvette's husband, had been on the Eiger with Yvette and Loulou Boulaz in 1962 when, along with Michel Darbellay, the four climbers had been foiled by bad weather and had had to retreat from the Ramp after three bivouacs on the face. Michel's rope mate, Jean Juge of Geneva, was a professor of chemistry, a respected and accomplished mountaineer, and president of the *Union Internationale des Associations d'Alpinisme*. At sixty-seven he was the oldest climber ever to have attempted the Eigernordwand.

On the third rope was Michel Darbellay, who had been to the Eiger half a dozen times before, and indeed had been the first to climb it solo—back in 1963. He was now climbing in his capacity as a professional guide, having been hired by an amateur Swiss climber, Louis Frote, to take him up the Eiger's north face. On the fourth rope was Tomas Gross, twenty-five, a Czech by birth but now a student in Geneva. Despite his youth he was a superb mountaineer with many solo and winter Grade-VI climbs to his credit. His partner was Natacha Gall, who had, the preceding March, partnered Gross on a ten-day winter climb of the west face of the Dru, outside Chamonix.

The four ropes reached the Flatiron by noon and took a lunch break at Death Bivouac. On the north wall that same day there were three other pairs—French, Austrian, and German. The Swiss climbers crossed the Third Icefield and encountered a thunderstorm on the Ramp. While on the Ramp the German pair, Hans Engel and Hans Kirchberger, combined with Darbellay and Frote to form a rope of four. The climbers avoided the Waterfall Crack by taking the Terray Variant, got up through the Ice Bulge, and decided to bivouac on the left-hand side of the Ramp Snowfield.

That night Jean Juge's rucksack slipped off a ledge and went tumbling down the face. Among other things he lost a down jacket, an anorak, a wool sweater, and a bivouac sack. The next morning the ten climbers made it across the Traverse of the Gods, with Michael Vaucher now leading the way up the Spider, step cutting for the nine who followed.

In the Exit Cracks the Austrian rope of two, Rudolf Friedhuber and Karl Pfeiffer, caught up with the rest of the party, now making a string of twelve climbers in the cracks. All that day Jean Juge suffered increasingly from hypothermia. The weather had turned noticeably colder, and without his down jacket he shivered almost constantly. Again and again he had to be hauled up on the rope, even over moderate passages, and again and again one or another of the party had to massage his face and hands at each stance. All twelve climbers bivouacked that night in the Exit Cracks, and everything possible was done to keep Juge warm. Despite the attention he was unable to sleep, and periodically one or

Jean Juge climbing on Mont Blanc du Tacul a month or so before his death.

another of the climbers would hear him moan in agony over the cold. The increasing cold and Juge's condition notwithstanding, the climbers reached the summit the following afternoon—in the teeth of a raging snowstorm. After a brief rest they started down the west flank, but Jean Juge was at the end of his strength. The others now realized that he would have to be either carried down or airlifted off. The three women climbers, along with Darbellay and Frote, continued the descent and made it down off the mountain by 10 P.M. They alerted rescue workers to Juge's plight, though obviously nothing could be done that night.

In the meantime Michel Vaucher and Tomas Gross stayed with Juge in a snow hole that they had excavated high on the west flank. The next day, a Tuesday, the weather was still too tempestuous for them to hope for a helicopter rescue, and the three men stayed put. Wednesday morning brought clear skies, and an SRFW helicopter soon appeared, lifted Juge off the flank, deposited him at Kleine Scheidegg, and then came back for Vaucher and Gross.

The experience did nothing to cool Juge's ardor for big-wall climbing. In August of 1978 Jean Juge, seventy by then, formed part of a rope that climbed the north face of the Matterhorn. However, while on the descent of the Hörnli Ridge, he collapsed and died, evidently of a heart attack brought on by exposure. It was probably how this grand old man of Alpine mountaineering would have wanted to go, setting a record, the oldest man to have climbed the north face of the Matterhorn, as well as the oldest to have climbed the Eigernordwand. The youngest to have done the Eiger north face was probably a seventeen-year-old Austrian, Georg Hasenhüttl, who did the route with two others on a four-day climb in August, 1974.

The year 1976 ushered in the Czech era on the Eiger. Like the Japanese of 1969 and 1970, the Czechs were all over the face on several different routes. They had first appeared on the Eiger as far back as 1961 when Radovan Kuchar and Zdeno Zibrin had done the Heckmair Route on a four-day climb. A handful of Czech mountaineers had made ascents in 1968 and 1971, but in 1976 they were out in force. On February 19 six Czech climbers, Martin Novak, Leos Horka, Petr Gribek, Jan Martinek, Milan Motycka, and Vladimir Starcala, started up the Japanese Direct line. They climbed Himalayan style—two were route finding, two fixing ropes, and two ferrying loads from one camp to the next. They established bivouac caves at the head of the Second Icefield, at the Center Band, at the Sphinx Pillar, and a final one under the head wall. They emerged on the summit at noon on March 5.

Unroped, they started down the west flank. Novak, close to exhaustion with frostbitten hands and feet, lost his foothold on an ice slope and helplessly slid 800 feet before he was brought up short on a ledge. His hands, desperately scrabbling at the ice to stop his plunge, were a mess; the flesh was peeling off in shreds. In addition he had severe friction burns on his back and buttocks. While the others were trying to get down to him, an SRFW helicopter, with Günther Amann at the controls, happened to fly by on a routine patrol. With Amann were his usual helper, Adolf Rüfenacht, and the guide Ueli Sommer. Amann, on his daily patrols over the previous week, had been keeping an eye on the progress of the six-man Czech team. Today he was pleased to see that they had reached the summit and were now on their way down the west flank. But there was something odd about the group—of course! There were only five of them. Where was the sixth climber? Then Novak was spotted on his ledge, hundreds of feet below the others, making distress signals to the helicopter. Amann brought his craft around and, with the help of Rüfenacht and Sommer, succeeded in plucking Novak from his stance. Because of the climber's condition, Amann flew Novak directly to the hospital in Interlaken. Providentially, the Czech climbers were all subscribers to the Swiss Air Rescue Service, with the happy result that the rescue operation didn't cost them a penny.

Novak's condition, especially his battered hands, graphically demonstrates the plight of a climber sliding out of control and desperately trying to arrest his plunge. One climber in Yosemite, killed in a slab fall, was found to have both wrists broken, both arms broken, one shoulder dislocated, and several fingernails ripped out.

During the summer of 1976, a five-man team under the redoubtable Jiri Smid, seconded by Czechoslovakia's foremost woman mountaineer, Sylvia Kysilkova, along with Josef Rybicka and Petr Plachetsky, pioneered a new direct that sliced up the right-hand side of the Rote Fluh and came out on the west flank a few hundred meters below the summit. It took twenty-six days to do a route that now became the fourth direct on the face. With the 1938 Heckmair Route, and the North Pillar line and its variants, there were now at least six routes up the Eigernordwand.

On the same day that the Czech foursome started their new direct, another four-man Czech team, consisting of Petr Bednarik, Pavel Cicarek, Pavel Sevcik, and Jindric Sochor, did the first summer, and third overall ascent of the John Harlin Direct. The route had been considered suicidal in the summer because it ran directly up the main path of rockfall down the face. But the Czech team was lucky with the weather—a cold snap with little sunshine meant much less rockfall than normal—and the Czechs completed the route early in the afternoon of their seventh day, reaching the summit in a snowstorm on August 9. One of the climbers had earlier lost his rucksack, ice axe, and bivvy sack, and nearly all had been "pinged" by small stones, though fortunately none of the four suffered anything worse than the usual scrapes and bruises on such a climb, a remarkable escape considering the "dump chute" route they took.

Not so lucky were a pair of Nuremberg climbers, Werner Haser and Kurt Stör, who started up the face on July 17 of that same year. They bivouacked the first night at the Swallow's Nest, the second night at the Brittle Band, their third high up in the Exit Cracks, and reached the summit at 10:30 in the morning of their fourth day. On their descent of the west flank, Stör slipped on the ice and started to slide, dragging Haser with him. The pair went flying down an ice slope and out over a cliff, to fall a total of 600 feet. Stör was killed outright. Haser, severely injured, suffering several broken bones, had to be lifted off by an SRFW helicopter. Kurt Stör was the forty-first Eiger fatality.

In January of 1977 the Czechs were again on the wall when Jiri Smid, Jaroslav Flejberk, Josef Rybicka, and Miroslav Smid put up another new route to the left of the Harlin Direct. The team had bad weather and twice had to retreat from the face. One 500-foot cliff section above the Ramp took ten days to complete, and the climb itself wasn't finished until February 26, the last twenty-one days having been spent continuously on the face. It was the seventh route up the Eiger's north wall.

In September of 1977 Alex MacIntyre, an English law graduate just back from a climbing trip to Afghanistan, met a twenty-two-year old American, the Yosemite climber Tobin Sorenson, in the Bar National in Chamonix. After some initial probing (What have you done? Where?) MacIntyre found out that Sorenson was thinking of an Eiger solo on the 1938 Route. MacIntyre had twice previously attempted the Harlin Direct, only to be driven back each time by excessive avalanching. He explained the attractions of the route, Sorenson was interested, and the two agreed to meet later at the Hotel des Alpes in Alpiglen. In the finest mountaineering tradition both climbers were broke, and made their separate hitchhiking ways to Grindelwald. Then, in another climbing tradition that goes back to Sedlmayer and Mehringer, who split firewood in return for lodging in a mountain hut in 1935, MacIntyre and Sorenson washed dishes and did odd jobs for Mme Lydia, proprietor of the Hotel des Alpes, in return for room and board. "I washed my way to food and favor," MacIntyre later wrote. The pair waited for good weather, and while waiting, they were found by good fortune in the guise of a TV director shooting a commercial for Timex watches. They were hired as "technical advisers," picking up excellent wages for eight days work, and the weather turned fair just as the TV job was over. The pair celebrated the completion of the Timex commerical at a party in Grindelwald that didn't end until 3 A.M. At 7 A.M. they took the train up to Alpiglen and then hiked up the pastures to the foot of the face. They were attempting the fourth overall ascent of the Harlin Direct, and the first by an American. (John Harlin had been killed before completing the climb.) Curiously enough, MacIntyre and Sorenson had never climbed together prior to that day.

They started up the face at 10:30 A.M. and reached the Eigerwand Station windows, where they found a crew of three workers clearing snow away from the windows so that train tourists could enjoy the dazzling views. The pair went inside for a drink of water, and Sorenson learned that one of the workers was also a local guide who, learning of their intentions, informed them that, in his opinion, the Harlin Route was impossible. "But so are we," Sorenson is supposed to have answered in good California Zen fashion, and the pair climbed on.

They bivouacked that night at the head of the First Rock Band. Their second night was spent at Death Bivouac, their third near the top of the Central Pillar, and their fourth at the head of the Fly. The fifth day they reached the summit at 3:30 P.M., five days over a route that had taken almost two months on the original ascent. However, MacIntyre and Sorenson were able to take advantage of bolts placed by previous parties and were fortunate in that cold weather meant very little rockfall on the face. Six weeks later, in early December, Sorenson soloed the north face of the Matterhorn in nine hours. In 1980 he was killed when he fell on a solo climb of Mount Alberta in the Canadian Rockies.

In November, 1977, came one of the most spectacular rescues yet from the face. On the eighth, two Spanish climbers, Fernandez Jesús Domingo, twenty-four, and Miguel Pérez Tello, twenty-one, started up the Heckmair Route. By now, of course, the Heckmair or 1938 Route was old hat, having seen over a hundred successful ascents. The Spanish climb, however, was unusual in that it was the latest in the year that anyone had ever tried to climb the face. The cold weather, of course, meant little rockfall, but if ropes weren't fixed on the route and left for a quick retreat and if a bad winter storm blew up, grounding helicopters, climbers could easily perish before being rescued. Indeed this almost happened to the Spanish pair, who, climbing very slowly in winter conditions, took four days to reach the Ramp. At the head of the ramp, Pérez, leading the pitch, fell almost a hundred feet, breaking both legs. Jesús managed to hold his partner, and then somehow hauled him into a sheltered place on the Ramp.

Down in Grindelwald the chief of police and head of the guide's rescue unit, Kurt Schwendener, grew worried when no further activity was observed on the part of the Spaniards on the Ramp. On November 14 he called the SRFW, then alerted three local guides—Rudolf Kaufmann, Ueli Frei, and Hannes Stähli—to prepare themselves for a possible rescue. At this point no one was aware of Pérez's incapacitating injuries, but everyone assumed that deep snow was preventing the Spanish pair from either continuing the climb or retreating.

The weather turned bad on the fourteenth as a three-day storm moved in. People began to talk of the Spanish rope of Rabada and Navarro, who had lost their lives on the Spider in 1963. Was another *spanische Tragödie* in the making? Pérez and Jesús had now been nine days on the face. It was assumed that their food supplies were exhausted and that the long, cold November nights were rapidly sapping their last resources of physical strength.

On November 17 the storm clouds began to break. By 4 P.M. the weather had cleared just enough to allow a flypast by the helicopter. The pilot maneuvered to within thirty feet of one of the Spaniards, who, motioning to his mouth, indicated that they had no food. There was no sign of the second climber, which led to speculation that he might have fallen to the foot of the wall. Others surmised that the second climber was in a snow hole, too ill or exhausted to drag himself into view.

The next day brought clear weather, and the rescue workers held a conference. Could the helicopter get close enough to the Ramp to lower a rescue worker, or would the overhanging wall above the cleft block the chopper's approach? Photographs of the face were intently studied. Everyone agreed that speed was now vital, so a direct lift-off from the Ramp was decided on. At the same time, two dozen guides readied themselves for a possible winch recovery from a spot on the Lauper Ridge above the head of the Ramp Snowfield.

The pilot Günther Amann, with the guides Rudolf Kaufmann and Hannes Stähli, flew as close as he dared to the wall that towered above the Ramp. Kaufmann was lowered on the cable, but despite his and the pilot's efforts, he was unable to find a spot on the heavily iced-up rocks of the Ramp secure enough for him to stand up on. He couldn't even get his crampons to stick. He signaled a retreat, and the copter made a big looping turn and came in for a second approach. This time Kaufmann was lowered to a snow bench some forty feet below the Spaniards' position, and some thirty feet out on an angled side wall from the Ramp. Kaufmann was able to steady himself at the stance long enough to hammer in an anchor piton. Then he helped Hannes Stähli as the second guide was lowered and anchored to the wall. Both men now made the dangerous traverse to the Ramp, then climbed the cleft up to the Spaniards' position, where they found that Pérez, with both legs broken, was unable to move. This meant that he would have to be lowered down the Ramp with ropes, then somehow maneuvered across the traverse to the snow platform. At least one more guide would be needed. Kaufmann called Schwendener on his two-way radio and outlined the situation. And now a new complication sprang up, as clouds were beginning to

move in again and snow flurries were already slanting across the face. Kaufmann radioed for food and sleeping bags. If they couldn't get Pérez off that day, and the weather turned bad, it might be another three or four days before the chopper could return. The guide Ueli Frei was winched down from the helicopter and joined the other two guides as they slowly worked Pérez down the Ramp. Kaufmann, still worried about getting off the face before the weather closed in, called for yet another guide, and twenty-six-year-old Edi Bohren was airlifted to the snow bench. With him he brought sleeping bags and food—just in case. Bohren was met by Frei, and the pair fixed a rope across the traverse to the Ramp. Snow flurries continued to boil around the face and dark clouds were settling lower and lower and turning more leaden by the minute.

Jesús was brought to the platform and the chopper called in. Bohren said that Jesús spoke no French or German and, presumably because of the language barrier, wore a grin of gratitude and desire to please throughout the whole operation. Minutes later he was lifted off and ferried down to Kleine Scheidegg. Now Kaufmann and Stähli brought Pérez down the Ramp with all the gentleness and care that they were capable of. With the help of Frei and Bohren, they worked the trussed-up Spanish climber across the traverse to the snow platform. The chopper was overhead, and Pérez was swiftly strapped into the harness and lifted off. Now all that the guides had to worry about was getting themselves off the face. They gathered up their rescue gear and stuffed it into sacks. In the meantime the sky kept getting darker and darker—so dark that the hotels of Kleine Scheidegg were no longer to be seen. Then the men heard the welcome sound of copter blades chopping the air, and once again the cable was dancing down in front of them. Ueli Frei was lifted up, then the cable came down again. Edi Bohren hooked himself in. Before he was even reeled up into the cabin, the helicopter was sliding away from the face, as pilot Amann now raced the dark.

At the Kleine Scheidegg, Bohren and Frei were no sooner out of the aircraft than they were surrounded by a swarm of Spanish hotel workers, who couldn't do enough to show their gratitude for the rescue of

---

Local guides at helicopter pick-up point on the Ramp (1), with injured Spanish climbers. (2) Guide at Ramp belay and (3) Spanish bivouac.
BILD-NEWS

OVERLEAF: *(Left) Rescuers Ueli Frei (with radio) and Edi Bohren (right) waiting to lower Pérez, both of whose legs were broken, to the ramp where the helicopter sling could reach him. (Right) Pérez being lifted out of the ramp by helicopter.*
EDI BOHREN PHOTOS

their compatriots. A quarter of an hour later the helicopter returned with Kaufmann and Stähli in the near dark of a late-November afternoon. The most difficult helicopter rescue yet from the Eigernordwand had been accomplished successfully. It was probably the local guides' finest hour.

Just how much the techniques of winter ice and snow climbing had improved was startlingly demonstrated when a twenty-five-year-old Frenchman, Ivan Ghiradini, became the first climber to do a solo of the three great Alpine north faces—all done over the winter of 1977–78. The Matterhorn took him nine hours, the Grandes Jorasses three days, and the Eigernordwand six days. On the Eiger, Ghiradini took a hundred-foot fall in the Exit Cracks but was unhurt. Between March 3 and 9, 1978, the Japanese climber Tsuneo Hasegawa also soloed the 1938 route.

On March 5, 1978, the Czechs were back again with a six-man rope that attempted to put up a new route, a so-called super-*direttissima*, on the face. The earlier Czech Direct of 1976 came out on the west flank, several hundred meters below the summit. The new route meant to correct that defect by going straight up past the Fly to the peak. However, bad weather forced the climbers to retreat from the face. Then the team doctor, Petr Jirko, came down with pneumonia and had to withdraw. A second climber, Dietr Smejical, suffering from severe frostbite, had to be airlifted off the Second Icefield.

Finally, on April 28, Jiri Pechous, the team leader, and Jiri Siegl left their camp just above the Central Pillar for a final summit push. Following them up the fixed ropes, cleaning the route, were Viktor Jarolim and Heinz Skopec. When the latter pair reached a pillar above the Fly, they found two rucksacks and a ten-foot length of broken rope. Jarolim and Skopec looked all over for any signs of their rope mates, then started abseiling, searching the face as they descended. They were caught in a bad storm and forced to hole up for two days in a snow cave, but finally made it down safely. The bodies of their companions were found a month later at the foot of the wall. Pechous and Siegl were the forty-second and forty-third Eigernordwand victims.

In July of 1978 a banquet was held in Grindelwald to celebrate the fortieth anniversary of the original climb. Guests of honor were the two survivors of the original ascent, the seventy-two-year-old Anderl Heckmair and the sixty-six-year-old Heinrich Harrer. Also present was Michel Darbellay, who, in 1963, had made the first solo climb of the face.

Pérez on arrival at Kleine Scheidegg (hotel in background).

SWISSAIR PHOTO

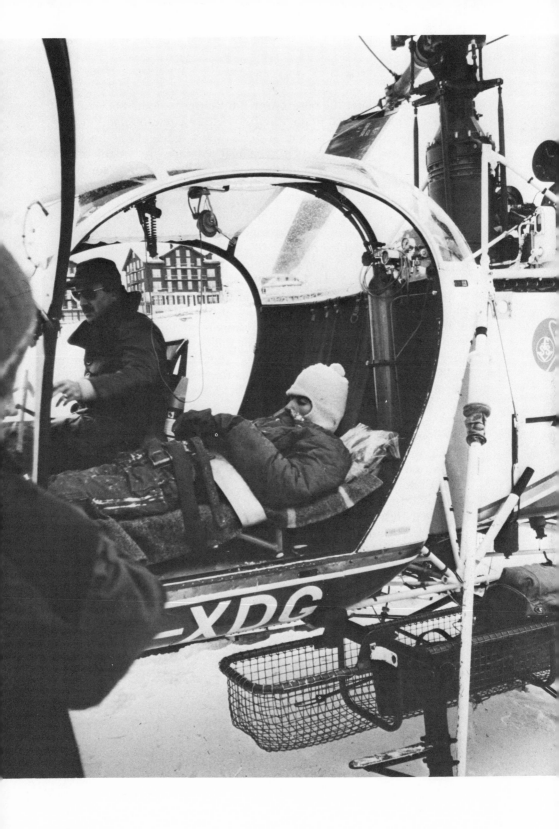

Two months later the bergführer Edi Bohren, who had been one of the four guides airlifted to the Ramp to help rescue two Spanish climbers the preceding November, and his fellow guide Fritz Imboden, started up the north face. They bivouacked their first night on the Ramp, not far from the Spaniards' bivouac, and reached the summit at 4 P.M. the following day. It was a more or less routine climb. There were no falls or injuries, no lost equipment, no sudden storm. In fact they essentially free climbed the route, using pitons only for protection against a fall. "There was an old rope strung across the Hinterstoisser that I might have pulled on once or twice, but very gingerly," Bohren explained. "I certainly didn't rely on it to bear my weight." The climb was notable for one reason, however, and Bohren had said he felt "more responsible" on the Eiger climb than on any of the other equally difficult climbs he has done. The twenty-seven-year-old Edi Bohren was climbing in front of the hometown folks, and actually became the first Grindelwald native to climb the Eiger's north wall, 120 years and a few days after Christian Almer and his namesake (but no relation) Peter Bohren had first climbed the Eiger with Charles Barrington. "It's not surprising that it took so long," Bohren said. "Our fathers could only afford to climb when they had clients, but the really good amateur climbers didn't need guides. And with the others, you couldn't climb routes like the Eigernordwand with them anyway, so the older guides never got to do the big walls. Also the local guides, during the fifties and sixties, took part in too many searches at the bottom of the wall, found too many broken bodies. There isn't much left of a climber by the time he hits the bottom of the Nordwand. It wasn't the greatest inducement to go up on the face themselves."

Bohren, who works in his father's shoe store in Grindelwald, cheerfully admitted that the younger Swiss guides have a much easier life. "There's a lot more money around now," he said. "We can take off any time we want for a few days climbing, here in the Oberland, or Chamonix or the Dolomites. I myself spent last summer climbing Mount Logan and Mount McKinley. The older guides never got that kind of experience." McKinley at 20,320 and Logan at 19,850 feet are, respectively, the highest mountains in North America and Canada.

The climbing year of 1979 opened with a six-man English rope of climbers attempting a winter ascent of the 1938 route. They started the climb on February 19 and six days later reached the Spider. However, here they were stormbound, ran out of food, and, suffering from exhaustion, signaled for rescue down to Kleine Scheidegg. Several days of bad weather kept the helicopters grounded, but finally, on February 28, the six were successfully airlifted from the snowfield. It was the highest point on the face from which a helicopter rescue had been carried out.

On the morning of August 22, 1979, the pilot of a light plane on a normal pleasure flight over the Bernese Alps, radioed that he was having technical difficulties with his aircraft. Half an hour later he called again and said he was flying straight into the Eiger! A short time later spectators spotted wreckage high up on the north face of the mountain. An SRFW helicopter flew past and reported bits and pieces of the machine scattered up and down the wall. Although the pilot's second radio call, that he was flying straight into the Eiger, gave rise to reports that he had committed suicide, it was also theorized, with somewhat more logic, that he had been blinded by ice glare coming out of an aerial maneuver of some kind and recognized the face in front of him only when it was too late to take evasive action. Helicopters of the SRFW later retrieved parts of the aircraft, and parts of the pilot's body, which was mangled beyond recognition. There had been no passengers in the plane.

A month later two American climbers, Larry Bruce and Steve Shea, of Boulder, Colorado, were well up on the face, making a normal ascent of the 1938 route. A short distance below them a pair of English climbers, Nicholas Kagan and Ian Wade, were climbing normally when Kagan, a doctor in his flatland life, found what he recognized as the shoulder of a human. Not aware of the airplane crash, he was completely mystified as to how it had gotten there. That high up on the face it could hardly have come from a climber, yet who else would be up there? It wasn't until months later that he learned of the plane crash and the origin of his gruesome find.

Fatalities dropped off sharply in the 1970s, down to seven from seventeen during the 1960s, and this despite the fact that the number attempting the climb must have at least quadrupled. The lion's share of the credit for this lowered fatality rate has to go to the helicopter rescues that could now be staged from almost anywhere on the face. Pérez, for example, and several others, would surely have died in the days before such rescues. There were other factors that helped to make the Eigernordwand climb safer—the use of two-way radios, more accurate weather forecasts, a greater knowledge of diets and the physiological effects of cold and altitude, new climbing techniques, especially on ice and snow, better-conditioned climbers, improved climbing gear and clothing, and a better knowledge of the face itself.

And while it may now appear that the Eiger has been thoroughly mastered, it is doubtful whether it will ever become as easy as the Hörnli Ridge on the Matterhorn, where, on one day alone, 300 tourists made the climb. The Eigernordwand, "the meanest mountain on earth," as a writer for *Reader's Digest* once called it, will always be sui generis, the Final Exam for most Alpine climbers, the ultimate mental and physical test of a mountaineer's potential as a human being.

32

Climbing Standards

All the great Alpine faces have been climbed, and most of the world's great peaks have been mastered. Those still unvanquished retain their status largely because they are to be found only in out-of-the-way corners of the world that require costly expeditions to reach—Antarctica, the Himalayas, the Andes, Greenland, and the like.

What's ahead then for the Eiger? The Eiger *third-classed,* that is, climbed solo, without ropes, pitons, carabiners, or any other form of protection? As this book was being finished, it was reported that Eric Jones did something like that on September 14, 15, and 16 of 1980, becoming the first British climber to solo the Eigernordwand. He used a self-belay system and rope protection on the Ice Hose, the Waterfall Crack, and another short pitch—a total of 200 protected feet of climbing in a 10,000 foot climb. The rest of the time he climbed with his rope coiled. He bivouacked twice and found the Waterfall Crack and Ice Bulge the hardest pitches of the climb. And that perhaps ends the era of Eiger challenges, which brings us to the newest frontier in mountain climbing, "free" or "clean" climbing. With the bolted ascent of Cerro Torre, direct-aid climbing reached a dead end. Any mountain face, anywhere in the world, could now be mastered with a ladder of bolts. So a movement toward clean climbing began, a reversion to Victorian "purist" ideals. It started mainly in America and England, though "clean" climbers have quietly practiced their art through the years in half a dozen different countries. The craft has come full circle, and the age of direct-aid, artificial climbing seems to be over. Aid, of course, will still be used, particularly in "siege" climbs, but the trend is swinging sharply to free climbing as more and more aid routes are being climbed free.

"Clean" or "free" climbing has been defined as climbing in which equipment such as pitons, nuts, slings, and ropes is used *only* to protect against a fall, and not as handholds or footholds or as a pull-up, or resting place. The ultimate free climb, of course, is a solo without any kind of equipment, or even any kind of clothing. Because of the danger of such free soloing, it's doubtful whether it will ever become popular with the average climber.

Clean climbing is full of ethical problems. Some consider the use of chalk dust to absorb perspiration in the fingertips as a violation of clean-climbing ethics in that it defaces the rock, leaving behind a white smear. Some climbers won't repeat a climb on which they've fallen until a certain amount of time has passed, on the grounds that the climb was beyond the climber's ability, because he fell. Other climbers, trying to put up a new 5.11 or 5.12 route, expect to take as many as a score of falls before they master the crux move on the climb.

The first revolt was against the piton, when the English climbers in the early 1950s began to substitute artificial chockstones, metal nuts on a sling that could be easily removed and, more important still, did not deface the rock in any way. In California, during the early 1950s, a grading system sprang up, confined to Class-5 free climbing, and subdividing routes into ten categories of difficulty: 5.0 to 5.9. However, as free climbing progressed and standards kept getting raised, new classifications had to be found, and, in defiance of the decimal system, 5.9 shaded into 5.10, then became 5.11 and 5.12. As free climbing continued to improve, 5.13 was added, though there are only a few such routes in the country, one in the Shawangunks in New York State ("Supercrack"), plus a couple in Colorado. A rough comparison of different climbing grades follows. UIAA (*Union Internationale des Associations d'Alpinisme*) is an umbrella group of various national Alpine societies.

American	English		UIAA	Australian
5.0 to 5.2	D	Difficult	II to III	4 to 8
5.3 to 5.4	VD	Very Difficult	IV	8 to 9
5.5	S	Severe	V−	10 to 11
5.6	HS	Hard Severe	V	12 to 13
5.7	VS	Very Severe	V+	14 to 15
5.8	HVS	Hard Very Severe	VI−	16 to 17
5.9	XS	Extremely Severe	VI	18 to 19
5.10	XS	Extremely Severe	VI+	20 to 21
5.11	HXS	Hard Extremely Severe	VII−	22 to 23
5.12	HXS	Hard Extremely Severe	VII	24
5.13	HXS	Hard Extremely Severe	VII+	25

The world-wide movement to convert aid routes to free routes goes on. Through gymnastic training, climbers have improved their ability, technique, and endurance. One California climber, for example, does 1,200 pull-ups a day, in "sets" of 50 and 100. Another climber, John Gill of Boulder, Colorado, was not only capable of doing half a dozen one-arm pull-ups, using either hand, he could also do one-*finger* pull-ups, using his index or middle finger. Other free climbers are experimenting with Zen and transcendental meditation to help them become better rock climbers.

Speed-climbing competitions, to see who can climb a particular route the fastest, has caught on in Russia and in some Eastern European countries, but has so far been largely ignored in the West, probably because Western climbers, despite all their ethical splitting of hairs, oppose rules and regimentation of any kind. The problem of ethics, of course, really doesn't exist in direct-aid climbing, in which anything, short of scaffolding, is considered legitimate to help get one up a mountain face.

Climbing is an unusual sport in that it has no official body upholding rules and regulations, no organized competition, no score keeping, no referees to interpret the rules, no annual trophies or medals, and no restrictions on the number who can play. A climber's reputation is therefore based almost solely on what his peers think of him—how other climbers rate his style, ability, technique, and courage. For that reason, it is one of our purest sports. And whether climbing is primarily a sport or, as some people claim, an art—or a science or a hobby, as others affirm—the Eigernordwand has furnished and will continue to furnish a stage on which these definitions are dramatically interpreted.

In Memoriam

Year	Name	Nationality
1935	Karl Mehringer	German
1935	Max Sedlmayer	German
1936	Edi Rainer	Austrian
1936	Willy Angerer	Austrian
1936	Andreas Hinterstoisser	German
1936	Toni Kurz	German
1937	Bertl Gollackner	Austrian
1938	Bartolo Sandri	Italian
1938	Mario Menti	Italian
1953	Paul Körber	German
1953	Roland Vass	German
1953	Uli Wyss	Swiss
1953	Karlheinz Gonda	German
1956	Manfred Söhnel	German
1956	Franz Moosmüller	German
1957	Franz Mayer	German
1957	Günter Nothdurft	German
1957	Stefano Longhi	Italian
1961	Adolf Mayr	Austrian
1962	Barry Brewster	English
1962	Adolf Derungs	Swiss
1962	Diether Marchart	Austrian
1962	Tom Carruthers	English
1962	Egon Moderegger	Austrian
1963	Ernesto Navarro	Spanish
1963	Alberto Rabada	Spanish
1965	Tsuneaki Watabe	Japanese
1966	John Harlin	American
1967	Roland Travellini	French
1967	Günter Warmuth	German
1967	Fritz Eske	German

Year	Name	Nationality
1967	Günter Kalkbrenner	German
1967	Kurt Richter	German
1967	Hans Herzel	Austrian
1967	Kurt Reichardt	Austrian
1969	Martin Weiss	Austrian
1970	Angelo Ursella	Italian
1972	Masaru Miyagawa	Japanese
1972	Furukawa Masahiro	Japanese
1974	David Knowles	English
1976	Kurt Stör	German
1977	Jiri Siegl	Czech
1977	Jiri Pechous	Czech

INDEX

Index

Page numbers in **bold** face refer to illustrations.

ABOUT THE AUTHOR

Arthur Roth started climbing several years ago, at the age of fifty-four, and has since climbed in the Bernese Oberland and Leysin in Switzerland; in Chamonix, France; in the Shawangunks of New York; in Boulder and El Dorado canyons of Colorado; and in Yosemite Valley in California. A "free" climber, he is currently seconding 5.7–5.8 and leading 5.4–5.5. He cheerfully confesses that he often climbs in a state somewhere between sheer (le mot juste!) panic and stunned disbelief, but somehow, a true adrenaline junkie, he keeps coming back for more.

He is the author of over twenty adult, mystery, and young-adult novels. He lives in East Hampton, New York, at the flattened-out end of Long Island, where the only things to climb are ten-foot-high stone railway bridges—which he does, with his twelve-year-old son, Mark. They are currently collaborating on a climbing guide to Long Island railroad bridges.